*For Clare, who has taught me the true value of life,
and for Teil, Raphie and Ella, for helping me make the
most of every minute.*

'They feel all the love given to them. They have a great sensitivity for love. I am sure of this. There are many mysteries, and one of them is the girls' eyes. I tell all the parents to look at their eyes. The eyes are talking to them. I am sure the girls understand everything, but they can do nothing with the information.'

DOCTOR ANDREAS RETT

PART ONE

1

Patience

July

'Ladies and Gentlemen! We're Gary, Mark and Howard. We're what's left of – Take That!'

The crowd erupts. The group sitting in front of me – demob-happy mums in their late thirties, bottoms berthed on royal blue plastic seats, all sipping overpriced Chardonnay from white paper cups – suddenly thrust their bulk heavenwards, spraying lukewarm wine onto my feet as they do so. But I say nothing.

All I can see now for what seems like miles is a sea of waving hands; all I can hear is a cacophony of catcalls; and all I can smell are the combined fumes of booze, cheesy nachos and sweat. Through the hubbub, I can just make out the early strains of 'Pray', which is one of my favourites. I start to sway along as it ramps up both in volume and beat. Music always makes me move; it's like my body doesn't know how to do it until it's been given a rhythm.

I close my eyes so that I can ignore both the drunken ladies and the two bored husbands I've just spotted a few metres to my left, arms crossed, faces like thunder. What a waste of money it was bringing them here. Why would you even bother? A night off from those charmers would feel like a jail break, surely?

I open my eyes so that I can check up on Gill. She's standing up like most of the audience, waving her dimpled arms in the air, the loose flesh beneath them flapping around like a net curtain, a beat or so behind her hands. She has long since forgotten I'm here. The atmosphere and the music have carried her away.

That makes two of us.

Gary Barlow's voice is so familiar, it's etched into my childhood like declarations of undying love on a school desk. 'Pray' was released in 1993, when I was four. It's a perfectly ordinary pop song really, with a catchy chorus and soaring vocals, but it means so much more to me than the sum of its parts.

Now don't tell Gary this, I think it would hurt his feelings, but I'm not here for the music. Or even the totty. The boys – lads – men, whatever term you prefer, are lovely to look at, but in all honesty, it's the memories that go with their songs that have brought me here. Take That's music is the soundtrack to my life. And when you can't be the main actor in what's happening to you, your memories form a parade in your head, as if you're a film director assembling a storyboard.

Listening to music is a trigger for me, a little bit of magic that allows me to jump right back into pictures from the past, like the children in Mary Poppins launching themselves into those drawings on the pavement. First drawing: Eliza and me wallowing in the paddling pool in the garden, surrounded by parched grass on an idyllic summer's day. Second drawing: her crying because she didn't win the running race at her ninth birthday party. Third drawing: she's practising plaits on my hair in our bedroom. (Both of us got chickenpox in the same week and she experimented on my hair to pass the time. Whenever someone tries to tame my unruly blonde mane into plaits now, I still feel the itch.)

I am pulled back from my memories by a change of song. It's louder this time, one of the band's new singles. The bass is so strong that the floor beneath me is vibrating with the beat, and both the repetitive rhythm and the musky aroma of the assembled mass of bodies are overwhelming.

I notice that Gill has finally decided to stop dancing and look my way. I don't think she likes what she sees. I possibly look a bit green. Or red, maybe? I'm definitely a bit hot and I feel slightly dizzy, now that I think about it. I don't want fuss, though. I hate fuss.

'Are you OK, Patience? Do you have a bad head?'

Gill is sitting down next to me now. I notice that a sweat-tsunami is forcing an inexorable path southwards from her armpits – she's not accustomed to exercise, our Gill – and the resulting odour, both ripe and rampant, makes me nauseous.

Piss off, Gill. Please. I want to enjoy this by myself. This is time I will not get back.

Through the waving arms of the women in front, I can just about make out the band gyrating suggestively with some lithe female dancers. Strobe lights shine out into the crowd, flash-flash-flash in quick succession. Hundreds of thousands of tiny pieces of ticker tape are then blasted into the air, falling down slowly, gracefully, like ash.

It starts to feel stifling in here, airless. Lights emitted by thousands of mobile phones begin to blur. And then there's a cloud above my head, a swirling cloud that seems to be made up of dust, glitter, dry ice, smoke and baked breath. I'm floating now, and Gary Barlow is beckoning to me.

I'm coming, Gary...

Then the sound of the band starts to dull and all I can see is darkness. I feel a thump as I hit something. There are heavy, frantic footsteps. I can just about make out what someone is saying.

'Call an ambulance, quick! Some girl in a wheelchair is having a massive fit.'

2

Louise

July

As Louise pulled into the hospital car park, she registered a flash of pink and red in her peripheral vision and slammed on the brakes. Her tyres screamed in protest and came to rest just a few centimetres from where two small girls stood, as if frozen, blinking in disbelief at the car bonnet which now loomed over them. They wore pyjamas and flip-flops, and each clutched a small plastic unicorn. The girl in pink's left arm was constrained by a sling.

After a few beats of Louise's now frantic heart, the girls sprang back into action and continued to run across the car park, their short legs pumping hard, mischievous smiles returning swiftly to their faces. And then their mother sprinted in front of Louise's car, her arms stretching out to grasp at invisible hands, her mouth fixed wide and open in a silent scream.

Breathe.

Louise put on the hand brake and took a moment to focus on inhaling and exhaling, trying to rid herself of the extra adrenaline.

Beep. Beep-beep-beeeep.

The driver in the car behind her apparently wanted to pass. Reluctantly, she put her car back into gear and swung into a nearby space. After she had turned her engine off, she closed her eyes and lowered her forehead, resting it on the steering wheel.

Thud.

Thud. Thud.

Louise raised her head. The woman who'd just run in front of her car was now banging on her window.

'*Do you hear me, you stupid old cow?*' the woman shouted, the glass distorting her voice, so it sounded as if she was underwater. '*You almost killed my kids.*'

Louise inhaled deeply once more and opened her door, forcing the woman and her two wide-eyed, chastened children to back away towards her bonnet. Instead of rising to the bait, however, she remained silent.

'*I said. You. Almost. Killed. My. Kids.*' The woman took several steps forward, invading Louise's personal space.

'*So, what have you got to say? Anything?*'

Louise raised her eyes and looked directly at the woman, whose two girls were now attempting to hide behind her ample, dimpled, Lycra-clad thighs.

'You should have been holding on to them,' she said, quietly.

'*What?*'

'You should have been holding on to them more tightly,' she repeated, louder this time.

'I'm sorry. I must have misheard you. Are you blaming *me?*'

'If you had been holding their hands, they wouldn't have

been able to run off. I had a split second's warning. It almost wasn't enough.' Louise had lost control of her breathing pattern completely now.

'You were going too fast,' the woman spluttered. 'It *was* your bloody fault. This is a car park, not a racetrack. And there are sick people here. My daughter has broken her arm!'

'Then you have no idea how lucky you are,' Louise said, her hands now scrunched into two angry balls.

'What?'

'*You have no idea how lucky you are.*'

'Yes, I heard. I just couldn't believe it. Are you saying I'm lucky that you didn't run my kids over? It's the opposite, you bitch – you're bloody lucky you're not in a police cell.'

'No,' Louise answered. '*You* are lucky. Those girls – those girls, they can *run*. They can run away from you. They have legs that work and arms that heal. You are *lucky*.'

'And you're a nutter. *Insane.*' The woman shook her head, a look of disgust rendering her face a caricature.

'I have to go now,' said Louise, swallowing hard to suppress tears of anger and grief. She reached into the car for her handbag, turned away from the woman and began to walk away. 'Sorry,' she said, as an afterthought, not looking back.

Louise sped up as she approached the hospital entrance, almost breaking into a run as she made her way along the labyrinthine grey, scratched and scraped corridors of the ageing building, greeted as she went by the familiar twin smells of disinfectant and dinner. Her speed masked the fact that she was shaking. It was not the first time she'd had a similar row with a stranger, but each time it happened, she was deeply disturbed. And it was far worse when she was tired.

Louise had been up for hours. She had watched the dawn arrive through her thin curtains, the pole hanging on by a thread on one side, its struggle against gravity almost over. She'd heard the dawn, too; the intense summer heat had forced her to open all of her windows wide, and the birds, such as there were in suburbia, were rejoicing in the rising sun. Lying uncovered in her sweat-soaked sheets with a growing headache, Louise had felt no such emotion.

Pete had finally worn her down on the subject of respite care a few years previously, but she had never reconciled herself to Patience's fortnightly visits to Morton Lodge. Her two-day stints there were supposed to give Louise a break, but, in reality, they just created a void that sleep always refused to fill. Caring for an eternal child meant that her circadian rhythms had permanently reset to accommodate frequent night-wakings and early rises; she lived perpetually in the twilight zone of the new parent. Even at the age of sixty-one, with nobody to care for but herself.

As she strode along the network of anonymous corridors, she tried to subdue her anger, despite knowing that it was a battle she would lose. She had too much to be angry about, and that woman's rant was the least of it.

Like, why the hell hadn't Morton Lodge called her last night? Patience should never be left alone for that long. She'd have been so frightened. And, crucially, it would also have meant that she could have cancelled the job interview she had arranged for that morning at least twelve hours beforehand, leaving her with a semblance of dignity and the possibility it could have been rescheduled. They'd never take her seriously now, would they? They'd give it to someone else, who didn't have caring responsibilities that lasted a lifetime.

Also, she thought, why had Patience been able to fall out of her chair in the first place? Why hadn't she been wearing a seatbelt? Bloody Gill! She was lax, that one. She had been a fool to trust them to take Patience to that concert. She had let her guard down and that mustn't happen again. Louise filed the issue in her mind to deal with, firmly, later. What really mattered now was that Patience was still alive. That was the only thing that ever mattered.

Louise came to an abrupt stop and stood back against a wall to let a porter pass. He was pushing a hospital bed and in the middle of it, swallowed up and almost camouflaged by sheets, was a child who couldn't have been more than six. The little girl had no hair and her skin was almost translucent. Following behind were, Louise presumed, her mother and father. Both of them looked like they hadn't slept for weeks; their faces ashen, their eyelids leaden, their clothes crumpled. As the bed trundled further down the corridor with the parents part-walking, part-stumbling behind, Louise knew that she wasn't alone in wishing that she'd never set foot inside a hospital.

When she reached ICU, she recognised one of the nurses, Jayne.

'Good morning,' Louise said, forcing herself to pause and be pleasant, even though every cell in her body wanted to propel her forwards, towards Patience.

'Hi,' replied Jayne, with a smile of recognition. 'How are you?' Louise made a grimace and Jayne, nodding her understanding, gestured down the hall.

'She's down here. Shall I take you?'

Louise did her best to return her smile, despite her intense anxiety. She followed her.

'How are you doing?' she asked the nurse, out of politeness.

'Oh, well, thanks. Henry is weaning now. He's a little tyke.'

Louise now recalled that Jayne had just returned to work after the birth of her first baby. Over the years, Louise had got to know a great deal about the lives of the staff on this ward; there had been engagements, emotional breakups, illnesses, marriages, pregnancies, divorce. In return, they had witnessed her darkest moments – when she had been pared down, monosyllabic, raw. They had looked into parts of her soul even Louise didn't want to see.

'Ah, really? They grow so quickly, don't they?' Louise replied, robotically. This ward was a theatre for life's dramas, all right. And she had stage fright, as ever.

The nurse guided her into a side room. Patience was lying in bed, staring at the ceiling, her piercing blue eyes and alabaster skin making her look like a doll. Her long, curly blonde hair was piled up on top of her head in a messy bun. Her roots looked dirty, almost black in parts and Louise grimaced. She washed Patience's hair every day when she was at home.

Patience's hands were clasped firmly across her chest, but they were both still, as if frozen in place. Her knees were bent, sticking up like Toblerone triangles under the thin brown blanket. Her legs were almost always stuck in that position now; it took hours of massage and warm water to persuade them to retract. Louise could also see significant bruising on her arms and upper chest. She must have fallen hard, she thought. They'd put a drip into Patience's left hand, and an oxygen monitor chirped intermittently beside her.

Louise approached the bed and manoeuvred herself so that Patience could see her face, and then smiled. She waited for the usual response from her daughter – a glint in her eye, a small smile, or even, on occasion, a laugh. In the absence of any other communication, these fleeting expressions had become their language. But there was nothing coming back from Patience, not even a flicker of recognition. Louise's heart began to race. Wasting no time, she walked out of the room and marched up to the nurse's station.

'I need to speak to Patience's doctor,' she said. '*Now*, please.'

'Mrs Willow,' replied Jayne, her earlier smile slipping, 'Patience was seen by a duty doctor only an hour ago. They said she was stable. They'll check back on her in a couple of hours.'

'Right. I'm afraid I disagree,' said Louise, her hands now placed firmly on her hips. 'This was her first ever seizure and there's something not right. She's disappeared within herself. I think she's in pain. Can you call a more senior doctor? Maybe a neurologist? Is there one on shift?'

The nurse sighed.

'Mrs Willow, I really don't think—'

'*Please?*' Louise's tone and expression proved persuasive. The nurse paged the senior doctor on call and Louise went back into Patience's room to wait. She sat down next to the bed and took hold of her daughter's hand.

'Patience, my love?' Her voice was so soft, she was almost whispering. 'Patience... It's Mummy. I know you're in there, somewhere. I think you're in pain. Am I right?' Louise waited for a squeeze of her hand, even though she knew that it would never come. Patience couldn't control her hands. And yet, she always waited. Just in case. She realised she had spent almost all of Patience's life waiting for a miracle.

'I'm so sorry I didn't come last night. I didn't want you to be here, all alone. Hospitals are scary, I know that. But they didn't tell me, Patience, *they didn't tell me*. But I'm here now – and I promise I won't leave you.'

She stood up and leaned over her daughter once more. Patience was still staring blankly into space, her eyes unfocussed, like an infant about to succumb to sleep. Louise planted a kiss on her forehead and smiled at her again, even though she knew that Patience was in no mood to give her one in return.

Turning around, she glanced at the clock, and realised she should be on her way to her interview by now. To distract herself from both her daughter's pain and her apparent unemployability, she walked over to the room's small window, which overlooked a tiny square. It was cast into shadow for much of the day by the wards and consulting rooms surrounding it but several patients – identifiable by the hospital gowns that were poking out from beneath their coats – were sitting on a garden bench, smoking. One was still attached to a drip. Imagine if your own actions were responsible for your disease, she thought; imagine living with that guilt. It was bad enough living with something that people insisted you could never have prevented.

Louise turned away and returned to her chair. Noticing that Patience appeared to have dropped off to sleep, she switched on the small TV beside the bed and flicked through the daytime television options.

It was a fruitless search. No programme was engaging enough to numb her pain. She turned the TV off in disgust, stood up abruptly and began to pace around the room, tracing a crescent moon on the lino as she skirted purposefully around the bed, back and forth, back and forth. A few minutes and many fruitless steps later, she was interrupted at the cusp of the moon's shadow.

'Mrs Willow? They tell me you want to see me.'

Louise looked up to see a short, balding man in his late forties standing in front of her, his white coat stained with what looked like juice, but it may have been blood.

'Yes, I do,' she said, standing up. 'Are you a neurologist?'

'I'm sorry, no. But I'm a consultant in A & E. We saw Patience there last night.'

'Right. Well, my daughter is in a lot of pain – and the thing is, Dr...?'

'Ian. Call me Ian.'

'The thing is, Ian, you don't seem to be doing anything about it.'

'Mrs Willow, I understand you're upset.' He cleared his throat. 'It's a lot to take in,' he continued, after a pause, 'but I've had a good look at Patience and I think she's fine. She's recovering from the seizure very well. We're still not sure why she had it. It's possible—'

'She's not fine!' Louise snapped. 'I can tell. I know I don't have a medical degree, but I have been her mother for thirty years, and you're just going to have to take my word for it. You need to do something to help her, *please*. What painkillers can you give her?'

'You can *tell*?' There was obvious reservation in his voice. He thought she was nuts, clearly. People generally assumed that being non-verbal meant that Patience was a closed book, but over the years, she had developed an instinct about how she was feeling. It wasn't foolproof and she'd give anything to talk to her daughter properly, but most of the time, she knew when something was wrong. The powerlessness and guilt that came with not knowing exactly *what* was wrong gnawed away at her, however.

'Yes, I *just know*. Just one look at her tells me she's extremely uncomfortable. I don't think she's breathing right, either. I can't tell you exactly where the pain is, *Ian*, because of course I'm not psychic and I'm not a doctor. But I'm her mother and I'm telling you that she's hurting, *Ian*, and I want you to help her.'

'OK, Mrs Willow, fair enough. I'll chase up her test results, order some more and ask the nurses to start giving her some pain relief. It can't hurt.'

Louise began to breathe more easily. She managed to mutter a thank you before she collapsed back into the chair beside Patience's bed.

'It's going to be OK, Patience,' she said. '*Mummy is here. Mummy is going to make sure you feel better. Don't you worry.*' Louise took her daughter's hand again and closed her eyes. Her headache was receding now, but exhaustion, her constant companion, was not.

*

Jayne found Louise sleeping, her head lolling towards her chest, when she came in a few hours later to do her observations. She thought of waking her to let her know about the X-ray, the one that showed Patience had broken her collarbone. But she looked so clearly in need of rest, that she left it for the duty doctor to explain on his afternoon rounds.

3

Eliza

July

Eliza cried as she grappled with her keys and wrestled with the lock, her fingers refusing to cooperate. In fact, she'd been crying for hours, but her sobs rose to a crescendo as she finally pushed open the door to the flat, only to hear the telltale chime of the other set, which were lying on the tiled floor of the entrance hall.

The air in the flat was dense, smelling of baked dust. She ran through to the lounge, opened the sash window and leaned out, hoping that the fresher air would calm her. But it was a close, humid evening, one of those nights in London where everyone seemed to be having a barbecue or a drinks party, and the distant sounds of kids playing and adults laughing turned out to be more than she could bear. So, still sobbing her big, uncontainable tears, she swung back into the room, and delayed opening her eyes for a second or two, knowing what was to come.

When she did look, it was no surprise to find that books were set at jaunty angles on the shelves, leaning into each other as if embarrassed by their depleted numbers. The CD shelf had been decimated, and her modest collection from her uni years – Coldplay, Keane, Oasis – were lying like islands amongst a sea of scratched paint. He'd loved music and had amassed a huge CD collection. 'The sound quality is so much better than downloads,' he'd always explain, repeatedly, to whoever would listen.

She began a mental inventory of everything else that was missing. Several framed photographs had vanished from the mantelpiece and, in the main bedroom, there was a circle of clean surface on her bedside table surrounded by dust, a reminder of the alarm clock that had stood there only this morning. The wardrobe doors were partially open and she could see that she now had plenty of room for her 'unnecessarily large' collection of clothes. That was another thing he had liked to say to her, regularly.

She moved into the small galley kitchen and opened the cupboards. She had been left with a sum total of four plates, one mug, some chipped water glasses, and the set of blue wine glasses they'd been given for Christmas that she suspected he'd never liked. There was no sign of the kettle or the toaster. Cereal for breakfast tomorrow then, she thought.

Then she noticed the note on the counter, propped up against the tiled walls with a broken egg cup. It was written on standard A4 lined writing paper, ripped from a pad they always kept for shopping lists and notes for the cleaner. The handwriting was precise, tidy. Like him. It read: *I'm sorry. Take care of yourself x*

That kiss at the end simply took the piss, she thought. Resisting the urge to rip it up, she grabbed it and threw herself down onto the sofa, rereading it until its contents began to swim in front of her eyes. What on earth was the point in saying sorry? How could any words be appropriate at all?

She looked down at the cluster of diamonds currently decorating the third finger of her left hand. He had chosen it alone, insisting that it was traditional to do things that way. She had not argued, even though she would have preferred a solitaire. Even so, it would be strange, taking it off. She had only ever done that to wash it, to get rid of the London dust that collected among its constellation of tiny stars.

She wondered where he was right now. Most likely, cosy in the flat in Oxford they had chosen together, just as a stopgap – or so she had thought. What an idiot she was! Or was he out with his mates, elated after moving everything he owned (or, to be more specific, the stuff that he'd liked) out of the flat he had barely lived in for months? He'd be overjoyed too, now that he no longer had to put up with her, the gigantic failure in life that she was proving to be.

Eliza thought then about all of the people who needed to be told; almost a hundred people who had just been sent an expensive ivory card, embossed with the image of a lily, with the text printed in one of those curly-wurly fonts, made to look like calligraphy.

She knew that most of the people on the guest list were still weighing up whether they could afford to attend the event next summer; they'd only had a few responses so far. She was certain, however, that no one doubted it would go ahead. After all, they'd been together for so long and they were both in the latter part of their thirties – it was time to knuckle down and start a family now, right? Everyone thought they were a solid couple, about to have 2.4 children, destined to walk along Southend pier on a tandem Zimmer frame. How could she explain that, behind that perfect façade that they'd had for more than a decade, things had gone horribly rotten, horribly wrong?

Oh fuck! She could not – *would not* – tell her mother.

'*Oh goodness, I'd almost given up on you two getting married.*'

That comment from her mum had really smarted. She would never forget it. It had seemed to Eliza that Louise had embraced her future son-in-law with more enthusiasm for her elder daughter's choices than she had ever previously managed. They had waited seventeen years for him to propose, after all. And the obvious happiness that had followed their announcement – the joy her mum had shown in the planning, in the shopping, in the deciding over the past few months – she was about to take all of that away, wasn't she? She was going to have to take the source of her mother's only happiness away.

Ed was everything that a son-in-law should be, she thought, and that made it so much worse. He showed every sign of progressing up the career ladder, right to the top. His ambition was a great counterbalance for her distinct lack of it. Eliza knew that she was not destined for success. But she had been destined to become the power behind his throne, however; the strong woman backing up her man.

Had been. Had.

She fished out her phone from her handbag and turned it on. She had ten missed calls and several voicemails. She'd turned the ringer off last night after he had stormed off. He'd said he'd call her to talk about it when she had calmed down, and, well, she hadn't quite got there yet.

This radio silence was a complete about-turn because for almost two decades, he had been pretty much the only person she called. When she got a new job, she called him. When she saw someone wearing a terrible outfit on the street, she called him. When her acidic boss said something crass and hurtful (as she often did), she called him, and he always made her feel better. And now she had the ultimate emotional catastrophe on her hands – and no one to call.

Speaking of her boss – work today had been a complete washout. She still wasn't sure why she had gone in at all, except that calling in sick would have meant sticking around to watch their home being decimated. She hadn't trusted herself to maintain her dignity while he set about dismantling their life in front of her.

She had managed to get her act together enough to sit through a client meeting and to induct a new work-experience girl, but by mid-morning she had become robotic and rudderless. And Jenny had noticed. She was so bloody on top of things, Jenny, and of course she could see that Eliza wasn't. She had asked her if something was up when they were queuing together for a coffee; Eliza's carefully formed poker face had crumpled and she had run to the toilet for sanctuary. Her annual appraisal was coming up, and she knew now that it wasn't going to be stellar, because crying in the office meant you were weak. She knew this was Jenny's opinion because she had said something similar to her about Aggie, a colleague who'd recently come back to work after failed fertility treatment.

Eliza got back up off the sofa and returned to the kitchen and opened a cupboard, taking one of the chipped glasses out. After a quick glance in the fridge she reached inside and pulled out pretty much the only thing left – a half-empty bottle of gin – and poured herself an extremely generous measure. Then, having unearthed a warm and almost flat bottle of tonic from the back of a cupboard, she went back to the window and sat down once more. She drank the mixture slowly, hoping the tear-induced hiccups would subside before she had to make the inevitable call to set off the bush telegraph.

In the distance she could see trains heading south from Victoria to Clapham Junction, the occasional flash as they switched tracks. There were so many perfectly ordinary lives out there, just beyond her window. But, inside, her own little existence had just become extraordinary. Extraordinarily bad, that is.

Her phone rang. It was the first contact she'd had from the outside world since she'd left the office. She snatched it up.

'Ed?'

'Eliza? It's not Ed, it's Mum.'

A deep breath. She swallowed hard, and tried to sound calm. Happy. Engaged.

'Oh, hi. How are things?' she said, sitting back into the sofa in preparation for her mother's habitual lengthy monologue about her sister, her father, and a new favourite, their 'difficult finances', which she suspected was a hint about the cost of the wedding. Oh well, she thought, that's one less thing for her to worry about now.

'Eliza, I've been trying to get hold of you all day,' her mother said. 'Why don't you answer your phone? You've got to come! It's Patience.'

4

Patience

July

Jesus, woman, can you please stop stabbing me with that bloody needle.

One of the nurses – KatyJayneSamEmma (I've given up, they are all blending into one now) – is making a hatchet job of trying to get a line into my right hand. My veins are feeble and minuscule – it's one of the crosses people like me have to bear – and she's having difficulties finding a vein at all. But instead of admitting defeat, she's absolutely going for it, puncturing my skin with wild abandon, playing a numbers game.

'I'm sorry, Patience… almost done.'

Ouch bloody ouch, woman. Stop lying to me and find someone who can actually do it.

'Actually, do you know what? Your poor hand has had enough of me. I'll call a doctor and see if they have more luck. OK?'

I don't know who she's expecting a reply from, but actually, it's nice that she's trying. Most people don't because I can't respond and they assume, therefore, that I'm not really there. To the vast majority of folk, you see, I'm a ghost. I can be in a room, right there in front of somebody, and they don't see me at all. I am privy to intimate conversations, erotic confessions, devastating truths. And when I'm not being invisible, I get far too much attention. People who accompany me get stared at.

On the plus side of things, I'm also a handy plus one. I get people better seats at the theatre, more convenient parking and much better service at Disney. These are not things people have told me, by the way. These are things I've worked out for myself. I've had a lot of time to do it. Thirty years, so far; three decades of ever-decreasing muscles, fruitless operations, myriad different personalities sitting patiently in front of me, spooning in mashed-up beige food, and then washing my scar-littered body in a hospital-grade bath with a door.

I'm not unhappy, though, despite it all. The thing is, being forced to sit down for almost my whole life has had an incredible side effect. Unlike 'normal' folk (and frankly, what is normal?), I have no choice but to properly appreciate the joy that surrounds me. And soaking up all of this joy means that I laugh a lot. I think people around me take that to mean that I'm a bit simple, but actually, it's the opposite. I'm pretty complicated. As I say, I see everything, and I know what it all means, too. I've joined up all the dots. I know what Eliza did. And I know what Dad is hiding, too. But I'll never tell. Not because I'm a super-trustworthy person; I'm pretty certain that I'm the gossipy sort. It's just that I can't talk, can I? So I'll never be able to pass on any secrets, no matter how juicy they might be.

So having assessed the status quo, as it were – my

involuntary silence, my extensive disabilities – you might wonder why I'm still here, the pathetic excuse for a ghost that I am.

Two reasons. Mum and Dad's devotion is the reason I'm still alive, no question. Their love has kept me well and I want to pay them back by sticking around. It's a very simple exchange.

And then there's the time-shifting. I'm not claiming to be a time traveller, I'll leave that to the great Doctor, but I do have the ability to drop in and out of consciousness at will. This means I'm never bored, never lonely. I just disappear inside myself somewhere, into a world where my arms and legs work brilliantly and, even more astonishingly, I have a voice.

It's a nice voice. Warm and rich, not squeaky or whiny. I could listen to myself all day. That's why I'm talking to myself, you see. I sound fabulous, and it's the only conversation I'm ever going to have, after all, so I make the most of it. I imagine I'm narrating my own autobiography. It would be quite a racy read, I reckon; I get to say whatever I want about whoever I want, and no one is ever offended. It's almost a superpower.

So – in my special world, my personal world, I exercise my vocal cords and my working limbs in a network of cherry-picked locations, all under a reliably warm sun or gently falling snow, the kind you want to catch on your tongue. Oh yes! My tongue works well in there, too. It's not a stupid wedge of spam any more. No, I can stick it out, roll it around, make clicking noises on the roof of my mouth to accompany the music I've chosen as my soundtrack. Which is mostly Take That, of course. So when I look like

I've switched off a bit, you should know that I am actually running through a field of daffodils, or sledging down a hill, or wandering through a glasshouse full of hundreds of beautiful butterflies.

Oh, sod it! The doctor's here and he's carrying a tray with yet another needle. It's poking over the edge, taunting me.

'Patience. Hello. I'm Paul Roberts.'

He would be handsome if he didn't have such a stupid beard.

'I hear your veins have been proving tricky. Let's see if they can withstand the Dr Roberts' magic...'

Oh God, he loves himself. And here we go again. The needle pierces my skin and the nerves dispatch pain up to my brain with incredible accuracy and speed.

Argggghhhh...

Right. Distraction, distraction – where were we? Butterflies. Yes.

I adore butterflies. There's a buddleia bush outside my window at home which attracts them and I eagerly anticipate their arrival in spring and mourn their departure every autumn. I am mesmerised by their vibrant colours, their mirrored patterns, their rhythm. I envy their freedom to float from one bud to the next on a whim, their ability to cast their ugly, tubular bodies aside in favour of miraculous painted wings. A few years ago Eliza bought me a mobile made up of glass butterflies. It hangs above my bed at home and, when the sun catches it, it paints bright splashes of colour onto my cream walls, like a stained-glass window, or a piece of abstract art.

Butterflies are one of my 'small joys'. Whenever I spot one of these joys, they always call me out of my internal world and bring me back to the present. I have hundreds of them, such as a spider spinning an intricate web over one corner of my window, its labours casting an ever-increasing maze on the wall; a song coming on the radio that I actually like; our dog, Tess, a languorous black Labrador, licking my toes. When you're only ever the recipient of things, ever the object and never the subject, you are forced to digest them, to ruminate on them, to really see them…

… *Fucking hell, he's still at it.*

'Almost done…'

Liar.

'Nearly there…'

Still lying.

'There we go, all done! I told you that the Dr Roberts' magic would win the day.'

He's smug, but I like him.

I can feel the cool fluid rushing in now, at last. I'm going to have a horrible bruise there though, aren't I? And that means I'm going to be in pain, because my hands are a magnetic pair, attracting each other without my say-so. They're going to grind into each other whether I want them to or not. Currently, for example, my left hand is desperate to reach its opposite number, despite the fact that my right hand is tethered to a drip. Mum keeps trying to stop it, because I could easily pull the line out by mistake. And who wants to go through that palaver again? I definitely don't. But even so, this enforced separation makes me feel strange, like a circuit has been interrupted.

And it seems that epilepsy makes me feel really strange, too. I went a bit cuckoo there for a while, even more cuckoo than I am normally. It's unusual to develop epilepsy so late. I hope that's not a sign that I'm going downhill. I wonder what they'll give me for it? Rosie, in the respite care bungalow, has epilepsy and she has to take a special tablet. Perhaps they'll give me that to control it. But as I can't take tablets and I struggle with liquid, they'll have to give me suppositories again, won't they? I hate those bloody bottom bullets. My bum is a fun-free zone, all practicality and no pleasure. No one's ever looked at it for fun, least of all the five families (I counted) who were pushed aside at the concert as I flailed at the railings, my pad and sexy gauze shorts clearly on show.

While we're on that theme, you should know that the view from that 'disabled row' *was* pants. I always imagine a 'disabled row' to be made up of chairs missing several legs and lots of bolts, but – I digress – we were miles away from the stage. The band looked like toy soldiers. We were also at least twenty metres away from any other seats; we had our very own disability fallout zone, in case we had something catching. Having said that, it was also within easy reach of the bar (for the carers) and the disabled toilets (for the incontinent), so there's that.

I have had better seats at gigs. At my first, at the Birmingham NEC in the 1990s, we sat at the front, just to the side. We were so close to the stage that when Robbie came to sing to our section, I could make out the beads of sweat dripping down his chest. I remember grinning at him like an idiot, hoping to catch his eye, momentarily forgetting that I was not a buxom teen wearing a tiny crop top and a winning smile. He would only ever look at me in pity. Not just him, of course. Everybody does.

I need to distract myself from that thought, so I'll return

to the hospital room for a bit; there's a small joy there, waiting to be appreciated. There's a bird, I think it's a blue tit, sitting on one of the branches outside my window. It's looking straight at me, at the strange blonde girl in the big bed and at the knackered-looking woman by my side.

I'm not able to turn my head very far, but I know that Mum is still there. She is always there. She's only left me for a couple of hours to go home to shower and change. I opened an eye when she returned a few hours ago and she looked dreadful; the lines around her eyes seemed even deeper than usual and her hair was pulled back roughly into a ponytail, wisps of it frizzing out at all angles. That's just like her, going all the way home for a shower and not even taking the time to brush her hair before she came straight back again. She doesn't look after herself. In fact, I'd say that she's been deliberately damaging herself for some time now.

I wonder if I should make a noise so that she knows I'm OK? I should probably put her out of her misery.

Someone's coming.

It's Eliza. *She* doesn't look good either. Well, to the average person she probably looks OK, but I've been watching her intently all of my life, and it's clear to me that something is up. The make-up is a little too new, her eyes are suspiciously pink, and she's dusted powder all over her face, the pallid hue absolutely failing to mask a shiny red nose.

'Mum! Thank God I found you at last! The nurses were all vague and the information desk people were useless. I tried calling you but you didn't answer.'

Eliza walks over to Mum and bends down and kisses her cheek, before turning towards me and taking hold of my left hand. Mum looks at Eliza then, although not very closely. I don't think she's really looked at Eliza properly for years. 'I'm sorry, darling, I had my phone on silent. Having a nap,' she says.

'Mum, you *must* go home for a proper sleep. It's getting late. Have you been sitting here all day?'

'No, no. I've been having regular breaks.'

Liar, liar.

'Where's Dad?'

'He's on his way back right now. But only for a flying visit. His boss wants to go on holiday. You know how it is.'

I know how it is. Dad working overseas means that Mum is mostly a single parent these days. In fact, Mum and Dad seem to me to be single people who only live together on special occasions. It seems to work, though. Well, they're still married, anyway.

'How is she doing?' asks Eliza, stroking my cheek.

Mum sighs, a sound that I know well. It is a sign that signifies drama, something this family is never short of. That's all my fault, by the way. Just so we're clear.

'I think she's going to be OK, but they say she has epilepsy now. I really thought we'd escaped *that* particular evil, but it seems not. They're going to do an MRI to check for anything nasty in her brain, but it's most likely just a random change in her make-up. They want us to medicate. I'm fighting it. I think it will sedate her.'

'But surely she'll keep having fits if we don't give it?'

'Who knows? This could be a one-off. What if it's a one-off and we give her lots of unnecessary drugs she doesn't need? No, I think we wait,' she says, winding down the drama in her voice. 'Watch, and wait. And then there's the broken collarbone.'

'It's broken? Wow.'

'They only found it because I insisted they chase up an X-ray. Seriously, I think they just see someone like Patience and then decide she's not worth the effort. If I hadn't been here…'

Eliza is now staring out of the window. Mum notices, eventually. 'Anyway,' she says, changing gear, 'they are going to fit her with a sling; apart from that, it's just painkillers and ice packs. Poor Patience. It must really have hurt.'

It does hurt. It's still throbbing.

Eliza sinks into the chair on the other side of the bed and looks plaintively at me. There is silence for a short while. She reaches into her bag for her phone and looks at it. Whatever she was looking for, it doesn't seem to be there.

'Why didn't you pick up your phone when I called you this morning?' Mum asks.

'Just like you, I had it on silent, Mum. I'm sorry. Stressful day at work. I didn't want to give my boss any more reasons to complain about me, so I put my phone out of sight.'

A little too quick with that answer. A little too ready with that one.

'Is she being difficult again? Are you having a hard time of it?' Mum asks, with genuine concern in her voice, but she's still looking at me, not Eliza.

'No, it's fine, honestly, just short-term crappy.'

'And how's Ed?'

'Oh, he's great, Mum, thanks, just working hard too. He says he's sorry he can't make it today, he really wanted to, but he's tied up.'

Far, far too light-of-voice with that one, I think. There's definitely something up.

'Lou? I'm so sorry, I got on the first flight I could!'

I open one eye and see Dad standing in the doorway, the strip lights in the corridor casting him in shadow.

What time is it, I wonder? I nodded off there for a bit. The lights aren't on over my bed and it's definitely dark outside, so it must be late. Or very early.

'Pete?' Mum says, with a yawn. 'What time is it?'

'It's 2 a.m.' The latter, then.

'Oh. I think I was asleep.'

Poor Mum. The nurses seem to think that because I'm an adult, she doesn't deserve a camp bed, so she's been forced to spend the night on an upright chair, propped up against a concrete pillar. She's lucky, I suppose, that they didn't try to enforce visiting hours.

'You were. Sorry to wake you.'

Dad walks over to Mum and she stands up gingerly; they embrace.

'I'm so sorry I wasn't here,' Dad says, his head resting on her shoulder, his arm rubbing her back. 'I'm so sorry you've been dealing with this alone.'

'Don't be silly,' Mum replies, shrugging. 'It's always a risk, with you being away. The main thing is that you make the effort to come home and be here with us when we need you. That's what matters.'

Dad looks at me. I open the other eye and can just make out his expression in the twilight; he looks worried, sad and old. He is a handsome man, Dad, but he seems to be ageing rapidly now. I hate it. I want him to live forever.

'Oh, you're awake, Patience,' he says. 'I'm so sorry I woke you. But I'm here now. We're both here.'

'Did you get my message?' Mum says. 'About her collarbone?'

'Yes, I got it when I landed,' Dad replies, walking over to get a plastic, stackable chair from beside the door. 'Bloody hell. That's insane. How on earth did she manage to do that?'

'My guess is that Morton Lodge didn't want to tell us how bad it was, because she obviously wasn't wearing her seatbelt. It's negligence, isn't it? I told you we couldn't trust those carers with her. If only we could have her at home all of the time, she'd be safe.'

Dad puts the chair down next to Mum and sits on it. 'Now come on, Lou. You need those breaks. Everyone does. And those carers – they *do* care about her, we've both seen it. Everybody makes mistakes.'

'Well, mistakes with Patience can be life-threatening. They shouldn't be making them.'

'To be fair, they wouldn't have expected her to have a seizure. None of us expected that.'

'No.' Mum sounds a bit defeated. She does that when someone cuts through her defences. It's something only Dad can really do.

They both look at me for a moment, in silence.

'Do you think the seizures… do you think they're a sign of things to come?' Dad asks, quietly.

'I hope not,' says Mum. 'She's got every other bastard symptom of Rett syndrome, I was hoping she might see out her days without this one.'

'What if...?'

'I know, Pete. I know. But let's not, OK? Let's not go there. Not now. She's recovered from everything else. She's a fighter.'

I can just make out Dad reaching for Mum's hand and her accepting it. And then there is quietness and a feeling of unity in the darkness.

I close my eyes and drift away somewhere deep inside, temporarily escaping my pain.

5

Louise

August

'Who's a lovely girl? *You are.*'

Tess stared up at her with a look of apparent devotion, her black velvet ears framing wide, glossy, doting eyes, prompting a fleeting flicker of happiness in Louise. She had resisted getting a dog for years, concerned about the additional responsibilities that came with it. But she had discovered, belatedly, that the constant companionship was well worth the effort. It was reassuring to know, on the nights when Patience was away and with Pete being overseas, that there was another warm, sentient being in the house with her. If Tess hadn't been there, Louise knew that she would have become overwhelmed by the memories, frustrations and anxieties that haunted her home. They lurked around every corner, ready to flood into the silence.

Louise opened the back door so that Tess could go out for a pee. The Labrador gave her a grateful look before bounding out onto their weed-infested lawn, which was drenched in morning dew. The grass, such as it was, was now several inches high and needed cutting, but it would have to wait for Pete. He was long gone, of course; called back to Qatar almost as soon as he'd arrived. He couldn't afford to lose his job, not with the way things were, so she had let him go without a fight. She was used to handling these things alone now, anyhow.

Louise remained by the door for several minutes, her addled brain not yet capable of issuing more instructions to her body. She had been woken up half an hour ago by the rattle of Patience's first conscious breaths from the baby monitor on her bedside table, after only a few hours' sleep.

In truth, she was still in hospital mode, losing consciousness only fitfully, fearful that Patience's condition might deteriorate the minute she allowed herself to switch off. The carers who had been sent to nurse Patience at home for the first two days after discharge had not been able to persuade her to go to bed.

Patience hadn't had another seizure yet, and that was something to cling to. Louise had been told that there was a chance that it might be her one and only; she dearly hoped that it would turn out to be so. She was still waiting for the referral to go through to the neurology team. That battle was still waiting to be fought. It had joined a long list of future battles for which she felt increasingly ill-equipped. Louise's armoury was dented, battered and bruised: remaining on a war footing for years had taken an inevitable toll.

It was one of life's heavy ironies that they had tried so hard to have Patience. They had desperately wanted a second child, but it had taken them five years to conceive her after Eliza. Louise had suffered several miscarriages in the intervening period, each one a physical wrench and an emotional low.

They had named her Patience because they had required so much of it, waiting for her to arrive. So when she finally did – puffy, blotchy in all shades of red and pink and with a swollen face only a mother could love – they were simply relieved the battle was over. If only they'd known that it was just beginning.

Patience had inherited Louise's blonde wavy hair and her dad's hazel eyes, rimmed with long eyelashes. Once she'd recovered from the shock of birth, it was obvious to everyone, biased or not, that she was beautiful. All their thank-you notes for the gifts lavished on her by family and friends had included a line about how lucky they were to have two beautiful, healthy daughters. And just as she had done with Eliza, Louise had started to make a keepsake book of baby memories for Patience, keeping a first lock of hair, her wristband from hospital, prints of her little feet. She'd also provided a somewhat edited account of her birth, and had written about what her first days at home were like – or at least, what she could remember through the blur of the post-partum exhaustion. But now it was all hidden away in a box in a dusty cupboard, with only the first ten pages filled; the rest of the book – the bits about baby's first steps, baby's first day at nursery, baby's first words – remained unfilled. There had seemed no point in writing more, because Patience would never read it.

It had taken about eighteen months of Patience's life to acknowledge that something was genuinely amiss, but the signs had really been there from the beginning. They had both seen them and then decided, individually, to try not to notice, she thought. Patience had never rolled over or crawled, preferring instead to shuffle about on her bottom.

She and Pete had tried so hard to get her to form words properly, to imitate the sounds they'd made. Patience had tried so hard to please, too, managing to say 'Da-da', and attempting 'duck'. ('Dut, dut,' she'd said, over and over again, with a beaming, mostly toothless smile.)

On impulse, Louise had once lugged an enormous tape recorder and microphone into the kitchen so that she could record Patience attempting to talk at dinner time. She was very glad now that she had. They hadn't known it then, but it had turned out that they were to be Patience's only words.

Louise had dubbed that tape onto a CD more than a decade ago, and she still listened to it sometimes, when no one else was around. It always made her cry, but the wormhole it invited her to plunge into – a portal that transported her from the reality of her silent, frozen daughter back to the memory of a chubby toddler smothered in yogurt and ketchup and delighting in her own voice – was worth every tear.

Once Patience's words had been snuffed out, however, things got even worse. She then began a hideous stage of crying incessantly, as if in pain. Janet, Louise's mother, had been a regular visitor in those early days, taking a break from the apparent trials of being a vicar's wife. She had referred to Patience's cries and developmental delay as 'her little bit of trouble', as if overtly trivialising it would persuade God to deal them all an easier hand. Louise and Pete, meanwhile, continued not to talk about it at all.

But as the months went by, a proliferation of sleepless, fearful nights, punctuated by Patience's piercing screams, had driven her to see her GP.

It had taken a great deal of courage to spit out the words;

to explain, in terms she hoped the doctor would understand, that her daughter was not 'normal'. But Dr Cooper, nearing retirement and head of his practice, had told her that he didn't think she had anything to worry about. But she had persisted, had refused to accept the platitudes he had offered. So he had referred her to a paediatrician at the local hospital – to get rid of her, she now realised.

And so it was that in that hospital on a dreary day in the early 1990s, seated on that stained grey chair with Patience on her lap, Louise had been dealt a body blow. And it hadn't been a diagnosis; instead, it had been a decimation of her character.

'I can find nothing specifically wrong with her,' that paediatrician had said, so forcefully that he had almost been spitting. 'She is perhaps just a little slow; she's not as bright as her sister, clearly. But you really must try, Mrs Willow, not to be such a neurotic mother.' He had said those actual words out loud – 'a neurotic mother' – as if he had been chastising a child.

She'd been alone at that appointment, and had been so overwhelmed by this assessment that she'd been unable to utter any retort at all, although many were forthcoming afterwards. She knew, absolutely knew, that Patience's problem was not in her head, and this doctor, with his greasy side-parting, sparse moustache and repugnant odour of cigar smoke, was somehow suggesting that she was responsible for her daughter's plight.

Pete hadn't been working overseas then, but he had been working long days, trying to make their eternally loose ends meet. He'd often come home late at night to find her sobbing on the sofa. But that day had been worse than most, and he had taken one look at her despair and, in a rare fit of rage, had found the telephone number for the consultant's private secretary (his NHS phone was permanently on answerphone), dialled it and demanded that the blasted man call him back.

Pete's anger had jolted the doctor into action. Louise suspected that he had yielded when challenged by a fellow alpha male and, in an effort to get him off the phone as soon as possible, he had promised a referral to a specialist centre for further testing. The appointment that had followed, the one where they had given her 'trouble' a name, had begun it all. Or ended it all, if you looked at it another way, she thought. It had certainly put an end to hope.

After taking a few deep breaths to galvanise herself into action, Louise turned around and opened a chipped melamine cupboard door in search of teabags. She dropped one into a mug, then flipped the button on the kettle and switched on her laptop, which was in its habitual spot on the table. As she waited for it to boot and the kettle to boil, she opened the back door once more and walked around the side of the house, clasping the box they used to store the recycling to her chest.

She opened the lid of their large green recycling bin and the smell of unwashed yogurt pots and food tins, baked and fermented by the summer heat, hit her like a tsunami. She held her breath and rested the box on the rim, tipping it up gently, letting the empty wine bottles fall into it one by one, each one playing its own part in an avant-garde melody. When it was empty, she took a step away and inhaled deeply before meandering back around the building, taking in their ramshackle garden shed, the pile of roofing tiles mouldering in the corner, the dark patch on the ground which marked where the guttering leaked.

They had bought the house, a three-bedroom 1960s-era semi-detached, in the late eighties, brimming with plans and dreams. It had been in a state, even then, but Pete had reckoned that he'd have the time and money to do the work it needed between building contracts, and Louise, although slightly doubtful, hadn't cared too much. She had been so delighted to move back near her parents, to the area she had grown up in, that she had completely ignored the dodgy bathroom, the perilous electrics and the cramped kitchen.

She had approached her transition from parent to carer in a similar manner. She had ignored the reality of their situation for as long as she could. You could argue that parents were also carers, she thought – that they were part and parcel of the same thing – but you'd be wrong. Parents care for children who gradually pull away from them; carers care for someone who only grows to need them more.

The kettle clicked off as she re-entered the kitchen. She opened the fridge in search of milk for her tea, but there was none. Its grimy shelves were home only to a collection of mouldering jars and the drawers beneath were hosting a collection of vegetables which were closer to compost than cooking. She slammed the door shut and poured hot water into her mug, splashing hot water on her fingers as she did so.

But she did not pour cold water on the inevitable burns, because she had something more important to do.

She walked down the corridor into Patience's room,

which was at the front of the house. It was the only room that they'd found the money and time to refurbish in the past decade. It had previously been an unloved front room, dominated by brown shagpile carpet, yellow and green geometric wallpaper and a selection of dark-brown utility furniture. Now, however, thanks to Louise's careful selection of decor in varying tones of cream and pink, it had transformed into a boudoir fit for a princess. It was still dark in there, thanks to blackout blinds – another recent purchase – but Princess Patience's blonde hair was visible as always, fanning out behind her on her pillow, like a halo.

'You've woken up again, my love, why didn't you tell me? I didn't hear you. Hang on a sec…' Louise carefully rolled her onto her side and wiped around her mouth with a tissue. It was important to keep moving her, in case of bedsores, and to keep her mouth dribble-free, to avoid similar on her face. 'There you go. Much more comfy. Look, I'll put the radio on for you. Beth should be here in a minute to get you up. And I'll send Tess through when she's done her business. I know you two like to see each other before breakfast.'

Louise returned to the kitchen and sat down in front of her laptop, mug in hand. There was an email from Pete. She'd read that later when she had more time, and give him an update on Patience's recovery. Then underneath, another job rejection – nothing new there.

But under that, there was something entirely unexpected. She paused and took a large gulp of tea, allowing the hot liquid to sear her oesophagus, jolting her to lucidity as it went. She had to read the email several times before taking it in. Then she snatched up her phone.

*

'Shit,' said Louise, on her third circuit of the hospital car park, two hours later. 'Shit, shit, shit.' She'd almost had that space, but some bastard in a black Range Rover had reversed at light speed to secure it instead. Damn hospital car parks, she thought; she was clearly condemned to do battle in them for all eternity.

She caught sight of an old lady in a Nissan Micra pulling out of a space about fifty metres ahead. Finally, a chink of light in this pit of despair. She could see someone circling back around in an attempt to seize the spot, but she was not letting her rightful place go this time. Her foot hit the accelerator with force and, when she reached the space, she staked her claim alongside it with a screech of brakes, bidding her bitterly disappointed rival farewell with a nod and a triumphant smile.

It was only after the other driver had retreated, however, that she realised how tiny the much-prized space was. There was a large 4x4 parked on one side, and a family-sized saloon on the other, each hugging the lines. Her own car was significantly larger than the old lady's Micra, but she had no choice but to try to fit it in. There simply was nowhere else to park. And being late for this, on top of everything else, would be disastrous.

Louise put her car into reverse and began to turn, keeping a close eye on her side mirrors as she did so. She also took a couple of deep breaths, willing her heart to slow its frantic pace, and her ears to stop ringing. She sighed with relief when her boot squeezed between its two close neighbours, and began to straighten up, willing the car to find an equilibrium.

Then – crunch.

'*Shit*,' she said once more, but louder this time, and with even more emphasis.

She opened her door a few inches and eased her body through the gap between the two cars, flinching when the plastic moulding of the door compressed her torso. When she'd finally released all of her limbs from its grasp, she walked around to the rear of the car to assess the damage.

It turned out that there was a low wall marking the end of the space and her bumper was currently impaled on it, bent and bruised. It would undoubtedly be expensive to fix. Everything to do with cars seemed to be. Where they'd find the money, she had no idea, but there was no time to worry about that now.

She ran through the car park and into the building. She scanned the email once more. Room 465, it said: presumably that was the fourth floor? She checked her watch – she had five minutes left – and hammered on the button by the lift.

'That lift's out of order,' said a passing hospital porter. 'I don't think they've called anyone about it yet. You'd be better off walking. They're all up the spout. Everything here is.'

Louise noticed that the lift button wasn't lit and it didn't seem to have budged from the sixth floor. He was probably correct.

'*Fuck!*' she said, shifting her swear words up a gear. She searched for the stairwell, and began to climb. She hadn't had time to eat breakfast that morning; in fact, she'd barely finished her cup of black tea. As she panted her way up four floors, a familiar headache came back to the fore and a wave of nausea washed over her. Then she felt tears begin to form. They were tears of frustration, of anger, of despair.

She just wanted somebody to listen, to take her seriously, to say yes, just once. Was that too much to ask?

By the time she reached the fourth floor, she had tears coursing down her cheeks and beads of sweat forming on her forehead. She rubbed her face with her sleeve, depositing foundation on her jacket as she did so. She checked her watch once more. She had two minutes to get there. There was no time for a diversion to the loos to patch her face up.

She exhaled deeply as she finally reached room 465, saying a prayer of thanks as she did so that Beth had turned up on time that morning. Some of the carers on the roster were incredibly flaky; they'd had a series of young women recently who'd taken to calling in sick with almost zero notice. That meant that Louise had no choice but to drop everything and stay with Patience. It was something she had become accustomed to and nowadays it didn't even matter much. She had nowhere in particular to be. She didn't bother making any plans, because she knew she was too unreliable. Her friends, such as they were, had stopped asking her to meet up with them long ago.

Louise knocked on the opaque glass door and a muffled voice inside the room asked her to enter. Inside, a bespectacled man in his sixties, with bushy hair and a crumpled shirt, sat behind a desk, an untied red bowtie slung over his chair.

'Mrs Willow, thank you for coming in to meet me so speedily,' he said, standing up to shake her hand. He gestured towards a blue plastic chair wedged between two filing cabinets, bidding her to sit down. She did so, taking in the tiny room crammed wall-to-wall with piles of papers, unlabelled box files and perilously stacked books.

An awkward silence followed. Louise broke it first.

'Professor Larssen, I just wanted to apologise for not making the first interview date. My daughter…'

'Yes, I know that.' Louise was startled. 'Oh yes, I know she was ill. When you didn't turn up I rang your home and left you a message asking you to call me back. I spoke to a carer, I think. Didn't you get it?'

She genuinely couldn't remember. It felt like that entire period hadn't actually happened. She had sleep-walked through most of it.

'Anyhow, could we start, Mrs Willow, with you telling me why you want this particular job?'

Louise blinked at him and took a deep breath. 'I-I saw the advert and I thought… well, I'd enjoy that.'

'What exactly would you enjoy?' He hadn't taken his gaze away from her. She began to sweat in the heat of his undivided attention. This was excruciating.

'Let me be straight with you, Professor Larssen. I don't remember the exact particulars of the job. I only got your email a couple of hours ago and I was so keen to see you. I mean, you've waited quite a long time to see me. I'm sorry I couldn't make the last interview, I really am. You see, I've always wanted to pick your brains. But Patience has been ill, as you know, and I just haven't had the time to do… research.'

The word salad had tumbled out of her mouth before she could stop it.

'I see.' He leafed through a pile of papers in front of him. He took out a document and ignored the other papers which fell onto the floor one by one, pouring down like a waterfall.

'I've been reading through your CV,' he said. 'Am I right in saying you worked as a nurse before you had your children?'

'Yes. But that was more than thirty years ago.'

He nodded. 'And since then, you've been volunteering?'

'Yes,' she answered. 'At Patience's school, then later, at the local day centre. I did general admin, rosters, fundraising, a bit of first aid.'

'Interesting,' he said, uttering the word, but sounding to her like he barely meant it. He was clearly thinking about something else. Louise studied her shoes, still shining from the rigorous clean she'd subjected them to before her last unsuccessful interview, for an admin job at a firm that fitted bifold doors. She'd literally applied for every job she could find in the local area over the past few months, not really caring what it was, or whether she was suited to it. She just wanted to earn some money, because she could see how things were. Pete tried to hide it from her, but she wasn't a fool.

The one thing she could recall about this job was that it was more allied to her skillset than most. It was a position with the team who ran Professor Larssen's clinic, although she'd forgotten the precise details. It might be a job as the office cleaner, she thought, for all the attention she'd paid to the advert; it was his name that had drawn her to it.

She had known about Professor Larssen for years. She and Pete had poured over his early papers into Rett syndrome and its causes, particularly after the discovery of the gene fault which caused Rett, in the 1990s. They had even tried to get Patience signed up to some of the drug trials his team had run over the years, but she had been refused a place each time, mostly for being too old, or not having the symptom they were hoping to treat.

When she looked up from the floor, the professor was running his finger slowly down the side of the paper, ignoring her. Sitting there in awkward silence made Louise feel incredibly exposed, given her ignorance of this role's details and her lack of recent experience in the workplace. She'd had enough bruising encounters in interview rooms in the past month to last a lifetime and, at that moment, she felt like giving up. She couldn't take many more blows. This was clearly a waste of time, she thought. She felt her frustration rising, like a ball of fire in her throat.

'Professor. Let's be honest here,' she said, pulling herself up straight and tugging her shirt down over her stomach. 'Most people can't be bothered to read past the first line of my covering letter. I've been out of paid work for a generation and I'm getting on a bit. Trying to salvage a career this late is really a vanity project, isn't it? You're thinking it, and so am I. So the question is, why are you bothering to see me at all?'

Professor Larssen looked directly at her.

'My dear, I'm too old and too busy to afford to do things for no good reason.' Louise held his gaze and stared at him accusingly. 'I think you'll be able to help me,' he said. 'You'll be aware of my work?'

She nodded.

'Yes.'

'You'll know then that for the last couple of decades, I've been investigating Rett syndrome. And you were kind enough in your application letter to tell me that Patience has Rett.'

Louise nodded, wondering where on earth this could be going.

'Well, after the discovery of the faulty gene at the root of the problem, MECP2, twenty years ago, teams like mine began the next phase – working out if there was anything we could do to mitigate its effects,' he continued. 'We've looked into repurposing existing drugs, for example. But to cut a very rambling story short – I'm given to rambling, you might have noticed – we're at a critical stage with a new trial and I need someone who can talk to parents. Because I'm not very good at it. As you might have noticed also.'

He peered at her over his reading glasses. Then he cracked a smile. 'You must forgive the disorganisation and my sparse conversation with you on the phone this morning,' he continued. 'But there it is. That's why I'm so interested in having you here. Largely, to help me sort out this mess,' he waved his hands in the direction of the overflowing piles of files, 'and then to help me do something quite exciting.'

'What is it that you want me to help you to do?' she asked, her tone softer and more polite.

'It's the parents, and their children. We've been developing a therapy which may help people with Rett syndrome, like your daughter. We've had promising results in animal trials and we're now preparing to move to the human testing phase. We're looking to recruit families for them and we need – *I* need – someone who is better at communication than I am to help me do it. And someone who understands a bit about medicine. And Rett.'

'What sort of therapy? Is it a new drug?' she asked, pulling herself up in her chair.

'Oh no, my dear, no. This is gene therapy. We've tried

it on mice so far and it appears to completely reverse the syndrome.' Suddenly, everything was in sharp focus. Louise was aware of the individual leaves on the trees outside the window, the sound of phones ringing far down the corridor, the layers of dust on the desk.

'Reverse it? Completely?'

'Evidence so far suggests that, but it's too early to say with certainty, of course. We need to try it on humans now,' he said, seemingly oblivious to Louise's astonishment.

'H-how do you do it? How does it work?' asked Louise, struggling to get the words out, feeling like she was straining for air.

'We inject them with a virus which carries a healthy copy of the gene that's faulty, and causes it to rectify itself.'

'Just like that? So you'd just inject this into someone who has Rett syndrome and they'd get better? Be completely normal?'

'That's the tricky bit,' he said, pulling up his glasses and rubbing his eyes. 'We don't know. We obviously observed physical changes in the mice, but how that effect will transfer into humans, we cannot tell. Other genes we haven't yet discovered could yet be at play. So it might simply ameliorate their symptoms, but still leave them severely disabled. Or it could just do nothing. This is just phase one. At this stage we will mostly be testing the dose and checking for side effects.' The professor paused to sip his tea. He baulked and put his cup down. Perhaps it was cold. 'Ideally, of course, we'd get to Rett sufferers before they show signs of the disorder in childhood, but as you know, the disability is not screened for yet as part of amniocentesis.' Louise noticed that he appeared to be doodling star shapes on his own notes.

She'd often wished she could revisit Patience's first months and freeze time, so that she'd never find out what was to come. What if it had been possible then to test her and treat her, so that she could have developed normally? The idea was so glorious that it made her angry that this was now even a possibility, however remote. Patience had lived with this hideous disease for thirty years. Louise had been forced to watch her blonde-haired angel descend into paralysis and silence, slowly, painfully, inexorably. What if she'd never had to? And more than that, what if someone could make it all stop, even now?

'So the volunteers you want for the trials, I assume you'll want them young, then?' she said, drawing on her (failed) attempts to secure Patience a place on numerous drug trials.

'Actually, we can't do the trial on children. It wouldn't be ethical. So we are looking for adults, this time. We actually need a wide age range for the trial to be as encompassing as possible, Mrs Willow.'

'Louise. My name is Louise.'

'Louise. There's another thing I must mention. If you take this job, I can give your daughter a place on the trial, providing, that is, that she meets the criteria. If you want her to do it, of course. It doesn't come without risk.'

Louise did not hesitate.

'I'll take the job,' she said.

6

Eliza

August

'When you chose that backdrop for the photos, didn't it even bloody occur to you that it might look bloody ridiculous?' The fire-breathing dragon – her boss, Jenny, who was five years her junior and absolutely gloried in it – was in full swing. 'I mean, could you not see that the juxtaposition of a no-entry sign and a cactus next to the company managing director at the launch of a new industrial lubricant might be a bit, you know – unfortunate?'

Eliza wanted to laugh, but swallowed hard instead. This made her splutter, generating a noise which sounded more jovial than she had intended.

'We'll probably lose the account, Eliza, and I am fucking fed up to the back teeth with your lack of attention to detail. Your head's in the fucking clouds. It's not bloody screwed on.' Jenny liked to swear, but she was also quite posh, and the combination was often unintentionally funny. 'Come and see me tomorrow morning, first thing. I need time to think about this.'

Eliza didn't hang around after that pronouncement, in

case she started up again. She grabbed the coat from the back of her chair, clasped her phone to her chest, muttered something about missing her train, and left. Once safely outside the office, she felt the first tears of frustration and embarrassment begin to fall. She ducked into the toilet and locked the cubicle door. When she could be certain that no one could see her, she let the metaphorical taps open and cried with abandon, gulping for air, before hammering so hard on her legs that she left angry scarlet marks on her thighs.

She really, really needed to stop crying, she thought. This was ridiculous. She was thirty-bloody-six years old. Time to grow up and get a grip. No man, and no job, was worth this. Other people her age were married, raising kids, paying off a mortgage, climbing up the career ladder. Meanwhile, she barely managed to pay her rent each month and her chances of marriage and kids now looked about as likely as finding a reasonably priced house in Clapham. She had wasted so many years, hadn't she? All those years waiting for Ed to propose had been a complete and utter waste of time. She had clung on like a fangirl to her idol, desperately hoping that her dreams would eventually come true. It was humiliating, frankly.

When the waves of sobs had subsided, she listened carefully to check no one was outside before walking to the sinks and gingerly checking out her appearance. It wasn't good. She had layered on mascara that morning in an attempt to look more alive. Now she looked like a goth who'd stood for far too long at a bus stop in the rain. The manufacturers of her apparently waterproof mascara should be sued. She was fishing around in her gargantuan handbag for tissues and moisturiser to try to remove the gunk when her phone beeped. It was a message from Katy.

Wench, where the devil are you? I've got a bottle in front of me all to myself, and I look like a wino.

'Shit,' she said, out loud. She'd forgotten she was supposed to be meeting Katy after work. Her encounter with the dragon and her post-Ed hangover, which so far was worse than anything booze had ever managed to impose on her, had removed her so far from reality that she couldn't even remember her evening plans. Bugger! Eliza grabbed a tissue, tidied up as much of her make-up as she could, and dashed out of the door. She typed a hurried reply to Katy, apologising, as she ran down the stairs.

She emerged into a beautiful late summer's evening. All around her as she walked, weary London workers were pouring out of their offices at the end of a long, mind-numbing day, longing to peel off damp, shiny suits and agonising heels and kick back for the evening with a pint and an attitude. The street smelt of chips laced with vinegar and mayo, sweating gin and tonic and the sweet sadness of accidentally dropped ice cream from Luigi's Gelato Emporium, which was just down the street. Above the buildings nearby, the Shard loomed large, reflecting the sunshine.

Eliza's love affair with London had begun long ago. Her parents had taken her on a rare weekend away without Patience when she was eleven, their destination of choice the capital. It had been booked to celebrate her mum and dad's wedding anniversary, but to Eliza – the recipient of her parents' undiluted attention for forty-eight hours – it had surely been all about her. Even the train journey had seemed tinted with magic. It had been February, and there had been a light snowstorm followed by a frost across most of the Midlands and South-East. Frozen fallow fields, punctuated by mighty oaks, ice-encrusted wooden fences and large red-brick farmhouses had quickly given way to an urban landscape of graffiti-strewn bridges and tunnels, forgotten canals and trundling tube trains; for Eliza, it had been love at first sight. The sheer volume of people around her, all seemingly experiencing lives of infinite possibilities, filled her with excitement and hope. And as the train pulled up into a dirty, fume-filled Paddington station, she decided that London would eventually become her home. Here, she could become whoever she wanted to be.

And that was why she had applied for a place at King's College, right in the centre of the action, to study English. Which meant that she had unwittingly started herself on a trajectory which would end with Ed dumping her just after they'd finally got engaged. If she hadn't gone to that university, had instead chosen the convenient, red-brick campus of, say, Birmingham, she might have met a bloke called... Jake; studying, oh, maybe geography, and together they might have settled down, produced two globe-trotting children and studied maps together, or whatever it was that geography graduates did. But instead, it had been London and Ed, and there was absolutely nothing she could do about that now.

After employing what Eliza called her 'London walk', which was, in reality, more of a jog, she finally arrived at the wine bar which Katy had appointed for that evening's meet-up. She winced at the sign outside, which invited customers to enjoy 'it's beer garden'. It was hard, she felt, to take businesses seriously when they couldn't even use an apostrophe properly.

Shrugging off her distaste for grammatical inaccuracy, Eliza walked into the bar. Its windows were all open onto the street, but once she entered she realised that their ventilation efforts were in vain – it was bloody boiling in there. Katy was sitting in a booth near the window, tapping on her phone, her black, glossy hair reflected in the chrome pendant lamp above her head. A bottle of white wine and two glasses – one half full – were on the table. Eliza smiled broadly at her as she leaned in for a kiss, hoping that her earlier brief make-up fix was convincing.

'Blimey, love, you look awful.'

So it hadn't worked, then.

'Cheers, that really makes me feel better,' Eliza replied, smiling, despite everything. Then she let herself be hugged – and this caused the tears to fall once more.

'It's been pretty shit, then?' Katy said, after she released Eliza and fetched another tissue from her own bag for her to use. 'All sorts of shit? Or just Ed shit?'

'All sorts of shit,' Eliza answered, sniffing.

'Work? Patience? Your parents?'

'Every bit of that. Mostly Ed, I suppose, but then I made a huge, hammering error at work today for which I'm going to pay dearly.'

'Is your boss still a witch?'

'Yes, I think she'll be eligible for a broomstick upgrade soon. She's next level,' said Eliza.

'That company seems like a pretty shit place to work, if you ask me,' said Katy, taking a slurp of wine, her right eyebrow raised. 'Toxic. Do you regret leaving NewHome? They seemed nice.'

'Hmm,' replied Eliza, pouring herself a glass of wine. She thought back to the small homelessness charity in Brixton where she'd cut her PR teeth. She'd been a one-woman band in a tiny office with no aircon and a smelly fridge, but she'd loved the stories she'd placed in the media, and the characters she'd worked with. If only they'd paid more, she thought, she could have stayed. But she and Ed had been wanting to buy their own place, and she had needed a better salary. And he had encouraged her to move to a corporate environment, because he said it would be more 'stable'. More fool her, she thought. All that effort for a future that never materialised.

'And how is Patience now, after the accident?' asked Katy, changing the subject, to Eliza's relief.

'Better. Back at home with Mum, epilepsy – if she's even got it at all – under control, it seems. But Mum's stretched to the limit, as ever. She was close to exhaustion for a bit there, trying and failing to sleep in the hospital, refusing to let any of the carers come and do a shift.' Eliza leaned over and accepted another tissue from Katy's bag.

'Won't even consider letting her go in for extra respite care either, hey? Sounds about right. Have you been home to check up on her?'

Katy had known Eliza since primary school, and had been a regular visitor to the Willow family home throughout their childhood. And that meant that she knew, without Eliza having to explain, all about her family's complicated dynamic. She understood how her mum functioned – or often, didn't function – and how Dad fitted into the mix.

She also knew how Eliza felt about Patience. All of it, even the jealousy and resentment she'd felt on really bad days, as a teen. She was deeply ashamed she'd ever felt that way, and so it was a relief to her that only her best friend really knew about it. Katy never brought it up explicitly, however; she just had a way of acknowledging it silently and dismissing it at the same time, and Eliza loved that. It was wonderful to feel heard, forgiven and understood. And mostly, it was just a relief not to have to go through it all again. It had been hard enough to deal with the first time.

Katy had also been Eliza's flatmate for two years before deciding to move in with her boyfriend – now fiancé – Matt. Matt and Ed knew each other, but had not become friends; it was something that had always bothered Eliza. Eliza saw Katy reach for her own engagement ring and begin spinning it. Eliza moved her own hands onto her lap.

'Not yet. I haven't felt right, since Ed – but I will.' Eliza winced internally as she spoke. In truth, she felt incredibly guilty about not going home to help, but heaven knows, she had a full-time job and an emotional mess of her own to deal with. It wouldn't be fair to burden her mother with it, on top of everything else. 'But you're on the money re respite care,' she continued. 'She resists it as much as possible, even though she's knackered. But Patience has been staying at Morton Lodge a bit more since she was discharged from hospital. Dad is trying to encourage her to do it.'

Katy gave her a sympathetic smile. 'So your dad's still working away, then?'

'Yes. They still need the money, I think, not that they talk to me about it. They never seem to have enough cash. I think Dad wants to retire soon. So they need the tax-free salary.'

'I see,' Katy replied. 'How do they feel about the wedding being off?'

Eliza took a large gulp from her wine glass. 'They don't know. I haven't told them yet.'

'*You haven't?* But it's been a month!' Katy made an incredulous face.

'I know, I know! It's ridiculous. But I haven't found the right time. Mum and Dad were so caught up with Patience and then Dad flew back to Qatar and I came back to work – and well, I don't want to tell them on the phone.'

Eliza had decided not to tell her the real reason, which was that she was determined to win Ed back. This was just a blip. Pre-wedding nerves. They were meant to be together, she just knew it, and she was sure he would come back with his tail between his legs, very soon. And then she wouldn't have to tell her mother anything about it. It would be like nothing had ever happened. They could all carry on as before.

'*Hang on a sec!*' Katy's eyes flew down and settled on Eliza's left hand, which was now lifting up her glass. '*You're still wearing your ring!*'

Eliza blanched, put her wine down and put her hand back on her lap. Damn it, she thought; I should have remembered to take it off before coming out.

'And you've had loads of weekends free – you could have driven to see your mum to tell her then.'

'I don't have weekends free. I have a gym class on Saturday morning and I'm finally getting good at hot yoga,' said Eliza, trying to deflect the question.

Katy snorted.

'Oh, come on, Lize. The last time you went to the gym, you fell off the running machine and twisted your ankle.'

Eliza eyed her friend. Katy always knew when she was lying. 'Yes, well, I could have gone home, I suppose,' she said. 'But I didn't want to. As I said, I haven't really been myself.'

Eliza pictured the scene: her mother in floods of tears, a visible demonstration of her devastation at the cancellation of the wedding; and, of course, the deposit they would lose. Their wedding had been the one ray of sunshine her mother had had to look forward to and it had tangibly improved her mood. Also, there would be no grandchildren now, would there? Talk about a double whammy. Eliza knew that Louise really wanted to be a grandma and Patience could obviously never manage that one, could she? It was up to Eliza to provide the next generation, and she'd blown it.

'Don't want to? Why? Come on, Lize, this is insane.'

'I don't want to give her something else to be upset about,' she said. That, at least, was the truth, she thought. 'Mum *needs* this wedding. You know how she is; she thinks Patience is going to die at any moment. It's the only thing that's keeping her going.'

The two friends eyed each other. 'Eliza, you have a wedding booked for next summer. I'm getting married too, so I know how enormous an undertaking it is. If you are going to get any money back on it at all, you need to cancel it, *now*. Does Ed know that you haven't cancelled it?'

'I have no idea. We haven't been in touch,' replied Eliza.

'Bloody hell! Has he cancelled your honeymoon?'

'Probably. *He* sodding booked it.'

'Has he given you your share back?'

'No.'

'You need to ask him for it! How are you affording the rent?'

'I'm thinking of advertising for a lodger. I just haven't got around to it yet.'

'What a bloody mess! And don't you have a food tasting scheduled for next week? Have you cancelled that at least?'

Eliza didn't reply.

'Jesus, you're still going, aren't you? You're still going to try the sodding food for your reception even though you're not actually going to get married?'

'I am *waiting*, for *Mum's* sake,' Eliza said, loudly. 'I am delaying this so that I can spare her the shock. She's had enough shocks.'

'Eliza, it's been four weeks – *four weeks* – and Ed has not come back. You haven't even spoken to him. Don't you think it might be time to come clean? And *come on*, your parents will cope. I doubt they love him as much as you think they do. He's a knob.'

'He's everything they want in a son-in-law, Katy.' There was a snort from the other side of the table, but Eliza was thinking about her mum's delight when they'd got engaged. It was something she thought of, often. 'Look, he's been a part of my life for so long that I no longer really function without him. And there's so much that's great about him – he's so successful, he knows what he wants... And I find myself wanting to send him messages myriad times a day with just general observations about weird men I see on the tube, or YouTube videos of mad cats, or disastrous interviews on the *Today* programme – and I can't. And it bloody hurts. So we must be a real thing, mustn't we?'

'It *will* hurt,' Katy said, then took another swig of wine. 'You were together for years. Christ, almost fifteen of the buggers! But that doesn't mean he was right for you. He's behaved like a tosser and he doesn't deserve you wanting him back.'

Eliza suspected that this was the polite version of what Katy was really thinking. She wasn't usually one for holding back.

'I'm afraid I don't have your strength, Katy. I can't do it. I need him. And anyway, you don't need strength, you have Matt. You should try being me. Ed was my *One*. The only one who'd have me. Everyone else has run a mile.'

Katy's mouth dropped open.

'You are genuinely saying that you would still marry him after this, if he came back with his tail between his legs and asked you to?'

'Yes. He's the only guy I've ever loved. And the only guy who will ever love me.'

'Eliza, my dear, you are deluded. I love you, I really do, but you are deluded.'

'Cheers.'

'You know I'm saying this because I care. I properly care. More than he does.' Katy had reached out to put her hand on Eliza's.

'I know. I know. But I can't say goodbye to all of this, just yet,' Eliza replied, looking firmly into her wine glass, and not at her friend. 'I waited too long for it.'

'OK. I've had my rant. But please think about it. Let's try to move on,' said Katy, reaching for the drinks menu. 'Firstly, let's order cocktails. And then tell me what on earth you did to incur the wrath of the boss from hell.' Eliza managed a genuine smile before filling her in on the desperate details of her workplace faux pas, cactus and all.

*

It was several hours later when the pair tumbled out of the bar and into a minicab home. They dropped Katy first, at the studio flat she shared with Matt in Vauxhall. She planted a kiss on Eliza's cheek as she opened the door. 'Courage!' she said, as she got out. 'This too shall pass.'

As the cab drew away from the curb, Eliza felt a rare surge of hope. Being with someone who knew her almost as well as Ed had made her feel less alone, if only for a short while. Perhaps she would survive this after all.

That feeling of hope lasted only a second or so.

Her phone beeped. Eliza pulled it out of her pocket, convinced it would be a message from Katy, saying she'd forgotten something. But it wasn't Katy. It was from Ed.

Hello there. Sorry I haven't been in touch. I wondered though – would you like to meet up to talk? I think we need closure.

All the best friends in the world couldn't protect her from herself now.

7

Pete

Pete held several paper towels under the tap for a few seconds, flapping at the sensor impatiently to persuade it to vent forth. When they were sufficiently damp, he wiped his face and neck, noting the brown staining, a confirmation of the sand and dust he'd just removed. He'd performed a similar ritual at the airport in Qatar, but desert dust was hardy stuff and he wanted to feel properly clean before he went through passport control.

He hated Heathrow at this time of day. It was heaving, despite the late hour. Several large aircraft had just landed, the e-gates were inexplicably shut, and the queue at immigration, now being ushered, loudly and doggedly, into a semblance of order by a member of Border Force, snaked out far beyond the maze of cordoned corridors. Pete reckoned that pausing for a while would make very little difference to the time he'd spend in the queue.

He reached into his bag and pulled out a soft grey V-neck jumper. It was only ever used on trips back to the UK, and it had come to signify homecoming to him. He also considered donning a scarf, but decided that no self-respecting Brit – even an expat Brit – could get away with that in summer.

It was a warm evening by local standards, but these days he wasn't much used to temperatures below thirty centigrade. The two men using the urinals next to him were wearing shorts, sandals and T-shirts, but he felt freezing. He pulled the jumper over his head, noting that this was the point at which he had to change gear. If he tried to live his Qatar life in Oxfordshire, his wife wouldn't recognise him. More to the point, he didn't really recognise himself.

He checked his reflection in the mirror before leaving. God, he thought, I look old. And tired. His good looks, if he'd ever had them, were long gone. He'd got the first flight out he could, just a few hours after his ten-hour early shift had finished. He was getting too old for twenty-four-hour days. Retirement was too far away for his liking.

When he emerged from the toilets, the queue was a little more manageable and his line moved fairly quickly. He bypassed baggage reclaim as he'd only brought a small bag for the cabin, then walked through the double doors, past customs and the railings holding back the assembled melee of taxi drivers, hotel reps and family members, to the hire car desks. It was a well-practised manoeuvre. It was a long drive for Louise, so he had a privilege card with a company who rented him cars cheaply. He wasn't ever home long enough to justify them owning a second car.

As he stood outside, waiting for the courtesy bus, his mind turned to Patience. When he'd last seen her she'd been in a hospital bed, staring despondently at the ceiling. He'd hated having to leave, but James, his boss, had been texting him hourly for updates, nagging him to return as soon as he could. Louise had assured him that she had it sorted and could cope without him, and she did, always. She was so organised, so dedicated, so crusading. She had to be; he'd been out of the country for work for much of the past decade.

The transfer bus arrived and he jumped on, eager to be embraced by its warmth. The journey around the airport perimeter was smooth and unhindered by traffic. When he arrived at the car hire office, he found it deserted. The sole member of staff manning the desk looked at him in disappointment as he entered, sighing as he winched his ample buttocks into a standing position before swigging the dregs of full-sugar coke from a can. He barely made eye contact as he tapped Pete's details into his computer and zapped through a list of inflated, optional insurance policies, to which he clearly did not expect a positive response. Within minutes, Pete was driving out in the direction of the M25, having been handed the keys to a mid-range, minimum-trim, low-powered commuting car, just like all of the others.

London's orbital motorway, so often clogged with thousands of frustrated motorists, was almost entirely empty. He did his best not to delight the average speed cameras as he headed north and then west on the M40, opening his windows a crack and breathing deeply as he entered the green belt just outside London, savouring the scent of grass and pollen. Qatar's air never smelled of either.

It was 2 a.m. when he reached the house, so he was surprised to find that the lights were still on downstairs, as if welcoming him back. She's made a conscious decision to do this, he thought; how wonderful. Back in the early days of his expat existence, she had often greeted him at the door, whatever the hour, with a smile on her face and her best underwear concealed beneath a dressing gown, waiting to be unwrapped.

When he had finally located the correct key for the front door on his ring of assorted keys from two continents, he turned it in the lock and pushed it open. He could see Louise sitting at the computer in their office, with her back to him. So, she had waited up for him, too! His heart swelled. He desperately needed a hug. He went for weeks in Qatar without any human physical contact at all.

She gave no sign that she'd heard the door, so he tiptoed through the hallway and into the study, aiming to surprise her. As he drew near, he realised that she was typing frantically. He moved further forward and tapped her gently and swiftly on both shoulders.

'I'm ho-ome!'

He had almost sung it.

'Oh, hi, Pete. I'm working. Sorry. With you in a minute.'

He was stunned.

'I've got this urgent thing to do,' she added, turning her head around very slightly as an obvious afterthought, and receiving his kiss on her right cheek.

'More important than welcoming me home? Grrayt.' His Brummie accent, severely eroded after years of living in the south, came out when he was riled. He walked out of the room and into the kitchen. There, he opened the fridge, reached for a cold beer, and opened it. Then he glanced towards Tess, who was asleep and dreaming in her crate, her legs miming a frantic run.

'How was your flight?' his wife asked mechanically

from next door, as the click-click-clack of the keyboard continued.

'Hot, cramped, tiring.' It was a familiar response, usually met with a kiss and a directive to have a shower while she made him a cup of tea, or something stronger. He resolved to have the shower anyhow, but walked down the corridor to check on Patience first.

She was sleeping soundly on her back, her arm lying across her chest in a sling, her mouth wide open, her breathing shallow. He stood in her bedroom doorway for a few moments, taking her in. Even though he had received regular updates from Louise while he'd been away, every time he returned he needed to see her for himself, straight away. He feared that he'd find her worsening, or weaker; he didn't entirely trust Louise to tell him the truth when he was in Qatar – not out of malice, but out of a desire to protect him. He knew that she shielded him from a great deal, understanding that hearing about her struggles would make him feel even worse. He hated having to work overseas, and she knew that.

Content now that his daughter was showing no signs of ill-health, he returned to the study, his beer still in his hand. 'Lou, why are you still awake at this ungodly hour, anyway, if you're not waiting for me?' he said to his wife's back. '*What on earth are you doing?*'

'I'm sending in an application for something important. You'll like it, I promise. I'll tell you in the morning.'

'Can't it wait?' He placed his hands on her shoulders. 'It's gone two.'

'No. The sooner I do this, the better things will be,' she replied, her own hands remaining fixedly on the keyboard.

'For all of us. Towel's out in the bathroom,' she added, her voice light.

Pete spotted a few key words in the document she was typing.

'A medical trial? What sort of medical trial?'

'Go to bed, Pete. It's a long story. As I said, better saved for tomorrow, when you're not tired.'

'Is there something wrong with Patience? Or you? Are you ill?'

'No, actually, I'm better today than I've been in years.' Louise swivelled her chair around to look at him, dislodging his hands from her shoulders. He saw that there was defiance in her eyes – and something else he couldn't quite discern.

'I've got a job,' she said.

'A job? What brought that on? You know you don't need to work.' Pete took a swig from the beer bottle.

'No, but I want to. I've been applying for a few months now, and today I got offered a job. A *good* one.' Louise smiled.

'Bloody hell, Lou. You could have told me.' He watched as her smile turned into a scowl.

'You're hardly ever here now, and anyway, I didn't want to get your hopes up. I've been out of it so long, it was a very remote possibility.'

'So what is it?' he asked, perching on the side of the desk, trying to defuse the situation as best he could. He knew that he should be pleased that she would be earning a wage, but somehow, news of her having a job had suddenly made his life in Qatar seem less necessary, and that made it so much harder for him to bear.

'At the hospital. A medical research assistant.'

'But you're a nurse.'

'*Was* a nurse. Years ago. This uses some of those skills, though.'

'When are you starting?'

'Tomorrow – no, later today. And this application is part of it.'

'You're going to take part in a medical trial yourself?'

'No, Patience is.'

'*Jesus*, Lou. You didn't think to talk to me about this first?' Pete took another swig and glared at her.

'It's a trial with Professor Larssen, Pete. You know, the one who ran all the drug trials for Rett? We applied for a few. But this one is different. And it's the best thing that could ever happen to her, seriously. The thing is, I had to make a quick decision, and you were in the air at the time. But you'll love it, I promise. Just give me a chance to explain it to you, tomorrow.'

'I'll love our daughter being experimented on? *Really?* I see.'

Pete remembered applying for those drug trials. Patience had been younger then, and the last vestiges of hope had not yet escaped him. But now? Now they were settled and they were coping – and frankly, he was glad that he'd lost all hope that Patience would 'get better'. That hope had almost destroyed him.

He had finished his first beer and decided that the time was right for a second. He marched back into the kitchen, retrieved another bottle from the fridge. He stood still for a minute, concentrating on both his rapid breathing and the cold, numbing liquid. When he returned to the study, Louise had resumed typing.

'What is it, then? *Tell me*. What are they going to do to her?'

'You really want to do this now?'

'Yes, I do. After a seven-hour flight and a two-hour drive, I'm still wide awake and *raring to go*. Let's do this now.' His nostrils flared.

'It's gene therapy. Scientists reckon they can reverse Rett syndrome.'

Pete took another swig and swallowed hard.

'Reverse it, *how*? Are they going to wave a wand? *Say abracadabra?*'

Louise chose to ignore him.

'They inject a virus with a copy of the gene, without the Rett fault. And then... It fixes it.'

'That's not possible.'

'I am telling you, it is. Or at least, it may be. The experiments they've done on mice are very promising.'

'You're going to make our daughter have experimental treatment that's only been tested on *mice*? Bloody hell.'

'There's really no need to be like this, Pete.'

'There's every reason. Because I love Patience as she is. I have come to terms with it, after all of these years. This is who Patience was always meant to be. It's time you started believing that too, Lou. You have to let the hope go.'

'Why the *hell* would I do that?' replied Louise. 'This new trial is amazing. It's extraordinary. Denying Patience this chance would be betraying her. This could change her life. It could unlock her. She could maybe find a way to learn, to speak again.'

'Christ, Lou, this sounds like science fiction! Have you even *considered* what the risks are? God knows I'm no scientist, but even I know that experimental trials are full of risks.'

'They will take all the necessary precautions.'

'Precautions, *bollocks*,' said Pete, finishing up his beer. 'Look, I'm knackered from travelling all day to get home to spend a precious week with my family. I'm going to bed. You have obviously decided that I don't need to be consulted. Thanks a lot, Lou, thanks a lot. I work my arse off halfway across the world for you. And here you go acting like we're divorced.'

There was a prolonged silence while they eyed each other warily. Finally, Louise spoke.

'I often feel like I am,' she said.

'Then there's no point discussing this further, is there?' he said, slamming his beer bottle down on the table, storming out of the room and stomping up the stairs.

He heard her call out his name as he went, but he could tell that it was a half-hearted effort, so he didn't bother to reply. As he snatched the towel that had been laid out for him on the heated towel rail, he heard the clicks of the keyboard start up once more.

Pete was woken up in the morning by what sounded like two furious blackbirds sumo-wrestling on the telephone wire outside their window. He turned to check the clock on his bedside table and discovered that it was only 4.30 a.m. But still, it was 6.30 a.m. in Doha. Normally he'd be up, dressed and in the car on his way to the building site right now, ready for a 7 a.m. start. So this was practically a lie-in, he reasoned.

He turned over to look at Louise. She was comatose beside him, her blonde, highlighted hair ruched by her pillow, the remnants of mascara forming a half crescent under her eyes, her lips parted. Her breathing was shallow and rhythmic. It was difficult to believe that the defiant, angry woman he'd been met with last night was the same woman lying beside him. Her face was relaxed now – her dreams were clearly offering her respite – and the lines on her face, forged by decades of stress and exhaustion, were much smoother. They might almost be called laughter lines now, rather than the physical evidence of sorrow.

She had always made him laugh. That was one of the first things he'd noticed about her. They had laughed their way through financial crises, family crises and parenting crises, as only a couple genuinely, *really* in love, can. It had made the hardships they'd faced over the years more bearable. Even a few weeks ago, when Patience had been in hospital, they had found comfort in each other.

Where had it all gone so wrong, so quickly, he wondered. Maybe it had been building for a long time and he hadn't noticed. It didn't help that he had taken yet another foreign contract, of course. He wasn't around to absorb the daily worries with her, to gauge how she was feeling from one moment to the next. What had he missed?

Maybe she was angry about his decision to take this latest expat posting? But she had always been supportive of his employment choices before. She knew he didn't want to work for his brother, and she knew that the Middle East was where the money was. She understood that their future retirement relied on this contract. No, he didn't think it was about that. And it couldn't be the menopause, could it?

She'd gone through that a decade ago. It had been awful for her, he knew that, but she had come out the other side some time ago and he was glad.

Could it be Eliza getting engaged? Perhaps that had prompted her to reminisce, to regret that their married life hadn't panned out the way they had both hoped. They had both planned to enjoy their children while they were young, to have family adventures, and then to wave them off into adulthood, enjoying their retirement together, alone.

In reality, of course, their family adventures had largely been limited to long drives in their converted car, isolated picnics and days out to disability-friendly museums, and he was the only one of them to set foot on a plane in the past decade. He had not been able to offer her the life she had wanted, he knew that, and Patience, wonderful as she was, came with lifelong responsibilities.

Could it be Patience that was bothering her so much? After all, judging by her behaviour last night, she was obsessed with this trial, this insane *alchemy*. But Patience was on a fairly even keel at the moment; aside from that seizure, she had been fairly stable for a long time now, and the carers who looked after her both at home and in the respite care place treated her well. They had a system going and it seemed to be working. And Louise was a coper. It was who she was.

No. It *must* be about money, he thought. She was going to have to go out to work now, adding to her already considerable daily stresses and strains, just to bring in a few paltry quid. And he was entirely to blame for that, he knew.

He leaned over then and kissed her softly, not wishing to wake her. He had not been able to do so last night, and it had felt wrong. Then he rolled over, and stood up as quietly as he could. His back ached, and he rubbed it. He decided to ignore it. It ached every day now, a sign that he was well past the age where physical labour came easily.

He tiptoed down the stairs, hearing the bottom one squeak loudly as he did so. Shit, he thought; I really need to get around to fixing that. He decided that he'd do it later, when Lou was up. He had a little list of things he needed to sort around the house, actually, and he was determined to finally get around to them during this visit. Perhaps it would even cheer Lou up a bit.

He headed towards the kitchen with breakfast in mind, but was distracted by the sight of the computer's screen lighting up the study. Lou had still been down here when he'd fallen asleep last night, and she had obviously failed to shut it down when she'd finally made it to bed. He walked towards the computer and put all thoughts of coffee and toast out of his mind. She'd printed the information and application documents for that trial and they were sitting in a pile on the desk. He took a seat and began to read.

He scanned the first page, which was an introduction to Professor Larssen and his team. The next page was an introduction to Rett and gene therapy. It explained in simple, layman's terms what caused Rett syndrome – a mutation on a gene called MECP2. That gene, it said, made a protein which people need for the brain to function normally. Patience and those like her didn't have enough of this protein, so their brains were severely damaged as a result. It sounded so straightforward when put like that, he thought. Almost comprehensible.

And then it mentioned those damn mice. Everyone in the

Rett community knew about those poor rodents. In 2007, researchers at Edinburgh University gave Rett syndrome to a few mice (*lucky mice*, he thought), and then replaced the protein they were missing. And instead of carrying on as their visibly disabled selves, they got better.

This apparent miracle had fired up Rett families around the globe, each and every one of them desperate for a 'cure'. He remembered Louise coming to him that day, tears in her eyes, summarising the news as if she was announcing the second coming, or Aston Villa winning the league.

But instead of giving him hope, he had actually felt frightened. He still felt guilty about that instinctive reaction, because it was clearly so counter-intuitive. Why wouldn't anyone want their disabled daughter 'fixed', after all? But the thing was, he didn't see her as broken. He saw her as whole, as a person in her own right, her own special variety of normal.

Things had gone quiet after that research had come out, and he'd been glad of that. Those researchers had suggested gene therapy as a possible avenue, but the technology was in its infancy then, seemed to be something only for the next generation, not for theirs. And he had come to terms with that, definitely. Patience was her own person. She was who she was. And he loved her for it.

He turned over to the next page. Here, Larssen's team explained how they planned to carry out the gene therapy, using a virus that they injected directly into the spine. Pete knew from personal experience – a lumbar puncture he'd needed due to a meningitis scare years ago – that this could be both painful and frightening. The lumbar puncture would happen in hospital, the guidance said, followed by a few days in a ward for observation. Then, if they seemed stable, nurses would keep an eye on trial participants when they got home.

He turned over once more. This page was a list of possible side effects and risks. His throat tightened as he read it and he flipped frantically through several more pages of warnings and saw that Lou had already signed her section on the permissions page. So she had given them the go-ahead already, having read this. Who was this woman? What had she done with his wife?

He stood up and marched out into the hall. There, he dug deep into the pocket of an old coat that was hanging on a hook, pulling out a packet of cigarettes and a battered yellow lighter. Then he walked past the dog, still asleep in her crate, to the back door. He unlocked it and strode out to the end of their garden, bashing the weeds underfoot. When he reached the wire fence that marked their boundary, he pulled a cigarette out of the pack and lit up, inhaling deeply. Lou thought he'd given up smoking a few years ago. In fact, he *had* given up, mostly. But at times of stress, he lapsed. Understandably, he thought.

He surveyed the scene around him. Beyond the wire fence was the back of next door's ageing concrete garage. All sorts of detritus had been shoved between that wall and the fence over the years: planks of wood; dead snails; old drink cans; rocks they'd dug up when trying to establish a flower bed. He turned around and noticed that their red swing frame, once Eliza's greatest joy, was now covered in rust and leaning over at a worrying angle. It must have finally wrenched itself out of the concrete base, he thought. He had stood behind that thing through countless summers, pulling Eliza back as high as she could go before releasing her, addicted both to her screams of joy and repeated cries of, 'More, Daddy! More! Higher!'

After Eliza had outgrown it, they'd fixed a special seat onto it so that Patience could come outside and enjoy the garden, too. She had learned to push herself backwards and forwards with her own legs, an achievement he had felt incredibly proud of. When she'd first done it, he'd sat down on an old plastic chair opposite her for at least an hour, marvelling at her ability to propel herself, wiping away tears.

He turned around a little more and took in their dilapidated shed, which had been painted a jaunty shade of blue on one particularly optimistic spring day. It was now more grey than blue, and not a fashionable shade of grey by any means. Jesus, it needed condemning, he thought.

Suddenly, he was seized by an idea. He was home and he was awake – and he had time to kill. This was a great opportunity, he decided, to get some of this sorted. This garden was full of junk, piles of dog poo and riddled with weeds. It was about time he took it to task.

It felt as though someone had given him a shot of cocaine. He felt energised, determined, super-human. He threw his spent cigarette over the boundary to languish with the other detritus, opened the shed and began grabbing items from inside, chucking them over his shoulder one by one. They landed in a scatter-gun pattern over the patio and lawn. But no bother; most of them were destined for the tip, anyway, he thought. Then he grabbed a shovel and searched through the grass for piles of dog poo, lobbing them in the bin behind him as he went along.

Then he hauled the mower from deep within the shed, filled it with some of the petrol that had been languishing in a can by the shed door and pulled the starter handle. He heard something turn over inside, but the engine remained silent. So he yanked it once more, and the engine flew into life, petrol fumes and dust rising in a cloud as it did so. It irritated his throat and he coughed, but it did not deter him. He dragged the mower back towards the edge of the lawn, took a deep breath, and set off. He heard the machine protesting as it was forced to ingest several months' worth of grass, but he forged on, pushing it with all his strength, determined to finally take control of the garden, to take it on in battle, and win. Later, he'd have a go at the house, he thought. Today would be a day of getting things done.

'What the bloody hell are you *doing*?'

Pete was suddenly aware that he was not alone in the garden. Louise was standing next to him, wearing only her white cotton nightie and a pair of blue slippers.

'Sorry!' he shouted over the noise of the mower. 'I can't hear you properly.'

'*Just turn the bloody thing off!*' yelled Louise, right next to his ear.

He leaned down with reluctance and turned the engine off. When the noise had faded, all he could hear was the gentle tweeting of birds, the barking of a dog in the distance, and the harsh breathing of his wife. She was glaring at him.

'*It's five thirty in the morning,*' she said, in a voice that was a hybrid of a shout and a whisper. 'What the bloody hell are you mowing for? You'll wake all of the neighbours. We'll get a letter from the council.'

Pete looked around and saw the telltale twitching of

several bedroom curtains in neighbouring houses. He took a deep breath.

'As if that's the worst of our problems,' he said.

'What do you mean?'

Pete swallowed. 'I *read* that document. I *read* that list of risks for the gene therapy trial. Did you actually read it? *Did you?*'

'Of course I read it.'

'Well then,' he replied. 'Are you OK with Patience getting cancer from it? Or an infection that she can't fight? Or, you know, dying? That was on there, too.'

'Lower your voice, Pete,' said Louise. 'Everyone on the street can hear you.'

'I don't *care*,' he said, shaking with rage. 'This is too important. You are risking her health and her life with this ridiculous trial. *I will not stand for it!*'

Pete waited for Louise to react, either with violence, or shouting, or tears. But she didn't. Instead, she turned around and walked calmly towards the house.

'Where are you going?'

'Inside. To get ready for work,' she answered calmly, opening the back door. 'It's my first day today. Since I'm up already, I might as well leave early, and miss the traffic.'

The door closed behind her and Pete was left standing alone in the garden, sweat pouring down his face. Or at least, he had thought it was. It took him a minute to realise it was tears.

8

Patience

September

'So I told him, absolutely not. No way was I going to do that.'

'Too right.'

'For a start, it would hurt.'

'Yes!'

'Honestly, some men are disgusting. No, make that *all* men are disgusting!'

'Did you tell him about Kevin?'

'No, there's nothing to tell, is there? Except for, you know, that thing that happened round the back of Aldi...'

I always wish I could ask questions during these conversations. Like, who the flip is Kevin? And why on earth did you let him do anything to you behind a budget supermarket? Have some standards, ladies! Demand Waitrose at least.

You see, it isn't just music that forms the soundtrack of my daily life. Given my ghostly status, I get to overhear all kinds of great stuff, like that conversation between Magda and Jane as they changed my bed. They are outrageous, that pair.

Given that I can't talk, overheard conversations and noises shape my day. Right now, for example, I can hear clattering dishes in the kitchen; the postman leaving parcels outside the front door; Rosie, one of my fellow respite care inmates, yelling in the bathroom. She despises having her hair washed.

The downside of being great at listening, however, is that I also have to hear Mum and Dad arguing. They bicker pretty much constantly when he's home nowadays, mostly about the day-to-day minutiae of my needs and how they fit in (or, let's face it, don't fit in) with their daily needs. Mum definitely believes Dad doesn't do enough to help. His frequent absences for work make her resentful and she has high expectations when he returns. In fact, I think they're so high, it's not actually possible for him to meet them.

And of course, I also hear things that I'm not supposed to hear.

Secrets.

I know all of Eliza's secrets because she has told me. I'm the vessel she keeps them in. And Mum, bless her, I don't think she has any secrets; she has no time for intrigue. But Dad – he's a closeted sort, you know. He keeps his cards close to his chest usually. He's let his guard down only once in my hearing.

Mum went away on a weekend break for carers a few months ago, run by a charity. Dad had invited his brother Steve around to our house for company while she was away. Dad and Steve's childhood was tough, I think, and whenever they meet, it's like a pressure cooker letting off steam – they give each other permission to vent. They were sharing a twelve-pack of beer in the lounge, watching football, talking loudly over it. They were so loud, in fact, that I could hear them clearly in my bedroom down the hall. And what I heard Dad say, well, I'm guessing he doesn't want Mum to know.

I am worried about it, mostly because I don't think they have ever kept secrets that big from each other before. They really only deal in little white lies, like hiding presents they've bought from each other, or not mentioning that the other has got a bit fat, or those bottles Mum has started secreting in the understairs cupboard. But this is in an entirely different league.

I'm supposed to be napping right now, but I'm not tired. So instead, I'm lying on my back examining the ceiling. There isn't much else to do in this position, is there? One of the carers recently stuck a few Take That posters up there, so I have something to look at when I'm in bed here, a bit like they do for people at the dentist who need distracting from the cavity they're filling. These posters are a small joy, so I'm here, in the present, examining them. I count them left to right – one, Gary, two, Robbie, three, Mark, four, Jason, and finally, five, my current favourite, Howard. This poster is very out of date, of course. Not only is there no Robbie any more – except for their reunion tour, of course, I've got that DVD somewhere – there is also no Jason. His departure was a bit of a shocker. I found out about it from the *This Morning* presenters, Phil and Holly, who were chatting about it on TV. I was being given a drink at the time and I almost choked, prompting a quick whack on the back and a precautionary visit from the doctor.

I sobbed when Take That announced that they were breaking up in 1996. Partly because they wouldn't be making more music, of course, but also because I'd just heard that I was actually set to meet them, in real life. It was supposed to be a surprise, but of course, everybody talks about me in front of me, don't they? Eliza had written to the Take That fan club about me (that's sisterly love for you – that must have hurt) and the lads had decided that I was worthy of a personal meeting. I remember so well the flurry of excitement, a jostling to decide who would come with me to my little audience. Even Eliza expressed interest. And then they announced that they were splitting up, didn't they? And our meet up, my once-in-a-lifetime opportunity to actually dribble on Howard Donald, was cancelled. I was distraught.

Not that the band ever really broke up in our house, mind you. That old VHS just kept on rolling, replaced with a DVD version eventually and replenished with eBay finds when scratches made the earlier versions untenable. I am a cinch to buy for every birthday and Christmas. In my bedroom, you see, those three middle-aged men I saw perform at the O2 are still a group of five, all smooth-skinned and skinny, sleeping with groupies in hotel rooms and being re-dressed and redesigned by stylists daily, like dolls.

Here's Beth. I like her. She has purple hair and tattoos.

'Patience, welcome back! I hear you've been a very ill girl! So nice to have you back with us for a break. We were so worried about you. Now, let me see… What would you like to do? Watch a DVD? Now where is that Muppet one you like – oh, I'm sorry lovely, Magda was supposed to reorganise them all back into their boxes, wasn't she? She's got man trouble, I think. We'll look in a bit. Now – when did we last take you to the toilet? Was it lunchtime? Crikey, best get on with it then, hadn't we?' And Beth's caring monologue continues, brightly, breezily, without pause, because she will never get a response.

I lie there as she checks to see if my pad is dry and then she rolls me over and sits me up. It feels good to not be lying down for a change, despite the fact that my back muscles are totally pathetic. I was developing a sore patch after all that lying down in hospital, and crikey, yes, I really do need the toilet again. It stings down there, in fact. Beth calls Magda in to help her with the hoist, which transfers me from my bed to my wheelchair. And as she pushes me into the bathroom, the relief to be moving again, escaping bed, makes me smile.

'Ooh, look at you, Patience. Smiling away!' she says, as she manoeuvres me through the door frame. She definitely thinks I'm simple. They all do.

Magda is now back again, fresh from being sent to find a cloth. I have a bit of dribble running down my chin, you see.

'My lovely Pat! Oh crikey, look at you,' she says, wiping me. She's the only person who calls me Pat. I hate it.

I suspect that Magda is the cause of things being a bit 'off' here this weekend. For example, I was given the wrong breakfast cereal this morning – shredded wheat instead of Weetabix. I had always fancied trying them; Ellie has them, but I've never previously been allowed them, due to the choking risk. In the event, however, they were a bit of a disappointment. I reckon that's what cardboard tastes like. I'm so fed up of eating mush, though, that I'll take what I can get.

So yes, something is definitely up. I think it's the endless staff shortage, frankly. A rather limp and useless teenager, Karen, left last week after only a few months. Magda is an agency carer plugging the gap and, as sweet as she is, she doesn't know her arse from her elbow – or the difference between breakfast cereals, when it comes to that.

Things are about to change, however. I overheard Maggie, the care home manager, tell Beth that someone new was starting today. Staff turnover here in the respite bungalow is high, always – the pay is low and the hours antisocial – so the hiring of a new member of staff is always a reason for celebration at Morton Lodge.

And here is another reason to celebrate. I've finally been hoisted onto the toilet. I've been wanting to go for hours. I let go of a welcome stream of urine, exhaling in pleasure. It stings at the end, mind you, but the relief was worth that small amount of pain.

I wait while Magda wipes my bottom, pulls up my leggings and then hoists me, with the help of Beth, back into my chair. Then she pushes me into the dining room where Beth is mopping up Ellie after a very late lunch. Ellie is a tremendously messy eater, with more usually hitting the floor than making it into her mouth. She has cerebral palsy. I overheard Maggie saying it had something to do with being deprived of oxygen at birth. She's got something on me, though – she can move her arms deliberately, albeit in jerky movements. She can also manage some words; slow, slurry, but definitely there. I envy her. She looks at me sometimes when we're alone together in the TV room, and I wonder if she knows that I can understand her.

Magda has just come in to get us, to put us in front of late-afternoon daytime TV, which is as inane and vacuous as morning daytime TV. I enjoy catching the occasional afternoon news bulletins on BBC1, a welcome relief from the endless antiques programmes which seem *de rigeur* at this time of the afternoon. Just now I'm having to watch a show in which Den and Belinda – a couple in their sixties who probably applied to the TV production company because they had run out of conversation – pretend to look shocked at the goodies their tangoed presenter is finding in their garage.

'*Ooh, Belinda, look at that! I would never have thought that old chamber pot of my gran's would have any value!*'

'*I know! But will it sell for the reserve price at the auction?!*'

I do hope they've washed it...

The front door bell! A very welcome distraction. I watch as Maggie runs to get it. Maggie rarely runs for anything – at eighteen stone, it isn't something she takes to easily. It's only a matter of seconds before I understand her urgency. Walking alongside her down the hallway, towards the day room, is a man. A very handsome man. He has curly brown hair, left long on the sides, cut just above his collar. His eyebrows are strong and sleek and his jaw is purposeful; I can see the muscles in it dance as he swallows. Come to think of it, doesn't he have a look of Howard Donald?

'So you've worked in care homes before?' asks Maggie, craning her neck upwards to gaze at him through her stubby blue eyelashes, preening her mousy, frizzy mane as she does so.

'Yes, several,' he answers in a voice laced with chocolate, as she reverses him into her tiny office, like a spider closing in on her prey. She doesn't shut the door, though; she probably needed to sit him in the doorway so that there was enough space. This means that I can hear everything they say.

'But I've only looked after men before,' he continues. 'That's originally what I applied for here, to work next door, with the men.'

'Yes, I'm sorry about that,' replies Maggie. 'But we're short of staff at the moment, so I snapped you up for here. You won't be able to do the personal care with the girls, of course, but there's lots you *can* do, and we definitely need you. Do you mind coming over?'

'No, no. I'm happy to help wherever's needed,' he replies.

'You're doing a college course, is that right?'

'Yes, sort of. I'm doing my GCSEs again, part-time,' he replies. 'Very late. I'm having a bit of a career rethink. It depends on my grades, really.'

I hear Maggie laugh. 'Well, don't do those exams too quickly! Lord knows, we need you here. Shall I show you around the place?'

I move my head as far as it will go to watch them come out of the office and head down the hall. I hear Maggie showing him our bedrooms – all as close to a home from home as you can manage with hoists and medical beds everywhere you turn – and into the bathroom, complete with its padded bath with a side that lowers so you can be lifted into it, and its extra tall, comfortable toilet. Then they turn and head my way.

'This is Patience,' says Maggie. 'Patience, this is Jimmy. He's going to be working here from now on.'

Jimmy squats down and looks straight at me. 'Yes, I'm the new boy,' he says, grinning. I feel the colour rise in my cheeks, but I don't think they notice. I have a rash on my cheeks anyhow, from the cream they use to get rid of my burgeoning beard. The joyful effects of hormone imbalance are another glamorous element of my existence, by the way; it's not all about my bum.

'Hello, Patience. I'm Jimmy,' he says. He's already been introduced, of course, but it is nice that he decided to do it in person, face to face, on my level. 'I'm a bit new at this, so please be gentle with me.'

I can behave in no other way, fella.

'Actually, Jimmy, Patience is due a drink,' says Maggie. 'Could you do that, do you think? Beth will show you how to make it up.'

'Sure,' he says, putting his hand on my shoulder. 'I'll go and get it and I'll be right back.'

Maggie smiles with approval and goes back to her office, singing to herself quietly. She's out of tune. I want to smile, but decide to keep it in. They'd probably assume I'm smiling because I like this bloody auction programme and make me watch it every day for all eternity. It's not worth the risk.

A few minutes later, Jimmy comes back bearing a plastic beaker full of chocolate milkshake, which he's forgotten to put the thickener in. Bingo, this one's a keeper. I detest that stuff. It's like drinking lumpy custard.

He pulls up a chair next to me, grabs a handful of tissues from a box on a nearby table and proceeds to tip the glass into my mouth.

'Now here goes, Patience. I'm sorry if I get this wrong and make you choke.'

I laugh before I can stop myself, and splutter. It probably sounded more like a choke than a laugh.

'Now then, lovely, don't give me a heart attack! Are you OK? Are we good?'

He cradles my face as he asks me that. I look straight at

him, composed and ready. Jimmy tilts the glass once more and I try to drink it more carefully. This has the dual benefit of making sure I won't choke – my tongue is a constant hazard – while allowing me to savour the attentions of this lovely man. If you have to spend your life being cared for, you might as well be cared for by someone nice to look at.

After Jimmy goes off shift, I feel flat. He brightened up the whole place, and this rubbed off on the other staff, who all, magically, became more enthusiastic, more hard-working, more helpful. But I can't let this low mood colour the rest of my day, because I have a visitor this afternoon.

Her name is Janet and she's a music teacher at one of the local primary schools. When she's not torturing herself by trying to persuade six-year-olds to learn the recorder, she works as a music therapist. I always look forward to Janet's visits. She has a mass of curly hair and smells of flowers, and I know that I'm not going to have to switch off during her session, even if it goes on for ages. She brings all sorts of percussion instruments with her, things that even I can use, like bells which I can wear around my wrists and drums I can try to hit with my clasped hands. Each impact, each jangle, sends a shockwave of joy up my arms and legs and into my brain. And when she puts on a backing track for me to play along to, my limbs fizz and I rock side to side, miraculously free of pain.

This sensation only lasts as long as the music does, however. When it's over, I go back to being frozen, brittle, rigid. For I am only truly alive while the music lasts.

9

Louise

September

Louise tiptoed down the stairs, hoping that by avoiding the squeaky step, she might also avoid waking Pete, sleeping in the spare room. They couldn't bear to be near each other now. She didn't have time for another fruitless argument this morning, not if she was going to make it to the conference centre in Birmingham on time. Since accepting the job last week, she'd been out of the house every day and, given Pete's current attitude, that was something of a relief.

She had been full of trepidation on her first morning at work, worried she'd be viewed as a dinosaur, she'd been out of the workplace for so long. However, Professor Larssen was an incredibly loyal employer, and most of his team had been working with him for two decades, so everyone had been welcoming, respectful, even. Her colleagues respected the knowledge she had about Rett and had asked her advice on all sorts of aspects of the trial. They were cracking on with the recruitment for it now and she was an important part of the process, communicating with parents and discussing their concerns.

Being consulted, being respected, being valued: she realised now that she had wanted a job not just for the money, but also for the recognition that came with it. She had forgotten how good it felt to be valued as an individual. She had been dismissed as only 'Patience's mother' for far too long. Motherhood was an extraordinary privilege, she knew that, but she also felt that mothering a disabled adult was like wearing an invisibility cloak. Your herculean efforts went entirely unnoticed by society. In this job, however, she was actually being *seen*.

There were some really impressive women on the professor's team, she had discovered; some really successful women, and she had found their different paths both fascinating and inspiring. The most prominent of these was the professor's wife, Magda. She was a scientist – a geneticist – originally from Hungary. She had brought up two children while learning a new language and forging her own career. She was as chaotic as her husband, but she had a brilliant mind, a sparkle in her eye and a laugh like a hyena. Louise had warmed to her immediately. She hadn't laughed so much in the past year as she had done in the past week.

There wasn't much laughter at home, though. The hideous mix of angry silence and flaming rows that had defined Pete's home leave had been exhausting. She had started leaving early every morning to avoid seeing him at breakfast, leaving him to wake Patience and deal with the carers all day. Having him at home had at least meant that she could deputise that responsibility for a short while.

Today was leaving day, however. When he'd gone, she'd

be entirely in charge of Patience once more, and that would be some juggling act, mixing caring duties with her new job. But on the bright side, she'd be able to reclaim the house for herself. Over the past few months, his intermittent home visits, previously eagerly anticipated, had actually begun to feel like an imposition.

She couldn't put her finger on what exactly had changed, but something definitely had. She felt she couldn't be herself with him around, couldn't relax. He hovered over her while she ate, and she even felt guilty pouring herself a drink in the evening to take the edge off a stressful day. It felt like he was watching her constantly, looking for things to criticise. And everything he'd done this week had driven her to distraction: his insistence on recognition for any housework he'd done; his piecemeal efforts to fix the house's many problems; his dogged determination to try to change her mind over the gene therapy trial.

This trial had unearthed something long-buried between them, something ugly. Despite her anger, she had privately tried to see it from his point of view. In truth, she had struggled to sleep in recent days, Pete's words dominating her thoughts and refusing to let her rest. She had never really disagreed so vehemently with him before, and this upset her deeply.

She stopped at the bottom of the stairs and looked in on Patience. She was sleeping soundly now, after a difficult night. Patience had woken her up at about 1 a.m., crying out in pain. She had come downstairs and found Patience's arm out of its sling and wedged up against the wall. Her collarbone was still healing, and she knew that it must still hurt. She'd given her a suppository of paracetamol and sat with Patience in the dark, stroking her hair until she'd fallen asleep.

Louise felt utterly determined to give Patience the chance of a different life. She wanted to rid her of this pain, this silent torture. The professor had taken her through every risk the trial posed, had answered every question she had with understanding and concern. The list of possible side effects Pete had seen was alarming, she knew that, but it was also unlikely that any would occur and, in her view, the possible gain was so extraordinary, so mind-blowing, that it was worth the risk.

Louise crept into the kitchen and filled up the kettle. So far, so good. There was no sign of Pete. While she waited for it to boil, she grabbed a piece of paper from a notepad on the side and wrote him a message, wishing him a safe flight. She was furious with him, no question, but she still loved him. She could hardly let him leave without a goodbye of some sort.

And then the back door slammed.

'Ah, Lou,' said Pete, reaching down to unclip Tess from her lead, 'I hoped I'd catch you.'

'Unlike you to walk the dog so early,' she said, still facing away from him. She crumpled up the note in her hand, chucked it in the bin under the sink and then turned on the hot tap, to begin the washing-up, all without turning around to acknowledge her husband.

'I couldn't sleep and she looked desperate when I came down. Also, I needed the fresh air.'

Louise busied herself rinsing and scrubbing and did not respond.

'Lou. Please. Stop doing that. *Look at me.*'

Louise noticed that one of the mugs had coffee residue almost welded to its bottom. It must have been drying out in the sink for several days, she thought. She squeezed washing-up liquid into it and brushed it with vigour.

'Lou. I'm going today. *Please.*'

She took a deep breath and turned around, still holding the mug and the brush.

'I know,' she said, still brushing.

'I don't want us to part on bad terms. I won't be back for a month.'

'Yes,' she said.

Pete took two steps forward, so that he was just a few inches away from Louise.

'Lou, we won't get anywhere if we don't talk about things. I really don't understand why you won't. Things haven't always been like this. We used to discuss things, remember?'

Louise still did not put the mug down.

'Look, Lou, I want to understand why you feel like this. Why you're so determined to go ahead with the gene therapy, even when I don't want you to. I want you to explain. Can you try?'

Louise stopped scrubbing the mug.

'I *have* tried. But it makes no difference.'

'You haven't tried, Lou, you just keep on telling me that it's the right thing for Patience and that I'm being an idiot for thinking otherwise.'

Louise checked her watch. She needed to leave in fifteen minutes. This would at least have to be quick.

'Well, that's because it *is* the right thing to do, Pete. And I simply don't understand why you don't see that.'

Pete moved around Louise and began to make tea,

reaching into the cupboard for two clean mugs. 'But Patience is mostly well, Lou, she's stable, happy, we have funding for carers to look after her at home, it's the status quo we hoped for. I don't get why you feel things have got so bad.'

Louise turned around again and waged war on the washing-up once more.

'I think that's because you don't *want* to see,' she said to a soundtrack of clinking crockery. 'When I went to see her in the hospital after that fall, she looked... blank. Absent. And I catch her looking like that often now, even at home. I think maybe she's in pain a lot, Pete, and we aren't helping her because we don't know where it is. What if that's her future? You know, a slow but hideous slide downwards into constant pain? This gene therapy, it could give her the ability to tell us how she's feeling, couldn't it? That would be amazing. It would change everything for her – and for us. No more guesswork. And you know, maybe she wouldn't need as much care? She could be more independent. The relentless round of social workers, doctors and physiotherapists and sleepless nights, that could end, too.'

'It sounds to me, Lou, like this is more about you than it is about Patience.'

'How *dare* you!' said Louise, relinquishing the washing-up and turning towards Pete, who was now getting milk out of the fridge and pouring it into the mugs of steaming tea. 'How *dare* you suggest that I'm being selfish. I haven't had time to think about myself for decades.'

'Lou, I'm not saying that. I'm sorry. You know I didn't mean that.' Pete took the teabags out of the tea and dropped them in the bin. He presented one of the mugs to Louise, who took it, muttering an automatic thank you. She checked her watch once more.

'You're not listening to me properly,' said Louise. 'My interest in this trial is about Patience alone. You and I both know how hard caring for her is – but it's a labour of love. Everything I do is for her. And I'd do it all again if I had to.'

Pete nodded, looking not at Louise, but at the steam rising on his tea.

'Anyway, I've got to go in a few minutes,' she said. 'We're holding the information session for the parents of prospective trial participants today. Perhaps you should come,' she added, glaring at him. 'You might learn something.'

'I've read the literature, Lou,' said Pete, his tone suggesting he was determined not to rise to the bait. 'So I know the facts. And that's what bothers me. There are too many risks.'

'They are risks that are being mitigated. They will be incredibly careful. No expense is being spared. They will be monitored intensively. The professor—'

'Yes, I know you think the sun shines out of his arse!'

'The professor would not be doing this if he didn't feel it would bring about a great result.'

'He *would* say that, Lou, wouldn't he? He needs bodies for his trial. So just stop and think for a moment. Patience is content, happy at home, being cared for by others, you aren't having to do most of the heavy lifting. What is so wrong with things as they are? Why are you willing to risk so much for this tiny chance of a change that, frankly, seems pretty petrifying to me?'

'Why so petrifying?' asked Louise, cradling her tea.

'Just *think*. She's an innocent, is Patience, isn't she? She's one of the world's most wonderful, innocent souls. She doesn't have a dicky bird what's going on around her, and that's a good thing. And if this experiment works – *if* – you are potentially giving a severely disabled body a brain which absolutely doesn't match it. Imagine how frightened she'd be. She'd be a prisoner in her own body. It's disturbing, Lou. I can't sleep for thinking about it.'

Louise thought about the baby she had held, in those days before the regression had robbed her brain of its potential. She remembered the light she'd seen in Patience's eyes, the intelligence, the promise. Her intense determination to sit up, to grasp toys, to mount her trike and push herself along. They had video of her doing that, of her laughing as she traversed their patio, her hair billowing behind her, her smile conveying the joy she clearly felt at finally being able to do something that Eliza could do, too. Louise ached to be back behind that camera, witnessing it. She longed to hear Patience speak again, even if all she ever said was no, the way Eliza had done for one memorable month as a toddler. This trial could return Patience's stolen future to her. Why on earth couldn't Pete see that?

Louise checked her watch. She *had* to go. She put down her tea – she had hardly drunk any of it – and looked at Pete.

'Well, I can see that we're not going to agree,' she replied, finally. 'But you know how I feel and I'm not going to change my mind. So I'll talk to the professor about next steps.'

'There won't be any, Lou, because she's simply not going to do it. I won't give my permission.'

'I'm told that we won't need it,' Louise replied, picking up her handbag from the kitchen table, and doing up her jacket.

'*What?*'

'There are ways of getting round that, I'm told.'

'You can't be serious! You're prepared to go ahead without my approval?'

'Absolutely. I will do whatever it takes, Pete, for Patience. Now, I must go.'

Louise walked swiftly to the door, with Pete in pursuit.

'Lou, we have to talk about this. This is serious. Critical. We need to work as a team on this...'

'It's too late for that,' said Louise as she opened her car door and sat in the driving seat. 'It seems we're on opposing sides now.'

And as she turned on the ignition and reversed out of the driveway, Louise forced herself not to look at Pete. But as she drove away, her rear-view mirror captured him in the open doorway, staring fixedly at the car until she was out of sight.

One by one, they entered the room, some holding hands, others clutching cups of coffee and phones, searching the rows of chairs for faces they recognised. There were hugs between some, who were obviously old friends; looks of suspicion between others. They knew that this was essentially a competition and that some of them would lose.

Louise had made a spreadsheet of their names, their ages, and their addresses, so she knew who they were. But she wasn't prepared for their faces. The women and men who were making their way through the open double doors into the medium-sized, strip-lit conference room she'd rented for the event, all had expressions of fear, tinged with something unmistakable – hope.

She knew that look well. She'd borne it long ago, back when Patience had been a baby. But it had been wiped right off her face during a regular reunion of her birthing class friends which she'd gone to once – and only once. Louise had watched as five babies born in the same month as Patience bounced up and down on podgy legs, hauled themselves up against the chairs in a local café and babbled joyfully, blissfully unaware of each other and entirely dedicated to their own enjoyment.

Patience had spent the entire event in Louise's lap, crying. She hadn't been hungry, or wet, and she hadn't had wind; she had just cried, angry tears dripping down her cheeks, which were red, the blood under her skin bursting to the surface. Louise had left early, telling the woman next to her that she needed the toilet. She had picked up her coat, strung her bag over her shoulder and walked out of the door of the café with Patience dangling from her hip, never once looking back.

Louise remembered, too, the fierce determination she had felt when driving past the local primary school, the one her mother had spotted when they'd decided to buy the house.

'It'll be a nice little walk for you all in the mornings,' she'd said, doused in glorious innocence.

Louise had willed her youngest daughter to speak properly, to walk properly; convinced that if she believed it enough, Patience would start school there in two years, just like her peers, just like Eliza. She had maintained that hope until her place had been refused, and a row had ensued. Back then, Patience could stand a little bit, could sit cross-legged and listen. But try as she might, the school had stood firm and Patience was given a place at a 'special' school, fifteen miles away from home instead. It had been nice enough. It had actually been loving – caring, even. But it was not 'normal'.

Every morning a minibus had pulled up on the gravel outside their home. Inside there were three other children, each locked, it seemed to her, in their own personal prison – a wheelchair, a chest brace, a body ravaged by oxygen starvation. She'd watch as Patience was loaded among them every morning, a shooting star being sent out into a cold, unbidden galaxy. It depressed her beyond measure. At least Patience was unaware of her reality, though, and that was a comfort.

It was around that time that she had been forced to give up her nursing career for a different kind of work. Patience's school holidays eventually became an impossible gap to cover. The paltry offering from social services of a carer to help put her to bed nightly was not enough and the constant changing of staff in what was a low-paid, stressful job meant they had usually only just taught someone how to look after Patience before they left for a more rewarding role elsewhere. The crunch point came when Louise had got back from picking up Eliza from a friend's house to find their latest visiting carer, Jean, smoking in their conservatory while Patience slept in a soiled nappy in front of *EastEnders*.

Just after she had given up work, a social worker had come to visit. She'd seemed relieved to hear that Louise planned to be around more. She had gone through the care package they'd been offered – a carer every morning and evening, to do the dressing, feeding and undressing – and confirmed that that was all they could expect at that point. 'Unless, that is,' the woman had said, with a steely look in her eye, 'you decide you can't cope.'

Louise knew a mum who couldn't cope. She'd met her through a local support group for families with disabled children. She had always been so well turned out; painted nails, glossy hair, clothes spotless and ironed. And yet she had apparently cracked one day and walked out of her house, leaving her disabled son sitting inside alone in front of the TV. She'd called social services before she left and told them to come to pick him up.

He had been taken to a residential school and Louise had visited it with her once. It had been built on a brown-field site within a stone's throw of the M5. The windows were triple-glazed and its outside space amounted to a tiny courtyard overlooking a supermarket warehouse. She had hated it from the minute she'd parked the car outside, had to wipe tears away from her cheeks before anyone else could see. She had resolved then that she would never send Patience away. She was their child, and she belonged at home. All sacrifices were worth making to make this her continued reality.

And so, while her peers were all packing their bags and heading off to university without a second glance at their childhood bedrooms, Patience spent most of her days embedded in a special armchair in her childhood playroom, watching repeats of *The Muppets*. The entire family had become inextricably locked into her never-ending childhood. And despite the fact that she lived in Neverland, she was forced to leave her special school at nineteen. The family found themselves thrown into a hinterland of 'adult provision', discovering that there was neither the money in the system – nor the inclination – to make the days of disabled adults worth living.

It had been a time of great cruelty. As Patience's youthful good looks faded, so did her appeal to almost everyone around her, even her own grandparents, and Louise's friends. She was no longer a cute, blonde angel. Her face could no longer launch fundraisers or inspire charitable acts. She became invisible, and so, by proxy, did they.

But unlike the parents of her generation, who were all led to believe that their Rett children would die before they reached this ghost-like adulthood, these parents, gathering in this anonymous conference centre out by the ring road, shuffling along rows of grey stackable chairs, had good reason to expect their disabled children to live almost as long as them. And crucially, they knew what they were dealing with. Patience had been given a diagnosis based on a list of symptoms; the children of these families had been diagnosed using genetic testing.

These families knew, absolutely, which gene fault had waged war on their daughters' – and in a few rare cases, their sons' – brains. And because of Louise's new employer, they were now being presented with the tantalising prospect of fighting back. They were being offered hope, and Louise knew how powerful that was.

Having hope bludgeoned out of you was a body blow. It was an experience that she had never fully recovered from. She remembered exactly where she had been, and how she'd felt, when it had happened.

It had been a stifling, muggy day in the long, hot summer of 1992...

*

Louise had opened the window to try to usher some fresh air into the car. Instead, however, she had ended up inhaling the exhaust fumes of the double decker bus waiting at the lights in front of them. She'd rolled the window back up and looked in desperation at Pete, hoping that he could somehow find a shortcut to escape the traffic. He'd reacted with a sudden swing to the left and embarked on a series of detours down narrow residential streets flanked by closely spaced parked cars.

Finally, after a close shave with a moped and several shocked pedestrians, and at least two arguments in which one or both of them had threatened to get out and walk, the family arrived at their destination – the Royal Children's Hospital. Patience's initial appointment there hadn't yielded a diagnosis, so she had been invited back for a whole week of tests.

Pete pulled up directly outside the hospital entrance and unloaded Patience's wheelchair as taxis beeped and pedestrians weaved their way around it. It was her first wheelchair, bigger and more unwieldy than her old toddler buggy, and they were still getting used to it. It had to be stuffed into the back of their elderly Volvo estate, the boot only just closing over it. Louise stood on the pavement watching Pete struggle to unfold it, smelling the carbon in the air and absorbing the city's constant hum. The hospital entrance loomed large behind her. More bloody hospitals, she thought; it had better be worth it this time. Would the very best knowledge this city could provide be enough for Patience? Someone must know what was wrong with her, surely.

The chair finally unfolded, Pete bent over, reached into the back of the car and let out a deep grunt as he lifted Patience out. She was getting heavier and she showed no signs of wanting to bear weight or use her arms for anything other than wringing. The twisting motion required to move her in and out of the car was beginning to take its toll on them both.

Pete signalled that he was now ready for Louise to take over. She busied herself securing Patience in the chair, while he reached into the glove compartment for the orange disabled parking badge; another new, unwelcome but vital addition to their lives.

They had a routine now, a caring routine that neither of them had spoken of, but both understood. Speaking about it would make it all too real, too permanent, she thought. She preferred the silence.

Pete carried their bags, one slung over each arm, as she pushed Patience in the direction of the entrance hall and then into a large service lift to the second floor. Once there, they located Butterfly ward. All of the wards had names drawn from the beauty of nature, a stark contrast to the network of concrete corridors and brash metal reality of hospital life.

The ward sister took them to Patience's allotted bed. It was Pete who noticed that there wasn't anywhere for Louise to sleep; hospitals didn't usually offer accommodation for families back then. The utilitarian hospital bed, surrounded by optional curtains, had a small lockable cabinet next to it and a plastic, upright chair resting against the wall. Pete asked the orderly who had been making the bed next door where his wife should sleep and she had shaken her head solemnly, both acknowledging the problem and dismissing their query in one fell swoop.

Despite Patience's young age, there was clearly an assumption that parents would and should leave their children alone at night and find somewhere else to rest. Louise decided in an instant that she would challenge that assumption, and it seemed that she wasn't the only one. When she reached the nurse's station, she found another woman arguing with the ward sister about her own sleeping arrangements.

The woman, with her vibrant red hair, stilettos, long drop earrings and red lipstick, looked like she should be heading out for the night, not preparing to bed down in a hospital. However, she was also cradling a little boy in her arms, rocking him fiercely.

'Now you listen to me. *Just listen*,' she said, in a rich Yorkshire accent. 'I'm not going to the bloody cheap hotel down the road. I've never spent a night away from Patrick, and I am not going to start now. He's very ill, or else he wouldn't bloody be here, would he? And I'm going to be here for him, whether you make me lie down on the lino beside his bed, or whether you manage to rustle me up another blanket.'

Louise instinctively placed a hand on the woman's shoulder. She'd never done something like that before and probably would never be brave enough to do so again, but her instincts were strong.

'Excuse me, sorry, I don't mean to interrupt,' she said. 'I just wanted to show that I agree with you. I'm not leaving my daughter either.'

Both women glared at the sister, oozing defiance. There

was a short silence, punctuated only by the cries of children down the hall and the rattle of the tea trolley.

'The reason why we suggest you stay elsewhere is because we haven't anywhere comfortable,' said the ward sister, her tone reflecting her resignation. 'Space is at a premium here. But if you don't mind roughing it a bit, we do probably have a room you can use.'

She led the two women away down a long side corridor and opened a door into what looked like a meeting room. A large walnut effect table and chairs was placed in the middle, ringed with institutional style waiting room chairs. There were two large sash windows which overlooked an internal courtyard. It stank of cigarettes, had a bare bulb hanging from the ceiling, and was missing at least one set of curtains.

'You'll see why we don't advertise this as accommodation,' she said, looking at them, her eyes alight with challenge. Her gaze then fell on the little boy, who was now asleep on his mother's shoulder. 'But I do understand why you want to stay,' she said, softening. 'I have a little one too. Look, I'll go and get whatever I can find to make your stay a bit more comfy. What do you need? Sheets? Pillows?' Louise, still a nurse at heart and at home in a hospital environment, resurrected her workplace efficiency and sprang into action.

'Yes, please. Definitely sheets, pillows, blankets. And do you have any tape? Drawing pins?'

The ward sister nodded and left.

'I'm Serena,' the woman in the stilettos said. 'And thanks for that. I was about to crumple.'

'You didn't look or sound like that to me. You sounded bloody fierce,' replied Louise. 'Even I was scared.'

Serena smiled at that; but it was only a half-smile, with deep pain clearly loitering just beneath the surface. Louise studied the other woman closely. In those moments before, she had seemed such a powerhouse, such a visible source of energy, but she now appeared broken. Her immaculately applied eye make-up was smudged. A small tear was creeping slowly down her cheek. Louise decided that it might be best to ignore it.

'Come on, let's make this place acceptable,' she said. 'I know it's a bit like polishing a turd, but never mind. Let's polish it anyway.'

Serena sniffed. 'Yes, let's. Thanks.'

'Oh, come on, it's nothing. You were the one who fought the fearsome sister,' said Louise.

'But you were the one who didn't cry.'

They smiled at each other, and were still doing so when the sister returned with sheets, blankets, pillows and drawing pins.

'Here you are, ladies. Hope you have a reasonable night. There are showers down the corridor to the right, the staff use them. Is there anything else?'

Serena had recovered her composure. 'No, I don't think so, but we'll let you know. Thanks.'

The ward sister nodded and left. Serena spun round to Louise and smiled. 'Now, why the drawing pins?'

'Ah,' answered Louise. 'Old student nurse trick. We'll pin the sheet to the window to create a curtain. I'm buggered if the secretaries who work opposite are going to get an eyeful of my boobs in the morning.'

*

Their week in hospital had been a seemingly endless cycle of discussions with consultants; blood tests, brain scans, X-rays and ultrasounds. It felt to Louise as if they'd seen every doctor in the hospital. She'd also slept fitfully, not due to her unusual sleeping arrangements – she and Serena had eventually managed to borrow some mattresses and had made a reasonably comfortable den for themselves – but due to the regular wake-ups from nurses who wanted one of them to come to see their children, who were distressed by their surroundings, and light sleepers to boot.

This whole experience had only really been bearable because of Serena, she thought, as she packed up her belongings ready for the long journey back home. Poor Serena – you wait years for a diagnosis for your child, and then when you get one, it's the one you most fear.

'How do I look?'

Serena spun around to face Louise, after a lengthy spell spent in front of the mirror they'd erected on top of a filing cabinet. She'd done a reasonable job, but no make-up could mask her swollen, bloodshot eyes.

'You look lovely,' replied Louise, not missing a beat. Serena needed all the encouragement she could get. 'Do you really have to go now?' she asked.

'Yes. Alec will be here in a few minutes. He's taken the day off to come to get us. And it's not like the doctors can do any more, is it?'

Louise saw that a tear was forming once more in her left eye, and that her right eye was set to follow.

'Oh, Serena!'

Her new friend reached into her pocket for a tissue, and blew her nose.

'I'm OK. I knew that it would be this, to be honest. I just knew it. I kept telling our GPs that something wasn't right, that it was more than him just having dodgy balance, or laziness, or whatever. I knew it.'

Serena's son, Patrick, it turned out, had Duchenne Muscular Dystrophy. He was four years old and Louise knew that a diagnosis of Duchenne meant an early death.

'I know. But you've still had a huge shock, even if you expected it.'

Serena nodded and picked up her bag. Louise hugged her.

'Write to me, OK? And call me. You've got my number.'

'I will. I promise. And good luck with the seminar today.'

The end of their stay loomed, and still they had no diagnosis. The only thing left to do was to attend the hospital's weekly seminar for unsolved cases. They actually called it something far more erudite, but essentially it was for no-hopers, Louise thought. *Abandon hope all ye who enter here.* If all of the UK's medical might hadn't found Patience a disease to call her own, she doubted whether a group of old white men scratching their heads together would have any more luck. But still, they'd been kind enough to spend all of this money and time investigating Patience's case, so it was only fair that she played along, she thought. It couldn't hurt.

Following the ward sister's instructions, Louise pushed Patience in her wheelchair down a dimly lit corridor in the basement. She found the room number that had been written down for her and pushed the door open to reveal a large lecture theatre. There wasn't room for the buggy inside, so she parked it in the corridor and lifted Patience out and rested her on her hip. Barely more than a toddler, it was still possible for her to do this, but she knew from the twinges in her back that their days walking around like this were numbered. As she made her way back in, a junior medic spotted her and gesticulated towards a free seat at the back, so she headed in that direction and grabbed it, sitting down with Patience on her lap.

A portly man in his early sixties made his way to the podium. As her eyes adjusted to the low lighting, Louise realised there were about twenty people seated in the first few rows and a few other relatives and carers were dotted around the room further back. The man didn't introduce himself. He probably reckoned he was too important to need an introduction, she thought. Instead, he simply began to read from a pile of notes on the lectern.

The first case, he said, was about child A, who'd been referred due to an awkward gait, and bones which were not growing normally. The child had been tested for everything they could think of, but to no avail. Her problems continued. Did anyone have anything to suggest?

A quietly spoken, grey-haired woman in the front row suggested something Louise couldn't quite hear; there was some nodding among the pack and a brief discussion ensued. When they were finished, the speaker summed up the case and announced that they had decided to refer her case notes to a clinic in Edinburgh that had recently reported a similar case. Passing the buck, thought Louise. Always passing the buck.

The man referred once more to his list. He sounded bored. 'Next, we have child B, a three-year-old girl who appeared to be developing normally at her one-year check, and who went on to gain some skills before regressing. Repetitive hand movements are present and she has no speech. Her gait is awkward, she has a slightly smaller head than average and she can't walk independently. We've put her through all the usual tests – MRIs, blood tests, etc, and we've found nothing. Anyone got anything?'

Louise heard a shuffling of papers, and a voice, a male voice, began to talk.

'I've been thinking a lot about this one,' he said. 'I realised after I met her that I'd heard of something similar before, at a conference I went to last month in Austria. A paediatrician called Andreas Rett gave a speech talking about girls who'd been attending his clinic who all had similar features – repetitive hand movements and the regression, mostly – and I wonder whether this might be the same thing. I've looked it up though, and there haven't been any cases identified in the UK yet.'

Louise could almost hear her heart thrashing away in her chest.

The man on the stage chuckled. 'Oh, Giles, always trying to make a name for yourself! You've always got to be the first, haven't you?'

Louise felt a wave of rage take hold of her. 'Stop laughing, please!' she shouted, her voice hoarse. 'Please stop.'

The group fell silent as she spoke from the gloom at the back of the auditorium. 'You are the first person who's suggested anything that sounds remotely like what Patience has. Please, please tell me more.'

★

Later that day, in that doctor's cramped office lined with medical textbooks, after a cup of lukewarm, milky tea, they had finally been given a name for it. Rett syndrome, named after the Austrian paediatrician who'd first recognised it as a disorder.

When Giles Rivers, a senior consultant with twenty-five years of experience in paediatrics, had given Patience's 'trouble' a name, it had echoed against the walls of his office and ricocheted in Louise's ears. Pete, who'd made the journey to the hospital after a rushed phone call from Louise that morning, was struck dumb, staring blankly at his wife, willing her to say something.

Back then, the name had meant nothing to either of them. Dr Rivers told them that it meant nothing to most doctors, too; it had only been recognised relatively recently. Patience was to have the dubious honour of being one of the first children in the country to be diagnosed with it. Louise then asked the question that she had been suppressing for months. Years.

'Will she die?'

Dr Rivers had paused for a moment as he formulated his answer.

'I don't really have any answers for you,' he said, looking somewhere over their shoulders, into the distance. 'Except, that is, to say that the oldest girl Professor Rett has seen – it seems to only affect girls – was in her thirties. Many don't get that far I'm afraid.' He paused, removing his glasses and rubbing them on his handkerchief to clean off a smudge. 'Looking at the evidence we have, I think it's unlikely Patience will walk. It's also extremely unlikely she'll ever be able to speak.' Then he paused and took a sip from his teacup. 'I'm very sorry.'

'But she did speak, for a bit. A few words… but that stopped,' Louise replied, hoping that perhaps this nugget of information would somehow persuade the doctor to change his diagnosis.

'Yes, that's quite common, from what I've read. The girls regress. They learn things, and then they lose those skills. It's… very cruel, like that.'

'Does she know what I'm saying to her? Does she understand?'

'It's not thought that most girls with Rett syndrome develop mentally much beyond their very early years, Mrs Willow,' he said. 'So her level of understanding now is likely to remain constant throughout her life. She will probably always have the mental age of a toddler.'

'Why is she… like this? What made her this way?' asked Pete, voicing his own personal, long-considered, burning question.

'We don't know what causes it,' the doctor answered, looking directly at him and avoiding Louise's gaze. 'We assume it's a genetic fault, rather than brain damage from birth or whatever, but at this stage, we're really in the dark.'

He's trying to tell me it's not my fault, Louise thought. But I feel like it is, and it could be. I had a few drinks whilst I was pregnant, the odd cigarette. Didn't I once fall over in the car park at work when I was eight months gone? Or what if I caught something from a patient? It could be my fault she's like this, she thought.

Then the appointment was over. Every anxiety, every tear, every sleepless night had built up to this and it was over in less than twenty minutes. Dr Rivers had booked them in for a follow-up appointment in six months' time and suggested they seek out physiotherapy for Patience. And that was it. They were dismissed.

'Take her home and make her life as comfortable as possible,' he'd said, as they got up to leave. Louise realised how similar his advice sounded to that meted out to the relatives of elderly patients on the geriatric ward she'd worked on during her training.

Pete had taken Louise's hand then and they had left the office swiftly, collecting Patience from the ward and making their way to their car. Their conversation for the long drive home was sparse; perfunctory. Neither of them knew what to say. They were both living out their own personal horror, and they needed time to process it individually. Louise had looked across at her husband several times during the journey and had seen Pete's teeth grinding, a clear sign that he was under stress. In her, the emotional trauma manifested itself in nausea and a thumping headache that no painkiller could touch.

When they arrived home, he had gone upstairs to their bedroom and shut the door; Louise knew better than to follow. She went to put the kettle on, partly because she was thirsty and hoped it might help clear her head, partly to mask the sound of muffled sobs coming from above...

Back in the present, in a room full of parents who had probably gone through many of the same emotions and experiences, the atmosphere was tangible.

Professor Larssen had asked Louise to organise the meeting in Birmingham so that all of the parents hoping to enter their Rett children into phase one of the trial could find out what it was about. They'd had an overwhelming response to their adverts on social media asking for participants and today was about whittling them down to those who were really committed.

She knew, because she'd seen all of their addresses, that several of the parents had driven more than four hours to be at the seminar. One pair had even got a flight. She also knew, as a fellow carer, about the hoops they'd have had to jump through just to leave the house. You needed to find someone you really trusted and who was trained properly; these people were expensive and rare. But these families knew that this was a meeting that could change their child's life forever so it was worth paying through the nose for.

When the room was full, Louise nodded to the professor, who she had now learned to call Philip. He walked up to the podium to begin and she dimmed the lights for him, then took a seat at the back to watch.

'Good evening, ladies and gentlemen,' he began, 'and welcome to Birmingham. I know some of you have travelled very far, so we will try to keep this as short as possible. There will be time for questions at the end. I'm going to start with a brief presentation.' The professor hit a button on his laptop, triggering a video, recently released by an American charity which was raising money for the research.

On screen was a little girl with the face of an angel, crowned with blonde curls. She sat centre screen, perched on her mother's lap. If you took a brief glance at her, you wouldn't know there was anything wrong; but if you looked closer, the wringing motion of her hands and her grinding teeth told a different story.

The voice-over explained that her name was Crystal and that she was five years old. She had been diagnosed with Rett syndrome at the age of three.

'The doctors told Crystal's mom that she had no awareness,' the voice-over stated, 'but they were wrong.' In front of Crystal was an iPad and she was gazing intently at it. 'How are you today, Crystal?' her mother asked. There was a pause, and her daughter continued to look at the iPad. 'I'm feeling fine,' came an electronic voice from the device. 'Can I have some chocolate now?' Crystal's face broke into a smile.

There was a flutter of laughter in the room, infused with amazement. On screen, Crystal was being taken in her wheelchair into the kitchen.

'Eye gaze technology is great. It's shown us that people with Rett syndrome do have things to say,' the voice-over continued. 'But it can only go so far.'

The parents watched Crystal's mother break a chocolate bar into tiny pieces before putting it in the microwave for a few seconds to soften it. Then she fed it to her daughter by hand, piece by piece.

'We believe that we can do better than this. Much better. Groundbreaking gene therapy offers us the possibility of reversing Rett syndrome's symptoms. We believe that if we get it right, nobody on this earth will need to suffer from this horrendous disease any more. We will set people like Crystal free. They will have normal lives.'

Crystal was again on screen, sitting serenely as her two younger siblings played with their toys around her chair. 'We need your help to carry out a groundbreaking trial to see if our belief is right. Donate today.'

The final shot was a close up of Crystal's face, with the crowdfunding link superimposed on the screen. The screen faded to black and the parents' attentions switched back to Professor Larssen. There was silence in the room.

'It's quite something, isn't it?' he said, breaking that silence. 'It sounds almost like science fiction, I know that. But the fact is, we do have the money to do this trial now, here in the UK. This charity says our regulations are more favourable for it, so it's taking place here. I must caution you and say that it may still prove to be science fiction. It's my job, as a doctor and a scientist, to tell you that. I'm perfectly clear that we could be barking up the wrong tree. I am not living with false hope – and I want you to be the same. You have to understand that those promises, those hopes on screen, they could be wrong. It's very possible they are. But they could be right, and for that reason, I believe that everyone with Rett syndrome deserves this chance. Now, let me give you some details about the practicalities…'

Professor Larssen went on to give enrolment details, age requirements, fitness levels, family history, the legal specifications. As this was to be a phase one trial, he said, families needed to understand that they were going to be giving a relatively low dose of the virus – therefore, results might be limited. He went on to explain that the viral vector would be injected into them via lumbar puncture, which might be 'uncomfortable', and that they'd need to spend several days in hospital afterwards, followed by close monitoring at home.

Children taking part in the trial would need their parents' consent to take part, he said. On the other hand, adults like Patience would need a letter from their doctors and approval either from both parents, or from someone else representing their interests, a so-called 'consultee'.

The professor made it clear that there were a limited number of places available on the trial, and that he and his team would be selecting their subjects carefully. Except for Patience, of course, who had a guaranteed slot already. Louise was incredibly grateful for that. She still hoped she'd get that signature from Pete giving it the go-ahead, but if that didn't happen, she had a backup plan...

The session drew to a close. Professor Larssen stopped talking and invited questions. The first one came from a shaven-headed man sitting several rows from the back.

'So, you said you weren't sure this will work. Does that mean you think it's pretty likely that it won't? Are you basically telling us it's a waste of time?'

'No, no, nothing like that,' the professor replied. 'I am actually fairly optimistic. I do think this has a good chance of working. Don't get the wrong impression. I am merely trying to equip you with all the facts. As I said, we are only going to give a low dose this time, so it may not have a dramatic effect. But it also means it is safer.'

The man didn't ask another question. Louise saw him turn to his partner and whisper something in her ear. Then, another hand shot up at the front of the group. This time it belonged to a black woman with beautifully plaited hair piled artfully on her head.

'You said in your talk there might be side effects. Can you tell us more about those?' she asked.

'At this stage, it is almost impossible to tell what they might be,' Professor Larssen replied. 'But trials we've done in the lab suggest this is relatively low risk.'

'But what are the actual things that could go wrong?' the woman insisted.

'As I said, we will try to remedy the Rett genetic defect using a viral vector. That's a virus which will enter the body and target the specific gene that needs fixing. The risk is that we could affect more cells than we mean to, or we somehow damage some other part of DNA. Or we could "overexpress" the gene and cause too much protein to be produced, and that can be harmful too.'

'So what does that really mean? What could happen to my daughter?'

'In most cases, hopefully very little,' he replied. 'But there is always the risk of something serious, like cancer, potentially. I showed you the list on the slide earlier and this is also explained in detail in the information packs you'll collect on your way out.'

'Are you saying my daughter could develop cancer as a result?'

'It is one of the risks we've identified, yes,' he replied.

There were no further questions.

One by one, the parents stood up, picked up their coats and bags, and filed out of the room, taking an information pack from Louise as they left. When they'd all gone, she walked round the chairs checking for lost property, and then put the remaining packs carefully back into her own bag so that she could return them to the office in the morning. She walked over to Professor Larssen to tell him she was leaving. He was making notes on his script, which Louise had printed for him several days ago.

'Thanks, Louise. Well done. Excellent turnout, I thought.'

'Yes, we didn't have any no-shows,' she said, fiddling with her bag strap. 'How many of them do you think will apply?'

'Oh, probably all of them,' said the professor, looking up from his writing and raising an eyebrow.

'Really?'

'Yes. We're their only hope, aren't we? It wouldn't have mattered if I'd told them there was a strong chance their children would come out of it with webbed feet. They'd still do it.'

Louise was startled.

'That seems incredible,' she said, putting her hands on her hips. She thought for a second. 'But I suppose you're right. I feel that way about Patience.'

'Well, there we are,' the professor said, packing his laptop and script away and picking up his briefcase. 'I'll see you tomorrow, Louise. Thanks for today,' he continued, walking to the door. 'Good work.'

Louise waved goodbye as he headed out into the lobby. After he'd gone, she spent a few minutes throwing abandoned paper cups in the bin and straightening chairs.

As she hoisted her bag onto her shoulder and walked towards the door, she thought back to that morning, to that awful row she'd had with Pete. He had accused her of putting Patience forward for the trial for selfish reasons. And while she absolutely disagreed with that, she did recognise that her decision to forge ahead with it, to completely ignore Pete's concerns, was an act of defiance.

She had spent a lifetime caring for others and acquiescing to their views, but now – now was her time. Something in her had changed; she had found a new energy. And she was going to use that to pursue what she believed was right, whatever Pete thought, because Patience's future happiness depended on it.

10

Eliza

November

Eliza's day was going incredibly well – really, extraordinarily well – until the hairdresser rang her to cancel.

'I'm so sorry love, Letty's broken her finger and we need to cancel your appointment today, but I'll book you in for tomorrow, OK?'

It was absolutely not OK. She needed her hair blow dried for tonight, on pain of death. Her long brown mane – unruly, and neither straight nor curly – only looked good when it was blow dried properly, and she couldn't do it herself. She had long admired Patience's effortless glossy blonde hair and wished she'd got that particular gift in the genetic lottery. Although she acknowledged, of course, that she'd done pretty well in the whole able-to-walk-and-speak genetic side of things.

Her attempts with hair straighteners usually resulted in limp yet frizzy hair which looked as if she'd just walked home through drizzle, and her blow dries were akin to Bridget Jones' hairdo after that ride in an open-top sports car. Neither was the look she was

going for this evening. This evening, she had to be hot.
Very hot.

She was finally, finally getting together with Ed for dinner
tonight for the 'closure' he apparently wanted. It had taken
weeks and weeks to arrange. Evidently, he was very busy
and she had pretended to be, too, just for a few of the dates
he'd suggested, just to appear unbothered. She hoped she'd
been convincing.

She had not told Katy about the meeting. This absolutely
was not because she was ashamed; it was something she had
to do for herself and for her relationship, and Katy didn't
need to know, because she'd worry. And tell her not to do
it. Anyhow, it was imperative that she had nice hair. She
had bought a new outfit during her lunch break yesterday.
Nothing too overtly sexy, because that would be sending
out the wrong message. But she had found, in Zara, a nice
black skirt and a gorgeous frilly red top; with tights and
heels, the hair was to be the icing on the cake. It wouldn't
work without it.

She was supposed to be bashing out a press release for
that afternoon, but instead found herself sending multiple
Facebook messages to salons in the area, begging them
to see her. Twenty messages later and a near-miss with
Jenny (she'd just managed to flick up the Office doc she'd
been working up in time) she had managed to secure an
appointment at Chez Julienne down the road. It was twice
the price of her previous option (and wasn't Julienne a way
of cutting vegetables?) but beggars couldn't be choosers –
and anyway, it was impossible to put a price on confidence.

She had dashed out of the office during her lunch break
in order to make it on time, passing on actually eating

anything. Her Australian stylist, Laura (Julienne was on his or her own lunch break, clearly) ushered her towards a plush chair next to the mirrors and wrapped her in a gown.

'So, where are you off to tonight?' she inquired, her tone implying that she actually cared. You got what you paid for in this place, clearly.

'Nowhere particularly special. I'm just meeting an ex for dinner.'

'Wow. Ex-husband?'

Eliza laughed nervously.

'Ah, no. We never got that far. Ex-fiancé. We were supposed to be getting married next summer, but...'

'Ah, I see. What happened? Did you call it off?'

Laura was clearly a straight from the hip sort of girl. Eliza laughed, aware that Laura was watching her in the mirror.

'No, sadly,' she replied, after a pause. 'He said he wanted... closure.'

'Is he a recent ex?'

'Yes, sadly.'

'Hence the hair.'

'Yep.'

'Show him what he's missing, that sort of thing?' suggested Laura.

'Exactly.'

'So as well as the cut and blow-dry, can we offer you any colour today?' said Laura, as she examined Eliza's hair. 'We have some really cool temporary rinses which are excellent for hiding those silver flyaways.'

'Er, no thanks, I'm fine with the highlights I already have,' Eliza spluttered. Jesus, she thought, do I really look that old? She had the odd grey growing around her parting, sure, but she tweezered them out whenever she spotted them. But shit, she was only four years off forty. Was she actually over the hill? She realised with horror that she might be.

'So did you have kids, you and your ex?'

'Ah, no. We never got that far, either.' God, woman, please stop asking these questions, she thought. I can't cope with them today.

'Probably best, eh? It gets messy with kids. And they're exhausting. I have a son, he's three. His dad left us last year. It's a bit… shit. To be honest.'

Eliza suddenly felt sympathy for her inquisitor.

'I'm so sorry.'

'Ah, that's OK. He was a bastard. Like yours, eh?'

'Yes, like mine,' Eliza replied, trying to smile.

Laura reached for the shampoo bottle. 'So, do you have any brothers and sisters?' she asked, switching tack.

Ah, she's decided to opt for 'safe' small talk, Eliza thought. She hated it when this happened. It was always a toss-up – should she lie and say that she had no siblings, or boast about a gorgeous brother who worked in the City instead? Or, should she be honest and then have to accept the hairdresser's sympathy, mitigating the ensuing awkwardness by explaining, in painful detail, her sister's inabilities, and her family's pain?

'I have one sister,' she replied, hoping that might be the end to it.

'Ah. Are you close in age?'

'She's six years younger than me. It took my parents a while to get around to procreating for a second time.'

Laura laughed. 'That's like my brother and me. He's ten

years younger. An accident, ha.' Eliza tried to produce a chuckle, as it seemed appropriate. Laura began to rinse the shampoo out of her hair. 'So, what does she do, your sister?'

Ah, here we go, Eliza thought. The yawning chasm beckoned.

'She's disabled,' she answered, resigned to her fate. 'She lives near Oxford. In residential care.'

Laura turned off the water and paused. 'Oh, I see. What's she got? My cousin's autistic, so I know a bit about that sort of thing.'

Not about this sort of thing, Eliza thought. She took a breath.

'She can't walk, talk or do anything for herself,' she answered, as Laura wrapped a towel around her head. 'I always say: imagine a baby in an adult's body and that's her.'

There was an awkward silence. Laura beckoned her over into a chair in front of a mirror. She busied herself with her duties – removing the towel and bringing over a pile of magazines – but was silent. It was a reaction Eliza not only understood, but expected. It was always like this. People had no idea what to say.

'Would you like a coffee?' Laura asked, finally. 'We do a great cappuccino here.'

To avoid further conversation, Eliza pretended to find her magazine, full of the airbrushed lives of the rich and famous, tremendously interesting. It worked; Laura stopped talking to her as she brushed, trimmed and blow-dried her hair. But as she was holding up a mirror to show her the back of her hair – sleek and just on the right side of bouncy – Laura spoke once more.

'Good luck this evening,' she said, smiling at Eliza. 'You look sensational. But don't give him any joy. He's an ex for a reason. They always are. I have been there, and I know. Look at him, head held high, and repeat to yourself, "I am worth more than you".'

'Right,' replied Eliza. '"I am worth more than you." Got it.'

She tried reciting the mantra to herself, under her breath, when she emerged from the comforting, luxurious cocoon of the salon half an hour later. Her hair now looked sensational, but her face told a very different story. She was already mentally preparing herself for that evening, for the enormous effort she was going to have to make to appear untainted, unbruised. Fortunately, the location of her desk in the office – tucked away in the corner, handy for hangovers, tears and lazy days – worked in her favour and none of her colleagues questioned her unusual silence, or unusual expression, that afternoon.

At 6 p.m., after the room had emptied of most of her colleagues, she retreated into the bathroom. She had her make-up bag with her and a small holdall which contained her outfit. And as she exchanged her white underwear for black satin, she began to feel a new resolve. Things might have gone stale between them, but that was simply because she hadn't tried hard enough. She had become lazy, she thought. So, to quote Laura – tonight, she'd show him what he'd been missing.

Half an hour later, she caught a bus to St Paul's. Ed's chosen venue was a steakhouse near to the London branch of his firm, where he'd had meetings that afternoon.

A year ago, Ed had decided to retrain as a lawyer after an aborted first career as a teacher. Having passed his exams in the June, he'd moved to Oxford in July to start his training at a well-regarded firm with an office near the Cornmarket. He'd been delighted about the move and the challenge ahead; she'd been delirious with tears. He had told her not to be silly – and had proposed to her after a celebratory meal in their favourite Italian restaurant. He had said that their future was bright.

They'd decided not to give up the London flat, as her job kept her in town. So she'd had to lead this strange half-life, half in London, half in Oxford, a foot in both camps. Exhausting, but worth it. Being together was always worth it, of course it was. They had lived together for more than fifteen years, after all, and distance was nothing to a couple who were so grounded, so devoted, *so together*.

She'd taken to doing most of the travelling, as they (or, he?) had decided that Oxford was a far more pleasant place to spend a weekend. It had been an extraordinary challenge to cover two lots of rent, but it had been the right decision. Or at least, she had thought it had been. Now it just seemed as though she'd taken the mesh off the top of a very deep wishing well and simply chucked all of her cash into it. His decision to leave her had given with one hand financially and taken away with the other: she no longer had to share the cost of the rent of the Oxford flat – on the other hand, she now had to shoulder the London rent alone.

Eliza's route to the restaurant took her down a street lined with plane trees, planted there with great hope more than a hundred years ago, because of their resistance to the city's pollution. At the time, London's toxic air had caused thousands of deaths each year. Now, they were just a welcome note of colour in a grey man-made jungle, turning from bright green to shades of amber, floating down onto the pavement, forming a golden carpet. But despite their beauty, Eliza could never understand people who preferred autumn above all other seasons. The colours of the leaves aside, the season really signified the impending darkness of the winter and a long wait for rejuvenation – hardly a reason to celebrate in anyone's book. Not only that, but the damp leaves were not the safest surface for her new black patent stilettos and she occasionally found herself reaching for the tree trunks, railings and street lamps for stability and support.

The restaurant was fronted with black glass two storeys high. It didn't take long to spot Ed among the crowds of people gathered for fine wine and well-aged meat, even in the low light cast by hanging chrome pendants; brown closely-clipped hair, a smart suit, obviously tall, even when sitting – yes, that was him over there, at a table near the bar.

'Hello,' she said. He looked up.

I am worth more than you. I am worth more than you. I am worth more than you.

'Hi, thanks for coming.'

He'd spoken as if she had arrived for a meeting to discuss writing a will. His formality made it feel even more awkward a meeting than she had let herself imagine. She dropped into the chair that was proffered, smoothed her skirt and swept her hair away from her face. Then she took her compact out of her bag and reapplied her lipstick using the mirror inside. When she looked up, she saw that he was staring at her.

'Is that a new top?' he asked.

'Yes. I liked the colour.'

What else was there to say? He hadn't mentioned her hair, but then, he hadn't noticed when she started adding lowlights, then highlights, then layers – it wasn't his thing. They examined the drinks menu for a minute or two, encased in a bubble of silence that was exclusive to their table alone. Ed broke it first.

'So I asked you here because I felt that we didn't really get to say all that we needed to say.'

I am worth more than you, I am worth more than you.

'You *could* say that. *You* walked out.'

'Yes. And I'm sorry about that. But I just felt we weren't getting anywhere. We were going around in circles and you were so upset...'

'Of course I was upset. You told me you didn't know what love was.'

'Yes, I did.'

It had happened when they had invited a couple of long-standing friends over for the evening. It had been a Saturday and Ed had been up from Oxford, on a rare weekend visit to the capital. They had seized upon the opportunity to invite old university friends over for an Indian takeaway and a large quantity of beer. Callie and Max had also met at uni and had been together for more than eighteen years. They had got married several years after leaving, and were now parents to eight-year-old Rupert and four-year-old Julia. Their dinner with Ed and Eliza was a rare escape from the binds of parenthood.

'I do envy you both,' Callie had said, necking the wine. 'Look at your tidy flat, right in the centre of London, and that inevitable lie-in you're both planning in the morning. Absolutely magic.'

'Yes,' Max had interjected. 'Meanwhile, we had to move out to zone six to afford a house and it takes us about ten hours to get into work. If the trains run at all. And our idea of a fun evening now is a night at a friend's place eating food from Khan's Balti – no offence.'

'None taken,' Ed had replied, quickly. 'But Khan's is obviously the best takeaway in London town.'

'Obviously,' said Max. 'I don't know why it doesn't have a Michelin star.'

There had been much drinking that night. Wine, beer and spirits. Max and Callie were demob happy, had a taxi booked home and were not afraid of their hangovers in the morning. Which was probably at least part of the reason for Ed's awful behaviour later.

They had all collapsed onto the sofas after the meal, clutching their glasses. Eliza had opened the window and turned off the main light, and for a while, they had all gazed out at the view of south London, thousands of streetlights beaming out in the partial darkness of a summer's evening, mapping each street.

'Big year coming up next year for you guys, then,' Callie had said, after a while. 'Finally saying I Do. So exciting. Do you remember that time, Max?'

'Sorry, when was that?' Max joked, as Callie playfully punched him in the arm. 'Yes, that I do. It was quite the time. They were the best days, actually. The best.'

'Yes, you're so lucky to have it all yet to come. That's

such an amazing time, when it's just about you two and the love you have,' mused Callie. 'No ankle biters nipping at you, nagging you to feed them three times a day, that sort of thing.'

'So pesky,' replied Max, kissing her and rubbing her leg. He gave his wife a look which made Eliza wince. Ed had never looked at her like that. And right now he was staring into the distance, impassive. Callie had filled the space that was looming large.

'Anyway, yes, it's amazing, that feeling you have, just before you get married. I'm guessing you guys are right in that bubble now,' she'd said, looking at Ed.

'I'm not sure I know what love is, really,' Ed had replied, after a pause, in the same tone of voice he'd have used if he didn't know what time the bus was coming, or what food to order. Eliza's stomach lurched.

'Oh, come on mate, don't go all heavy on us,' said Max. 'We all know how you feel about Lize.'

'Yes, I know; we're getting married and that's great, it's the right thing to do – but I mean, I don't think I understand the meaning of the term, really. Not in the way you guys are using it. I never have.'

At that point, Eliza had got up, walked to the bathroom and slammed the door shut. She took several deep breaths, trying to subdue the adrenaline which coursed through her body, before collapsing onto the toilet seat, her head cradled in her hands. She had only heard the muffled responses to Ed's pronouncement, but got the feeling that Max and Callie had decided that it might be time to leave. This was confirmed when they walked past the bathroom in the direction of the bedroom to retrieve their coats.

Callie had whispered at the door, 'We're off, Lize. But I'm on the phone, OK? I'm on the phone. Whenever. Speak in a bit. Love you.'

She had gone then. They both had. It had been very silent after that. Well, until Ed had put on some Coldplay dirge, loudly, to fill the void. Eliza had used the cover of the music to repeatedly hammer her head into the bathroom door, desperate to exorcise the disturbing thoughts which were now running rampant through her head.

Half an hour later, Eliza had emerged from the bathroom to find Ed in the lounge, staring at his phone, a small rucksack beside his feet. He had looked up at her and said, without any further explanation, that he felt it might be best to go back to Oxford.

'Are you any clearer now?' She wanted Ed to give her answers. Or at least, she thought she did.

'I don't think so,' he said, looking around for their waiter. 'I need time to figure that one out. But what I am certain of is that I don't want to get married yet.'

'*Yet*? Ed, you're in your late thirties. We've been together since uni. When *will* you be ready?'

The waiter arrived to take the drinks order. Eliza stared directly down at the table and did not look up.

'We'll have a bottle of the Chilean Merlot. And a bottle of sparkling water,' said Ed, before bidding the waiter to leave them. 'Have your parents cancelled the venue?'

'I don't know,' she replied, her voice hoarse. 'Have you just brought me here to talk logistics and refunds?'

'Eliza, I'm just being practical. They spent a lot of money on that venue. And I know money is tight.'

Yes, they had. The venue – the venue that would have been – was a stately home fifteen miles from her childhood home, bang in the middle of the rolling Cotswold hills.

Langland Manor was actually somewhere her parents had taken them out to at weekends when they were kids. The house was open to the public on Saturdays and it was also one of the first places in the county to provide a disabled toilet for visitors – a prerequisite of any Willow family trip after Patience got too big to be lifted into a toilet cubicle. So, about twice a year, in fine weather, they had all mounted an expedition to view the house's manicured lawns and carefully laid-out vistas, before retiring to a wooden picnic table beneath apple trees to eat the packed lunch Mum had made; always egg and cress sandwiches, crisps and apple juice. And possibly Jaffa cakes for a treat.

It had been a relief, eating outdoors. Patience was a messy eater, but no one really noticed her table manners (or lack of them) there, with so much space. No one was really close enough, not even the inevitable staring, curious children, and what Patience hadn't managed to eat, the birds had loved. Those picnic tables had had a fine view of the house's Georgian facade, which in itself had been built on the carcass of a rather fine Tudor manor house. And while her mum and dad had bickered over Patience's feeding efforts, wiped her face and hands and debated about who was going to push her up the slope back to the car, Eliza had stared at that house and soaked up its beauty, its stories.

She had always loved historical buildings. It was not the decor or the furnishings. It was the layers of human drama they had contained within them which inspired her. And when she and Ed had decided on it as a wedding venue, she had felt she was adding her own scene in that multifaceted human play. Well, it had certainly taken a dramatic turn.

'Thanks for your concern,' she said. 'I'll pass it on.'

She wondered idly whether wedding insurance covered being dumped. Ed was right; her parents were set to lose a lot of money that they'd saved up for so long, simply because of her inability to persuade a man to marry her.

The waiter returned, bringing with him the wine, the glasses and the food menus. He poured Ed a glass and waited patiently as he sniffed it, rolled it around the glass and put it to his lips and sipped.

'Mmm. Nice,' Ed said, satisfaction in his voice. Two full glasses were poured for them as they waited in silence.

Finally, Ed spoke. 'So, I suggested we meet because I wanted to explain why I said what I said.' He took a sip of his wine. 'And why I left. I feel like we need closure.'

Eliza raised both eyebrows, and half-laughed.

'Bloody hell, Ed, have you finally been reading those relationship books I bought? Closure! Is there any point? I mean, I feel we got closure when you packed your bags and took half the items in the flat. More than half, actually.' As she spoke, Eliza knocked her newly poured glass of merlot with her left arm, and they both watched in horror as it tumbled to the ground, spilling its overpriced cargo all over the tiled floor, the glass smashing into hundreds of tiny pieces.

As a flock of waiters ran towards them bearing paper towels and a dustpan and brush, Ed glared at her. He looked around anxiously as the clean-up took place, aware that the couple next to them – who had not spoken a word since they had arrived a quarter of an hour ago – were listening in to everything they said to each other.

'You seem really angry,' he said, almost whispering now. 'I get that you are. But let's try to be calm. At least in here.'

Eliza swallowed hard.

'I'll do my best. Tell me then, why you left me.'

'Let's order food first and I'll try to explain.'

Another glass was brought for Eliza and more wine poured. And after about thirty seconds of reading the extensive menu, Ed told the waiter that they were ready to order. He reeled off his choice – scallops, followed by a medium rare fillet steak, with blue cheese sauce and fries – and then looked across the table at Eliza with anticipation, like a conductor preparing to lead an orchestra.

'I'm… I'm not feeling very hungry,' she said, cautiously. 'I ate a late lunch. Can I skip the starter and just have the mussels for main?' The waiter asked if she wanted to have garlic bread with it, but she declined. After that, he smiled in her direction – she detected a possible note of sympathy there – took both menus and walked away in the direction of the kitchen.

'Not like you not to be hungry,' said Ed.

'Situations like this do that to a girl,' she snapped. Did Ed look slightly guilty? It was possible. But he'd always been good at hiding how he really felt. That was at least part of the reason why she hadn't seen any of this coming.

'So, as I said, I asked you here because I wanted to explain,' he continued, unbidden, picking up a piece of bread from the basket a waiter had just left, and tearing it apart. 'I'd like to start by saying how sorry I am that I did it the way

I did it. Coming out with that stuff in front of friends. It wasn't my intention. Anyway, I wanted to say also – I love you. But I think I'm not *in* love with you. Not the sort of love that Max and Callie were talking about. Not those sorts of feelings that withstand two kids, wrinkles, endless drives down the M40. I'm trying to look forward here, to the future – and I realise I don't see us in it, like that. Let's be honest here. Do you?'

Ed's gut-wrenching summary of his feelings was interrupted by the waiter bringing the food. Eliza looked down on her steaming pot of mussels and felt bile rising.

'Yes,' she said.

Ed waited while the waiter positioned the plates, refilled their water and then retreated.

'Sorry?' he said, his whisper harsh.

'Yes, I see,' she replied, thinking: *I see us getting married next summer, I see us having a family, I see us eventually settling in Oxford or somewhere else together and me working part-time for a PR agency. I see us buying a house with enough room for a vegetable patch and a downstairs loo so Patience can visit with Mum and Dad. I see Christmas decorations hung on the front door and you swinging our children up in the air in the living room, just missing the light fixings.*

'Yes, I see,' she said.

'You see?'

'I see where you are coming from, I suppose. We had gone stale.'

'You could put it like that. But were we ever like Max and Callie? Were we ever in love enough to make that promise to be together for the rest of our lives?'

'You made that promise when you proposed to me. Why did you do that, if you didn't want to marry me?' she asked. She looked down at her pot of mussels, at those little bodies which had been boiled alive, and realised she couldn't face eating them. Instead, she reached for her spoon and drank some of the sauce from the bottom.

'I thought I did,' he answered, slicing into his rare steak, blood spilling out as he did so. 'Looking at it objectively, you and I are the perfect partnership. You're intelligent, you're fun, we don't drive each other mad. You're very attractive.'

Eliza felt her face begin to glow red.

'But, you know, perhaps I'm just not the marrying kind.'

'So you're saying that it's not me, it's you?' She looked up at him, her statement dripping with irony. Ed ignored her tone.

They paused to let the waiter take their plates. He looked concerned when he saw that Eliza hadn't eaten her mussels. 'I'm just not hungry,' she said, by way of apology. He nodded and took them away.

Eliza excused herself and made her way to the toilets. She threw herself into a cubicle, locked the door and paused briefly, looking down at the bowl, before vomiting copiously. Afterwards, she leaned down over the sink and sucked in and swilled some water around her mouth from the tap, before spitting it out. She watched it spiral down the plughole, along with small splatters of brown, orange and red sick. And when she looked at herself in the mirror in front of her, she could see that her face betrayed the truly sorry state of her beleaguered, emotionally damaged digestive system. Her skin was almost translucent, her eyes bloodshot and dull. It took her several minutes to restore relative order with the help of concealer, powder and lipstick, and a hard pinch on each cheek.

When she emerged from the loos, Ed was entering his pin into a credit card reader at their table. He stood up as she approached, and handed over her coat.

'I asked for the bill. Thought it best.' Eliza gave him a grateful smile and followed him as he made his way to the door and out into the street. When she had caught up with him and stood next to him, she fought the urge to reach out and hold his hand. It had been such an instinctive gesture for so many years. Instead, she placed her hands in her pockets. Ed turned to look at her.

'Which way are you going? I'm staying at a hotel near Blackfriars. Fancy a walk?'

Eliza had actually been planning to catch a tube from St Paul's, but decided not to mention it.

'Sure. I can get the bus from the bridge,' she said, following him. Their walk took them through a network of quiet, tiny streets with names referencing their historic past; Dean Court, New Bell Yard, Addle Hill. The roads were so narrow that no parking was allowed, and, as it was now 9 p.m. and all but the most dedicated of workers had gone home, it was as if they had the City to themselves. Except – a Toyota Prius was ripping down Addle Hill at some speed; its driver probably lost and late for a fare.

Eliza had no time to see it. She just caught something white and large in her peripheral vision. It was Ed who grabbed her by the hand, forcing them both into the side of a wheelie bin, nudging it under an archway. Eliza toppled over, falling awkwardly onto her left side with her arm underneath her. The car did not stop.

'Are you OK?' Ed asked afterwards, slightly breathless, holding out his hand to Eliza as the Prius disappeared around the corner and out of their lives forever.

'I think so,' she replied, allowing him to pull her upright. She felt shaky. It was the adrenaline. 'I'm going to be bruised tomorrow, but that's all, I think.' She added, 'Thank God.'

'Yes, thank God for that,' he said. He did not let go of her hand. They carried on walking down the road, together, not talking. When they reached Ed's hotel several minutes later – an ugly concrete square overlooking Upper Thames Street – he turned towards her and drew her in for a hug. She felt a further surge of adrenaline pass through her as he did so.

'Do you want to come in for a bit?' he asked, into her ear. 'I spotted some good whisky behind the bar. Might be good for the shock.'

She nodded and allowed herself to be led inside. It was the most natural thing in the world to do.

11

Pete

There were some Christmas carols playing in the background, very quietly. The well-known tunes, etched on his brain since childhood, were being performed on the godforsaken panpipes and the arrangement was appalling, but they were there, and for that reason alone, Pete stopped in his tracks to listen to a particularly dreadful rendition of 'Ding Dong Merrily on High'.

He was in the lobby of his hotel in Doha and the music was incongruous, because there was not a single sign around him that the festive season was nearing. Through the glass revolving doors, he could just make out a palm tree which was being buffeted by a light breeze. The sun had just set and the sky was now a dark brown, an improvement on the shade of dark-yellow urine that had been hovering over him outside today. Inside, the faded leather on the seats was also brown, and the beige walls, upholstered in damask, were as insipid and uninspiring as the flaccid offerings in the hotel's daily breakfast buffet: all you could eat for fifty riyals. If you could face eating it, that is.

He suspected that one of the reception staff was behind the musical choice. Most specifically, he suspected Edward, a forty-year-old from the Philippines. Always full of an inimitable joy from who knows what magical reserve, he welcomed Pete effusively every time he arrived back in the country. He was behind the desk right now, but his face was not giving anything away. Smart move. Acknowledging Christmas here was something of an underground movement, he thought.

There were several men in local dress – full length white robes known as thobes – having a very sincere business meeting to Pete's right, and he could smell the expensive oud perfume that at least one of them was wearing. It was overpowering and spicy, like incense.

To his left, a group of white expat men were arriving through the doors, most likely on their way to one of the restaurants in the hotel, which all served alcohol, a relative rarity. They were all dressed identically: chinos, deck shoes, short-sleeved shirts, and each had closely cropped hair. They nodded at him, and he nodded at them, looked down at his own outfit – chinos, a red checked shirt and brown shoes – and smiled wanly. Wherever they came from in the West – the USA, Europe, Canada – they seemed to be united not only by a common dress code, but also a common purpose. Money.

Many, like him, worked for long stints out here without their families, to provide for a better life for them at home. Out here, so the saying went, an expat had two buckets: one for money and the other for shit. When either one filled up, it was time to go home. His shit bucket was filling rapidly these days, but his money bucket was still too far from the brim. He was skilled enough, after years spent learning his craft on building sites, but he had no qualifications to speak of, and that had always severely affected his earning potential. His finances kept him awake at night, kept him here. It had only been in the past few years that he'd finally managed to earn a decent wage, to be able to put a pot of money aside for a rainy day. And even then, he couldn't be trusted with it. Even this contract wasn't going to be enough to fill the abyss he was staring into.

He ran his hands through his almost entirely grey hair, short on the back and sides and bald on top, recently shorn at the small Indian-run barber's down the road. Vikram – thirty, a father of four from Kerala, reliably attentive – also counted those men as clients, no doubt. It was a small town. Or at least, the Western expat bit of it was.

Pete was hungry and seeking a quick and easy dinner that would allow him to get an early night. He had to be up before dawn tomorrow to catch the first flight home, and after a long day in the dust, he had only another couple of hours of life in him before he would gladly welcome oblivion. Knowing that a club sandwich was as speedy and relatively tasty as this hotel got, he made his way into the café just off the lobby.

Pete selected a small table next to the window and caught the eye of the waitress, Sandra, as he sat down. She came over immediately and he ordered without even glancing at the menu. Sandra smiled and retreated, leaving Pete looking out of the window beside him. It was one-way and mirrored, and its dark tint meant that the evening light, which was fading fast outside, appeared to have dimmed already.

It had been a hard week. A hard month, come to that. James, ever keen to impress their local CEO and the UK office, had promised that they would complete the new hotel by June, but it was perfectly clear to Pete that they'd need a miracle to finish it by next Christmas. The supplies just weren't coming in fast enough and the labourers were exhausted and demoralised, six months into three-year contracts and *they* wouldn't get home to see their families in India and Nepal for another eighteen months. They'd been working extra-long days to make up for hours lost during Ramadan, and their one day off a week was generally spent holed up in their camp on the outskirts in the city because James had cut back on free bus transport on Fridays to save money.

Pete knew that his decent salary, furnished apartment and ability to fly home once every couple of months made him a very lucky man. But knowing this didn't make his essentially 'single' life any easier. Even being aware that he was, by accident of birth and opportunity, very lucky indeed, Pete was exhausted, physically and mentally. As each visit home approached he became less tolerant of life in the Gulf. He knew that he needed to get out regularly to reassess and restore the diminished parts of his soul, and he yearned for the day when he didn't need to accept another contract.

His attention was caught by movement on the other side of the glass. He could just make out a woman getting out of a cab, paying her fare and walking up the steps into the lobby. Was it – was it *her*?

His stomach lurched. She was about forty, with brown hair swept up into a bun. She was particularly notable because there were hardly any Western female visitors at this hotel who weren't with their families. This woman was wearing a dark trouser suit, an odd choice in this climate. Qatar's weather leant itself rather more to loose cottons. He'd often wished he could get away with wearing the local dress to work – a white cotton robe was definitely the way to deal with the desert – but sadly, not so practical on a building site.

As the woman faded behind the tinted glass into the hotel lobby, Pete's phone buzzed, distracting him, and he looked down. It was a message from Louise, another of many. She was asking which flight he was booked on tomorrow. He had not told her yet. In fact, they hadn't actually spoken since he'd sent that email objecting to the gene therapy trial. He knew that she was angry – she'd made that abundantly clear – and it was an unspoken rule between them that they never embarked on an argument when he was overseas.

In the past, video chats had helped bridge the gap a bit, but a recent decision by the government to block these calls meant that he now relied on text messages and emails, and these were a very poor substitute for face-to-face conversations. It was also impossible to make up properly afterwards. Their marriage had always been an affectionate one, and not being able to touch each other, to embrace and say sorry, was a real problem for them both. And when he was being honest with himself, really honest, he had no idea whether he could find the strength to say sorry, or to even meet her halfway on this one. He believed absolutely that she was in the wrong. In fact, she seemed to have taken leave of her senses in recent months. She was no longer someone he recognised.

What communication there had been between them since his last trip home had been in terse, written messages, largely to organise the so-called 'best-interests' meeting which was scheduled for the New Year. It was a statutory requirement that everyone with an interest in Patience's care should get together to discuss major issues that affected her well-being. There would have been such a meeting with or without his objection to the trial, but there was no doubt that the strength of his feelings would affect that meeting and its decision, and Louise resented this deeply.

He had wondered, in recent months, whether he should consider backing down for the sake of his marriage. He loved Louise very much, even now, and he didn't doubt her love for him, either, or for Patience. But he couldn't ignore his nightmares, like the one where Patience was swept away and he couldn't save her, or where she was buried alive, unable to shout to tell others she was there. He did not want to lose her, and he did not want to put her through pain and distress. She mattered too much.

'Your sandwich, sir.' The waitress had returned with his drink and meal, both of which were placed in front of him with a winning smile. Pete smiled back and began to eat as soon as she had turned her back; he was starving.

Christmas. Louise was the queen of all of that stuff. His input was rarely required. He just had to turn up. And he would turn up, definitely; he was booked on a flight tomorrow. The office PA had organised it for him several days ago.

Patience would be coming home for Christmas, as always. If she was well enough, that was, but she'd been in reasonably good shape since her seizure in the summer, so he had reason to hope. It was exhausting, having her back at home, physical work without cease, but it wouldn't be

Christmas without her, and he absolutely wouldn't let the fact that he had to work thousands of miles away get in the way of their festive reunion.

His current job out here had come about by accident. Quite literally. The previous incumbent had died in a head-on collision between his work truck and a Toyota Landcruiser. He'd been killed outright and Pete had been on the flight out to interview just a week later, probably arriving just as that poor man's battered body was being loaded on for return to his family.

Danger lurked everywhere out here, in his professional opinion. His role was to keep his colleagues safe at work, but he had no control over the standard of driving, the quality of the electrics, the frankly often shoddy installation of air-con units. He worried about the labourers particularly, in their packed dormitories, poorly insulated and under-cooled, cables strung between windows and across roads, sharing what power there was far too thinly. When he'd decided to take this contract, he'd made a judgement that his tax-free wages were worth that risk. But he knew that the blue-collar workers rarely had a choice. They needed to work here so that their families could eat.

He could see one labourer now – not one of his company's, but one employed by the sub-contractors who maintained the hotel's grounds – on his hands and knees, picking up fronds discarded by the royal palm trees from the spiky goose grass below. He hadn't even been given a mask. He just had a piece of cloth tied around his mouth and nose to try to protect him from inhaling the dust.

'May I sit here? Is this free?'

The woman he'd seen getting out of the taxi a few

minutes ago was standing next to his seat. He looked up and sighed with relief. It wasn't her after all.

Up close, he could see that she was older than he'd thought originally, but in good shape, with make-up apparently unaffected by the elements, and nails painted a fresh shade of coral.

'Of course, go ahead. I'm almost done here.'

Her accent was Antipodean. She sat down opposite him and reached to unbutton her jacket, removing it slowly and hanging it over the chair, sweeping stray strands of her hair away from her face as she did so.

'You're Pete, aren't you? I think I saw you at work this morning.'

Pete could not place her.

'I'm here for a few days from head office. Auditing the accounts – you know, the head of finance here is new and they wanted me to come and give him a helping hand.'

Pete gave no response, but she carried on regardless. 'I'm sorry if I've interrupted your moment of peace – but there weren't many other places to sit.'

Pete looked around him. It was certainly busy, but there were several other tables with a chair free.

'No, that's fine, as I say, I'm almost done.'

He looked up at her and she returned his gaze. He was about to smile to signal friendliness, and then he remembered.

She had smelled of cherries and spice. She had been wearing a red shift dress, made from what may have been linen, although he was far from expert on those matters. It had been slightly too tight around her hips, causing it to form gentle waves around her middle.

Pete wondered whether it would be rude to leave immediately. But he had to be up early and he was not in the mood for empty small talk. Or empty flirtation, for that matter. It was lonely out here, he knew that, but he had no doubt she'd find other company. He wiped his mouth with a paper napkin, took a final swig of juice, and stood up.

'In fact, you're in luck. I'm not that hungry. You can have the table all to yourself.' He stood up and made to go.

'Good night, then, Pete.'

'Good night.' He walked briskly up to the bar and asked for the bill. He would never find out her name – and that suited him fine.

12

Patience

December 23

Fleetwood Mac is playing in the kitchen. That's a bad sign. Mum's a Christmas traditionalist, a lover of carols, festive schmaltz, on the harp, the ukulele, whatever. This is not the season for Fleetwood Mac's *Rumours*. This does not augur well.

I'm lying in my bedroom at Mum and Dad's, the one Dad converted from the dining room when I was about ten. It's downstairs, so there's no need for a lift, and I'm within earshot of the daily comings and goings, which is nice for them as they can keep an eye on me, and nice for me as it means I am not really alone. This is not a big house and the walls are thin, so I don't miss much, even in here.

The bed I'm in has a specially designed mattress which helps keep my circulation going, and it raises and lowers, just like the ones you get in hospitals. Mum has done her best to try to hide the medical nature of the bed, mind you. Some years ago she made a headboard out of MDF, tie-dye material and some staples, and stuck it at the top end. It's fraying seriously now and it's not really convincing anyone, but I love that she tried.

Most of the room is dark (I'm supposed to be having my afternoon nap) but Mum has left my Christmas tree lit. It's small and made from green plastic, and it's ancient. I think it was Eliza's first. A string of coloured lanterns, stylish circa-1970, are draped around it. They look like sweets that have been left out too long in the sun, sticky and losing their definition around the edges. The tree is topped with a star made from tinsel, probably something Eliza brought back from Brownies. It's set at a jaunty angle and I long to straighten it.

The door is half-open into the hallway and I can just make out Mum shuffling about the kitchen, her slippers scrubbing the heavily marked lino underfoot. She's making mince pies, I think, but so far she just seems to be succeeding in making noise. I watch as she reaches into cupboards and slaps baking trays, jars, canisters and spoons onto the laminate surfaces, slamming the yellow oak doors closed in turn, like a percussion section tuning up. Every so often she pauses and checks her phone, and mutters.

Dad is supposed to be here by now. That's what Mum told me in her stilted monologue during the drive home yesterday. She said he was due on the afternoon of the twenty-third of December, a later flight than she'd expected. But there would still be time, she promised, for our family outing to see the lights, for hot chocolate. These two things have become family traditions – crucially, they were things I could actually take part in – although the chocolate has to be partially cooled these days and artificially thickened. But sometimes Mum adds rum to it and I like the taste.

I'm off to respite care tomorrow. Just for the night; I'll be back here in time for lunch on Christmas Day. It gives Mum and Dad a break while they get everything ready. They've done it this way for years, ever since they had a stand-up row with my grandparents over the turkey and trimmings, Mum's mum and dad sitting aghast at one end of the table, Eliza covering most of her face with a napkin at the other. To be honest, I don't mind going there, not one bit. Trust me, when you've witnessed your parents at each other's throats for decades over, say, what sort of socks you should wear today, it's nice to have a breather.

Mum's frantic baking activity is linked to her plans for this afternoon. Frank and Julie, our neighbours, are due any moment. They come around every Christmas. They haven't got their own family and they're now retired, so I think they find the chaos of our home a welcome change. Or perhaps something like aversion therapy? This house would put anyone off having kids. For a start, I'm still lying here, like Miss Havisham's mouldering wedding cake, at least ten years after I should have left.

Frank was an architect and Julie was the practice nurse at the local doctor's surgery. They're a nice couple, very approachable. They usually make an effort to get down to my level to say hello, which not everybody does. Julie sometimes even does my hair for me; she used to run a mobile hairdressing business on the side. I could do with a bit of colour now, I think, judging by how I looked last time I got to look in a mirror. I have a tendency for frizz, and I can see a few grey hairs starting. At least my hair is blonde; those greys will be hard to spot for a while.

There's the doorbell. Mum's just slammed the oven door shut, so there'll be fresh mince pies for our guests, at the very least. She takes her apron off in one swift movement, dislodging one of her special festive earrings, a flashing Christmas tree. It's probably fallen down her top. Wonder how long it'll take the neighbours to spot it?

She's raced to the door. I can hear her exchanging pleasantries with Julie and Frank. 'Happy Christmas, both! No, he's not here yet, delayed I think. But hopefully soon. How's Alfie?' Alfie is their dog. He's an Alsatian and I like him. He looks at me like he knows I can understand. Maybe he can, too? They're clever, Alsatians.

They're moving in the direction of the lounge, and they pass my door. Mum looks in and sees that I'm awake. 'Ah, Patience, you're back with us,' she says, brightly. 'I'll just take Frank and Julie through and I'll come to get you.'

Getting me out of bed is a palaver. I need rolling and hoisting. Mum had to apply for a grant to buy the hoist system in my room. If you imagine a Brio railway track, it's like that, only stuck on the ceiling. It cost thousands, but it does at least mean that she can manage me with just one helper, so I can still live here most of the time. I like it, mostly; Mum's cooking is delicious, the TV always has Take That on, and it smells of home, of Tess the dog and of dust. It's a little lonely, though. I rather like the madness of the respite care home. There's always something going on and they take us out – to the shops, to the theatre, to church. They treat us like adults.

While Mum's embroiled in the complicated process of transferring me from my bed to my chair, she hears keys in the front door lock.

'Pete? Is that you?' A few seconds later, Dad appears at my door.

'Hi, Lou,' he says, coldly, not really looking at her. 'And hi, Patience!' he adds, transferring his gaze to me, his tone transformed. 'My lovely girl. How are you?'

I'm pleased to see him, of course I am. It's been a month – and although I love Mum, it's a little dull when he's away. I smile.

'Why didn't I hear from you?' she demands. 'Why are you so late?'

He's not looking at her, he's still looking at me.

'Sorry. I had a lot on at work and it was all a bit last minute.'

He leans in to kiss me on the cheek.

'Too last minute to reply to my texts and let me know when you'd be here?'

There is an ugly pause.

'Yep.'

'Pete, don't be like this.'

'Like what?'

'Cold. We've barely spoken in the last month. But come on, you're home and it's Christmas, Patience is here, Eliza and Ed are coming over for Christmas day – there's so much we need to discuss about the wedding – come on, let's get things back on track. And I need to talk to you about asking Eliza...'

'Back on track? Like, you know, before you decided to sign Patience up for something that could kill her?'

What? Oh My God, this is news to me... and... and... I am having my period and I feel paranoid every month at this time anyway. What? This is going to tip me over the edge.

'*Be quiet, Pete!*' Mum rasps at Dad. 'Frank and Julie are just down the hall. And it's not going to kill her, don't be ridiculous.'

'*They're here, are they? Lovely,*' he says in a forced voice, before adding in a quieter tone, a sort of harsh whisper: 'I am not going to pretend, Lou, that things are better. You have made it perfectly clear that you don't give a shit what I think, but hey, I'm going to keep telling you, anyway. This is an experimental trial. Who knows what it's going to do to her?'

Yes, what the bloody hell is it going to do, Mum? Mum?!

'*I've told you*, they wouldn't allow them to do this to humans if it was that risky,' Mum replies, ripping the Velcro from my waist with a little too much force. 'And it could be amazing. It could help her walk, or talk, or you know, use her hands again.'

'Those are pipe dreams, Lou. Absolute fiction. I'm surprised at you, with all your medical training, believing shit like this. They're playing mind games with you, promising you the world. It's snake oil. And I'm not prepared to let them play Russian roulette with our daughter's life. I'm just not going to let it happen. I won't sign that bloody document – and I'll be telling them exactly that at the Best Interests meeting.'

'For Christ's sake, stop it, Pete! Look, you're upsetting Patience. She thinks you're angry with her.'

I hadn't realised I was showing it. Dad looks over at me and I can see that he feels guilty.

'We can talk about this tomorrow. When our guests have gone.' Mum pauses, looking at him, pleadingly. 'Not now?'

Dad sighs, and his face softens a bit.

'Fine. OK. Tomorrow. I'll just take my stuff upstairs and get changed.'

Dad doesn't wait for a response. I hear him take a deep breath as he hoists his bag up and mounts the stairs, taking each step heavily. And when he reaches the top, he turns right, not left. He's heading for the spare room.

13

Eliza

December 24

Christmas Eve and London was emptying out. The city's hard-pressed workers had escaped via every available exit – train, car, plane, taxi – and it seemed like only those with nowhere to go remained. Sloane Square was damp and sparsely populated, discarded sheets from yesterday's Salvation Army brass band carol concert pasted onto its stone flags by the rain, like address labels on recycled packaging.

Eliza's journey home in a bus just heading down Sloane Street was surprisingly quiet. She was the only person riding on the top deck. This was fortuitous, because she had just been sick in her coat. She had been feeling nauseous for a day or two, and it was with a sense of inevitability that she had taken off her coat and placed it in front of her just now, waiting.

Vomiting incident over, she'd wrapped her coat up and placed it in her work bag, wincing. A major clean-up job awaited her when she got home. Could you even machine-wash wool? She doubted it.

It had been an awful day. Feeling sick had made it worse,

but really, it was shit anyway. Jenny had been an absolute cow and it was clear now that, slowly but surely, she was being forced out. Her responsibilities had shrunk to almost nothing and she was bored, bored, bored! Her last client had been summarily removed and given to someone else that morning. It was constructive dismissal, but given how off the ball she'd been since Ed had left, she didn't think she'd have much of a case for her defence. She was an unstable, unreliable mess.

Seeing Ed for dinner had not been 'closure' at all. Instead, it had just opened up a whole can of worms. All of the emotions she'd tried to suppress since he'd left her had risen to the surface in one enormous, overwhelming surge, and what happened after dinner had basically been the fairy on top of a really spindly Christmas tree that had dropped all of its needles. In that moment, when he'd drawn her to him, she had felt like she'd gone down a wormhole and emerged several years earlier, back when he had actually given a shit about her. For that moment, and about twenty minutes afterwards (it had never taken him very long), she had honestly believed that they were going to get back together.

But when he'd rolled off her and announced brusquely that he needed a shower, rather than gathering her in a loving embrace and telling her that he loved her after all and would never leave her again, she realised she'd been entirely mistaken. Lying there, still half-clothed and with her expensive blow dry now sticking up at odd angles, she had felt like a slut. She needed to get out of there, and fast.

She had got out of bed quickly, pulled on her knickers,

skirt and shoes, and followed him into the bathroom to wash her hands and inspect the state of her face. Steam was rising out of the shower cubicle and the mirror above the sink was obliterated by condensation. She rubbed a small circle clear with her hands – she knew that he hated her doing this because it marked the glass – and found that her carefully crafted smoky 'evening eyes' now resembled more a pair of black eyes. She was just reaching for a piece of loo roll to try to limit the damage when his phone, which he'd placed on the bathroom windowsill while he was in the shower, beeped loudly. She looked. Obviously. She had to.

'*Call me when you're done*' it had said, before a gap, and then there was an 'x', and then that jaundiced face-kissing emoji.

Eliza's bowels had churned, and she had thought she might throw up. It felt like every morsel of food and drink she'd had in the past twenty-four hours wanted to head to the exit by the quickest possible route.

This was clearly a mistake of gargantuan proportions. She had to get out of there, fast.

She'd swigged water from the tap to try to quell the vomit – if it made Ed's shower boiling hot, all the better – threw the tissue she'd used on the floor, ran out into the bedroom, grabbed her coat and handbag, and slammed the door behind her.

Ed had not texted or called to check that she'd got home safely, or to ask why she'd left so soon. She didn't know if he knew she'd seen the text or not, but he clearly didn't care either way, and that was enough.

It had hit her right then, like a freight train – a very delayed, very slow freight train – that they really were over.

He was not coming back and she'd have no choice but to break the news to her parents soon.

But only when the time was right, obviously. And that wasn't now.

It was all such a mess. Mum and Dad were still expecting them both to come for Christmas lunch, so she was going to have to cancel tonight, at the last minute; that way she didn't have to explain why he wasn't there. Like a child trying to avoid homework by pretending it hadn't been set, she had pushed tomorrow's festivities to the back of her mind, hoping that they would simply go away. It was how she dealt with most things that worried her. Anyhow, she had concluded that she'd have to call her mum tonight, pulling a sickie, and as luck would have it, that wasn't even a lie. The news might send her mum into a bit of a spin, but not half as much as finding out on Christmas Eve that her daughter had been jilted by her fiancé.

Ed was probably several sheets to the wind in an Oxford wine bar by now, flanked by besuited lawyers braying about some amazing divorce settlement they'd negotiated for a large fee. Or in bed with whoever had sent him that text, admiring her gorgeous blonde hair, or her impressively rounded breasts, or her bronzed, toned thighs. Or all of the above, probably. Wherever he was, he certainly wasn't going to be coming with her, dutifully, for a family Christmas chez Willow, anyway.

She stood up as the bus headed at some considerable speed over Battersea Bridge and pressed the bell to signal that she wanted to get off. The driver braked hard as he approached the stop and she lurched forward down the steps, clinging onto the rail to keep herself on her feet.

When her feet hit the pavement, she paused. She felt faint and thought she might be sick again. Oh, bloody hell. Where had she got this bug from? It was Christmas Eve and everything was going to shut soon. Time to take action. She looked across the road and saw the lit green cross of her local pharmacy. Good. It was still open. She walked carefully across both lanes of traffic and pushed the door. An automated door alarm played 'Jingle Bells'. There was no one else in there, so the pharmacist, a young Asian guy who'd served her a couple of times before, looked up immediately.

'Hello, there. Can I help?'

Eliza suddenly felt her face go cold and a wave of nausea rise.

'Got any sick bags? I'm so sorry...'

Before she had any idea what she was about to do, she was retching in the vitamin aisle.

'Oh crikey, you poor love, wait a sec!' He grabbed a roll of tissues and leapt out from behind the counter. He got to her within a matter of seconds and the wad of tissues he thrust into her arms managed to catch most of what came next. It was all over quickly. Eliza felt mortified, but gratefully, no longer felt like being sick.

'I'm so sorry. So, so sorry. Let me see if I can mop some of this up.' She gesticulated to the splatters on the floor which hadn't been caught by the tissues. She reached into her pocket to see if she had a clean tissue in there.

'No, don't worry, I'll have a go with some bleach in a sec. Hang on, let me go and close up. That way no one will walk in it.' He walked over to the door and turned over his OPEN sign to CLOSED. He was so calm and so kind that

Eliza found that she was starting to cry. The man – Rohit, according to his badge – noticed and went to find a chair. Returning with it, he urged her to sit down.

'It's totally fine, honestly,' he said. 'Now just sit down for a bit and I'll get you some water and more tissues.'

Eliza sat down gratefully and waited, a tear making its way slowly down the ridge of her nose.

'There you go, some more,' he said, standing next to her, with a concerned expression. Eliza began to mop up the tears, and took a grateful sip from the glass of water he'd brought her.

'I take it you were coming to see me about the nausea?'

'How did you guess?' she replied, her sense of humour returning. 'Yep. I feel dreadful. And it's Christmas tomorrow, so… is there anything you can give me to make it stop?'

Rohit thought for a moment.

'That depends on why it's happening. There are anti-emetics I can give you, but we usually recommend you see these things out. I can give you some mineral replacement sachets, some paracetamol, maybe a vitamin tonic, that sort of thing. But before I do – is there any chance you could be pregnant? I have to ask because it affects what I can give you.'

Eliza sat up a little straighter and looked up at him. 'Oh shit,' she replied.

She'd bought everything he'd recommended, including the pregnancy test which he'd pressed upon her. 'Just in case,' he'd said. 'I don't want to send you away with all that stuff without it. Not when everything's closed tomorrow.'

She had thought more about it after her outburst and had sought to reassure him that she was single, for a start, so it simply wasn't possible, and that she had irregular periods anyway. And yet she had accepted the test meekly and its presence in the paper bag she was holding made her uncomfortable.

She reached her flat, opened the door, threw her dirty coat down by the washing machine to deal with later, and walked straight into the bathroom. She paused in front of the sink, turned the tap on and swilled her mouth out, trying to remove the taste of vomit. Vomiting was becoming a habit lately, she thought. Not one that she'd planned, but it was like being dumped was a kind of gastric flu. She'd been off her food since Ed left and, when upset, she found herself being sick, more often than not. This latest episode was probably stress-related, too, she concluded. It must be.

She grabbed the paper bag, removed the pregnancy test, ripped it out of its foil pack and sat down on the toilet. It was a routine she'd practised a few times while she'd been with Ed, when her period had been late and she'd become anxious. But her period was always late and it had never been an issue. She'd always come out of the toilet, an expression of relief on her face, and headed straight to the kitchen to pour herself a glass of wine.

But not this time.

It hadn't even been three minutes and there were two very clear, unequivocal lines on that stick. Fuck! *Fuck, fuck, fuck, fuck.*

This just couldn't be happening, she thought; not again.

She did two things in quick succession. First, she got out

her phone and sent a quick text to her mum saying that she was throwing up and wouldn't make it tomorrow. Secondly, she wiped, stood up, got dressed again and composed herself, and grabbed her car keys.

14

Patience

December 24

I'm in the respite care bungalow for my traditional Christmas Eve stopover. It's a family detox, if you will, needed by all parties before the main event. The radio is on in the kitchen and it's so loud that I can hear it clearly from my room. I imagine that Lutsi, one of the agency care workers, is dancing to it, her skinny frame bobbing back and forth between dishwasher and cupboards as she clears up after dinner and puts everything out ready for our breakfast tomorrow. They've bought deluxe Christmas crackers to pull at breakfast, I think. I saw them when we were having dinner. None of us have hands that can hold them hard enough to pull them, so they'll put their hands over ours and try to simulate the action instead. I'm not really sure what the point of that is.

The local commercial station, Star, is playing wall-to-wall festive tunes. We've just been treated to 'Driving Home for Christmas' (the M40 isn't too clever right now, we're told by the DJ in a blithe tone which speaks volumes about his planned route home – it's definitely not a motorway) and now I can hear the opening bars of 'Fairytale of New York' by The Pogues.

It's my favourite of all of the Christmas classics. I love the contrast of its hopeful opening bars with the crushing defeat and anger of its lyrics. I've never been to New York, but would love to go. Hard squeezing me into a seat on a plane these days, though, sadly. My bum is quite big, and bendy I am not. You can do it, though, apparently. Rosie, one of the other visitors to the home, went with her parents to Disney World last year. They apparently pretty much got the red-carpet treatment, from check-in onwards. I'd love to try that, but Mum and Dad don't have the money and I don't need telling that dreams don't always come true.

Anyway, why go to Disney when you can have the five-star treatment right here in Morton Lodge, Oxfordshire's premiere care facility? They've gone all out on the Christmas deccies, for a start. I heard yesterday that in the next-door bungalow, which has permanent residents, they've stretched to a real tree; meanwhile in here, someone has draped some partially-bald neon-pink tinsel over the rails beside my bed.

Well, I say my bed. It's only mine this evening. I share it with a whole host of others, each allotted a few days here every month, to give our carers a break. Accordingly, the decor in here is completely anonymous and neutral, neither feminine nor masculine. They've chosen purple for the walls – or perhaps you'd call it lilac? And I'm lying under a blue duvet, which was just plumped up by Magda, before she said goodnight. She's left the light on for me, but not the wall-mounted TV, unfortunately, because I'm not actually that tired and I'd like to have watched something before bed. I'm not eight, after all. I'm a thirty-year-old woman, damn it, and I'd really like to be able to watch something dramatic, funny or even, frankly, something totally crap, before going to sleep.

And I really wanted Jimmy to be on shift tonight. I've stayed here twice a month since meeting him, and we've hardly coincided. I hear whisperings about him, though. He's obviously got them all pretty excited. He should be good for staff turnover, anyway; not many care homes have eye candy as tasty as him on their books.

I wonder if he's gay? Lots of gorgeous blokes are gay. He might be, mightn't he? It doesn't make much difference to me either way, of course, as I'm only looking.

And I wonder where he's spending Christmas? If he's gay, then most likely with a handsome blond Adonis who works as a gym instructor, or as a pilot. If not gay, probably with some awesome nuclear scientist, with boobs like jelly moulds. I bet he never once thinks about this awesome blonde, with boobs like... What *are* my boobs like? Last time I had a look, I'd say they were shaped more like balloons. Huge, saggy balloons that have been inflated for weeks and are dimpled and losing their shape. And can you get hairy balloons, I wonder?

What's that? Crikey, it sounds like someone trying the door that opens directly into the car park from my room. It might be one of those kids who lives down the road. They come into our cul-de-sac sometimes and lark around, getting as close as they can to the weird-looking folk, probably for a bet. As if we are vampires or monsters, and to be feared.

There's that noise again, louder this time. And now there's shouting.

'Argh! Why the fuck do they lock this?'

Bloody hell, it's Eliza. I hear her swear several more times and then stomp around to the front door. The doorbell rings, not just once, but several times, until Lutsi goes running to the door. I hear their conversation. Eliza is currently trying to explain why she's appeared at the home at 9 p.m. on Christmas Eve.

'Look, I'm so sorry, I was just passing and I wanted to – to check Patience was OK. She is here, isn't she?'

'I seeeee,' says Lutsi, her Estonian accent making her sound particularly doubtful. 'Yas, she ees here. Weell OK – shee's in bed, burt you might bee in lurck. Sometimes shee doesn't go off immeediately. Are you OK, Eliza? Are you eel?'

'I'm fine, thank you. Just tired, you know. I'll just go through, shall I?'

'Yas.'

Eliza almost runs into my room and shuts the door right behind her. It's just a matter of seconds before she flings herself onto the bed next to me, throws her arms around me and starts to cry.

'Oh, Patience, it's all such a bloody mess!' she wails into my pyjama top. 'I am such a disaster.' Obviously, I remain silent, because that's all I can do. She's used to this, and I know she'll tell me more when she's ready. I wait, listening to the radio, which is now playing Mariah Carey's version of 'O Holy Night'.

'So, two major problems,' she continues, still talking to my chest. 'Number one, Ed and I have broken up, and I haven't told Mum and Dad yet.'

Oh sweet Jesus, that's a relief! I couldn't stand Ed. He

never looked at me properly, in the eye, in all those years, not once. He's a shifty bugger.

'Second major problem – and wait for it, this is worse – I'm pregnant, and it's his. Ed's.'

Now this is justification indeed for her crazy drive to see me here.

'I'll have to tell Mum and Dad, won't I? I mean, about the wedding. I think I'll be able to keep schtum about the pregnancy and deal with that myself. But the wedding – I'll have to tell them because there's so much to unravel. But Patience, you know as well as I do that they will be so disappointed. Mum has been planning this since I was little, and she knows it will be her only chance to do the wedding thing. No offence, lovey.'

I am not offended, of course. We both know that I will never get married or have children, and we also both know that our parents have offloaded all of their dreams for both of us onto her, the poor thing. I don't envy her, I really don't. I think she used to resent me a bit when we were both living at home, and I can understand why. My caring needs and stalled development meant that she was simultaneously ignored *and* overloaded with expectations, and that's a really, really shitty combination.

'This is not the perfect life they have always wanted me to have, is it? And I can't go home tonight anyway, because I've told them I'm sick, and I can't stay in the flat, because the loneliness is glaring at me from the bare walls from where he removed his bloody pictures, and the cupboards from where he took his bloody cups, and I am just so bloody angry. And lost. And scared…'

We lie there for a bit, her stroking my arms gently, while

she snuffles. Her breathing becomes a bit calmer. She moves a little further over so that she doesn't squash me, lifts up the duvet and lies down on her side.

'So, I'm staying here,' she announces. 'With you.' And just like that, we are children again, and she's climbed into bed with me to tell me stories. I feel her warm breath on my neck and instantly feel relaxed. And in a tried and tested procedure, honed throughout our intertwined lives, we both fall asleep.

'Good morning, Patience! Rise and shine! Happy Christmas!'

He comes over to pull back my duvet.

'Oh, Jeeeeesussss. Sorry. I didn't know you were there.'

Ah, Jimmy. At last!

'Oh fuck, sorry, I'm not supposed to be here, am I?'

Eliza has sat up in bed. Luckily she's fully clothed, but her hair now looks lopsided and she has the imprint of one of my buttons on her cheek. Jimmy looks like he has absolutely no idea what to say. But he still looks gorgeous. He *always* looks gorgeous.

'I should explain – I'm... I'm... Eliza. Patience's... sister.'

Crikey, love, I can't believe it took you so long to remember your own name.

She is shuffling to the end of the bed now, but it's an effort to get out, because my bed guard is in the way and she doesn't want to leap over it and worry him even more. She looks red in the face as she tries to swing her leg over it to dismount.

Jimmy looks baffled.

'I came here late last night, you see. To see Patience, for Christmas, you know, and then I must have just... fallen asleep. They must have forgotten I was here... So sorry. What a mess. I must look a mess, I mean. So sorry.'

She's gabbling. She doesn't usually gabble.

Eliza has now managed to get one leg onto the floor and is now lifting her other leg over the guard at an incredibly awkward angle. She looks as though she's practising an obscure martial art. When she finally gets it on the floor, she brushes herself down and walks over to my sink to check her face in the mirror. She does not like what she sees and, to be honest, I agree with her. It's not her best look. She tries to wipe the dribble away from around her mouth with my face towel.

'Anyhow. Thanks for waking me nice and early,' she says, turning around. 'I'll definitely make Mum and Dad's in time for breakfast if I go now! Great! Nice to meet you, by the way. What's your name? I'm Eliza. Oh, sorry, I've already said that.'

'I'm Jimmy.'

'Great! Lovely. OK then, Jimmy. I'll see you again? So sorry.' And there she goes, out of the door as quickly as she came in. 'See you later, Patience,' she calls, as an afterthought.

When she's gone, Jimmy exhales deeply before coming over to me once more to begin the morning routine.

'Blimey, P,' he says. He calls me P now. I like P. 'She's a bit mad, isn't she? I can see you're the saner sister.'

I enjoy this statement a lot more than I really should.

15

Pete

Christmas Day

Pete had a crick in his neck. He also had cramp in his right leg, which had spent the night braced against the filing cabinet which was squeezed in between the extremely narrow single bed he was lying on and the wall. He knew that the cabinet contained document after document about Patience: her care, her medical history, their regular fights for access to therapies and funding. It was a solid, tangible testament to the hours his wife spent working, for free, for the benefit of their second daughter.

He was in their smallest bedroom, the one they laughably referred to as 'the spare'. It used to be Eliza's, plastered with posters, alive with angry music broadcast at high volume, dusty as hell and smelling of a mixture of Anais Anais perfume and hairspray. Since she moved out, though, it had become a dumping ground, home to family files, unused sports equipment and random detritus destined for the charity shop. The posters were long gone, but you could still see the remains of Blu-Tack on the walls.

Poor Eliza, this bedroom was tiny, barely big enough for a

bed – that's why they'd bought such a small one, he supposed – and a little desk. Having said that, he remembered her look of rapturous joy when they'd told her she could have it all to herself. She had told them she kept being woken up by Patience at night and had had enough of early wake-up calls accompanied by nursery rhymes.

It was incredible to think now that there had actually been a time when Patience had slept in a normal bed. A bunk bed, actually, beneath Eliza, in a room down the hall decorated with Laura Ashley print and a large border on the walls embellished with wildflowers and trees.

They'd lived in a false sense of security during her younger years, he knew that. Back then, Patience had been light enough to carry, she'd still fitted into children's nappies, and she could stand and put one foot in front of the other if they supported her. They had even taken her on holidays abroad, and people hadn't even stared that much.

But as she grew bigger, every day became a struggle, both a financial and a physical one. They'd realised that something had to give when they could no longer carry her up the stairs. He had even taken to going to the gym to build up his strength, but when Patience was eight and weighing in at thirty-five kilos, they had finally admitted defeat.

For a while, they'd put a bed in their front room for her and washed her with a flannel. It had been grim, unsustainable. They were told they were eligible for a grant from the council to fund work to build a downstairs bedroom and shower room, but it hadn't been enough to cover it all, and the work had cost far more than it should because they'd had to do it so quickly. So, they'd remortgaged to borrow more. It had hurt. Interest rates were high.

He had increased his hours to bring in more money, working as a safety officer on commercial building sites during the week, and at the weekend, did extra work on-site on other projects, sometimes bricklaying, sometimes roofing – whatever was needed. He'd only come home to sleep. Eventually, he'd bitten the bullet and applied for contracts overseas, which paid well but took him away for months at a time. And despite the fact that they'd desperately needed that adaptation, he knew that when Patience had moved into that room, a part of her childhood had died. In his mind, that was the dividing line. There was a time before, and a time after. In the time after, he was an absent father, an occasional visitor to the family home and nothing more. The provider. And not even a good one.

He leaned over the side of the bed and located his phone, which was lying on the grey, threadbare carpet. He really must get that replaced at some point, he thought; it was depressing. One more thing to add to his to-do list. He flicked the cover off the phone. It was 7 a.m. – time to get up. Patience wouldn't arrive for hours, and Eliza was poorly and wasn't coming, but he still knew he'd need to get up and show willing. Louise's energy was extraordinary, always, and she really had no time for people who didn't manage to keep up. She would have expectations for today and he would have to meet them, despite their ongoing row.

She had taken the news about Eliza's lurgy badly. She'd spent the past two days baking, decorating and cleaning in a frenzy, anticipating a family reunion akin to the ending of Charles Dickens' *A Christmas Carol*. It didn't seem to matter that she must know, rationally, that this was an unattainable goal; she kept on striving towards it, every year. It was a sort of voluntary blindness.

He swung his legs over the side of the bed, wincing as his body came to terms with being upright. Age had certainly withered him; his body, strong and athletic, the product of thousands of hours in hotel gyms around the world, was starting to refuse to cooperate and this new reality depressed him.

He stood up, stretched, and padded to the bathroom across the hall, where he had a welcome pee and retrieved his dressing gown from the hook behind the door. It had his name on it, etched in blue thread across the back, a gift from Louise for a birthday a decade ago or more.

As he made his way downstairs, he could hear that Louise was, as he had anticipated, already up and at it. She was wearing an oversized blue fleece dressing gown and an ugly pair of pink slippers which had been a free gift from the company that made Patience's incontinence pads. The cupboards were being discharged of their bounty; the oven pressed into action. Classic FM was on, and playing a steady diet of carols interspersed by Bach's *Christmas Oratorio*. In previous years, he'd have crept up on her stealthily before springing himself upon her with full force, delivering a huge bear hug, followed by a kiss. There would have been laughter, an offer of a cup of coffee, a wink.

But not today. Today, he walked into the kitchen and was greeted by the invisible curtain that had been pulled between them since he had flown in two days ago. His continuing refusal, as she saw it, to cooperate over the trial had apparently been the final straw for her, an unconscionable betrayal of not only her, but their daughter. He had tried to explain why he felt the way he did. After his initial reaction, which had come straight from his gut, he'd made a particular effort to read up on the topic, so that he could understand where she was coming from. The problem was, he had hated what he had found.

Where she saw boundless hope in the experiment which had apparently reversed the damaging effects of the faulty Rett syndrome gene in adult mice, he saw absolute danger. He'd digested the fact that nine out of the seventeen mice that had apparently been 'cured' had died soon afterwards, most likely before their time. He knew that Patience's head, and therefore her brain, was smaller than normal, and that she might need brain surgery if it started to grow as a result of treatment.

He'd made these points to Louise, slowly and deliberately, several times, but it seemed to him that she had simply refused to hear him. She must have been completely brainwashed by the doctor she was working for, Professor Larssen. He clearly needed her to be there, and was prepared to tell her what she wanted to hear. Pete suspected that he had recruited her to give his trial credibility in the eyes of prospective families, to give it a softer edge, to make it less about statistics and more about humanity.

Anyway, they were now set for a full-scale battle over it, it seemed. The 'Best Interests' meeting was in the diary and all the stakeholders in Patience's life were preparing to decide, boardroom style, what was best for her.

He wished, not for the first time, that he could ask Patience what she thought. Would she really want to submit herself to possible pain and suffering, to further possible operations, to an uncertain future? She seemed content, to him. She seemed happier and more settled than she'd been in years.

Louise had now moved into the utility room, where she was polishing a silver platter with vigour. He took the opportunity to walk into the kitchen and put the kettle on. He'd make his own coffee today.

He was plunging the filter on their cafetière when the doorbell rang. They weren't expecting Patience and her carer until about midday – so who on earth was it? He went to answer it, noting that Louise appeared to be feigning deafness.

It was Eliza. She looked tired, as if she'd been rubbing her eyes; most of her mascara seemed to have transferred to her cheeks and her hair was all over the place. Suddenly he saw her as sixteen again, incredibly grumpy after being forced to wake up for school, after a late night caused by angst-ridden phone calls and lots of pining while listening to Oasis. He had loved her then, despite it all, and he loved her now, too.

'I thought you weren't coming!' he said, opening his arms wide for a hug.

'I know,' she said, folding herself into him. 'But it was a false alarm. I was only sick once. And I couldn't miss Christmas Day, could I? So I set off as soon as I woke up.' Pete let her go and stood aside so that she could move into the hall.

'You must have left early. I haven't even had breakfast,' he added, as they moved down the hallway. 'Where's Ed?'

'Oh, he came down with the bug in the early hours,' she replied. 'I thought it best to leave him to it.'

'Yes. *Lou! Lou!*' Pete called out, not actually caring

where Ed was, or that he was currently vomiting his guts up. It was such an effort to pretend to like him.

'Guess who it is, Lou!' he shouted once more.

Louise came running, a bit like she used to do when he arrived home after a long time away.

'Darling! Oh, my darling, you're here! Are you OK? Crikey, you look tired. And thin! Do you want to go to bed?' She was looking at Eliza with great concern, sweeping the hair off her face and examining her in great detail, as if she was six, not thirty-six.

'Actually, Mum, that's not such a bad idea.'

There was a brief pause. Pete knew what the issue was; Louise was wondering where to put her. She couldn't have her old room, because he was in it, and Louise wouldn't want her to know that they were in separate rooms. She also couldn't sleep in Patience's room, in case she passed on whatever virus she had to her, and she couldn't sleep in the other bedroom upstairs because it was now Louise's office. An office that was more of a war room, really.

'You can have our room,' she said, a few seconds later. 'The bed's made up and I only changed the sheets yesterday. Head up there and I'll get you a hot water bottle. Go on. Don't worry. We won't be having lunch for ages. And presents can wait.'

Pete watched Eliza obey immediately, succumbing to the reassuring, loving control that Louise had always exercised over their household.

As she went upstairs, Louise gave instructions for him to follow in her absence. The oven needed to go on; the dishwasher needed emptying; Tess needed to be let out; and could he also empty the bin? Pete understood that his wife was not intending to tell Eliza that they had been arguing. They had always tried to keep any disagreements from her, as if finding out that they occasionally argued would damage her life's foundation.

At this very moment, however, he did not have the energy to maintain the facade. He made no reply. Instead, he stomped on the lever which opened the bin, grasped the liner within, tied it at the top and lifted it out, before walking to the back door, finding his outdoor shoes, and pressing the handle down with extraordinary relief.

It felt good to be outside. He could detect a faint scent of burning wood in the air, almost like incense. It had recently rained and their garden looked dank and uninviting, its beauty sleeping, waiting for someone, perhaps a handsome prince, to awaken it in the spring. Pete walked round to the side passage to their wheelie bin and placed the bag inside. Then he reached swiftly inside his top pocket and removed a cigarette. He had still officially given up, but only when he was home.

Qatar was a different matter. He was surrounded by smokers there. The locals smoked openly indoors and out, and the labourers on his sites bartered with cigarettes. They were almost a language out there, cigarettes, and it had eventually become easier to speak that language than not. He flicked the lighter open, lit one and inhaled quickly and deeply, moving further down the side passage so that neither he nor his smoke could be seen.

Pete had been smoking when he had proposed to Louise, he remembered. They'd both been at a fireworks evening at the local cricket club. She hadn't even looked surprised when he'd asked; she had just smiled at him, and they had kissed as Catherine wheels and rockets were set off in front of them and bonfire toffee circulated in parcels of wax paper. It was a kiss that had tasted sweet, smoky and full of promise.

Within six months, they were married at a grim-looking church near his mum's home in Birmingham, with a reception at the pub down the road. It had been a small do, nothing grand, but they had loved each other so much, it hadn't seemed to matter. His beloved mum had already been ill then and she had had no money to put towards it, even if she had been well.

Louise had just qualified as a nurse when they were married, and when Pete found a job through old friends in Birmingham, she'd found a job at Birmingham Children's Hospital. They had rented a small flat above the local laundrette while they both worked to save a deposit for their first house. There had been no central heating and they had kept a money box beside the bath, each putting a coin in it before turning the taps on each night.

He remembered how she'd reacted, the first time he'd taken her to see the flat he'd found for them to live in. The cramped, damp one-bedroom flat was a far cry from the comfortable rural vicarage she'd grown up in – he was more than aware of that and she knew it. But instead of reacting in horror, she'd taken his hand, laughed, and asked if he could pop out to buy some rubber gloves. She had started work straight away, turning that fleapit into a home.

It had taken them several years of hard graft, but they'd eventually saved up the deposit for their first house. Pete had wanted to stay in Birmingham. He'd had a great job there, with a chance of becoming a partner in his uncle's firm, when the time was right, but Louise had been insistent: she had wanted to move back down south to be near her parents. She wanted a family and she didn't want to do it in Birmingham, she'd said.

Pete had known what that really meant – I don't belong here. I've played at being poor and working class for a while, but the fact remains that I am not from here, and this is not who I am. And so, he'd moved south with her and it was his turn to feel out of place. They'd bought a crappy house they couldn't really afford, and he'd spent the next thirty years trying to make it into the home she'd always wanted. Except, of course, that it could never be that; it was a small suburban semi-detached in Kidlington, not a Cotswold cottage. He was an unwilling participant in an unattainable dream.

He took one more drag on the cigarette, before stubbing it out on the garage wall then disposing of it in the rubbish bin, hiding it under the bag he'd just put there.

'Pete, are you out here?'

Louise walked towards him, clasping her arms around her chest in response to the cold.

'Look, I wanted to say: let's not continue arguing, in front of the kids. It's Christmas Day. Let's just call a truce for today. It's not fair on them, is it?'

Pete looked up, trying to analyse what her mood was. He saw the defiance in her eyes and decided not to reply.

'And I needed to tell you – ask you – about Eliza,' Louise continued. 'I'm told that we need to appoint what they call a "consultee" for Patience, someone who is allowed to consent on her behalf for the trial. It can't be me, because

I'm involved with the project, and it can't be you, because you don't want it to happen. So…'

Pete glared, his silence speaking for him.

'That's all I wanted to say.' She turned and walked away. 'And by the way, you stink of fags,' she said, as she pulled the back door closed behind her.

Three hours on, the house looked as if Christmas elves had swept through it, leaving magic in their wake. The fire was lit; the air smelled of roasting turkey and spices; piles of presents were stacked against the furniture in the lounge. Five piles. One for him, one for Louise, one for Eliza, one for Patience and one, ludicrously, he thought, for the dog. There were also a couple of gifts for Patience's carer. They weren't sure who was coming, due to staff sickness, so there were chocolates and a bottle of wine for whoever they managed to send.

Pete had wrapped Louise's presents in a rush last night, using the odds and ends of the paper she'd bought to wrap presents for others. Looking at them now, they looked like an afterthought, which they absolutely weren't. He'd taken a special trip to the nearest mall in Qatar before he left and had chosen what he hoped were thoughtful, beautiful gifts. He just hadn't found anywhere selling anything remotely resembling Christmas wrapping paper so he'd waited until Christmas Eve to do it.

They had spent the day so far dancing around each other, taking care never to touch or to step over the fine line between cordial and friendly. She seemed in a happier mood, sipping on Prosecco and Buck's Fizz as she chopped, stirred and assembled. She had outdone herself with the catering, clearly having spent months researching recipes, sourcing ingredients and planning menus. It looked incredible, as it always did, but in truth, Pete would have been just as happy with a roast chicken, packet stuffing and ready-made Yorkshire puddings. Particularly if they could have a laugh while preparing it.

At midday, right on cue, the doorbell chimed once again. Louise went to get it this time and Pete heard her greeting Patience with an enthusiasm that contrasted so starkly with her current attitude towards him that it stung. He put down his current task – putting the pudding in a bain-marie to steam – and went to see his youngest daughter.

It took him a second to register what was wrong with the picture. Instead of Magda or Beth, there was a man standing beside Patience, a good-looking man, a man he didn't know.

'Hi, Mr Willow,' the unknown man said, moving past Louise and towards Pete, thrusting his hand forward. 'I'm Jimmy. Sorry for the surprise, I know you weren't expecting me but there's a bug going around and Magda's got it, so I got called in to cover.'

Pete had almost forgotten what day it was, until he looked down at Patience. She had a healthy colour in her cheeks, almost a glow, and she was smiling. He gave her a kiss and a squeeze, and instantly felt more festive.

'Call me Pete,' he found himself saying. 'And Merry Christmas. Now, let's all stop standing around in the hall. Come on through to the lounge. I hope you have time to stay for a drink before you have to drive back?'

All four of them assembled in their front room, the able-bodied sitting down adjacent to their particular mountain of presents. Patience's chair was parked in her usual space beside Louise, who had distributed glasses and then opened a new bottle of Prosecco, pouring generous measures into each glass. She was being a jolly, generous host.

Pete sat down in his designated spot at the far end of the sofa and admired the Christmas tree, which he presumed Louise had picked out, carried from the car and erected entirely by herself. It was at least six feet tall and incredibly bushy – how she must have battled with it. It was decorated with mismatched, sentimental ornaments which he could remember hanging with Eliza's help, back when her fingers were pudgy and her gait a waddle.

He looked over at the unusual young man who'd appeared at his door. There weren't many male carers around, in his experience, and that's what made him unusual. The business of caring wasn't something that seemed to attract many men. He was a young bloke, but not young enough to be caring during his gap year, or just trying it out as a first job – Pete reckoned he must be in his late twenties at least. Interesting.

Pete noticed then that Louise was refilling not only Jimmy's glass, but also her own, and with regularity. She was drinking much more than usual, he thought. The colour had risen in her cheeks, and was she flirting with Jimmy? She was laughing uproariously at a story he'd just told about Maggie at the care home, and it really hadn't been all that funny.

It was then that Eliza appeared at the door. She was still drowsy from sleep, her hair sticking out by her ears, and she was wearing some pyjamas he hadn't seen for at least fifteen years. They had a faded Mickey Mouse on the front and they were pink. They were also far too small – the top was clinging to her chest and finished a couple of inches before the trousers, which ended at mid-calf, began.

'Happy Christmas, everyone,' she said, in a tone far more chirpy than she obviously felt. 'I heard talking, so I thought I'd come down.' Pete watched as her gaze settled on Patience, then on her mum, and then finally, on Jimmy.

'Oh, hi!' she said, with surprise. 'I'm sorry, I thought it was just us down here. If I'd known I'd have got – got dressed.'

Jimmy seemed mortified and clearly didn't know where to look.

'Oh, I don't want to make anyone feel uncomfortable,' he said. 'I'll head off.' He made to leave.

'No, don't be sillllly, Jimmy,' replied Louise, her speech now starting to slur a little. 'Everyone is absolutely welcome. Absolutely. Now, Eliza, darling, you pop upstairs and get changed into something nice and we'll eat when you're done. You'll stay for food, won't you, Jimmy?' Eliza didn't need to be asked twice; she disappeared back up the stairs at a run.

'I'm sure he's got a home of his own to go to, Lou,' said Pete.

Everyone looked at Jimmy. Pete could see that he'd been put in an impossible quandary and that he was going to come out badly from this either way.

'I don't have other plans, but honestly, it's fine. I can eat back at the bungalow with the other staff. I really don't want to gatecrash your Christmas Day.'

'That's it, then! You're staying. How wonderful! Patience has brought a young man home. That's a first.' Louise, who seemed to find this hilarious, made her way into the kitchen with speed, her laughter receding as she did so. Pete turned to look at Jimmy.

'I'm really sorry,' he said quietly, genuinely feeling it. 'I think she's had a little too much to drink this morning. If you'd rather spend your day elsewhere, please do so. I'll explain to her afterwards.'

'No, it's fine,' replied Jimmy, moving so that he could sit next to Patience. He looked right at her. 'I really like P, she's fun. Why not spend Christmas with one of our nicest clients?'

Pete noticed a flicker in Patience's eyes. It wasn't fear, it wasn't pain, and it wasn't a need to pee – but what was it? He realised he didn't understand this new look of hers, and it made him curious.

An hour later, they all sat down to lunch. Eliza had reappeared some considerable time after she'd disappeared, wearing the clothes she'd arrived in this morning. It occurred to Pete that he hadn't seen any sign of a bag when she arrived. Had she come without any stuff, he wondered? Why? She hadn't said much and had declined the Prosecco, opting instead for coffee. And she still didn't look very well; it was pretty obvious that she'd dragged herself out of her sickbed to come to lunch to please her mother, and he was sorry she'd felt she had to do it.

'Oh Eliza, I'm so pleased you were able to come in the end,' cooed Louise, serving up vegetables, smiling broadly at her daughter. 'It wouldn't be Christmas without you.'

'That's OK, Mum. I'm glad to be here, too.' Instead of

looking at her mother, Eliza was looking fixedly at the floral decoration that adorned the centre of the table, an eclectic mix of Christmas roses, variegated ivy and tiny gold reindeer.

'I'm glad you came actually, for many reasons,' Louise continued, as she passed round plates. 'We – I – wanted to ask you a favour. I am entering Patience for—'

'Don't you think we should do this later, Lou?' Pete looked at her with both eyebrows raised. 'When she's feeling better?'

'Gravy, Jimmy?' Louise leaned over the table to dispense gravy from a jug, wobbling slightly as she did so. Then she turned to face Eliza.

'Now, darling, as I was saying – Patience has been entered into this amazing gene therapy trial. You know about gene therapy, don't you? It's the future of medicine. It's eventually going to cure lots of horrible diseases. Rett syndrome included.'

'Now Lou, that's not quite—'

'But your father disagrees with me.' Louise put the gravy boat down, unfolded her napkin and placed it in her lap. 'So, because of that, the people who are running the trial need someone called a "Consultee" to be appointed, someone who can speak up for Patience, because she can't speak up for herself. Someone to talk sense and give permission for her to take part. And it can't be either of us, of course, because of the disagreement. But you'll do it, won't you?'

Pete observed Eliza's reaction. She hadn't started to eat yet, but was instead running her hands over her napkin repeatedly, smoothing it down over her knees.

'Hang on, Mum,' she said, eventually. 'I need to think about this. And are you sure that I'm the right choice? Shouldn't it be someone professional? A doctor or someone?'

'Oh, it can't be them. The GP will be on the Best Interests panel already, anyway. It needs to be someone Patience is close to. Someone who cares about her. And the obvious person is you.'

'But what do I need to do?'

'Give the hospital permission for it to go ahead, basically,' Louise replied, staring directly at her daughter, apparently determined not to catch Pete's eye. 'And go to the Best Interests meeting with us. That's where we'll have the final vote.'

'Mum, I'm not sure it's a great idea for me to be—'

'Nonsense. You are the perfect choice. Look, I've got the contact details for the person you need to email. I'll give them to you after lunch. You can have a nice chat with them about it and then all you need to do is sign. Anyone for bread sauce?'

Louise turned to face Jimmy, who was sitting next to her, proffering a jug of sauce. He had said very little so far, opting instead for short, polite responses.

'So, do you have much family?' she asked.

'No, and they're all in Cornwall. So too far away to go to spend the day.'

'And no close friends here?'

'No, I moved here recently. I haven't had much time to make friends yet.'

'No girlfriend?'

'Not at the moment, no.'

'Are you gay?'

'Lou! I really think you should leave Jimmy alone.' Pete could no longer let it go.

'Jimmy is *fine*, Pete. And I didn't ask your opinion. Lots of male carers are gay. I was only asking.' An ugly pause descended upon the table.

'I just think Jimmy's looking a bit uncomfortable, Lou. I thought it was time to give it a rest.'

'I don't know why you're behaving like you're in charge here.' Louise refilled her glass, slopping some wine on the tablecloth. 'You just swanned in a couple of days ago, like you always do, and you'll piss off again in a few more days to that job of yours, leaving me with it *all* to deal with. You're not even a guest. You're a *visitor*.'

'Do you know what, Patience, I think I fancy watching the Queen,' said Jimmy. He stood up, walked over to Patience's chair, undid its brakes and began to wheel her out. 'You coming, Eliza?' Eliza looked grateful for the out and took it, following after him. Pete glared at Louise across the table.

'Brilliant, Lou, just *brilliant*. Best Christmas Day ever. You get pissed, insult Patience's carer and make the whole family feel uncomfortable.'

'*Uncomfortable*? Oh, *boo hoo* for you. After all of the hard work I've put into making this happen? The endless hours cleaning this shitty house, shopping for food, working out how to save pennies, always saving those bloody pennies. Why are we nearly at retirement with no money to speak of, Pete? After all the years of you working away all the time, leaving me at home to look after *our* daughter, where has it gone? Why are we so fucking poor? Are you spending it on *whores*?'

Pete remembered how understanding Lou had been when

he'd accepted his first overseas contract, how supportive she'd been of him.

'*Shhhh*, Lou, they'll be able to hear you in the lounge.'

The old Lou would have shut up at this point. In fact, she'd never have started this argument in the first place. But this was a new Lou that he didn't recognise, and she was on fire.

'I don't bloody *care*. Frankly, I've had enough of pretending. It's all about money for you, isn't it? It's not about family. And you're not stuck here in this prison of a home, *I am*. All that crap about hating being away. I bet you *love* it. Doing your bloody job, keeping people safe, people being grateful. Meanwhile I've been stuck at home for decades, my skills and ambitions festering and ignored. I bet you enjoy telling your friends how awful, dull and old your wife is. How she's *let herself go*.' She looked like she was about to vomit. Pete stood up.

'I'm going to go now, Lou. I'm going to get a cab to Tom's, and tomorrow morning, I'm going to go to stay with Steve. I'll ask Jimmy to take Patience back to Morton Lodge for the night. I think they have room.' He looked down at her. 'And when you've sobered up, I think we should talk.'

16

Patience

December 27

It's pitch black in here, which is odd. It isn't usually ever completely dark, because I have a dim bedside light which Mum leaves on for me all night. She's done it ever since Eliza and I were small and afraid of the dark. Unlike Eliza, I was never able to tell her that I preferred it off, that I actually find it easier to sleep in darkness. So it's remained on for the duration.

I've got used to it now, anyway. It's comforting, sometimes, especially if I wake up unexpectedly and I'm in pain. My right hip plays up a lot still, despite the hip surgery I had a few years ago, and my muscles get cramp sometimes, sending searing pain up my legs that I am unable to do anything about.

When I'm in the care home, there's always someone awake all night, checking on me, and I like that. It makes me feel safe. In fact, I enjoy my time there, in general. I suppose that might come as a surprise to many, but seriously, there's so much going on, and I love that. There are so many personal dramas to overhear from a touring cast of carers and fellow inmates – sorry, clients – and frankly the relief that I feel, not seeing Mum's exhaustion and stress up close and personal every single day, is extraordinary. She works so hard and I don't want to seem ungrateful – but some days, I just long to live somewhere else, away from the drama, of which I am, as we've already discussed, the cause.

When I'm at home and in pain at night, I cry out, because it's the only option I have. I know Mum is tired and needs her sleep, but I need her. She has pain-killing suppositories she gives me, which are unpleasant, but a necessity. I wish the doctor would give me something stronger than paracetamol, but I suppose they have no idea how bad it feels.

I feel a little odd tonight. Nauseous. That's why I've woken up, I reckon. I don't usually wake, unless I'm uncomfortable, and I think I've only been in bed a couple of hours, so it's not that. It might be nothing, it might just be that the unsettling atmosphere in this house is rubbing off on me. Things have gone wrong, very wrong, in the past week.

After the *Christmas Lunch Incident*, Dad left and he hasn't come back. Apparently, he's staying at his brother's house in Birmingham. Jimmy took me back to Morton Lodge soon after Dad left. They were surprised to see me there, I think, but they were fairly empty, it being Christmas Day and all, so I had my old room back for the night.

When Mum came to get me on Boxing Day, Jimmy gave her a nice thank you card, which she has put up on the kitchen counter. It's got flowers on the front. I wish I was able to open it to read it, because I'd love to know how he skirted around the *Incident* in it, amongst his profuse thanks. He's so diplomatic, I'm sure he managed it somehow.

Eliza left that afternoon, too. She told Mum she needed to go home because she hadn't brought any of her stuff with her. In normal circumstances, Mum would have seen through that lie in an instant, but these are not normal circumstances.

After we got home on Boxing Day, Mum just sat down on our sofa and stared into space for quite a while. She put me in front of the TV, turned it up very loud, and then went into the kitchen, from where I heard loud clatters of saucepans and plates, and occasional sobs.

The twenty-four hours since have been deadly. That period after Christmas, that annual anti-climax, it's a time of hangovers and regret in most houses, I know. But here, this year, it's been almost funereal. As the sun set on Boxing Day, Mum grabbed a large black bin bag from under the sink and started ripping down the decorations she'd taken weeks to put up. She did it with such force that she left the pictures on our walls awry, and she scratched the mantelpiece when she removed the angel candlesticks Eliza had made her in primary school. I watched her try to take the fairy lights down from the tree beside my bed. When she couldn't remove them easily because they'd become tangled up in the branches, she simply grabbed a pair of scissors, snipped through the wires and chucked the whole set into the bag. Then, when she was finished, she took several large black bin bags to the tip, and with them, a whole host of my Christmas memories.

Then there was the tree. I watched her wrestling it inside a few weeks ago, sighing and panting with the effort of putting it up. She had spent hours getting the light-to-tree ratio just right, tying ribbons on the ends of its branches, and hanging decorations all over its broad expanse with delicate green hooks. Now, she ripped them off in minutes, apparently not caring if they were unusable next year, and instead of putting the glass ones in egg boxes for safe keeping, they went into a large plastic bag with the rest. Once these were off, she tipped the tree over onto the floor and took the lights off over the top of it, ending up with a massive ball of wires, bulbs and plugs, resembling tumbleweed. I watched her chuck this into another black bag which she then hauled upstairs and flung into the roof-space, so an enormous challenge is lying in wait for next year.

Finally, she unscrewed the tree trunk from its stand, grabbed the tree right where our family angel had been perched just minutes before, and dragged it through the hall and outside into our tiny front garden, scattering pine needles and decorations she'd missed in its wake. It's still there, right outside my window, and sometimes the winter sun catches one of the small pieces of tinsel fibre in its branches and I catch it glinting. I see dog walkers looking at it curiously on their daily rounds, wondering why it's been put out for collection so early.

This nausea is getting worse. And there's pain now, in my bowels, I think. *Oh my God, I need to poo.*

This isn't a common occurrence. In fact, due to my inactivity, I generally have problems going to the loo and I'm given laxatives to help. One of the carers has to sit me on the toilet for up to half an hour most days before I manage to produce anything. It's both boring and awkward, but this, this is urgent, and there are no laxatives required.

I wail in the direction of the monitor. Oh God, I hope

Mum wakes up fast. This is bad. *Really* bad. The pain is ratcheting up and I'm not sure how long I can hold on.

Here she comes, stumbling down the stairs, unsure of her footing in the dark. I hear her fumble for the light switch at the bottom and she runs into the room, calling out as she comes.

'Patience! Patience!' She's with me now. *Thank God.*

'Oh shit, I forgot to leave the light on. *Shit.* Hang on...' She's leaning over the bedside table, looking for the switch on the cord. Then she overbalances and falls briefly against the wall, before righting herself. She succeeds in finding the switch, and we have light.

There are snakes at work down below. They are writhing inside me, and they are angry.

She looks dreadful. Her hair is greasy, her eyes are bloodshot – and she smells. I think it might be alcohol; I'm allowed a taste of her gin and tonic sometimes and it smells a bit like this. Sweet and sour.

But never mind that. There are slugs in my gullet, too, and they are trying to come out of the other exit. I gulp them back down, praying I can keep them at bay.

'Argggggh' my mouth manages to exclaim. 'Arrgggghhhhh.'

'Oh crap! Patience, I'm coming. What is it? What is it, darling?'

She looks at me, holds my head in her clammy hands, as if willing me to form words, but of course I bloody can't. She puts her hand to my forehead; no fever. She feels my pulse; it's racing. I can see her panic increasing. She must be worried I'm about to have a fit, or that I've already had one. But then I let out a huge rriiiiiippp from my bottom and she knows.

I can see Mum trying to work out what to do, battling the fog in her brain.

'I'm going to get you to the loo.' But Mum isn't supposed to operate the hoist by herself. Someone is supposed to be with her. Usually, a carer sleeps in. But we don't have night cover this week, because Dad is supposed to be here.

'Right then. Let's roll you over.' That smell grows stronger as she nears me and grasps my shoulders. I'm worried that she might not be able to pull me up to sitting, but she manages it, with a strength I haven't seen her display before.

The slugs in my gullet are nearing the exit.

It's then that she realises that her hoist is out of her reach. It's over by the toilet, a few steps away. I see her thinking about it, wondering what to do. And then she makes her choice. She leaves me sitting there on the edge of the bed, bending over towards my knees, just for an instant.

But an instant is enough. Within a second, I am falling.

Thump.

Crack.

I open my mouth as I'm about to hit the floor and a torrent of vomit emits from my throat. My pad fills with brown, stinking sludge.

And Mum screams.

PART TWO

17

Eliza and Patience

January 7

It was below freezing and the sun, weak but welcome, illuminated the ice crystals that had formed on the path outside Patience's respite care home, making it sparkle. As Eliza walked up to the door, she noticed that someone had planted bulbs all along the lawn to her right and there were shoots just poking through, hinting at the new life and warmth to come. She knew that some of the families of the residents took turns to look after this garden, and she was glad that they did. The building itself – a 1980s red-brick box of a bungalow – could never be called beautiful, but it was wonderful that its residents could look outside and see flowers, green grass, bees and butterflies.

Patience had always loved butterflies. She giggled whenever she saw one and followed them with her eyes. When they were both small, Eliza had caught one once, on a warm summer's day. She'd held it softly in her hands and carried it over to show to her sister. When she'd opened her fingers just a crack to show her, Patience had laughed with such intensity that Eliza had been shocked and let it go. It had flown right into Patience, bumping into her nose before heading back into the nearest honeysuckle. Patience had grinned with pure joy.

Patience's smile had always been an extraordinary tonic for Eliza. It was an innocent smile, a pure smile, and it was something that she desperately needed to see. Her office had shut down over the whole Christmas break and since leaving her childhood home on Christmas Day she hadn't seen a single soul. Surrounded by walls stripped of pictures and half-filled cupboards, Eliza had realised that her flat was now not so much a sanctuary, as solitary confinement. She desperately needed to see a friendly face, and that meant Patience. She'd been sent here from hospital to convalesce after her horrible vomiting bug and fall, and Eliza wanted to reassure herself that she was comfortable and recovering – and she also had something very important to ask.

She rang the doorbell and one of the carers, a woman who she didn't recognise, came to the door. Eliza introduced herself and the woman beckoned her in and told her to make her own way to Patience's room.

Eliza found her sister sitting in her chair watching a DVD of *The Muppets*. The DVD had been hers first, like many of Patience's collection. They must have seen it hundreds of times, but Patience showed no sign of getting bored of it. Eliza could see that her eyes were fixed on the screen, and her hands were still, resting, not wringing, a sure sign that she was concentrating. Eliza broke this bubble with a large kiss on her sister's cheek.

'Wotcha, Patience,' she said, placing her face right in her sister's line of vision. 'I'm back, the prodigal sister. Now, let me see how bad it is…'

Pretty bad, sis. Pretty bad.

Eliza tried not to wince when she saw Patience's face. Her alabaster skin was now black and yellow, and her left eye was only just visible through the swelling on that side of her face. They'd kept her in hospital for a few days after her fall, largely due to the horrible gastroenteritis she'd developed, which had left her dehydrated and exhausted. But they'd eventually been persuaded by Louise to discharge her here, with extra nursing support to keep an eye on her as she recovered.

Mum had wanted her back at home, but Dad had stepped in and refused to let that happen, emphasising his wife's need for rest and Patience's medical needs. That hadn't been the real reason though, Eliza knew. He hadn't said so out loud – to do so might have nudged the medical staff in the direction of a call to the police and all of the horror that would ensue as a result – but it was clear to both of them that Louise had been incredibly drunk while in charge of Patience and they were both still processing that.

When she and her father had met in hospital on that dreadful night, having bombed up and down their respective motorways after being woken by phone calls from a very sympathetic A & E nurse, they had looked at each other with mutual understanding. They both had to step up now.

Her mum had been sitting slumped on a chair beside Patience's hospital bed, her head in her hands. A nurse had been standing next to her, rubbing her back as she retched into a cardboard bowl, more from shock, apparently, than booze, although they could both smell alcohol on her.

Dad had taken decisive action as soon as he'd taken

in that distressing vignette. He asked the doctors to sign Louise off sick from work for a few weeks and Professor Larssen had been very understanding when Dad had called him to let him know, which she was pretty impressed by, as he had been fairly terse. They'd decided not to mention the booze, had just said that Mum was very unwell. The professor hadn't questioned it.

What on earth had gone on that night, though? And why was Mum drinking so heavily? What had triggered it? Or maybe it had been going on for months or years and they'd been too stupid to notice?

Eliza turned the TV off and spun her sister's wheelchair around to face her. Then she sat down on Patience's single bed, sinking into its extra-thickness mattress topper, a measure designed to stop her getting sore.

'So, hey. Sorry about turning the TV off, but I want your full attention. Here's where we are,' she began, moving her head from left to right to try to attract Patience's gaze. After a few seconds she caught her eye and Patience looked at her, straight on, as if she was taking it all in.

Spill. I have all the time in the world.

Eliza took a deep breath and spoke softly, so none of the carers outside in the hallway could hear. 'Firstly, I'm so sorry that I haven't been home more. I got caught up with my own drama. And so I feel like all of this mess is my fault. If I'd been here more often, maybe I'd have been able to see what was happening with Mum? Anyhow, I'm going to try to be around more from now on.'

Eliza took one of her sister's hands, noting how it relaxed as she did so.

None of this is your fault, Sis. Stop blaming yourself. You always do this, and you're wrong. If it's anyone's fault, it's mine. I'm the one with the bloody useless body.

'Secondly, I'm still pregnant. Or at least, I think I am. I haven't had a period and I feel as shit as it's possible to feel. I haven't told Ed, before you ask, and I haven't told Mum and Dad either, because – well, you know why. I'm not going to keep it though, don't worry. My life is enough of a mess. Wedding-wise though, I'm afraid, my lovely, that we're going to have to send your bridesmaid dress back, and that's a shame, because you look lovely in green.'

Eliza paused for the sardonic response she knew, just knew, that Patience would make, if she was able to talk.

I don't look good in any colour, you moron.

'Anyway, I am going to let Mum and Dad know about the wedding stuff soon. Possibly today. I'm on my way to see her now. I need to find out what's really going on with the two of them. I mean, have you ever seen it this bad?' Patience moved her eyes a bit. Eliza took that to mean that she agreed.

Erroneously, as it turned out.

It's always bad, sister mine. Surely you remember how bad it was, how strong and deadly the undercurrent often was, at home? That's why you escaped and moved to London, isn't it? But I don't blame you. I'd also escape, if I could.

When Eliza had driven to Oxford impulsively on Christmas Eve, she had thought, in the far recesses of her mind, that she might be able to tell her mum the truth – both about the wedding being off and about the pregnancy. She had wanted to do so, badly; she had longed for Louise to hold her tight as she wept, to hear her say that she was loved and that it didn't matter, like she had done when she was small, when something awful had happened at school. But she had known when her mum had met her at the door the next morning, with a look on her face more weary than she'd ever seen before, that she could do no such thing.

Growing up, Louise had been the driving force behind everything they'd done as a family; every celebration, every holiday, every nice meal. Outwardly, she had appeared to be incredibly organised, always full of energy. Neighbours and friends had openly called her superwoman. At home, however, her mask had sometimes slipped. And when it had, it had been miserable – for a teenage, hormonally-controlled Eliza, especially. She had struggled to empathise with her mother, embroiled as she had been in her own struggles. Eliza now realised, however, that it must have been incredibly exhausting to maintain that act daily, for decades.

That's why she knew that telling her mum the truth about the detritus in her own life might cause what was left of Louise's simulated stability to disperse completely. And she could never live with that. No, her secrets would have to wait a little longer to come to the surface, particularly because she also had to decide whether to take on the role of consultee for Patience in the gene therapy trial. She had taken her role seriously, doing all the reading she could about it, trying her best to understand the pros and cons. It was a minefield, she had discovered. She could see both sides of the argument very clearly.

In the one corner, there was Dad, determined to protect his daughter from even more harm; on the other, there was Mum, desperate to turn back time and take all of the harm away. She desperately didn't want to play piggy in the middle between her two warring parents, but Louise's forceful, persuasive personality had corralled her into a corner, as it had done many times over her childhood. She was only just beginning to realise that this was a pattern she was doomed to repeat.

The gene therapy trial team had sent her a form to sign. They needed her permission, on behalf of Patience, ahead of the Best Interests meeting where the final decision would be made. She had not signed it yet, because she hadn't made up her mind. That's why she was here. She wanted to ask Patience about it first.

'Anyhow, there's this thing I wanted to ask and I'm not really sure how to ask it. Or even, why I'm asking, because you have never been able to answer me, damn it. But I so wish you could. You always look so wise.'

Eliza looked down at their joined hands and shifted position on the bed. 'Anyway, here it is. Mum has entered you in for a gene therapy trial. You know about that, I think? Has anyone spoken to you about it? I expect they have.'

Nope.

'Anyway, the scientists are promising all sorts of amazing things. Talking, maybe, or walking. Can you imagine that? And it might be great for you, Patience, it really might. But Dad doesn't want you to do it. Because it's untested and – and they are going to test it on you.'

This again. Still no detail. What on earth does it involve and do I want to do it? Tell me. Tell. Me. I can take it.

Eliza assessed her sister's face. Patience's gaze was now focussed on the mural on the wall behind her. Did she even know she was there at all? She sometimes wondered. But she persevered.

'The risks are... worrying. You might get cancer. Or you might need brain surgery afterwards, to make room in your brain. Or you might just feel incredibly weird for a long time.'

Shit.

'But then, I suppose you might wake up the next morning, and be able-bodied, like me. Although that's not all it's cracked up to be, as you know. Anyway, because Mum and Dad are disagreeing, they have asked me to decide. On your behalf. And the thing is... I wanted to know... Do you want to try? Do you want to risk it? It'll mean a spell in hospital.'

Suddenly, Eliza was hit hard in the face by a memory of her own time in hospital; of blood, of pain, regret... She grasped Patience's hand tighter.

The two sisters sat in silence for a few moments, listening to the hum of activity elsewhere in the care home; someone was washing up, someone was moaning, and the TV was prattling on next door. Eliza was clasping Patience's hands which were, unusually, perfectly still. Then, Patience's gaze returned to her sister. Her expression was blank, but her eyes – were they wet?

Patience rarely cried, except when in pain. Eliza sat up and leaned forward.

'Oh, lovely, are you crying? Please don't cry.'

Of course I'm crying, dimwit. I'm crying because you are actually asking me how I feel.

Her face remained blank, but one solitary tear was forging a path down her cheek. Eliza reached for a tissue from a box beside the bed, and caught it.

'OK. I think I know what you want. I hope I do. I love you, do you know that? *I love you.*'

I love you too.

'Patience, my lovely! Have you time for that walk we planned at breakfast?' Jimmy, clad in tight black jeans and a grey V-neck jumper, had come into the room in full flow and stood stock-still when he saw that Patience had company.

'Ah, sorry, I didn't mean to interrupt. I was just coming to get P to take her for a stroll into town.'

Eliza didn't know where to look. Jimmy was undoubtedly attractive, if you liked that sort of thing; he had broad shoulders, a narrow waist, elegantly tousled short brown hair with just the right amount of floppy, and a mouth that appeared as though it was always about to smile. But it wasn't his appearance that made it hard to look at him – it was what he'd witnessed on Christmas Day. No one from outside their family unit had ever seen them behaving anything other than cordially to each other. Even at home, the family had always been on their best behaviour when there were carers present. In Eliza's mind, it was as if Jimmy had walked in on them all eating their lunch naked.

'I... er... meant to get in touch actually, after Christmas,' she said, standing up and then shifting awkwardly from one foot to the other. 'On behalf of my family, I just wanted to say that I'm – I'm sorry it was awkward... Very awkward.' Jesus, she thought, I sound like I'm reading a prepared statement. Her face began to feel hot. She looked at the floor. 'Things are very difficult at the moment. As you may have gathered.'

'Yes,' he said, looking straight at her. 'And don't worry, I wasn't upset and I'm not about to spread it all around the care home, if that's what this is about.'

'Honestly, I wasn't suggesting that…'

'Look, it's fine. Anyway, do you want to carry on this conversation outside, where no one else can hear? You can walk with us part-way, if you like.'

Eliza nodded her assent and waited as Jimmy placed a warm cloak around Patience's body, a hat on her head and mittens on her hands. Then he turned Patience's chair towards the door and she followed behind them.

The sky was a glorious blue, criss-crossed with aircraft contrails, and Eliza felt her mood improve instantly. It had been murky and damp for weeks and now the fog had lifted, both metaphorically and literally.

'Are you here for a break?' Jimmy asked, speaking for the first time since they'd started their walk. They were now approaching the crossroads near a church. He was holding Patience's wheelchair firmly as they waited for a break in the traffic.

'Something like that,' replied Eliza, tersely. The road was busy, and the traffic was almost stationary. A coach full of children was approaching them at a crawl. Eliza looked up and saw at least twenty young faces staring down at Patience. She could see that many of them were trying to attract the attention of the child sitting next to them, so that they could also gawp at the funny-looking disabled woman in the wheelchair. Several of them appeared to be laughing.

People always stared at Patience, and Eliza understood why: Patience looked different. Why wouldn't a child have questions? But it was the laughter that got to her this time. She was fine with curiosity, that was understandable, but witnessing such apparent hilarity at her sister's vulnerability triggered an unexpected rage that started in Eliza's toes and rose through her like a rocket. Without stopping to think, she stepped forwards into the road and hammered on the side of the bus with her fists. She was roaring indistinct, guttural words, and the cold, hard metal was Ed, and it was her boss, and it was her mum and dad, and it was Rett syndrome.

Then, two arms grabbed her by the waist and dragged her back to the pavement.

'What. On. Earth. Are. You. *Doing?*' asked Jimmy, gesticulating at the bus driver to carry on, nothing to see here.

'I'm just... I'm just... so...' she said, hyperventilating. She couldn't finish her sentence.

'OK, OK,' said Jimmy. 'Look, there's a church just here. Let's go inside and sit down and we can talk.'

He let go of her, then, and set off, willing her to follow.

The church was both warm and open. Jimmy pushed Patience towards a circle of chairs in one corner, next to some kids' toys and books. Then he moved a chair out of the way to accommodate her, facing her outwards so that she had something to look at.

'I'm sorry about that,' Eliza said, as if she was apologising for knocking into someone on the street. She took a seat opposite them and Jimmy wondered why she'd chosen to sit that way around, rather than sitting side by side.

'I'm so sorry that you had to see that,' she said.

Oh, my lovely Eliza. I so wish I could give you a hug.

Jimmy reached inside the bag slung across the bars of Patience's chair, and pulled out a Tupperware container. He snapped the lid open, and passed it over.

'Chocolate digestive?'

Eliza smiled with relief, glad of the distraction, of Jimmy's attempt to lighten the mood.

'Oh, yes… please.'

Jimmy is offering Eliza his chocolate biscuit stash. Uh oh. He never gives those out to anyone. I've changed my mind about him being gay.

'Chocolate sorts most things, in my experience,' said Jimmy. 'That, and crisps.'

'You are absolutely right,' Eliza replied. 'On both counts. But do you think chocolate is capable of fixing crazy?'

Oh my God, she's smiling! I love it when she smiles.

'I don't think you're crazy,' replied Jimmy, looking down at the box as he did so. 'Just very loyal.'

'No, I'm crazy,' replied Eliza, smiling now, her mood lifting. 'Have always been crazy. It runs in the family.'

That's it. It's official. They are definitely flirting.

Jimmy passed her another biscuit.

'So that's not the first time you've hammered on the side of a bus full of schoolkids?'

'Ha no, that's definitely a first. I'm not usually *that* crazy.'

Well, quite crazy, actually, sister mine.

They sat opposite each other for a moment, munching biscuits in companionable silence.

'My grandfather was a vicar, you know.' Eliza had stopped eating and was now taking in her surroundings. The church was Victorian and would have been quite dark without its lighting system, which was casting a warm glow on its vaulted ceiling. There were no pews; the nave was home instead to orderly rows of upholstered chairs which looked, she thought, as if they might even be slightly comfortable to sit in.

'But his church was nothing like this. We used to go there sometimes, when we were little. I remember it being cold, and the services seemed to go on forever. We stopped going when I was a teenager, though. Mum didn't want to go any more.'

'Why?' Jimmy asked. 'Why the change?'

'Not sure why, to be honest. I didn't really know them. We almost never saw them and they're both dead now. I think she fell out with God too. She never took us to church after that. To be honest, churches creep me out a bit. All of the graves everywhere, the dark corners, the ritual. It all feels… oppressive.'

'I'm sorry. I wouldn't have brought you here if I'd known. I always think of them as welcoming places. I've been going regularly since I was a kid.'

'No, it's fine. It's actually really nice in here,' she paused. 'Actually, it's probably just what I need. I need calm. Peace. Ritual. Ritual is good when the rest of your world is falling apart.'

'So your reaction back there wasn't just about protecting Patience?' Jimmy asked.

'No. I mean, I love Patience.' She stood up and walked over to her, planting a kiss on her face and then sitting down next to her, beside Jimmy. 'That goes without saying. But I think I just needed to be physically angry. It's been boiling up inside me for a while now.'

'What are you angry about?' Jimmy asked. 'If you don't mind me asking?'

'What am I *not* angry about? I told you, I'm crazy. There's a list.'

'It's pretty normal to be angry,' replied Jimmy. 'I'm angry, too. Or at least, I was. I think I'm getting over it now.' He leaned over towards Patience and retrieved a plastic beaker from the bag.

'Why? You seem like a pretty chilled-out person.'

'I wasn't so chilled out when my dad was dying.'

Ah. Oh Jimmy.

Eliza remained silent while she watched Jimmy check the screwed-on sippy lid was secured properly, before lowering it towards Patience and tipping it gently into her mouth. It contained chocolate milk, from what she could make out. For a brief moment, Eliza considered giving him a hug, but she dismissed that thought almost as soon as it arrived. What was wrong with her today? She had taken leave of her senses.

'I'm so sorry, Jimmy, that's awful,' she said, staying seated where she was.

Jimmy continued to give Patience her drink. 'There you go, lovely, nice chocolate milk. I forgot the thickener again. I'll be in trouble back at base. That's the first time you've called me by my name, by the way,' he added, addressing Eliza. 'And you've met me at least five times now. I even came for Christmas.'

'Really? I'm sorry. I didn't mean anything by it. I hope you don't think I was dismissing you...'

'That's OK. I think carers are a bit like nurses. We're in the background a lot, expected to be there, but not noted.'

I sincerely doubt that Eliza has failed to notice Jimmy. How could anyone fail to see him?

'Bloody hell, it's not that,' she replied. 'It's not like that at all! It's really just that I've been so tied up in my own disaster of a life that I haven't had much time to acknowledge anyone else's.'

'Have you had enough?' Jimmy asked Patience. 'No? OK, just a bit more.' He turned to Eliza. 'You mean, whatever's going on between your mum and dad, and Patience's accident?' he asked, turning his attention away from Patience, briefly.

'Yes, there's that,' she said, guilt creeping into her voice. 'But it's not just that. To be honest, it's so complicated, I can't really untie the knots in my own mind, let alone try to explain them to someone else.'

Eliza was visualising the tangled threads, each of which had its own figurehead: Ed, her boss, a wedding dress, her parents, Patience – and a baby dangling perilously off the end in a gigantic black buggy. It was a gargantuan mess that kept her awake at night and drove her mad during daylight hours. She could not untie it. The threads kept slipping through her fingers.

'Try. It might help,' he said, before turning back to Patience. 'OK, now, P, I think you're finished. Let me just find a cloth to wipe you up a bit.'

Eliza observed Jimmy's sensitive, gentle, committed approach to her sister, and felt slightly dizzy.

'No, it's fine,' she replied, too lightly. 'I don't want to burden you with my crap.'

'Look. I won't tell anyone. I promise. Let's do this thing that I did with friends when I was a kid. If I tell you a secret, something that seriously compromises me first, then you have a weapon to hit me back with if I spill the beans. Deal?'

Eliza looked at him and smiled. 'You're nuts. Seriously? You did that?'

'Yes, and it works,' he answered. 'So, I'll go first.'

Jimmy had rolled his sleeves up and his sculpted forearms and strong hands were dabbing a tissue all around Patience's mouth, mopping up spilled chocolate.

'I get the bus to work. Or I cycle. That's because I lost my driving licence last year. Drink driving.' She looked at him, checking to see that he wasn't joking. 'I'm serious,' he said. 'And they don't know at work. I didn't want them to think badly of me. I was going through a bad time. I was caring for my dad who was dying. Motor Neurone disease. Do you know it? It robs you of your abilities, bit by bit, day by day, until you have no control over anything at all. Dad suffered horribly and I was so angry. Raging. I got pissed one night and took off in my car. I crashed it into a wall. Luckily there was no one in front of it, or I'd be inside for manslaughter.'

'Wow,' said Eliza. 'Christ. That's – that's awful. I don't know what to say.'

'That's OK. I know it is. Now, your turn.'

Eliza sat and thought for a moment. Then she stood up and started to pace around in a circle, a metre or so away, looking down at the floor as she walked.

'It's easier if I don't look at you while I say this,' she said. 'I only ever usually confess to Patience. And she doesn't really respond too much, facially, you know.' Jimmy turned his seat around and sat in silence next to Patience, the two of them looking like a jury waiting for a plea.

Let's have it. Tell him, Eliza. He's a good listener.

'OK, so, my fiancé has left me,' she said, continuing to look at the floor, 'and I don't think there's any chance that he's coming back.'

'And you have a wedding booked, right?' said Jimmy, not missing a beat. 'I heard the girls at the care home talking about it. One of us has to come as a guest, with Patience.'

'Yes, there's a wedding booked for the summer. It needs to be cancelled, but I haven't told Mum and Dad because it would break their hearts. Before you ask. And they are going through enough.'

'I see. But won't it break their hearts whenever they hear about it? Don't you think you should just come out and say it? Get it over with? Get things cancelled so it doesn't cost too much?'

Yes, Jimmy.

'No.'

'Why?'

'Because I am their happiness. I am the daughter who is going to make them proud at a wedding reception, the daughter who's going to make them grandparents, the daughter who's going to have a fulfilling career that they can talk about with their friends. I'm in PR. I used to love it, but I bloody hate it now! I'm useless at it, but if I change career I'll have to start again and I can't bear that either. They are going to be so disappointed in me. They spent so much money paying for me to go to university. It's too late to change, and it's too late to find someone new now.' Eliza began to cry. Jimmy stood up and walked over to her.

'Look, he's obviously an idiot,' he said, putting his arms

on her shoulders and looking her right in the eyes. 'And there is no fixing an idiot. They are beyond help.'

He's making physical contact with her. Eliza is blushing. How do I feel about that? Not as bad as I'd feel if it was anyone else, that's for sure. But still, that will never be me, and that smarts.

'And I'm sure you do make your parents proud. Look how great you are with Patience. I'm sure they're not that bothered about the wedding.'

Eliza reached into her pocket for a tissue. 'I wish you were right,' she said, blowing her nose. 'But I've known my parents for thirty-six years, and I doubt it. And I'm a shit sister. I don't do nearly enough. Lots of siblings of disabled people are total rockstars, taking on caring responsibilities and stuff. All I have to do is support my parents, really, and I've well and truly failed at even that.' She began pacing once again, and Jimmy dropped his arms to his sides.

They are grown ups, Eliza, and you are amazing.

'Look, Eliza, for what it's worth,' he said, trying to keep up with her, 'I spent years trying to please my parents. I worked in Dad's business, putting up fences and gates all across the south-west, hating it every day, because he said it was what I should do. It was man's work, he told me. And I did it, for him. And then he got ill and died and left me, and I never want to see a fencing post for the rest of my life. I'm now finally doing what I *want* to do. You should try it.'

Eliza stopped and looked straight at him. A tear had wended its way down her face and was now hanging off her chin.

'I can't. I can't change. It's too late. In fact, I think I'm going slightly mental. And then there's this huge mess with Mum and Dad. I can't possibly add to their burden.'

'Are you certain you're not using this whole situation with your parents, the gene therapy, and Patience's accident, as an excuse? To avoid facing the reality that your relationship is over?'

Oh. I don't think that will go down well, Jimmy...

Jimmy had come right up to Eliza now and they were standing face to face near the altar. They were eyeballing each other.

'How *dare* you?' she replied, her face transformed from angst-ridden to anger-ridden. 'I share my deepest fears with you and you accuse me of using Patience as an excuse? One of my teachers did that when I was a kid, you know – he suggested that I was using her existence as an excuse for behaving badly. It wasn't true then, and it isn't bloody true now. My whole life has been about protecting others, caring for others – it has *never* been about me. *It will never be about me.*'

Eliza didn't wait to hear Jimmy's response. Instead, she turned and fled down the nave and out of the door and into the street. It was only when she slowed from a run to a walk that she noticed it had begun to rain.

18

Pete

January 12

'Break time, lads.'

This news was greeted with a limp cheer, the usually welcome prospect of milky tea and custard creams dampened by incessant rain which had welded thick cotton work trousers to their legs and forged rivulets along every contour of their bodies.

Pete wondered idly whether it was possible to get trench foot in a twelve-hour shift. He was only halfway through and the waterproofing on his boots had already failed. His feet were swimming in a cocktail of rainwater and sweat. He made his way to the Portakabin, jumping awkwardly over deep puddles and dodging the rutted remains of the property's garden, which was well on its way to becoming a quagmire. On reflection, he wondered whether he preferred being baked alive to being dissolved.

But he was not going back. James, never the understanding type, had put pressure on him to return to Qatar. James had his family there with him and so he had no idea what it was like to live on a separate continent from those you loved. It was then Pete had seen red; his family came before everything, even money. And the money wasn't even that good now. These were difficult times, world-wide, and work was drying up a little in the Gulf.

He had yet to tell Louise about it – and the inevitable impact on their finances – but they'd manage. They had to, because he could never leave her on her own for that long again, that was clear. Anyhow, short-term gigs like this one paid well enough, particularly if you were prepared to work long days and weekends, and he was fine with that. And he hated his digs, so it was a relief to be out.

His brother, Steve, had offered to put him up at his place, but he couldn't face it. He'd also offered him work for the family firm, the one he'd learned his trade in. Their uncle's building business, once a small family-run enterprise, was now a major force in the West Midlands, with Steve at its helm. Pete was grateful for the offer, but reluctant to take a wage from a firm he should, by rights, have been co-director of. It felt like admitting failure. Moving to Oxfordshire all those years ago so that Lou could be back near her family had cost him dearly. He had never replicated his uncle's success, never striven to be his own boss. Now here he was, near retirement with just a suntan, what seemed like an impending divorce, and a pokey semi-detached to show for it. More fool him.

The windows of the Portakabin were rendered opaque by steam, and when he opened the door, he was greeted by a wave of damp, warm air that reeked of cigarettes, Lynx deodorant, and fart. His colleagues, a random collection of temporary itinerant labourers working for cash, were huddled next to an oil-filled radiator in the corner of the room, perched on orange plastic chairs, cradling steaming mugs of tea. He went over to the urn and made himself a cup, before pulling up a chair to join them. To his left, Marek – a recent recruit – had laid out one of the tabloid newspapers the foreman had bought on a small, upturned box in front of him. He was checking out the racing news from the day before. The men loved to gamble, sometimes en masse, on payday. Minutes later, he shut the paper with some force – the result was obviously not to his benefit – and stood up and marched over in search of more biscuits.

Not in the mood for conversation, Pete picked up the paper and began to read. It was the local rag, a publication that was at least 70 per cent advertising and what little news there was came largely, he suspected, from press releases. He flicked through the well-worn content: local primary school holds art contest; animal sanctuary seeks sponsorship; police call-out for witnesses to a hit-and-run. He took a deep breath and closed it, looking for the first time at the front page as he did so. What he saw there caused a surge of adrenaline which drove him out of his seat and back into the rain, his sodden feet forgotten.

'Eliza! Thank God you picked up.'

'Dad?'

'We need to talk, Eliza. Do you have a minute? Can we video chat?'

'I'm at work, Dad. Is it urgent?'

'Yes, Eliza, it is.' Pete heard a shuffling noise, as Eliza pushed her chair back and began to walk away from her desk.

'OK, I'll call you back in just a second.'

Pete turned his car ignition so that he could turn on the heater and waited, his fingers strumming a belligerent beat on his steering wheel.

The video ring tone rang out from his phone and he picked it up.

'Eliza.'

His daughter appeared to be standing in a stair well.

'Hi, Dad. What's up? Is it Mum? Patience?' Eliza had dark circles under her eyes. She looks tired, he thought.

'No. Yes. Sort of. It's about the trial.'

'I told you, I've got to be *independent*. I'm not taking sides. I *can't* take sides. I've told Mum the same thing.' She was now leaning against the wall behind her, a look of resignation on her face.

'I know, I know. That's not it. It's not about that. It's about the trial itself. It's in the paper.'

'What's in the paper?'

'The local rag's done some actual journalism. They've looked into that guy who's running the trial, Professor Larssen, and guess what? The funding for his trial is dodgy. Big pharma, corruption – all that stuff.'

'Hang on, Dad, back up. What does it actually say?'

Pete grabbed the paper, which had been lying on the passenger seat, and began to read while balancing the phone on his lap.

'The Bugle *can exclusively reveal that Professor Philip Larssen, a world-renowned geneticist who's currently leading a ground-breaking gene therapy trial in Birmingham, is being investigated over alleged malpractice concerning a previous research project.*

'*Sources close to the eminent scientist have told* The Bugle *that Prof. Larssen has questions to answer about a source of funding for a recent trial of the drug Curlinapam, which is currently being considered as a treatment for Huntingdon's disease.*'

'Where was the funding from, Dad?'

'Some of it came from a dodgy Russian pharmaceutical firm, apparently, but it wasn't disclosed. Otherwise he wouldn't have been allowed to do the trial.'

Pete put the paper back down and held the phone up in front of his face once more, so he could see Eliza's expression. Both her eyebrows were raised.

'What makes them dodgy?'

'It says here that they apparently aren't that keen on being honest about side effects.'

'I see.'

'Don't you understand? It means that we can't trust this man.' Pete had now begun to gesticulate wildly with his free hand. 'We can't allow him to experiment on Patience. We have to stop it!'

'How certain are you that the story is correct? I work in PR and I know how journalists work – there may be another side to this.'

'Eliza, this man is out to make money. All of this stuff about making people's lives better' – Pete accidentally knocked his phone out of his hand, but kept talking as he rifled around in the footwell in his efforts to retrieve it – 'of helping Rett sufferers to throw away their wheelchairs and walk – it's rubbish. He just wants the cash.'

'You can't prove that.'

'Fine. I'll take a picture of this and send it to you. And

then, you have a think. Seriously. I know you want to be independent, but seriously, before you sign her life away, you need to read this.'

Pete located the phone under his left foot and lifted it back up triumphantly.

'OK, Dad, I get it.'

'So you won't sign it?'

'I'm not saying that. I'm going to go and see Mum first. See what she has to say about it.'

'She's brainwashed, pet. And not in her right state of mind. You know that as well as I do.'

Pete suddenly felt overwhelmingly tired. He put the phone down on the seat next to him and put his head in his hands.

'Dad? Are you still there?'

'Yes, love?'

'I'm sorry. About being made to take sides. I do love you, you know.'

'I know, pet. Just keep an open mind, Eliza. It's never too late.'

19

Eliza

It was dark when Eliza drew up outside the house, but the lights in Patience's bedroom were shining brightly onto the driveway, the curtains undrawn. Eliza locked the car quickly and used her spare house keys to let herself in.

'Mum?'

Eliza turned into her sister's room and saw that the bed, usually neatly turned down by carers, was a tumult of blankets and pillows.

'E-lise-sa?' The blankets stirred, and a head emerged. 'Sorrrry, was jussst havin' a nap...'

'Oh, Mum!'

As Eliza approached the bed, the stench of alcohol grew stronger. Then there was a clatter as she knocked over a bottle of gin which had been deposited on the floor beside the bed. It was empty.

'I'll get you a glass of water.'

Eliza hurried out of the room and went into the kitchen. Dirty plates and cups were piled up in the sink and the encrusted remnants of cheap ready meals littered the surfaces.

She opened the cupboards and finding no clean glasses, opened the dishwasher, only to be hit by the smell of rotting food and stagnant water.

Fighting the urge to vomit, she retrieved a glass from the upper level and washed it thoroughly under the tap.

She should have come sooner. She should have told work that she needed time off to deal with a family crisis. But after that incident with Jimmy in the church, and weighing up the abortion she knew she needed, she just hadn't felt up to it. Now she felt incredibly guilty. Her mum needed her and she had been wilfully absent.

She poured some water into the glass and walked swiftly back into Patience's room. Her mother was now sitting up in bed, rubbing her eyes. She was wearing pyjamas, even though it was only 7 p.m. Had she been wearing them all day, she wondered? Maybe all week? It certainly smelled like it.

'Here you go, Mum.'

Louise took the glass without looking at Eliza. She drank deeply, draining it in a few gulps.

'Checking up on me, are you?' she said, handing the glass back.

'Sorry, Mum. It wasn't deliberate. I decided to come on the spur of the moment, after work.'

'Hmm.'

'Mum, I'm here now. And I want to help.'

'Do you now?'

'Yes.'

Louise glared at her.

'Well, you can start by finding me some paracetamol. I'm not feeling very well today.'

Eliza located the tablets and took them to her mother along with another glass of water and a fresh set of pyjamas. Then she returned to the kitchen, turned the dishwasher on, emptied the bin and loaded the washing machine. After an hour, the room was at least sanitary. She considered their dinner options. As there was no food in the cupboards to speak of, she used an old takeaway menu she'd found behind the bin and ordered from it. They'd dine on Mr Wu's special set meal B tonight.

'Food should be here in half an hour,' she said to Louise, who was now sitting with her feet up on the sofa under a blanket, like an invalid. 'Are you feeling hungry?'

'Maybe,' Louise replied, pulling the blanket further up her body.

'Good. You need food. There's not much in the kitchen, Mum.' Eliza perched on the end of the sofa, by her mother's feet.

'I know. I haven't been feeling well, as I said. I haven't been able to get out.'

'OK.'

'And since Patience isn't here, I haven't needed to go shopping.'

'Right. She'll be coming home in a few days, though, all being well?'

'So they say. If they decide to trust me with her.'

Eliza put her hands on her mother's blanket, stroking the legs beneath. Louise pulled her legs towards her body in response.

'Mum, don't be silly. No one is saying they don't trust you. We just thought you needed a break. You're obviously under the weather.'

'Hmm.' Louise crossed her arms and looked down at her lap.

'It's cold in here,' said Eliza, rubbing her own arms to keep warm. 'Is the heating timer on the blink?'

'No, I don't think so. I don't have it on much, though. To save money.'

'It's freezing, Mum. And you and Dad aren't that short of cash. Surely you can afford some heat?'

'My bank account says differently,' Louise replied.

Eliza smiled, as if her mother had made a joke. 'Don't be silly, Mum. Dad wouldn't keep you short of money.'

'You reckon? You think because he's been working out there in Doha he'd have loads of cash to splash? Me too. But apparently not. At the moment, I'm getting through the cash he transfers in three weeks. The final week of the month is a wasteland.'

Eliza looked at her mother. She looked beaten. Exhausted. She definitely wasn't laughing.

'I didn't know.'

'No.'

'I should have come home more. I'm sorry, Mum.'

'You've got your own life to lead, darling, and a wedding to plan! I can't expect you to stay at home with me forever, can I? Anyway, Patience will always be here, won't she, so…'

Louise had meant that as a joke, and Eliza tried to smile.

'Is there anything I can do to help?' Eliza asked. 'I mean, I don't have much money either, but I could lend you a bit.'

Louise visibly softened. 'Don't be silly, darling, I don't want your money. This will pass. All of it. You'll see.'

'I think you're depressed, Mum.'

There was a pause.

'Maybe. Or maybe it's just a natural way to respond to what's happened? I mean, Patience getting hurt on my watch, and then your dad... Anyway, it will pass, I'm sure.'

Eliza moved up the sofa and leaned in for a hug. They sat like that for a few minutes, enjoying the feeling of mutual security it brought.

It was Louise who broke the silence. 'There's something you can do for me tomorrow, though,' she said.

'Are you sure you're up to this?'

It was the following morning and Louise had rallied significantly. She hadn't had a drink all evening. Eliza, meanwhile, had spent a terrible night in the spare room, battling with heartburn, nausea and guilt-induced insomnia. Louise looked at her with concern. 'I could have asked Philip if we could reschedule,' she said.

Eliza mustered every ounce of energy she had left and smiled at her mother.

'No, it's fine. As you reminded me this morning, Mum, time is of the essence. I'm fine. Just tired. It's been a tough week. But this is important.'

'OK,' said Louise. 'If you're sure. But let's go to the café first. You need a snack. You look peaky.'

Eliza followed her, grateful for any opportunity to rest. Louise led her around a corner and into a small coffee shop, furnished with metal tables and chairs.

'What do you want?' Louise asked. 'I'm buying, because you bought dinner.'

'Oh, just a tea, Mum,' said Eliza. 'Black.'

Louise headed off to order the drinks. While she was away, Eliza wondered whether now might be a good time to break the news about the wedding to her. After all, she needed to know, so that she and Dad could use the money for something else. And she seemed a bit better this morning, a bit stronger.

'There you go,' Louise said, presenting Eliza with a polystyrene cup of tea and a paper plate laden with a Danish pastry, glistening with white icing and glacé cherries. 'I got this for us to share,' she said. 'But it's mostly for you.'

Eliza's heart swelled, and her nausea evaporated. Suddenly, she was a child again, and Louise was taking her out for a special lunch, just the two of them, to celebrate her exam results, or the end of term.

'Thanks, Mum,' she said. 'That looks wonderful.'

Louise sat down opposite her and took a knife to the pastry, cutting it into thirds. Eliza remembered her doing this with meals she hadn't wanted to eat when she was tiny. If Eliza would agree to eat one third, she'd agree to eat the rest.

'Mum,' she said, suddenly deciding that this was the moment, this was when she would tell her, 'I—'

'I wanted to say how sorry I am,' Louise said, cutting in. 'It was unfair, me trying to make you take sides on this trial.'

Eliza took a deep breath. She must not be put off now. She had to tell her.

'It means so much to me, you coming with me this morning,' Louise continued. 'Do you know, you've been one of the only good things in my life in the past year or so? Amongst all of the shit, you've been a shining light. I'm so lucky to have you.'

And that was it. She couldn't do it. She just couldn't.

'I have been so worried about Patience, since her seizure last summer. I think that's what set me off, with the depression.'

'Have you seen a doctor yet, Mum? To talk about it?'

Louise sighed. 'I've made an appointment. I am going, as you have all asked me to. Next week.'

'That's great, Mum.'

They sat there in companionable silence for a few minutes, finishing the pastry. Eliza reflected that it definitely wasn't the first time she'd been unable to convey what she was really thinking to her mum; sadly, it probably wouldn't be the last.

'Shall we go?' Louise said suddenly – clearly, Eliza thought, to avoid having to talk about her mental health for one more second.

'Yes,' agreed Eliza. 'Let's get this over and done with.'

They set off together, Louise leading her daughter through the maze of corridors to a door several floors up, where she knocked, and they waited.

'*Come in*!'

Louise opened the door and held it for Eliza. She walked into the room and was hit immediately by a cloud of baked, stale air. It smelled of mothballs, dust and coffee. Sitting on a chair in the centre of this cloud was a man she presumed to be Philip Larssen.

'Good afternoon, Louise,' the man said, standing up gingerly and holding out a hand. 'I'm glad you're feeling a bit better.' He turned towards Eliza. 'And you must be Elizabeth,' he said.

'Eliza. Yes. That's me.'

The man smiled. It was a kindly smile, a genuine one.

'Sorry, yes, you prefer Eliza. I forgot. I forget a lot of things. Apologies. Anyway, please sit down.' He gesticulated vaguely towards one of two chairs in the corner. 'Thank you for coming. Did your mum explain what this was about?'

Eliza sat down next to her mother, who gave her an encouraging smile.

'Yes, she did,' she said. 'I'm here to find out more about the trial?'

'Yes. And then, as a consultee for your sister, to give permission – if you want to,' he replied. 'Now Louise. I'm sorry, my dear, but would you mind leaving us alone while we do this? As you're involved in the trial, you shouldn't really be here.'

Louise stood up and looked slightly flustered, as if she'd been caught shoplifting.

'Yes, of course,' she said. 'Shall I come back in half an hour?'

'Yes, that'll be long enough.'

As soon as Louise had disappeared through the door, he set about rifling through the papers on his desk.

'It must be here somewhere. I made sure I had a copy ready. Now, where is it...?' He lifted up a mug and a browned apple core. 'Here it is.'

Professor Larssen handed her a glossy brochure, which was now embellished with a circle of coffee on the front cover.

'This is the literature we've produced. Your role, as I'm sure you know, is to make a decision about taking part in the trial on your sister's behalf, because she lacks the capacity to do so herself. The Best Interests meeting will obviously rubber stamp it, but we're certain that your backing will swing it for us.'

Eliza began to flick through the leaflet, which was illustrated with beautiful photos of people who all looked a lot like Patience.

'You'll find more detail in there, but to save us both time, here's the executive summary, as it were. We are set to carry out phase one of a trial to see if gene therapy for Rett syndrome can be successful in humans. The disease has apparently been reversed in mice. We are uncertain if that will happen with humans, but we are going to run this trial to see. As it's phase one, we will be starting slowly, with a low dose, so the effects may not be dramatic. But there is also risk. Please turn to page six.'

Eliza did as he asked.

'These are some of the risks we've identified,' he said. 'It's quite a long list, a frightening list, I know. Take some time to look at it, if you like.'

Eliza examined the list, her breath becoming increasingly shallow as she read each entry.

Confusion

Autonomic disturbance

Raised intracranial pressure

Anxiety

Seizures

Depression

Death

'Death? That's one hell of a risk.'

'It's impossible to predict how any trial like this will go,' he said. 'We have to consider all possibilities. But please be reassured that we are going to take every precaution with this – we are not going in like a bull in a china shop. We have high ethical standards.'

Eliza nodded automatically, although she had not meant to. She was struggling to take it in.

'Yes – about that. I read the article, in the paper. About your previous trial,' she said, her eyes focussed and her back straight. She had to let him know that she wasn't a pushover.

'Ah, yes. Do you have questions?'

Eliza pulled herself up, and took a deep breath.

'Plenty. It sounded murky. You must know that. But Mum seems pretty certain that you're legit. Are you? Who's sponsoring this trial? And why have you got Mum involved?'

'This trial is being sponsored by an American Rett syndrome charity. They are doing the trial here because our regulations are a little more relaxed. But I promise we have no Russian backing. It's not some sort of "big pharma" conspiracy. We just want to find out whether we can do something amazing.'

'And the other trial? The one with the Russian backers?'

'I am confident that we will be cleared of any wrongdoing. It's all a storm in a teacup. Complicated bureaucracy, and whatnot. Be assured that our standards of care and assessment of that trial were as fastidious as they always are for all our trials. And as far as your mother is concerned, well, Louise has looked into that and is reassured. And in terms of her role, she is helping me, as you know, to talk to parents of Rett people. That's all.'

'Mum...' Eliza said, looking up from the document, signalling that she had finished reading the list. 'Mum really wants Patience to do this, doesn't she?'

'Yes. But this isn't about Louise,' he said. 'This is about Patience. And you are her advocate in this. You have to consider how she might feel.'

'And that's the huge problem with this, isn't it? Patience can't speak. We have *never* spoken. How am I meant to know what she feels?'

'You have grown up with her; you almost certainly know her better than anyone else. Your mother and father excepted, of course.'

Eliza thought about the secrets she had shared with Patience, the tears she had shed on her shoulder, the knowing looks that had passed between them over three decades. And then she thought about that tear in Patience's eye the last time she'd seen her. It might have been nothing – an allergy, an irritation, pure fluke – or maybe, just maybe, it was something else. She had felt, in that moment, that Patience was telling her to sign her up, to give her a chance.

And what about those hands that she had always wished could play cards with her? That voice she had always wanted to sing a duet with? Those legs she had always wanted to dance by her side on nights out? This was not only Patience's big chance – this was hers, too, her opportunity to get to know the sibling she had spent her whole life with, but didn't even *know*.

And if Patience was better, her mum and dad would be free – and she would also be free. Because Patience could make her parents happy, when she had failed.

Surely that was worth the risk.

Or was it?

20

Louise

It was a grey morning of steely skies and the air was pregnant with water, possibly hail if it grew colder still. The building she had just parked in front of was the day's perfect partner. Built in the 1960s, its concrete-clad Brutalist style, once considered honest and raw, now simply appeared bleak. Its gutters were failing. Along its flat frontage, water had poured over the top of the downpipes, leaving long streaks, like tears.

Louise walked through the glass-fronted entrance and spoke to the receptionist, who pointed her in the direction of a small anteroom, where she was to wait. There were two other people in there already, sitting opposite each other, both fixated on their phones, scrolling through social media posts as if they had just emerged from an internet blackout. Louise took them in; a man, mid-thirties, bearded, wearing trainers, jeans, a Superdry jacket, a rugged jumper. Opposite him, a woman, also mid-thirties. She was dressed for the office, her highlighted hair in a tight bun on top of her head, smart black trousers, an olive-green shirt, a grey jacket, a neck scarf. Her feet were squeezed into vertiginous pointed heels. It was incredible to think that they had, most likely, once stood opposite each other in a public hall or place of worship and promised to devote themselves to each other for the rest of their lives. Right now, it looked as if they could barely tolerate breathing the same air.

'Mrs Willow?'

A man had appeared at the doorway.

'Yes,' she replied. 'I'm sorry, my husband hasn't arrived yet.'

'That's fine. We can get settled and wait for him to join us. Is he on his way?'

Louise wanted to reply that she had absolutely no idea. They had not corresponded properly for weeks.

'Yes,' she said, her voice artificially light. 'Should be here any minute.'

She followed the man down a lino-clad passageway into a small room which was simply furnished with a standard lamp, three chairs, a small table and a plant, which Louise judged to be fake. There wasn't enough natural light in here to promote life. The man gestured towards one of the chairs, and invited her to take a seat. There was an overwhelming smell of artificial perfume, which Louise noticed was coming from a plug-in diffuser behind the lamp.

'Before we get going properly,' the man began, 'I need to introduce myself. I'm Nathan, one of the counsellors here.'

'Nice to meet you,' replied Louise, automatically. It wasn't nice to meet him at all, in fact. It wasn't at all nice to be here.

'Can you confirm for me your reason for coming here?'

'We've separated,' Louise said. 'Temporarily.' She looked down at her feet. 'I hope.'

The door opened.

'So sorry I'm late,' said Pete.

'No worries,' chirped Nathan, in a sing-song tone reminiscent of a primary school teacher. 'Take a seat over here.'

Pete clearly hadn't made an effort to dress up. He was wearing grey trainers which had once been white, baggy old jeans and a faded sweatshirt which she recognised as one he wore to do DIY. He didn't look like he'd shaved, either. Eyes cast down, he sat next to her on the other of the two low, cushioned, armless seats. That act – sitting down next to her – had been replicated thousands of times in their forty years together, a simple demonstration of mutual support and intimacy. Her arm almost reached out as a reflex to take hold of his hand, but she stopped herself; his proximity now only served to exacerbate the gulf between them.

'OK, let's begin,' said Nathan, looking at them with a neutral expression that Louise suspected he practised in the mirror. 'Which of you would like to start?'

'You go first, Lou,' said Pete, acknowledging her presence for the first time.

Louise cleared her throat, which felt constricted. 'Right,' she began. 'Well, we're here because Pete and I are... estranged. I mean, we've often lived apart for periods of time – he works overseas a lot – but he's moved out of our house here now.'

'Would you say that you have reached a crisis point?' asked Nathan.

'Of course,' she replied, her eyes widening. 'Isn't that obvious?'

'Not everyone who comes here is in crisis,' replied Nathan.

'Can I say something at this point?' asked Pete, looking at Louise as he did so. 'To be fair, me moving out is the symptom. It's not the cause, is it?'

'No, that's right,' said Nathan. 'Can you expand on what you feel is the cause?'

'I think it's crept up on us gradually,' said Pete. 'I mean, the crisis is new, but we haven't been in a good place for a good few months.'

'And why do you think things have come to a head?' Nathan asked.

'It's all this gene therapy crap,' replied Pete, almost spitting out the final word.

'It's not crap, Pete!' Louise leaned forward in her seat, knuckles clenched.

Nathan held his hands up as if signalling a truce.

'Let's go back. Can you tell me what you are so angry about, Pete?'

'Lou has got it into her head that our disabled daughter is going to be perfectly normal for the first time in her life – will do a Lazarus on us and just dance off into the sunset – if she takes part in an experimental gene therapy trial,' Pete replied, his voice raised and slightly hoarse. 'The first human trial in the UK. The very first – and therefore the most dangerous.'

'It's not dangerous, Pete. They are going to do it safely!'

'She wants to put our beautiful daughter through something that might kill her or hurt her, chasing an impossible dream. And it's being run by a charlatan who's being investigated for malpractice!'

'All of the regulations have been met, and the NHS is sanctioning this trial. Pete is very wrong on this.'

'I just feel, you know, like Patience is Patience. She was never supposed to be different, or normal, whatever that is. But she,' he glared at Louise, 'wants to put her through something awful, just for a dream!'

'Those allegations against Philip are false. Completely false.'

'And now she's got our other daughter – *our healthy daughter* – involved, and she's been manipulating her, too. And as for *Philip…*'

'Let's rewind a bit,' Nathan said. 'Often, relationships reach crisis point due to a lack of communication. How do you feel you've been communicating recently, Louise?'

'Well, we haven't been, have we?' she snapped. 'He's stopped replying to my emails and messages and now he's moved out, he's just refusing to engage at all.'

'It's always one-way with you, though, isn't it, Lou? Even when we lived together, you never took my point of view on board.'

Louise threw herself back into her seat and crossed her arms.

'Well, thank you very much. How can you even *say* that? I have always consulted you on everything to do with Patience. Even in the last few years, when you have almost never been home. And it goes both ways, doesn't it? All the time, you've refused to consult me about our finances, you won't even tell me how big your pension pot is, like it's nothing to do with me…'

'… and the perfect example, this gene therapy. You signed her up without even asking me.'

'... it's like you're hoarding money, getting ready to run. Are you? Have you stashed it somewhere?'

Nathan held out his arms.

'Right. Let's focus on that,' he said. 'What's your view on the family finances, Pete? Why aren't you involving Louise?'

Pete took a sip from his cup.

'I just don't want to worry her, that's all,' he replied. 'I have it in hand.'

'Do you?' said Louise. 'Then why do I have an overdraft?'

Pete looked horrified. 'Do you? Oh, Lou, I'm sorry, I had no idea. I'll do a few extra shifts. I'll have some more money with you by the end of the week.'

Nathan looked at Louise, inviting her to respond. She appeared mollified. 'OK, that would be helpful. But I'd still like you to tell me where we stand.'

Nathan switched his focus to Pete.

'Could you do that, Pete?'

Pete was rubbing his forehead.

'OK,' he mumbled. 'I'll come round soon and we can talk about it.'

Louise thought this to be very unlikely, but Nathan seemed satisfied. 'Let's talk about the gene therapy now, the apparent cause of your crisis. Can you explain what *your* thinking on that is, Louise?'

'Ridiculous. He's being *ridiculous*,' she replied, pointing a finger at Pete. 'Accusing me of manipulating our daughter. Eliza has her own mind.'

'Your other daughter aside – can you explain to Pete why you believe it's the right thing to do?' asked Nathan.

'I just cannot understand how he can consider passing up the biggest chance Patience has ever had for a better life,' she replied, dropping her arms onto her lap. 'She might be able to walk afterwards. She might be able to use her hands for something other than useless wringing. She might even be able to talk. *How can he not want this?*'

'How can *you* want to do this to Patience?' Pete was now looking straight at her. 'Put her through all this, when she's already been through so much? Why can't you just accept who she is and get on with things, as we've always done?'

'Perhaps you don't see it, Pete, as you're hardly around, but she's in pain a lot of the time. She's uncomfortable, she spends day after day just staring at walls and watching TV. She's not living. I want to give her a chance to *live*.'

Louise paused and took a sip of water, before taking a deep breath. 'And "we"? *We've always done?*' she continued. 'You've only been around about a quarter of the time at most. It's me who's been stuck at home holding the proverbial baby, washing her, feeding her, dressing her, nursing her when she's sick. And I've done it all because I love her. I'd do *anything* for her.'

'And I am working so that you can do that!'

Pete poured himself another cup of water from the jug on the table and sat back in his chair, sipping it, focusing on the cup and the floor and not Louise.

'That's interesting, Louise, what you said about being stuck,' interjected Nathan. 'That's very negative language.'

'Yes, because I *am* stuck. Completely. I was supposed to go back to work after Patience started school. That was always the plan. But I couldn't, could I? Someone had to be around. And so that person was me. And now I have nothing else. No career, no social life, and Jesus, I have only one friend. *One*. And I met *her* in a hospital.'

'Do you really think my world is so much better?' said Pete, coming back to life. 'I spend it out in the blazing sun and dust in whichever Gulf country I've managed to find a contract in, living out of a suitcase, coming home every evening to a crappy hotel room which looks just like all of the others. I live for those days when I get to come home. To you. And to Patience and Eliza. Every job I've ever done has been so that you could all live somewhere reasonable, so that you didn't have to work.'

'Reasonable? Good God, our house is falling apart, Pete. And it's in a dingy street near the bypass. It's hardly a palace.'

'If you wanted a palace, Lou, you shouldn't have married me!' The colour was rising in Pete's cheeks. 'You knew who I was, where I came from and what sort of life we'd have when you met me – and if I remember correctly, you said you didn't mind that I couldn't give you the life your father had. In fact, you said you were delighted that it wasn't going to be the life your father had given you. And you know that I was never going to be a middle-class Oxfordshire boy. I'm a working-class Birmingham lad. And proud.'

'Please get that chip off your shoulder,' Louise replied. 'It doesn't suit you.'

'I have a chip? Really? How about you look at yourself? Does it all come down to the fact that I'm not good enough for you, and so you're not going to pay any attention to how I feel about anything? When I think about all the work I've done to try to give you the life I thought you wanted – and now you're throwing it back in my face. I can't fucking believe it, to be honest.'

'Let's all calm down,' said Nathan. 'And try not to swear. It's not helpful.'

'Sorry,' said Pete. 'I got carried away.'

'Yep,' Louise replied, in a voice that sounded more like a sigh.

'Let's change tack,' said Nathan. 'And rewind right back to the beginning. How did you two meet, and what brought you together?'

There was a silence, during which Louise's mind was suddenly flooded with memories. Laughter over loud music; a hand brushing her hip; a smoky kiss.

'We were in a pub,' she replied. 'I was there with some of my friends and Pete was there with his. There was a band. We met on the dance floor.'

'What made you speak to each other?' asked Nathan.

'She smiled at me,' said Pete. 'It was a winning smile, you might say. I thought she was amazing.'

Louise tried not to meet his eye as he said that, so she looked down at the floor. She didn't want to smile, as that might make him think he'd changed her mind.

'That's physical attraction,' said Nathan. 'But we all know, those of us who've been married for decades, that being attracted to someone's personality is more long-lasting, so with that in mind, what was it that made you want to spend your lives together?'

Louise looked up and could see that Pete was wrestling with himself. If she was right, he was trying not to be rude to the counsellor, who he clearly felt was prying. Pete had always been a private person. But he remained silent, which surprised her.

'I thought he was funny,' she said, finally. 'And kind.'

Pete looked straight at her.

'I thought she was incredible,' he said, refusing to look away. 'I still do, to be honest. She's incredibly driven, a committed mother, a total powerhouse.'

Louise was dumbfounded. She had no idea how to respond. She wanted desperately to take his hand, but the environment they were in stopped her.

'But I *am* worried,' he went on, still holding her gaze, 'about you, Lou. I feel guilty that I've left you alone for so long. I can see now just how heavy a burden you've had to carry. I realise I've been too obsessed with providing, so I haven't been there, and I regret that. And the thing is, I'm worried that you're trying to cope now using – using alcohol.'

His words hit her like lightning.

'What I drink or not has nothing at all to do with—'

'It *does* have something to do with this, Lou, though, doesn't it? Patience is injured.'

Louise suddenly remembered the darkness, her feet giving way beneath her, a desperate plunge as she struggled to put her own body between Patience and the ground, a scream that hadn't even seemed like her own.

She set off like a rocket, getting up so quickly that she took both Pete and Nathan by surprise. She ran through the door and sprinted down the corridor, only stopping when she rounded a corner. There, she stood still opposite a fire exit, breathing huge gulps of air, taking in the white and green bar across the door, the patch of grass just behind it and the car park beyond; she contemplated pushing the bar and rushing out, fire alarm be damned.

'Louise?' Nathan must have tiptoed down the hall, as if he'd been stalking a rabbit. 'Would you like to come back in? I promise you'll get to put your side across. This is not about apportioning blame.'

'Sure,' Louise replied, 'it might do him good to hear some home truths.'

She took several more deep breaths and set off back down the corridor.

Pete looked relieved when she walked back in.

'OK, so now that we're back together – Louise, would you like to start up again?' said Nathan, walking the tightrope once again between consideration and condescension.

'I drink in the evening sometimes, to relax, to feel happy,' she replied, her body one big shrug. 'As I said, I don't get to go out, ever, so I drink at home instead. After a hard day caring for Patience, I need something to unwind. That evening, I'd only had a couple, but I suppose it was enough to send me off balance. I just lost my footing.'

'What about Christmas Day?' Pete asked. 'Did you drink that much just so that you could relax?'

'No. It was so I could feel *happy*,' replied Louise. 'Otherwise, I'd probably have cried.'

The room was silent for a few seconds, the only sound being the low hum of an air-conditioning unit.

'OK, let's change tack,' said Nathan, sensing that she'd said all she wanted to say on that subject, for now at least. 'What I'm hearing is that you are both angry about the life you feel you've had to lead. Would it be fair to say that you want someone to blame? Do you think you blame each other?'

'It seems like Lou is blaming me for making the decision to work abroad,' replied Pete. 'But it was a joint decision. I had to go.'

'Do you blame him, Louise?' Nathan asked.

Louise hesitated for a moment.

'No, I don't blame him for that, although I do wonder where his earnings are actually going,' she said. 'But I do blame him for not understanding how being at home all the time with Patience makes me feel. I don't think he thinks about how I am much, if at all. And I'm exhausted. Washed up. Old. Lonely.'

'Well, I feel lonely too,' replied Pete.

'And why is that, do you think?' Nathan asked.

Pete and Louise looked at each other for a moment.

'I think it's because we haven't been a functioning couple for quite a while,' Pete answered, maintaining eye contact.

Nathan turned to Louise.

'Do you agree?' he asked Louise.

'I suppose he's right,' she answered. 'But not in the way he's thinking. I imagine he's talking about sex. That's his main focus, I think.' Pete grimaced at her. 'No, don't look at me like that, Pete. You know I'm speaking the truth.'

'That's ridiculous,' he replied. 'Our marriage is worth a whole lot more to me than a sex life. If it wasn't, I'd have left years ago.'

'It seems we're getting to a crucial point here,' Nathan interrupted. 'Let's try to keep this conversation calm. I know this is an intensely personal subject.'

'OK,' said Louise, mentally brushing Nathan aside. 'Pete, what do you mean, you'd have left years ago? You seem to have checked out of our marriage already. When did you last sit with me and talk – properly talk? When did we last do something together that didn't involve a hospital or a supermarket?'

Pete looked despondent. Beaten.

'And now you're actively opposing me over the gene therapy, something we should be united about, because we are both Patience's parents, aren't we? Seriously, I just have no idea who you are any more. And if we *must* discuss our sex life, because I know Nathan's probably wondering about it now, well, yes, when is the last time we did it? It's like you switched that button off, a long time ago. You could be having an affair, for all I know. I wouldn't be surprised if you were, to be honest. It would be incredibly easy for you to do...'

Louise's sentence tailed off as she watched Pete grab his coat and march out of the room, not looking back.

'Oh dear,' Nathan said, a master of understatement. 'That topic obviously proved too much for him. We'll try to go back to that in a future session.'

Louise looked as though she had just woken up from a long slumber, her eyes alive, and energy coursing into her limbs.

She sprang up out of her seat. 'No, don't worry, I'll see myself out.'

21

Patience

February

There's a clear halo around my blackout blind, so it must be past seven, but I'm still in bed. This is not an ordinary state of affairs. In the normal way of things, I'd have had a pee on the toilet by now and Mum or one of the carers would be shoehorning me into leggings, soft socks and my uber-fashionable, medically prescribed Velcro-fastening chunky brown boots. If I have to wait any longer to go to the toilet, I'll have no choice but to pee in my pad. It's not a sensation I'm fond of. I've been toilet trained since I was a toddler, believe it or not; it's one of the 'normal' things about me. There aren't many, so I like to celebrate it.

Where is Mum, anyway? It's Saturday morning, so the carers won't come until later, but she usually sits me up and puts the TV on for me before they arrive, because my body clock wakes me up early every day of the week.

Ah, there's the doorbell. One of the caring staff has arrived at last. Mum will be embarrassed to be seen in her pyjamas, I expect.

There's the bell again. Still no Mum. Is she ill? Something

must have happened to her. Oh God, I hope she's OK. She's been strange since I got back home: absent, not talking to me much. I've been alone in my room a lot more than usual. There have been no impromptu disco parties in the kitchen this week, no sessions of us both watching *Pointless* on the TV, Mum shouting the answers at the screen, holding my hand and looking at me every time, as if to say, 'You agree, don't you? I'm right, aren't I?' She *is* usually right.

The phone is ringing now. They must have given up on the doorbell and decided to call instead. There's a handset upstairs in Mum's room, so she'll definitely hear it. If she's there, that is. It's stopped ringing now and I can hear a muffled voice, hers, I think, thank God, followed by uneven footsteps coming down the stairs. Is she hobbling?

It's her. She's still alive, then. But barely, by the look of things. Her hair is all fluffy, and it looks like a team of mice have been playing in amongst the strands all night, using sections of it as a ski jump. She's wearing a short cotton T-shirt nightie with a bear on the front, and it's stained with what might be coffee, or possibly it's juice? She's answering the door now, opening it a crack and peering outside with a squint, like a newborn witnessing its first sun.

'Lou! At last! I thought you'd died.' It's Serena, Mum's best friend. Why on earth is she here? She hasn't visited for ages.

'Serena? What on earth…?'

'I've come to look after you, my duck!' she replies, pushing the door open and, from what I can hear, forcing Mum into an embrace. I hear the wheels of a bag scraping over our threshold and trundling along our hall.

'What time is it?' Mum asks.

'It's 8 a.m., Lou.'

'Shit! I haven't got Patience up yet!' Mum rushes into my room, yanking the curtains apart and raising my blind with a turn of speed Usain Bolt would be proud of.

'Patience! It's Mummy! Good morning! I'm sorry, lovey, I'm a bit late today. But look who's come to see you! Auntie Serena is here.'

Serena slips into the room. Her glossy red hair – there's not a hint of grey, despite her age – is piled on top of her head, her make-up is precise, her nails primed and painted, and her green dangly earrings match her scarf and skirt. She is always well put together, ordered, sleek. She walks over to me and lands a kiss on my cheek. She smells of roses. 'Good morning, lovely girl,' she says, displaying not a hint of disgust at my morning breath. She's a pro.

'How did you manage to get here so early?' Mum springs into action with our usual morning routine as she talks, trying to persuade my legs to straighten before she rolls me over.

'I stayed overnight in a local hotel,' Serena replies. 'I decided it would be best not to disturb you last night.'

They exchange a strange look which, to be honest, seems a little hostile. This is unusual for them. Mum is at her most relaxed when Serena is around, her most happy.

'Has Pete been speaking to you?'

'No.'

'Oh, come on, who else was it?'

'I'm not saying,' replies Serena. 'But anyway, I'm here now. You need me, I hear. So here I am, like Mary Poppins, just more beautiful, obviously.'

Mum moves me into a sitting position, and asks Serena to help her attach the straps for the hoist.

'Hang on a sec, Lou – where are the carers this morning?'

'I told them not to come,' says Mum. This is news to me.

'Why on earth did you do that?'

'Patience and I don't need them at the weekends,' she says, avoiding Serena's gaze.

'But Pete has left,' Serena says, with emphasis.

'Who told you that? Him?' Mum is opening the straps and pulling them even more tightly. 'Yes, he's buggered off, but you know, situation normal.'

'There's nothing normal about this, Lou. And of course you need them at weekends. You need them all the time.'

'If I've learned anything in this life, it's that the only person I can trust is myself. And I don't need to hear them gossiping about me. They have no respect for me at all. So a couple of days without them is fine.'

She smiles down at me as she says this, the words coming out through gritted teeth. The hoist is currently lifting me across the room towards the toilet, as if Hermione Granger has cast a levitation spell. Serena follows our strange procession and, as I land on my porcelain throne, she asks a question I've been dying to ask myself.

'Where *is* Pete?'

'He didn't tell you? He's staying with his brother in Birmingham, apparently. All right for some. He's picked up some temporary work there, I think. I don't know when he's going back to Qatar, he hasn't said. We have the Best Interests meeting next week, so I suppose he's waiting for that.'

I do wish I'd been invited to this meeting, too. So far I've just heard that I'm going to be experimented on – both in snippets of overheard conversations, and from Eliza when she came to ask me about it, bless her – but no real details. I have no idea what they are planning, to be honest. What *is* gene therapy? Answers on a postcard, kids.

'Are you talking at all?'

As I let out a steady stream of urine, relief floods through me and I let out an involuntary shiver.

'Can you pass her dressing gown, Serena? I think she's cold.'

'Sure.'

'And no, we're not talking. We tried. We had a counselling session. It was a train wreck. He's a pig-headed, tight arsehole.'

'Should you be saying this sort of thing in front of Patience?'

'One of the things I am forever grateful for is that she has no idea at all about the messes adults make of their lives,' says Mum.

I mean, how wrong can you be?

She's pulled up my pyjamas, and now the hoist rises again and I'm transferred into my wheelchair. This routine is one Mum knows off by heart, but even so, she seems to be zipping through it today, every detail done in double time, every muscle in her body working at full pelt. She turns her back to me and I can see her shoulders are up. She should try to stop doing that. It gives her tension headaches.

'Why a pig-headed, tight arsehole?'

Mum takes hold of the chair and begins to steer me in the direction of the kitchen.

'Are you taking the piss?'

'No. I know you've always had your moments, but he's always seemed like a committed dad and husband to me.'

'Then I obviously have some filling-in to do,' Mum replies, stopping my chair abruptly and parking me by the kitchen table. 'Shall I start with the cheating, his financial lies, or his absolute refusal to back me over Patience's gene therapy trial?' The kettle clicks on, and some mugs are removed from a cupboard. 'Thank heavens for Eliza, though, and her common sense. Her views will carry weight at the meeting.'

'Infidelity?' asks Serena, her face startled.

Here we go.

'Yes. He hasn't owned up to it, of course, but he reacted oddly in front of our counsellor and the penny dropped. Suddenly I realise why he's been so absent for so long. And where the money must be going. He's seeing another woman. He must be.'

'Are you certain, though? He hasn't owned up to anything, has he?'

'I don't need to be certain. I know my husband. He's been hiding something for a long time. And his desire to work overseas, to be away for long periods, to avoid dealing with what needs to be dealt with here? It all adds up.' I hear the fridge door open and milk being poured into mugs.

'You are putting two and two together and getting five.'

'I'm not. I tell you, he's been sleeping with someone else.'

There's a telltale clink of crockery as Mum lifts a bowl out of a cupboard and pours Weetabix into it. Damn it, there are some Coco Pops in there, and I really fancy some. But no, they have to give me sensible, fibrous breakfasts, don't they? Bugger.

'Don't you think you should talk to him about this, to make sure you're not imagining it?' I can just make out Serena, to my right. She has both hands braced behind her on the kitchen counter and she's clenching and unclenching her grip.

'That's a lovely idea,' says Mum, sounding like it would be nothing like lovely, at all. 'But we'd have to be talking for that to happen.'

'But isn't the big meeting next week?'

'Yes, if he turns up. He'll probably bring a lawyer, knowing him. He pretty much suggested that I was an unfit mother, the last time we saw each other.' Mum plonks the bowl down in front of me and comes back into my line of vision.

'Lou... I wanted to ask. About the trial. I saw the article, about the guy who's leading it.'

'Did you indeed. Send that to you, did he? It's all rubbish. There's nothing in it.'

Mum sits down to my left and Serena takes a seat opposite her, to my right, bringing two mugs of coffee with her.

'Look, did he send you here to try to talk me out of it? That's pretty low.' Mum puts a plastic bib – a bigger version of the kind they use for babies – around my neck, and dips a large, flat plastic spoon into the bowl. 'He tried it on with Eliza, too. But I think she's on my side, still. So it should get passed at the meeting. It must.'

When I move my gaze away from the spoon to Mum's face, I see that she is starting to cry. Serena opens her arms and Mum collapses into them.

*

We are at the pub. Mum started bringing me here when I was eighteen, I think as a sort of gesture of defiance, as if she was facing off with Rett syndrome, saying, 'Look, this is one thing you haven't stopped her doing.'

When I first started coming, I got lots of stares, but the locals are used to me by now and I barely warrant a pause in an engrossing game of cribbage these days. It smells of old beer in here, and chip fat. The carpet, a festival of colour from circa 1970, is dimpled with cigarette burns and decorated with old food stains, which makes me feel a lot better, because I'm a messy eater. Also, they make a very nice home-made lasagne which mushes up just enough for me to eat it safely.

Serena is treating us to lunch. She announced this after she inspected the fridge this morning. Mum hasn't been too good with food shopping since Christmas. Come to think of it, I'm not sure I've seen her eating much lately, either.

Mum still has red eyes, but she's stopped crying now. After breakfast they wheeled me back into my room and put my TV on so loudly I couldn't make out what they were saying in the other room. There were raised voices, and there was definitely sobbing, along with occasional bursts of laughter. Their particular dynamic is something I will never understand. I do know, however, that their bond is deep, and that it has a lot to do with me and Patrick. Poor Patrick. He used to make me laugh. He was quite good-looking, too.

'I've bought you a Diet Coke,' Serena announces to Mum, before putting a pint glass filled to the brim with soft drink firmly on the table, and a small orange juice on the side for me. Then there is a silence between them which goes on for slightly too long.

'I'm not an alcoholic, Serena,' Mum says, in a tone just a shade harsher than a whisper.

'Okaaayyyyyy,' Serena draws that word out, her beautifully shaped eyebrows arching further as she does so. Then she lifts up her glass – is that sparkling water or gin and tonic? I can't tell.

'*I'm not!*' says Mum, getting louder now. 'And I know that addicts say that a lot, but I'm not. I'm just using it to get me through. Things have been impossible lately.'

Serena is pursing her lips and rolling her tongue around her mouth. 'Eliza told me that you were off your tits on Christmas Day.'

She says this deadpan.

'So that's who you've been talking to.' Mum exhales. 'And keep your voice down. I don't want anyone hearing.' She is now speaking in a very loud whisper, which is probably more audible than her normal voice.

'It's deserted in here,' says Serena, referring to the only other humans in the pub with us – two men over the age of seventy who are probably at least partially deaf anyway.

'Never mind. I don't want anyone around here getting more ideas. It's a small town and they are already gossiping enough.'

'Not about you drinking, surely?' Serena takes another swig from her drink.

'Shhhhhhhhh!' says Mum.

'*Sorry,*' Serena is now whispering comically. It must be the gin. 'Do you mean about Patience's accident?'

'Yes. Someone in the local shop asked me how she was recovering the other day. I hadn't told anyone she was injured, so someone has blabbed. Probably one of the carers.'

'They're probably just worried about her.'

'Hmm,' says Mum, pretending to examine the menu I know she memorised years ago, for several minutes.

'But, you know, to be honest,' she says eventually, very quietly, 'I think I'm *not* coping very well.'

'Oh, Lou,' Serena says. 'I can see that, my lovely.' She reaches across the table and rubs Mum's arm. 'I think you are in a sort of emotional storm. There's too much going on, isn't there? Sometimes it's hard to see out. But I'm here now. I'm going to help you get through it.'

'Thank you,' Mum says, softening visibly, before adding, in a whisper, '*I think I need it.*'

They smile at each other. They're not huge grins, not by any means, but I think they are smiles that old friends give each other when something is tacitly understood.

'Let's change the subject to nicer things, shall we?' says Mum. 'How much have I told you about my new job? And about the trial?'

'Not much. Your new job sounds exciting! Are you enjoying it?'

'Oh, yes,' says Mum. 'I love it. I mean, I've had a bit of time off sick since – since Patience's fall, but they are a great team. I feel so useful. And it's so wonderful to be paid for the work you do, you know?'

'That's wonderful,' says Serena. 'And I do know! If only carers were paid what they were worth, eh? We'd be millionaires.'

Mum laughs. 'Yep,' she says. 'And money of course helps make ends meet, so that's another weight off my mind.'

Serena doesn't reply to this, because I can see that she's thinking about something else.

'It's great about the job, Lou. But this trial. It sounds a bit scary.'

'Don't tell me he's got to you too.'

Mum snatches a napkin from the table and lifts the glass of juice up to my mouth with some speed.

'Who?'

'Pete, of course. He read that stupid article and now he's convinced that Philip is the devil incarnate. Shit!'

Ouch, Mum, that was my teeth. And yes, that was a clean dress.

I have most of a glass of orange juice in my lap. Mum is now mopping me up frantically, borrowing napkins from nearby tables.

'No. I make up my own mind, Lou, you should know that by now.'

'That may be,' she replies, still intent on soaking up liquid 'but you're wrong on this one. I work for the man. I know the truth.'

'Are you absolutely sure that it's not just a truth you want to hear?'

Mum stops mopping me up and glares at Serena. Oh crikey. Mum hates being challenged.

'After all of these years, and all of the things we've been through together, you really have to ask me that?'

I swivel my eyes left to right, taking in the fierce looks on both of their faces. I wouldn't fancy my chances against either of them in a dark alley. While they assess each other, I can only hear the insistent tick of the aged clock above the inglenook fireplace, the chink of false teeth onto pint glasses at the bar, and the crackle and pop of the carbonated bubbles breaking the surface in Mum's glass.

'Lou, I love you,' Serena says finally, breaking the silence. 'You know that. I'm just worried for you. For you all.'

'Well, you needn't be,' Mum snaps. 'We're fine. Patience and I are fine. This is Patience's big chance to live a full and happy life.'

Serena gets up so that she can go to place our order, and diffusing the tension as she does so, saying, 'It just sounds extraordinary...' She tails off, her tone of voice shifting down several gears.

'Serena...' Mum says, but Serena is already at the bar. When she returns a few minutes later, Mum looks chastened. 'I'm sorry,' she says, and she seems to mean it. 'I should have thought.'

'It's OK, Lou. I'd be the same in your place.' They both take sips from their drinks, and then Mum leans over and gives me some chocolate concrete from a plastic beaker she's brought with her. There is no orange juice left.

'Do you ever think about how it would have been, for both of us, if they hadn't been disabled?'

That's what that was about. It was about Patrick. There were no miracle cures for him, poor guy.

Serena is looking past my shoulder to the window, and beyond into the beer garden. I know from past experience that there are often children playing out there, their mothers sitting on the picnic benches sipping from cups of takeaway coffee which the entrepreneurial publican started selling a few years ago.

'Yes. I do. Although I don't think it's particularly helpful, is it?'

'Not helpful, no. But unavoidable.'

Serena moves her gaze from the garden back into the

room. 'We'd both have had successful careers, wouldn't we? And I might still be married. And we'd probably both be on the road towards having grandchildren now. Although, of course, *you* still are. How's Eliza doing? Wedding planning coming on?'

'Honestly, I don't know,' Mum replies. 'She's dealing with it. You know how she is: fiercely independent. Our savings have paid for the deposit on the reception venue – that stately home we used to visit a lot – and the dress. That was a nice bit, the shopping, the looking at venues. It was lovely spending that time together, just her and me. But she and Ed have got the rest covered. I am pleased they're finally getting married; Eliza's wanted it for a long time.'

'Has he improved at all? Ed? With age?'

'Not much,' replies Mum, wrinkling her nose, 'but there's no way we could tell her what we really think about him, is there? If we'd said that we think he's a control freak, that he's selfish – she'd probably have married him sooner, just to try to prove us wrong. We all need to make our own mistakes. She wouldn't thank me. And anyway, I obviously made a mess of my own choice, didn't I. So what do I know?'

'If you say so, Lou,' replies Serena, scowling at Mum.

My lasagne arrives, steaming hot and looks delicious, but Mum asks the barman to bring a cold plate and sets about decanting it and cutting it up so it doesn't burn my mouth. I am so hungry. I wish I didn't always have to wait.

'Anyhow, so that's the wedding, but this gene therapy trial is going to happen before that, hopefully. It's been given the go-ahead by the authorities and they've selected all of the participants now. We are very lucky that Patience is one of them.'

'And that's because you're working for them?'

'Partly, yes. But it's also because Patience is the right age for it – they don't want to start this trial with children.'

'Is that because it's so risky?'

Mum decides this is the moment to start spooning my lunch into my mouth. It's still slightly too hot.

'It has risks, yes,' she replies. 'But it's nothing to do with those allegations about Professor Larssen's previous trial, you know. And all trials have risks. This one has a few they are looking out for.'

'Like what?' Serena asks this with a light tone, but her eyes are locked on Mum as she says it.

'Well, probably the biggest is that there's a risk that if they do fix the gene fault and things start happening, the expanding brain won't fit...'

Oh bloody hell.

'... but this is just the first phase of the trial, so they will go in gently, only give a low dose. And anyway, there is surgery they can do to help.'

I splutter in shock. Mum assumes I'm choking and starts to rub my back.

'That's quite a worry,' Serena says. I can tell she's trying to tread carefully. 'But you still think it's worth it? With all those risks?' Serena is now tucking into her lunch, a Ploughman's, which is pretty much the only vaguely healthy thing on the pub menu. Mum still hasn't had a mouthful of hers. She's too busy feeding me.

'Wouldn't you do anything you could to have Patrick back, living a normal life?'

'Of course I would.' Serena is now pretending to be fascinated by her food.

'There you go. This is my chance to give Patience the life she should have had, if that bloody awful gene hadn't gone haywire, wreaking havoc, destroying her brain and her body.'

'At least her disability isn't your fault.' Serena has put her knife and fork down and I think there are signs of tears. She hardly ever cries.

Poor Serena, she had no idea she was carrying the Duchenne gene.

'I gave it to him. I didn't know it but I gave my beautiful boy, the love of my life, a disease that killed him before he reached thirty.' Serena was now drinking slowly, looking somewhere over my shoulder, out of focus.

'You mustn't think like that. Before we knew Rett syndrome was just a random fault, I used to think that it was something I'd carried without knowing it and passed on. Or I thought, maybe it was something I'd had to drink or eat when I was pregnant. I wasted those early years blaming myself, and I bloody wish I hadn't.'

I've never heard Mum say this before. I had no idea she ever blamed herself for the way I am. *Oh, Mum.*

'It truly is amazing, what doctors reckon they can do to help, now,' Serena says. 'It's as though they're offering parents like us a chance to make amends.'

'But it's *Not. Our. Fault.*'

'No, OK. But they are giving you a chance to change the future, aren't they?'

'Yes.'

'In which case I'll be here for you, Lou. For you and Patience.'

From the sound of things, I think we're going to need all the support we can get.

22

Pete

February

Traffic had ground to a halt on the M5 southbound carriageway and the windscreen of Pete's hire car was becoming obscured by insistent snowflakes, each one larger, colder, firmer than the last. He had turned the wipers off because he'd been stationary for a few minutes now – there must be an accident ahead – and it was becoming harder to make out the lines between the lanes.

He was going to be late. He reached for his mobile phone and sent a quick text to Lou to let her know. She'd be delighted, probably. If he didn't manage to make it to the Best Interests meeting, who else was going to argue from Patience's side? He still wasn't sure what Eliza's decision was; she had refused to share it. But what he did know was that all that stood between Patience and the lumbar puncture needle was this meeting and the panel that would vote on her fate.

He also wasn't sure of the points of view of the other participants of the meeting – her lead carer, her GP, her social worker – but he knew that Louise was a powerful speaker, a force to be reckoned with. Pete had always felt glad of this in the past; that aspect of looking after his daughter was not his forte. Now, however, he vehemently wished that it was.

Best Interests meetings were strange affairs. It seemed ridiculous to him that being Patience's parent simply wasn't enough in the eyes of the law. Once she'd turned eighteen they'd been forced to make big decisions about her care by committee, because she wasn't able to make decisions for herself. To him, Patience was an eternal child, and so this insistence on consulting with professionals seemed ludicrous to him, an appalling imposition on his parental rights.

It was 9.37 a.m. Just over forty minutes to go before the meeting was scheduled to start. The car in front edged forward a few metres, so Pete put the car into gear and set off once more. Although he was maintaining a gentle pressure on the accelerator, his other foot was pushing hard against the floor, as if its impotent manoeuvres could force the traffic to part. If he missed this meeting, his Patience – his beautiful, innocent Patience – was done for.

Every night throughout her younger years, he'd performed a ritual. He would pick her up, fresh from a bath, towel rub and nappy change, cradling her in his arms like a newborn, and place her in bed. Sometimes, after he'd pulled the duvet up under her chin, he would kiss her, stroke her sleek blonde hair and then kneel there, as if in prayer, although he had no faith to speak of. When she had fallen asleep, her face would relax, released at last from the pain she seemed to be experiencing daily, from the horror of whatever was going on in her brain. She had looked angelic, lying there like that. Normal, even.

In the early years, he had hoped desperately that she might wake up cured, that everything that had gone before might be consigned to a passing nightmare. It had taken him years to give up that hope. The process had been a kind of mourning; he had gradually, painfully learned to relinquish all desire for her to be different, learned to accept her as she was.

To help him get over his grief for a daughter he would never have, he had examined her closely, questioning every look and every movement, and had come to believe that she was happy – content, even. She had passed through hell and come out the other side, and the life she had been left with, although it was far from the life he had hoped for, was a good one. For a start, music gave her obvious joy. And when he hugged her at bedtime now, she seemed to radiate calm. He believed she had found peace. And that, absolutely, was worth fighting for, he thought.

The pace of the traffic was picking up and Pete could just make out the exit sign for his junction through the snow flurries. He indicated left and slid sideways into the nearside lane, driving up the exit to the roundabout at a crawl. It was 10.07 a.m. and he was just a couple of miles away now; he might just make it, but it depended on how the roads were from here. These were residential streets, and both sides of the road were lined with schoolchildren making the most of a snow day, building snow-men, snow-women and snow-dogs with wet mittens, wearing oversized hats and with the promise of hot chocolate before lunch.

Now 10.18. A bus was resting, as if spreadeagled, across the road ahead. Only a tiny trickle of traffic was squeezing past it in single file, the overwhelmed driver standing by its bonnet trying to direct the traffic while speaking frantically into his phone, presumably summoning help. When he went back to his cab for a moment, traffic coming from the opposite direction surged forward into the gap and streamed through it, not giving any quarter to the opposing vehicles. Pete sighed loudly, pulled his car up onto the ice-encrusted pavement, and switched off the engine. He would have to walk from here. He retrieved a pair of thick gloves and his padded, down-filled coat from the back of the car and set off, pulling up his hood as he went.

How far was it from here? Perhaps half a mile, give or take. As he marched on, he looked upwards at the millions of flakes falling from the heavens. Each single one unique, each one following its own path, buffeted by the winds, onto the ground below. And each one set for extinction when the earth warmed. He stuck out his tongue and let one fall onto it, feeling it begin to melt on contact. It tasted a little like the sea.

He was almost there, but he'd need to run now if he wasn't going to miss the first fifteen minutes. His shoes, solid black lace-ups selected for smartness, were not made for jogging through snow. The left one had begun to leak, freezing cold water seeping into his sock. He tried to keep up a steady pace, drawing on the hours he'd spent in the gym in an endless parade of hotels, filling his evenings and sleepless nights with some purpose.

He checked his watch again – 10.33. The meeting had started now, but he could just make out the sign announcing Patience's respite care home ahead. He put on a further surge of speed, willing his feet not to slip and his legs to find the power to keep moving. Always an active man, his joints had begun to feel rusty lately, like an outdoor tap left unattended during the winter. He knew that he could no longer rely on his physical strength, an attribute which had been his calling card for decades. But this recession into old age didn't worry him as much as the fact that he didn't really have other strengths to draw on.

It was 10.40 when he rang the doorbell, trying to breathe deeply so that he could recover faster. He swallowed to try to subdue an irritation in his windpipe, the cold that had eaten into his lungs making him cough.

'Mr Willow! Good morning. We were wondering whether you'd make it.'

It was Beth. She was young, fizzy, joyful and he liked her. If she was coming to the meeting, he was glad.

'Yes, the snow,' he said, stomping his feet to shake it off his shoes.

'Yep, we're short-staffed this morning, several of the carers haven't made it in. So I've got to look after the residents with Lutsi, I'm afraid, but Maggie, the manager, is there.'

This was not good news. Pete did not like Maggie. When he'd first met her, they'd eyeballed each other and known instinctively where they both stood. She was also a Birmingham girl, judging by her accent and turn of phrase, and had probably grown up a few streets away from him, although he had never asked. But instead of this fostering understanding, their similar childhoods had made them suspicious of each other; two individuals who'd successfully escaped the estate, each afraid the other would unsettle the balance they'd fought hard to introduce into their separate lives. She didn't like him; he was sure of it.

Beth ushered him into the small office which doubled as a meeting room when necessary. The room was overheated and smelt of dust, disinfectant and coffee. A round table had been shoehorned into the rectangular space, which also accommodated a desk, two large filing cabinets and an assortment of mismatched chairs. Sitting in five of them were Lou, Eliza, Patience's GP Dr Aitken, care home manager Maggie and Patience's social worker, David, each cradling a mug of coffee. Pete took the last chair, which was wedged against a radiator.

'I'm sorry I'm late,' he said, sitting down. 'The weather made my journey very tricky.'

'That's OK,' said Dr Aitken, a wiry-haired woman in her fifties who combined an air of efficiency with maternal warmth. 'It's awful out there. Well done for making it. It looks like it was hard work.' Pete was sweating and, as he peeled off his layers, he realised his shirt was stuck to his back. 'Anyhow, as we're all here now, let's get started. I'm going to chair this meeting. Any objections?'

Everyone shook their heads.

'Great. Let's begin with a summary of the situation at hand. Patience Willow has been offered a place on phase one of a trial of a new gene therapy approach. This trial is promising the possibility of life-changing results. I say possibility, because as it's experimental, by the very nature of the beast it will be hit and miss. I've read the submission that the trial team put into the Medical Research Council, and I've provided copies here for reference – I'm assuming you've all read it?'

The doctor looked around and everyone nodded.

'Fine. Well, in summary, this is what the trial consists

of: Patience will need to be an in-patient in Birmingham City Hospital for at least three days. The therapy will be administered through lumbar puncture and she will need to be monitored for some time afterwards. Extra nursing staff will be sent to wherever she is after she's discharged so that they can keep an eye on her condition.'

The doctor took a large sip from her coffee. 'So the hows and wheres are taken care of. The whys – Professor Larssen, who leads the trial team, says in the proposal that his new therapeutic approach could potentially reverse Rett syndrome—'

'I want to stop you there,' said Pete. Dr Aitken looked affronted by his interruption, but he ignored her. 'We can't have this meeting without talking about Professor Larssen's past. You'll all have read the article in the paper a few weeks ago. His credibility is in tatters. There are serious questions being raised—'

'There aren't any being raised about *this* trial, Pete,' Louise said harshly, sounding like a primary school teacher chastising a child.

'If I may?' said Dr Aitken, 'I anticipated this would come up, so I took it upon myself to look up the last trial, to try to establish the facts. There are very few similarities between the two trials and, as we've seen, the relevant permissions for this one have been granted after a full and thorough evaluation. This trial has completely different backers and a completely different method. I believe that we should judge it on its own merits. Any thoughts?'

The doctor's piercing gaze did not invite the comment she had apparently asked for. Pete found that he could think of no suitable response.

The doctor cleared her throat, satisfied. 'So, to continue. In his assessment of the benefits of the new therapy, Professor Larssen talks of regaining the ability to speak, the ability to breathe normally, the use of hands, legs, feet. These are amazing possibilities. But he also talks of risks, and that's what we're here to discuss. Among these are depression, confusion, raised intracranial pressure – that's pressure building within the brain – and seizures, a particular concern given Patience's recent episode. Who would like to go first?'

'I will,' said Louise, leaning forward in her chair, her notes clutched in her hands.

'Go ahead, Mrs Willow.'

'You all know, I think, that I'm the driving force behind this. I'm working as part of the trial team at the university and they have accepted Patience onto the trial. She's incredibly lucky to get a place; two out of three families who applied were rejected. Sometimes that was because their son or daughter was too young, or too unwell, but often it was just sheer weight of numbers. The trial has been very oversubscribed because of what it might be able to achieve.'

Louise was gathering pace now. Pete knew that she would have rehearsed what she had to say until she was word perfect.

'Every check and consideration has been made in designing this trial so that it's as safe as possible. It's taking place in one of the best hospitals in the UK, with skilled surgeons and an amazing ITU. The charities that are supporting it have provided funding for vein viewers so that researchers will find it easier to locate their typically tiny veins for blood draws; they've also given us funding to cover hotel stays and transport costs. The trial team have also promised that any additional medical needs created as a result of the trial will be paid for by them, with every urgency. They are funding nurses to provide extra care for at least a month after the trial at the homes of all of the participants. In conclusion, I believe that we should not let this opportunity for Patience pass us by. This could change her life. She could be one of the first Rett people in the world to live free of the disease. Personally, I think that's worth the risks.'

Louise glanced around her, checking that her words had had the desired effect. Maggie was certainly looking impressed. She was generally on her side anyway, though, thought Pete. David had been taking notes throughout and he was now looking at them thoughtfully. He was harder to read.

'Who'd like to go next?'

'I'll do it,' said Maggie, taking a deep breath and sucking in her ample stomach before she went on. 'I don't have much to add to that,' she said, smiling at Louise, 'but for what it's worth, we think that this is an amazing chance for Patience. We did have concerns about the need for extra care after her hospital discharge, but this has been resolved with the pledge of funding by the trial team. Louise and I have discussed things and we're happy to offer Patience a bed here after she's discharged so that she can be monitored twenty-four hours a day.'

Pete looked across the table and saw David scribbling away. He'll like that, he thought. He'll like the idea of her staying outside the home – he'd been trying to persuade them to institutionalise her for years. And of course Maggie would love this trial. If Professor Larssen's Magic Medicine manages to cure Rett syndrome, the cash-strapped social care system will have a load taken off it. What's not to like?

'Thank you,' said Dr Aitken. 'Now, Pete?'

Pete reached into his back pocket and pulled out a folded A4 sheet upon which he'd written some headlines last night.

Fear

Life

Death

Future?

'I don't know if you lot notice, but when Patience is in a strange place, her face seizes up,' he began. 'I think she's frightened. I think anything new frightens the life out of her. I'm worried that the hospital, all the new folk around her, the strange noises, will distress her. Secondly, she has a great life already. It's not the life I wanted for her, of course, but she has a nice place to live, she loves music, she loves food, she has a loving family and she's not in pain most of the time. I believe her quality of life is good. Thirdly, you have all skirted past this, but one of those side effects listed in that document is death. I know it's far down and that means it's less likely, but it's still a chance. And I don't think anything is worth that. She has been through so much, so many operations and had so many close shaves to get this far, and I really don't think we should jeopardise her life, which we've fought hard for, for these promises which, frankly, sound like the good professor has plucked them out of thin air.'

He paused to take a sip from his coffee, which was now going cold. He put it back down and stared into it as he spoke. 'And the last point I have here is the future. I don't want to condemn Patience to a life of misery and pain. She's already had a seizure this year, just the one, but still – what if the gene therapy damages her brain and makes it worse?' Pete moved his gaze from the table to his wife, who was glaring at him. 'Don't look at me like that, Lou,' he said. 'I know what you're thinking – you reckon she has that right now – but that's where we differ. I think she's happy now. I think she's content. And I think this trial has much more to do with you and your wishes than it does with her.'

There was silence for a few seconds, during which, if he'd been sitting closer, Pete reckoned there was a good chance Lou would have taken a swipe at him.

'OK, thanks for that, Pete,' said Dr Aitken. She looked across to the other side of the table.

'Eliza? As Patience's consultee, you are acting on your sister's behalf in this meeting. Could you tell us whether you have decided to give your approval for the trial?'

Eliza cleared her throat and Pete took a deep breath. He had no idea what she was about to say, but whatever it was, it would have a profound effect on Patience, who was at that very moment sitting next door watching a DVD, absolutely oblivious to the fact that her future was being decided in this room.

'Aside from all of the things Mum has said, I want to say that I am a bit worried about that article, too,' Eliza began. 'I understand why Dad is so concerned. I really do. This is a huge thing, a frightening thing, to decide upon.' Pete gave her a grateful smile. 'I feel – I feel... I don't know how to say this...' She took a deep breath. 'I feel like Patience and I have a connection. We have grown up with each other, obviously. And I've spent a great deal of time talking to her, monitoring how she responds. I know there is some disagreement on this,' Eliza avoided her father's gaze, 'but I personally feel that she understands when we speak to her. And so I went to see her, to ask her what she wanted me to do.' The whole room, Pete included, looked at Eliza, hanging on her every word. 'And, well, instinctively I feel that she wants this. That she wants her chance. She as good as told me to do it, the other day. She cried.' All of the other attendees were silent, their attention rapt. 'That's it,' she said, her eyes cast down. 'That's all I wanted to say.'

Pete could see that Louise was smiling at Eliza.

'So you will be voting in favour of the trial, then?' the doctor asked Eliza.

'Yes, I will,' she replied, before looking across at Pete. 'But Dad, it was so difficult. I genuinely wasn't sure, until I saw Patience.'

Pete saw Louise's triumphant smile flicker.

'I know, pet,' he replied, his heart sinking.

'David – do you have anything to add?' asked Dr Aitken, after a pause.

The social worker shuffled his papers and looked up.

'I've read this document extensively and conducted my own research. I'm happy with the way it's presented, and I can see its obvious benefits. But Mr Willow's point about the risks is very concerning. Have we brushed them aside too easily? I'd be interested to know what you really think, Dr Aitken.'

'So it comes back to me,' she said, straightening her glasses on her nose. 'I have known Patience for a long time. She's a lovely lady, very smiley, seemingly very content. I do agree with Mr Willow that her current state is not a concern. She is fine presently. But I am also aware that she is deteriorating; her muscles are getting tighter every time I see her, her lungs are more and more prone to infections, and her breathing worries me. I feel that the trial would be worth the risk if it offers her relief in just one of these areas. So, for that reason, I am in support.'

She looked around at the five other people sitting at the table, all anxious to escape the room and its dense, constraining atmosphere.

'Shall we take a vote?'

23

Eliza

March

The waiting room was really trying hard not to *be* a waiting room. Its walls were a fashionable shade of grey, decorated with framed pictures of coastal views and wildflowers; there were scatter cushions on the unyielding plastic seats; and someone had put all of the healthcare information leaflets in a floral cardboard box. A digital radio was plugged in in the corner of the room, currently tuned into Classic FM. But all of the music, soft furnishings and Cath Kidston prints in the world couldn't disguise what this room was for.

It was full of women of assorted ages, all inspecting their fingernails, their social media profiles or the contents of their handbags. There were only two men here. Eliza judged them to be partners, not fathers; they were both young, and they looked petrified. Which was ridiculous, she thought. This was not their battle, not their dilemma, not their body.

'Elizabeth?'

Eliza reached under the chair for her bag, stood up and followed the nurse who'd called her name down a small corridor with four rooms going off either side. She clenched and unclenched her fists, trying to release the tension that had been building in them since she'd arrived. She realised that her palms were sweaty.

'We're in here,' the nurse said, in a lilting Scottish accent. She gestured to one of them, showing Eliza that she could enter and take a seat. The decorating fairies had also been at work in this room; it was painted lilac and there were at least two separate vases of good-quality fake flowers on display. The curtains, which were thin, unlined and made of a Laura Ashley floral material, reminded her of Patience's childhood bedroom. The sight of them startled her.

'Are you OK?' the nurse asked, responding to Eliza's facial expression. 'I know that this is a tough time for you, but we can speak freely here. You can tell me how you're feeling, and I promise I will never judge you.'

'I don't know how I'm feeling.'

She could feel her heart racing; her throat had suddenly gone dry.

'That's understandable. Lots of people feel like that.' The nurse paused. 'Would you like a glass of water?'

'Sure.' Eliza watched as she walked over to a water cooler in the corner of the room and came back with two plastic cups full to the brim. 'Thanks,' she said, meaning it.

'Would you like us to do a test to confirm the pregnancy?' the nurse asked, once she'd sat down.

'No. It's fine. I've done at least three.' Eliza found herself smiling at this, despite everything.

'Ach, OK. How about testing for STDs? Do you think you'd like that?'

'Oh God, I don't know. Probably. I have no idea what he's been up to. Yes please.' The nurse appeared completely unshocked by this statement. She must hear some stories, thought Eliza.

'When I say I don't know how I'm feeling, by the way, that's a lie,' Eliza added, sitting back in her chair and crossing her legs. 'I feel lots of things. Trapped. Unloved. Lonely. Abandoned.' She wasn't usually given to emotional outbursts, and the fact that she'd just shared that with the nurse made her feel even more uncomfortable. She was not herself at the moment and it was unnerving. She was not in control.

'Oh, sweetheart, that's a common feeling at this stage,' the nurse replied. 'It's such a scary time. Can I ask – have you at this point decided whether you want to continue or terminate your pregnancy?'

'That's what I meant. I don't know how I feel about it. But I do know I have to get rid of it.'

'You don't have to do anything. Would you like to speak to a counsellor before you make a decision? We have one available here.'

'I *do* have to do it. I have no one to support me. My ex certainly won't. And counselling won't change that.' Eliza was playing with her watch strap, opening and shutting the clasp as she spoke.

'There's lots of other support you can access.'

'I can't do it alone. I live miles from my family – and there's my disabled sister to look after. Mum doesn't have the capacity to care for me, too.'

The nurse reached for a folder on the table in front of her and brought out some leaflets.

'I want you to take a look at these brochures, sweetheart, and decide what you want to do,' she said.

Eliza was wringing her hands, refusing to look up. She didn't take the brochures.

'And what if my baby is disabled, too?' she asked, still looking down. 'How on earth will I manage then?'

'Is it hereditary, what your sister has?' the nurse asked.

'Not usually. And I've had genetic screening, anyway,' Eliza replied. 'I don't have it. But what if the baby has something else? There's so much that can go wrong.'

'The chances are that the baby will be fine,' the nurse replied. 'And even if it does have issues – there's so much that can be done now. Lots of support.'

Eliza looked up at her. 'Not enough,' she replied.

The nurse gave her a sympathetic smile. 'I can imagine,' she said. 'Look, if you decide that you want to terminate the pregnancy, you can call this number to make an appointment,' she circled a number on one of the forms, 'and then we'll go from there.'

As Eliza walked back down the corridor, clutching the brochures, she thought, not for the first time that day, about the other abortion clinic she'd been unable to avoid.

The roses her mum had brought her were red. As the sun came up through the ward windows, the petals were caught in its rays, projecting blotches of red onto the walls that looked like blood. She was the only girl on the ward with flowers, but other than that, they were all in it together, all guilty of the same sin. Fruit, ripening too early.

Michael had sat next to her in Maths. Well, more correctly, he'd been placed next to her, as Mr Wilson had a thing about controlling seating arrangements. Up close,

Michael (he was never, ever Mike) was intoxicating. He was tall, just over six foot, had deep brown hair which fell down over his face, and eyelashes that framed his eyes, which were little whirlpools of blue.

When they'd met later that day beside the science block, away from the prying eyes of both teachers and other students, he'd asked her if she'd like to meet up with him out of school. In a burst of unguarded glee, she had agreed immediately.

And so, in an Oxfordshire playing field as darkness approached, he had taken her hand and led her behind a tree, into an even darker corner by a hedge. Without preamble, he had lunged at her, her lower lip disappearing into his mouth like quicksand. There was frantic fumbling with buttons and zips, fingers ricocheting between her legs, a clashing of limbs and teeth, and then a transient, searing pain. From her bed of earth, Eliza had stared up at the dusky sky and blinked, disbelieving, watching a swarm of parched leaves fall in ever-decreasing circles, buffeted by the breeze.

They had not told Daddy. That was her decision and she was glad of it. She didn't want him knowing that she was such an idiot. Such a slag. He thought they were visiting Mum's friend Serena in Brighton, enjoying walks on the beach, games in the arcades, ice cream on the pier. Far from it. Instead, she had endured wave after wave of pain and had had to give birth to the sixteen-week old foetus because they had said it was too far advanced to do it any other way.

She did not look at it when it came out. She had been sitting on the toilet and the nurse had said, 'Sweetheart, just sit forward for a moment', and she had just pulled it out, without ceremony. The nurse had advised her not to look and she hadn't. Privately, she believed that it had been a boy.

They had left after breakfast the next morning and she had cradled those roses all the way home. They'd driven home to Kidlington together, her mother chattering away about everything she could think of, except the one thing Eliza wanted to discuss. 'Look at those glorious leaves,' she'd said as they drove past an avenue of trees in full autumnal bloom.

Eliza, already absorbed by a grief she would never be able to fully describe, had simply looked at her mother in despair.

Eliza and her best friend were sitting outside a café on the South Bank, making the most of some rare spring sunshine. Katy ran her ring finger around the rim of her coffee cup.

'Thanks for coming with me to the cake makers,' said Katy. 'I owe you one. I know weddings probably aren't your favourite topic right now, but I really needed to face that woman head on, and having you by my side helped. I really didn't want that fruit cake.'

Eliza tuned out and stared into the distance, watching a tourist boat slowing before the bridge and beginning to turn.

'Eliza? Liiiiiiieeezzaa? Earth to Lil?'

'Oh, sorry, I'm just tired. Really tired.'

Eliza saw that Katy was taking her in. She knew that her hair was greasy, her skin spotty, and that there were distinct dark rings around her eyes. She also looked thinner than ever. 'You don't look too good to be honest, hon.'

'Cheers.'

'I mean it. Are you sleeping OK? Are you eating?'

'Barely.'

'Barely to which?'

'Both.'

'Shit. Lize, you need to see someone about this. You've had a hell of a time recently, what with Ed leaving and your parents being at war and then dragging you into it. You need to see someone professional, not just me. Although I do love you, you know that.'

'I know.' Eliza took a large swig from her cappuccino and looked up at her friend. 'And I will do, when things are clearer. There's just been too much going on.'

'I know. When's the gene therapy starting, then?'

'Next week.'

Katy looked surprised.

'Blimey, they're not hanging around, are they?'

'No. Oh, I really hope I made the right choice, Katy. The one Patience would have made.'

Katy shifted her chair closer to Eliza and leaned in for a hug.

'I'm sure you did, lovey. You went with your instincts. Don't beat yourself up about it.'

'Hmm.' Eliza remained upright, resisting the embrace. She didn't feel like human contact today, even from a human she genuinely loved.

Katy released her and sat back in her chair.

'Will you go? When they're doing it, the trial?' she said, picking up her coffee once more, apparently unfussed at her friend's refusal to engage.

'I don't think so. Partly because I'm already in plenty of

trouble at work, and partly because I already feel like I've betrayed Dad by signing her up for this thing. I don't want to make it worse.'

'They really have a lot to apologise for, your parents,' said Katy.

Eliza raised an eyebrow.

'Why?'

'Oh, come on, Lize, I've known you since you were tiny. I've seen the mind games your mum plays, the guilt trips, the martyrdom. I've seen how your dad absents himself rather than dealing with it. And I've seen you try, over and over, to fix things for them, to try to make them happy. But you can't, lovey. Because it's *their* mess.'

Eliza sat in silence for a few seconds. There might be some truth in what her friend was saying, but frankly, she didn't have the brain power to process it right now. There was something else even more pressing to deal with.

'You know you just said you owed me a favour for the caterer visit?' she asked Katy, draining what was left of her drink, putting her hand in her pocket to feel for the leaflet from the clinic. 'Do you think you could pay me back by coming to an appointment with me?'

24

Patience

March

This is the night before everything changes. I'm tucked up in bed already, alone in the semi-darkness, watching the stars on the projector beside my bed form new galaxies on the ceiling. The projector was Jimmy's idea; he suggested it to Mum when he last came here to do a shift and I love it.

I'm in bed early because we're apparently getting up before dawn. Mum told Serena this afternoon that she was going to set her alarm for 5 a.m. I don't think we're leaving that early, but it does take an age to get me ready in the morning, so I suppose she's working backwards from that. Preparing me so that we can leave the house is like trying to persuade twenty toddlers to get dressed by themselves. It's an operation that takes patience, determination, coordination, and, crucially, lots of time.

Mum's saved on carers again tomorrow. She's roped Serena into coming with us to the hospital instead. And don't get me wrong, I have always liked her, but I do wish Jimmy was coming instead. I could do with something nice

286

to look at while they're slicing me up, or draining me of blood, or whatever it is they're planning to do.

It has been a breath of fresh air having Serena to stay, though. Quite literally – before she arrived, the house had begun to smell unpleasant. Now, it's aerated and clean, full of nice-smelling candles. She's been sending Mum to bed a lot too, which I think has helped. She needed a rest. She's also been feeding both of us her tasty home-cooked meals, which I've really enjoyed. There are definite limits to the ready-meal range at the supermarket. Mum is also smelling and looking better, although there's still no sign of Dad. Mum hasn't spoken about him at all recently. In front of me, anyway. He must be due back soon though, I'd have thought. He's been gone far too long this time. Surely he must be coming back for tomorrow? He's never missed a hospital appointment before and this one sounds... meaty.

I still have no real details about this procedure. My family seem to be literally tearing themselves apart over this, but no one has even thought to tell me what's going to happen. Except for Eliza, of course. When she asked me what I thought, I cried, not because I really wanted it – I don't know what it is they are really offering, after all – but simply because someone had actually asked me what I wanted. No one has ever done that before. So I shed a tear. And here we are.

Apparently, this might make me 'normal'. That idea sounds ludicrous even to me; how would an able-bodied person like Eliza cope with being imprisoned in my useless body? No miracle drug or whatever is going to be able to fix my bent spine or my wasted legs. And I wish I could tell them that I already understand; that I'm even able to read a bit. I don't need medical treatment to help me with that. I'm already normal in that way. And also, what on earth does *normal* mean? Is anyone normal? I've seen the way that 'normal' people live their lives – heavens, I've done little else but watch people since I was born – and I don't much like the look of the mess some of them make.

In some senses, you see, my life is perfect. Of course I'd love to be able to communicate, to be able to feed myself, to be able to scratch that itch. I'd love to get out of bed for a pee right now, as I'm desperate, and it stings. I have wanted these things for my whole life. But to counter that, I have a lot of stuff I love: my music; my family; a never-ending cornucopia of carers; regular food; no bills; no money worries; my glorious internal world – and zero concern about cellulite.

Over the years I've heard many doctors, carers, nurses and social workers debate whether I have a decent quality of life or not. So I'd like to state here, for the record, that I do. I don't have anything to compare my life to, of course, but then, who does? There are lots of able-bodied adults who seem to live lives filled with anguish, disappointment, unhappiness. I've seen enough TV to know that. And when I'm not feeling ill or in pain, I'm pretty happy. If I have either of those, though, it *is* shit, I'm not going to lie. But then I'm guessing that sort of thing is also shit if you're 'normal'.

I have a pain right now, as it happens. It's down below. I'm not sure exactly where, but it's like someone's pressing down on my tummy, and I need to wee all the time, but not much comes out. That can't be good, can it? It's a bit like the pain I had last year, although that was duller and it went, eventually.

I really must try to get to sleep. I have a trick to help me do this, especially if I've got any pain anywhere and I need distracting; I start to play Take That videos in my head. It takes me away from wherever I am, and I know them so well, I'm able to project myself into them. I'm in complete control of what happens, so I make sure I'm always gorgeous and sexy, and, obviously, also romantically involved with one of the boys behind the scenes.

Look! I'm now on a beach somewhere exotic, wrapped in blue silk, inexplicably holding a mirror to reflect the sun. Ooh, and now I'm in a café which for some reason is entirely sepia, sashaying past dancers to get to the piano, where I bop demurely as Gary plays. Oh, and here I am, dressed like I'm going to a funeral, wearing a thin black veil, living in a house where it's apparently snowing indoors and there's a smashed chandelier on the floor, behind a snowdrift.

That's one of my favourites, by the way; I love *Babe*.

The projector timer has clicked off. It's dark in here now. My cue. Good night, my internal monologue-diary-imaginary-friend-type-thing. I do hope you're still here tomorrow.

PART THREE

25

Louise and Patience

March

It was an ordinary ward, full of ordinary patients, most of them over the age of sixty. Quite an extraordinary venue for something with the potential to change a life forever.

Louise had been sitting on a very hard, very upright plastic chair for at least an hour, holding Patience's hand. She was wedged between a hoist and a large canvas bag containing Patience's clothes; she had packed several outfits for her but there was nowhere to hang any of it. Patience was awake but making no noise, and she seemed to have no interest in the offerings on the TV or on the iPad which Louise had brought to distract her. It was rare that Take That and Kylie provoked no response, but this seemed to be one of those times. It was as if she knew what was about to happen and she was taking this time to prepare herself for it.

We're on a ward chock-full of old ladies, all having hip replacements and whatnot. I'm the odd one out, the weirdo in the corner. I've seen them staring when Mum's attention is directed elsewhere. That's not often, mind you. She's been almost entirely focussed on me for hours now. She keeps grabbing hold of my hand and squeezing it far too tight. She's after a reaction from me, I think, something to reassure her that she's doing the right thing. I have decided not to give her one. It's a sort of protest. I have nothing else to give.

Louise wondered whether Patience was just reacting to her own anxiety. She loosened her grip on Patience's hand and watched as the capillaries in her skin responded to the release of pressure, large red angry fingers disappearing like ghosts.

Thank God Mum's let go! I thought she'd never stop. Perhaps she'll go for a walk or get a coffee; then maybe I'll turn my head and watch some TV. I'm bored. Really bored.

Louise felt exposed, sitting there by herself. Pete wasn't coming, of course, but Eliza wasn't going to be with them, either. To Louise, this felt like an enormous betrayal. Not of her – of Patience. She had voted for it, after all, but her apparent continuing ambivalence towards it was baffling to her. It seemed unfathomable that someone could grow up with a sister like Patience and not want her to have the best of everything, the best chances. Eliza really could be incredibly selfish sometimes, she thought.

At least Serena was here, which was amazing of her, given the memories hospitals held for her. It was in a ward similar to this that they had both held Patrick's hands for the last time, surrounded by visiting relatives, clinking teacups and squeaking trolley wheels, the thin cotton bed-screen separating burgeoning grief from the everyday and mundane. Louise had seen Serena's face alter when they'd walked in here earlier, but she had contained whatever emotion had threatened to boil over. She said she would go and buy them two coffees, and she had yet to return. Louise didn't blame her for feeling the way she did, and she knew she'd be back when she felt ready.

A member of the research team had been to see them earlier, a woman she knew only vaguely. She had been composed, overbearing, full of jargon. She'd shaken Louise's hand, taken a few notes, explained what was about to happen, asked her to sign yet more forms, and then disappeared to talk to the nurses on the ward about the procedure that was to come. Philip had said he'd come to see them tomorrow, when it had been done. But for now, it was just the two of them, waiting.

This stuck-up woman turned up earlier. She was talking about a lumbar puncture. What the fuck is one of those? I have no idea, but puncturing any part of my anatomy doesn't sound brilliant, let's be honest.

Louise watched as the other patients went about their daily business, unaware that something utterly groundbreaking was about to take place amongst them. It was a women's ward and a large number of them were elderly. There was a lady of about seventy-five at the end, in for a hip replacement. She had just had a cup of tea and a custard cream, delivered by an orderly pushing the tea trolley. He was currently at the second bed along, giving a hot drink to a much older woman with translucent skin and a whisper of hair on her head. Louise didn't know what she was in for. On the other side, a family group – presumably husband, son and daughter-in-law – surrounded the bed of a woman perhaps in her late sixties. She was incredibly jaundiced, the colour of lemon rind, but still talking. And finally, there was a woman in her forties opposite them with a head full of highlighted curls and a face covered in carefully applied make-up, sitting bolt upright in bed reading a copy of *Good Housekeeping*. She had told Louise earlier, when they'd bumped into each other in the ladies' loos, that she was in for a double mastectomy following a diagnosis of breast cancer. She was putting a brave face on her fear, just as Louise was.

Voluntarily bringing Patience into a hospital when she was not actually ill was an act of madness, Louise reflected. She'd never have considered it, ordinarily. She might even catch something in here, a superbug maybe, that might kill her. Was she actually mad? In the depths of the night, unable to sleep and with Pete's words at the Best Interests meeting riding roughshod on her conscience, she had thought she might be.

And was it crazy to hope for a miracle? Her father would have said not; but then, he'd been a Christian, and they believed in miracles. Louise had believed in very little for years, but this – she believed in science. And she believed in the little girl she'd held in her arms all those years ago, full of promise. She believed in hope.

And coming towards them, right now, was that hope in action – a small vial of liquid, sitting in a sterile basin, alongside a long needle. A red-haired woman wearing scrubs, her hair tied back neatly in a ponytail, was carrying this precious load. She walked up to them and put it down on a portable trolley beside the window, before pulling the curtains around Patience's bed.

Shit, my boredom may be about to be replaced with something far worse.

'Mrs Willow? I'm Dr Stevens. I do lumbar punctures every day, so Professor Larssen asked me to do this one. Has he explained what's going to happen?'

Louise held her gaze and responded, determined not to look as out of her depth as she felt.

'Yes, I've done a bit of work with the team, so he went through it with me.' The doctor looked relieved.

That's great, Mum, I'm glad someone has some idea what's going on.

'Great. Good. We're going to move Patience into a side room for this. Let me just go to fetch the porter.' She walked off, closing the curtain behind her. Louise glanced over at Patience and reached for her hand. Was it her imagination, or did she seem to be shaking?

A side room? How large a puncture are they planning to make?!

The doctor returned a few minutes later with a friendly-looking short, round nurse and a middle-aged, sagging porter who looked as if his breakfast hadn't agreed with him.

'Right, let's go,' said the doctor, signalling to the nurse and porter to take the brakes off Patience's bed and begin to push her in the direction of the corridor.

You know when you are so frightened about doing something that you wish someone else could take over your body and do it for you? That.

Louise grabbed her handbag and followed behind them in silence, aware that all eyes in the ward were currently trained on her back.

Their strange parade came to an end in a small windowless, strip-lit room just off the main corridor. The nurse and her reluctant assistant parked Patience's bed exactly in the middle of the far wall and Dr Stevens closed the door behind them.

This is a tiny room. It's hot in here and the lights are hurting my eyes.

'Carol here is going to come over and sit next to Patience and chat to her,' the doctor said to Louise, identifying the nurse for the first time. 'Wayne, you can go now, thank you.' Louise watched as the porter sloped out of the room. Then the doctor turned towards her once more. 'Mrs Willow, are you happy for me to turn Patience onto her side?' she asked. Louise nodded, finding that she had temporarily lost the power to speak.

Yeah, well, don't bother asking me, lady. I'm just the patient, after all.

Carol went to get a chair and sat on the far side of the bed so that Patience's head would be directly opposite her during the procedure. Louise watched as the doctor carefully rolled Patience over on the bed, placing cushions under her knees and behind her back, so that she wouldn't move. Then she squeezed some white cream out of a tube and placed it in a puddle on Patience's back, securing it with a plaster. Local anaesthetic.

'Hi, Patience, I'm Carol. I'm a nurse. I'm just going to sit here for a bit, while the doctor takes a look at your back.' The nurse was smiling.

The friendly-looking nurse has a megawatt smile, as if she's just been told she's won a lifetime's supply of crisps. She also has a lovely lilting Welsh accent, and I'd be charmed by it if I didn't have a fair idea about what's coming. Sit here for a bit, my arse.

'Carol, could you hold Patience by the shoulders and make sure she's completely stable?' asked the doctor, interrupting her.

Brace, brace.

'Yep,' she replied, manoeuvring so that she could brace herself against Patience's body. Louise took in her daughter's back, marked forever by the major spinal surgery she'd had when she was nine. They'd inserted a huge metal rod to straighten her out, so that she didn't have to spend her life doubled over, her lungs compressed by her own body.

The doctor removed the plaster from Patience's back, and wiped the cream away. Louise winced as she saw the vial placed in the syringe.

'OK, Patience, you're going to feel a sharp scratch in your back,' the doctor said. 'But it'll be over quickly.'

Oh my God, that hurts!

'Just look at me, Patience,' said Carol. 'Look at me. Where's this top from, by the way? I love the colour.'

Her efforts to distract a woman who can't talk are faintly ridiculous, I mean, how am I supposed to reply? And, oh God, another twinge!

'Argggghhhhh!' Patience had made her first noise of the day, and it sounded like a cry. Louise stood up quickly and walked around the bed, so that Patience could see her.

Fuuuuccccccckkkkkk

'I'm here, darling, I'm here,' she said, and she knelt down next to the bed, as if in prayer. 'Just look at Mummy.'

I can hardly look anywhere else!

'Arrrgggggggghhhhhhhh!'

The doctor had inserted the needle. Louise was whispering in her ears now, almost chanting.

'Mummy's here, and it's going to be worth it, I promise. Mummy's here, and it's going to be worth it, I promise.'

What on earth could be worth this?

'It'll be over in just a minute, Patience,' said Carol brightly. 'Just a few seconds more.'

'Done!' said the doctor, swiftly removing the needle and replacing it in the dish behind her. She then ripped her latex gloves off and asked Carol to help her place Patience back onto her back. Louise noticed that there was a tear in the corner of her daughter's right eye.

'She's going to need to stay on her back for at least twenty-four hours, as you know,' she said, looking at Louise. 'The nurses are going to come to fit a catheter, and they'll also attach a drip. She can eat normally, but we'll be monitoring her pretty constantly for the next few days. Do you have any questions?'

I have plenty.

Louise could think of none. She was focussed instead on the tear, which was now trailing down Patience's cheek. She reached for the pack of tissues on the bedside table and used one to wipe her daughter's face dry.

'OK, well then. Great. I know Professor Larssen said he'd be checking in on you. Good luck with it. I really hope it makes a difference.'

And with that, she picked up the dish, opened the door and strode away, already thinking about her next patient. Louise watched the door close and gathered her daughter into an apologetic embrace.

Mum is giving me a hug. I think she's crying. That makes two of us.

26

Eliza

March

The waiting-room-that-was-trying-not-to-be was still as un-convincing as ever. The radio was still tuned to Classic FM, and the *Gladiator* soundtrack was currently serenading the assembled gathering of women desperate for distraction.

Katy was gripping Eliza's hand. She'd taken hold of it as they'd walked up to the building and hadn't let go, even when they'd checked in at reception. Eliza thought that some of the other patients probably had them down as a couple, which would have been funny, if she was in the mood for laughter.

She was feeling decidedly unwell. The morning sickness had pretty much abated now, but had been replaced with a gnawing in her bowels, which she recognised as fear. She hadn't dared to eat anything today.

At least she didn't have to work. She had laid the groundwork for this carefully, and taken the whole week off, citing wedding preparations. This was obviously a hilarious irony on so many counts, but Eliza was, again, not in the mood for hilarity.

'This is awful, isn't it,' said Katy. 'The déjà vu.'

It was surprising that she hadn't raised it until now; Eliza had never told her not to, but it had just been an unspoken understanding between them, that what happened in the past stayed in the past. Her mum had told her never to tell anyone about what had happened in that clinic on the south coast and, for the most part, she'd kept that promise. But it was Katy who'd come to visit the next day and, seeing the look on her face, had known something appalling had just happened. It had been such a relief to tell her. She had provided the emotional support afterwards that her mum had failed to. In many ways, it had cemented their friendship.

It had turned out, in the end, that the thing by the tree – for that was the only way she was prepared to refer to it – had been a dare. She had been the unwitting star of a cruel show, designed by Michael and his friends. She had been an easy conquest, so easy. A pushover. He must have loved that. Unable to move schools to avoid him and his friends and the inextricable shame, she had instead shrunk into her uniform, stopped speaking in lessons, taken to hiding in the library during break. She had longed to be invisible.

She had also discovered after that that she was, for the most part, perfectly happy with her own company. Aside from Katy, she had made almost no other close friends, and that had been a deliberate choice. Other people could not be trusted, as Ed had so elegantly demonstrated.

'Elizabeth?'

It wasn't the same nurse as before. This one did not have a Scottish accent, and she did not exude the same warmth. Eliza and Katy stood up in unison and walked, still holding hands, down the corridor and into one of the rooms, this time, on the right. Sitting inside there was an older woman of Indian descent, dressed smartly in black trousers and a floral shirt, dark brown hair up in a bun, her stethoscope slung around her neck.

'Elizabeth,' she began. 'Can I call you Elizabeth?'

'It's Eliza.'

'Eliza. Good. I'm Dr Krisha. I see you've decided to go ahead with a termination. Can I confirm with you the date of your last menstrual period?'

'I can't remember exactly, but it was last November,' she replied.

'Right, so that makes you about twenty weeks pregnant,' the doctor said. She typed a few words into a form on her computer, and swivelled her chair towards Eliza. She looked her up and down, taking in her thin frame, her complete absence of bump. Eliza had been relieved that she wasn't showing, but now she saw that it was worrying the doctor.

'I'd like to do an ultrasound to confirm those dates, as you aren't exactly sure,' she said. 'Can you hop onto the bed over there for me?' Eliza had not moved.

'Why, don't you believe me, about the dates?' she asked.

'I do,' the doctor replied, softly. 'But I wouldn't know that, from the look of you. It's standard procedure; we need to know what we're dealing with, confirm dates. Did you do a pregnancy test?'

'Yes. Several.'

'Good.'

Katy let go of her hand at last and Eliza stood up, walked over to the couch and sat down on it, unbuttoning her trousers.

'Do you mean, you think I might not be pregnant at all?'

'This will be cold,' Dr Krisha said. She was squeezing gel over Eliza's lower abdomen and the nurse was fiddling with a screen, which was turned away from her. 'And sometimes, pregnancies end without us knowing they have, and that can be dangerous. So I'm just taking a look.'

Eliza lay back on the tissue covering of the bed and placed a hand over her stomach. She had never once doubted that there was a baby inside there.

'Could this be because I had an abortion when I was a teenager?' she asked.

'That shouldn't have any effect, but let's see what's going on.'

The doctor placed the transducer on her stomach and Eliza lay still, considering for the first time that her first abortion might have ruined her chances of ever having children. Throughout her twenties she had battled not to get pregnant again; now, she realised, it might all have been a waste of time.

There was a significant pause. The doctor was staring intently at the screen and the nurse, meanwhile, was tidying up a table of instruments on the other side of the room, in what looked to Eliza like a deliberate attempt to avoid her little bit of human drama. She wondered when the doctor was going to break it to her that the baby had died inside her, long ago. She must be working out the best way to go about it, particularly as she was planning to abort it anyway. It was an odd predicament to put her in, no question.

Ba-boom-ba-boom-ba-boom-ba-boom-ba-boom-ba-boom

The doctor exclaimed loudly and reached for a knob on the machine to turn the speakers down. But it was already too late. It took Eliza just a split second to realise that she was listening to a baby's heartbeat.

It was the most extraordinary sound she'd ever heard.

'Please can I see?'

The doctor looked over at her.

'Are you sure?' she said. 'We don't normally show—'

'Yes,' replied Eliza, almost begging.

The doctor turned the screen towards her and showed her the outline of a small human amongst the grey and black.

'It seems fine,' she said, as if that's what she'd been expecting all the time. 'You must just be the sort of person who shows late. But it's odd… Have you been eating OK?'

'I'm not sure.' She had barely eaten for months.

'You look on the thin side. The baby will have taken what it needed and it hasn't left you much. You need to look after yourself, too.'

She wiped the gel off with some tissue, told Eliza that she could get dressed, and pulled the curtain around the bed to give her privacy. Eliza's whole body was shaking, and when she sat back down on the chair nearest the doctor's desk, she could see that Katy had been crying.

'OK, so I took some measurements, and it would seem you were pretty much accurate regarding dates, so we can authorise the abortion – if you want to go ahead,' the doctor said, slowly, carefully.

'I think we both know that I'm not going to go ahead,' Eliza replied, enunciating each sound in each word, as if making sure that she was properly understood. 'Thank you,' she said, as an afterthought. 'For checking.'

'Not at all, I was just doing my job. You will need to

register with your GP as soon as possible,' Dr Krisha said. 'By the way – do you want to know what you're having? A boy or a girl?'

'Oh, no,' she said, instantly. 'I don't care. But is it healthy? That's all that matters to me.'

'As far as I can tell, it's perfectly healthy,' the doctor replied. 'But you'll need a full scan to make sure. Make sure you visit your doctor soon, as I said.'

'Thank you, I will,' she replied, rushing to get out of the door, to get away from that room as quickly as she possibly could. She took Katy's hand again as they left.

'I would have gone through it with you, if you'd really wanted,' Katy said, turning to face her friend, 'but I'm totally delighted I don't have to.'

It was six o'clock in the evening, and the rush-hour traffic had begun to thin out. Eliza glided over Albert Bridge and slipped past Earl's Court without effort, easing her way onto the M4 in good time. She'd had to dig deep for the particular soundtrack she had chosen for this journey, had been forced to take a box out from the top cupboard in her bedroom and sift through it all to find it, but it had been worth it. Her own copy of *Take That: Greatest Hits*, deliberately hidden from view for years, was booming out of the speakers, making her smile. This was not the time for guitar-led angst.

The nights were getting shorter now and there was still a remnant of sun lighting her way. Spring was making its presence felt everywhere, dormant trees emerging from their long sleep, stretching their fingers to greet the sun. It might just be an age thing, but Eliza drew so much comfort from this time of year now. Witnessing this annual resurrection, inevitable and yet for so many months almost unimaginable, gave her courage and hope.

And there was something else giving her courage. Hearing that heartbeat, the sound of that new life intertwined with hers, had triggered a sense of self-determination in her. It was time for a seismic change.

She arrived in Oxford in under an hour and a half and found a place to park just a short walk from the flat. It was dark now, the streets lit by lamps and light cast out of hundreds of living room windows, TV screens beaming their flickering light shows onto front gardens, wheelie bins and parked cars. She walked up to the door and knocked firmly, twice. She could hear a TV playing through the living room window, which was open a crack.

It was Ed who answered the door.

'Oh… hi,' he said, in a tone as enthusiastic as if she had been a Jehovah's Witness bent on saving his soul.

'Hello, Ed,' she said. 'Can I come in?'

'I've got…' he looked shiftily down the corridor '… company.'

'Yes, I thought you might have,' she replied.

Ed lowered his voice to a harsh whisper. 'Look, it's over, OK? I thought you'd have got the message. That was what the dinner was for. I'm sorry you're hurt. But I'm with someone else now. It's over.'

'But it's not quite over,' she said.

'How so?' His voice was getting louder again, his hushed tones forgotten in his rage.

'Ed?' A woman with sleek, well-cut black hair appeared in

the corridor, wearing a pink fleece dressing gown and bright pink, fluffy slippers. Wow, she's really got her feet under the table, thought Eliza. She's not even making an effort.

'It's OK, sweetheart, I'm dealing with this,' he replied. 'It's fine.'

'It's not fine, sweetheart,' replied Eliza. 'And I will not be dismissed by you, Ed, like a door-to-door sales rep.'

'I really have nothing left to say to you, Eliza,' he said. 'We are done. And by the way, I cancelled the wedding reception booking last week. Amazingly, your parents hadn't done it yet. They'll be getting a partial refund in the post soon – but do I need to send them a signed affidavit stating that I do not want to marry their daughter?'

Eliza took a good look at him, the man she'd spent twenty years with, the man she'd wanted to have children with, to share a park bench with when she was too old to walk far. His hair was thinning, she now noticed, and his forehead glistened with sweat.

'It's not fine, Ed, because I'm pregnant. You got me pregnant when you screwed me last November. Does she,' Eliza turned to look at the woman in pink, 'know about that? Were you together then?' The woman's face crumpled. 'Oh dear, that's a shame. But yes, I'm pregnant – yes, with your baby, before you ask. The baby's due in August. I'll send you a text when it arrives.'

Eliza turned her back and walked away then, not waiting for an acknowledgement. The door behind her slammed shut and she made her way back past the cars, the identical front rooms, the wheelie bins and the local cats. In the distance, she heard a woman shouting.

27

Pete

March

Pete's phone didn't ring much these days. And if it did, it was either his brother asking him to come over for a shift, a lost pizza delivery man, or someone on a crackly line enquiring about an accident that wasn't his fault. He'd found this room on Gumtree; a smoke-free home, no dogs, own TV, one load of washing processed a week. There was dense condensation on the windows every morning, and if he sat down on the bed too quickly, a cloud of dust rose to engulf him.

He hated it here, absolutely despised it, but it was better than having to admit to Louise that he had been too proud to ask Steve to put him up and there wasn't enough left over from the small amount he allotted himself each month to pay for something more decent. But he wouldn't tell her. He didn't want her taking him back home out of guilt.

It was ten o'clock on a Saturday morning and he was trying to get a lie-in, but the noise from both outside (teenagers on mopeds) and inside (thumping Bhangra from the room next door) was making this impossible. But at least this meant that when his phone *did* ring, he was able to locate it and answer it quickly.

'Peter Willow?' Jesus, his full name. Lawyer, policeman, or doctor?

'This is Dr Ramsden at Birmingham general. Your wife has asked me to call you. I have your daughter here on the ward and Patience isn't doing too well this morning, following the lumbar puncture she had a couple of days ago. Mrs Willow would like you here.'

Pete did not need telling twice. He slung his legs out of bed, threw on a shirt and trousers, swilled his mouth out with mouthwash and grabbed the keys to the fifteen-year-old Ford Focus he'd bought the previous week. He was only a few miles away.

'Lou?'

Louise was sitting beside Patience's bed in a side room, holding their daughter's hand. Her face was ashen, devoid of make-up, and her clothes looked like they'd been slept in. Pete walked around the bed and saw that on the floor next to her chair were several half-empty water bottles, two empty sandwich cartons and two crisp packets.

'They're worried about her breathing,' she said, addressing an invisible person in front of her, rather than Pete. 'Her oxygen saturation has gone down too far.' Pete sat gingerly on the edge of the bench and looked closely at Patience, whose breathing was rapid, each inhalation snatching just a tiny parcel of air. Her face was pale and she had a faraway look in her eyes, as if she was opting out of consciousness. 'I thought you should be here. In case,' she said, in monosyllables.

I should have been here long before this, he thought, the guilt of his decision to steer clear of the lumbar puncture procedure bubbling back to the surface. It was never far away.

'Is it that bad? What have they said?'

'They *aren't* saying, and that's what worries me,' she replied. 'But they didn't expect side effects like this so early.'

Pete got up from the bed. 'Back in a few minutes,' he said. He walked along the corridor that linked the wards, seeking out someone officially dressed. He eventually landed upon a man wearing a white coat and a name badge, who was scribbling frantically on some notes, leaning on the nurse's station as a support.

'Excuse me,' he said. 'Are you a doctor on this ward?'

'Yes, I am. For my sins.' Then the young man looked up at Pete's face, registered his distress, and backtracked. 'Sorry, I shouldn't have said that. Force of habit. But I am a doctor here. How can I help?'

'I'm Patience Willow's father.'

'Ah, yes. We spoke earlier.'

'I've just arrived. I wondered if we could have a chat about her condition?'

'While I'd love to help, that's been taken out of my hands, I'm afraid,' the young doctor replied. 'They've called in a consultant neurologist – he'll be here soon – and I believe that the man who's heading up the gene therapy – Professor Larssen, is it? – he's coming to see her, too. We are monitoring her, of course, but there's not much we can do, apart from that. This is new territory for all of us.'

'But what's going on? Is this related to the lumbar puncture?'

'We're assuming so. The trial team warned us there might be some response from the autonomic system – that's all the stuff the body does without us thinking about it, like breathing, digesting, the heart beating – so this isn't entirely unexpected.'

'So her heart could be in trouble, too?'

'Not at the moment, Mr Willow. That seems OK for now.'

'For God's sake!' said Pete, his words not aimed at the doctor, but at the situation at large. 'What a mess.'

'I've brought you a tea,' he said to Louise, as he entered the room. He'd found a machine in the corridor. She rubbed her eyes and took it from him, muttering her thanks. Pete took a seat next to her and the two of them sat sipping their drinks in silence for a few minutes, the frantic rhythm of their daughter's breathing their only soundtrack. Both of them were unable to take their eyes off the oxygen saturation readout on the screen next to the bed. It was hovering close to 80 per cent, but so far had not dipped further. They both knew that anything under eighty could begin to damage her organs.

'I suppose you blame me for this,' said Louise, finally.

'*No,*' he replied, with emphasis.

'Really?' she said.

'No, I don't. How could I possibly do that? You only did what you thought was right. I'm so sorry, Lou. I've been a shit. A blind, idiotic shit.'

He reached out his hand and Louise took it. He noticed that her eyes were filling with tears.

'Oh my God, Pete, what have I *done*?' she said, looking

at him with desperation. 'We could lose her. And it's my fault.'

'No. I blame the scientists for this,' he said, his colour rising. 'They knew. They knew this could happen. Have you called Eliza?'

'I left her a message. Maybe she's asleep, or busy with Ed. She seems very distracted these days. When are you going back to work, by the way? You haven't said.'

'I'm not. Not in Qatar, anyway. I jacked it in.' Pete took a gulp of tea, avoiding Louise's gaze.

'Bloody hell. Why didn't you tell me?'

'Because the only communication we've had in the past month has been in the presence of a counsellor,' he said, lifting his cup in the air for emphasis. 'And a shit one at that.'

'Knock, knock.'

An elderly man with white hair and glasses had appeared at the door, and he was smiling. He had sung those words, rather than tapping on the door. Oh, brilliant, thought Pete – a comedian.

'Sorry to disturb,' he said. 'I've just come to check on our patient here.'

'Has no one told you?' asked Pete, his hands gripping the metal bars beside the bed so hard his knuckles were showing, 'she's barely breathing.'

'Yes, Dr Ramsden has been ringing me with updates. Let me see her.' Professor Larssen approached the bed. 'Patience, I'm just going to take a look at you, OK?' Quietly and confidently, he ran through a series of checks, listening to her chest, checking her pupils, taking her blood pressure. When he was finished, he returned to his original position at the foot of her bed. 'Apart from the breathing, which is clearly a concern, she seems stable,' he said. 'We had expected some disruption to the autonomic system and we are hopeful it will pass quickly.'

'*Hopeful?* Who the hell made you God?' Pete was on his feet now, and he had the height advantage. 'How dare you use my daughter to experiment on and not seem the least bit concerned that she's clinging on to life?'

'Pete,' pleaded Louise. 'Please calm down.'

The professor appeared unmoved. 'I understand your concern, Mr Willow. Honestly, I do. But as I say, we believe that this stage will pass. It is a side effect we anticipated and, if necessary, we will help Patience out with some extra oxygen. But she is doing fine on her own at the moment. I am not unduly worried.'

'Well, that's nice for you. But I suspect neither of us will sleep tonight,' said Pete, gesturing at Louise. 'Just like always, you medics throw a diagnosis at us and then leave us to pick up the pieces.'

'*Pete!* Now is not the time for this. Come on, stop it.'

'And what will you do tomorrow if her heart starts to play up, as I'm told it might?'

'If it does, then we will deal with it, Mr Willow. We will give her the best of everything. I still hope for a successful outcome.'

'Well, bully for you!'

'I think perhaps I should go,' said Professor Larssen. He turned to Louise. 'I'm so sorry you are both being subjected to this worry, Louise. I can imagine how you feel. Please don't even consider returning to work any time soon. And remember, I'm available twenty-four hours a day. I've told the doctors to keep a very close eye on her and they will call me the minute anything changes. If not, I'll see you tomorrow.'

'Thank you, Philip.'

'Not at all. See you then.'

The professor was gone, leaving Pete still standing, wrangling with his ghost.

'He fancies you, doesn't he? Has he tried it on yet?'

'That's ridiculous, Pete, and you know it. And anyway, he has a very nice wife.'

'Whatever. It's that bloody man,' he said, 'who caused all this.'

'No, Pete,' Louise replied, 'that bloody man is trying to *fix* all this.'

Pete decided it was probably time to leave the hospital when the night shift arrived. No one had explicitly told him so, but it was clear that he was no longer welcome. First, a nurse wearing freshly laundered scrubs and a determined expression had dimmed all the lights, then the orderly who came afterwards, sweeping the ward with a grey, straggly mop, had sighed as he had circled the exclusion zone around Pete's feet.

The day-shift nurses had managed to find Louise a camp bed and some sheets and blankets and Pete had helped her make it up in silence, then had sat down beside her on a rigid plastic chair in the neon-splashed semi-darkness, keeping watch until she finally drifted out of frantic consciousness. They had spoken little since their argument that morning; they knew each other well enough to judge that now was not the time for anything vaguely resembling a truce. Instead, they had settled for companionable silence.

He was relieved to see Louise finally getting some rest after a day characterised by breath-holding and persistent pacing. Sleep appeared now to be weaving its magic on Patience also; her breathing seemed to have eased a little and he felt that it might be safe now to leave her for a few hours.

When he finally climbed into his car and drove the well-practised route onto the dual carriageway, he found that he had turned in the direction of Kidlington, not Aston. The route was firmly embedded in his memory and anyway, Louise was away, and Tess still needed to be fed and walked. He could be useful at home, he thought.

When he pulled into their road, however, he saw that there was another car parked in their weed-splattered driveway. Louise hadn't mentioned that anyone was staying – so who was in the house? Had Eliza bought a new car, perhaps? She hadn't said.

'Eliza?' Pete called as he pushed the front door open, noting that their porch was looking unusually tidy, the usual bonfire of mismatched shoes notably absent. He saw then that there was light leaking out under their living-room door. He walked swiftly along the hall and pushed the door open. Inside, the television was on, broadcasting Scandi Noir to a sleeping, supine redhead on their wizened leather sofa.

'Serena?'

'Eh?' Serena stretched and rubbed her eyes. 'Oh, Pete,' she said, taking in who it was. 'Sorry, I drifted off. What time is it?'

'I'm sorry, Serena, I just didn't expect to find you here,' he said as Serena swung her legs over the side of the sofa and pulled herself upright. 'Lou didn't say.'

'No, well, I hear you're not talking much at the moment.'

Instead of replying, Pete decided to leave the room in search of booze. This was still his house, after all. But instead of their usual well-stocked, chaotic fridge, he was greeted by clean, ordered and pared-down shelves – with not a beer in sight.

'*I've emptied the fridge of all alcohol!*' shouted Serena from the lounge. Pete sighed, and settled for a can of lemonade instead. When he returned to the lounge, he took a seat in an armchair opposite her.

'Look, I wanted to say thank you, for coming to help Lou out after Patience's fall,' he said, hugging his can tight to his chest.

'That's what friends are for,' Serena replied, smoothing her hair down with her hands. 'Honestly. I knew she was alone, so…'

'I've just come back for the night,' he said, wondering why he was bothering to explain himself. 'It seemed too late to go back to Aston.'

'I thought you were staying with Steve?'

'No. He didn't have room,' he said, aware that she would see through this lie immediately. Steve pretty much lived in a mansion. 'I'm in a bedsit for now. Until we settle things.'

'I see.'

Not knowing what to say next, Pete turned his attention to the TV, where a young, attractive blonde woman was, predictably, about to be murdered in a particularly grizzly way.

'Lou's had a breakdown, I think,' said Serena, who was also now looking at the screen, on which mist swirled around a dark, forbidding forest.

'Yes,' he replied. 'I feel such an idiot for not spotting it. I've spent so many years seeing her as the strong one, I'd forgotten how vulnerable she is underneath.'

A man had now appeared in vision; he was wearing a dark cap which obscured his face.

'Yes, she's a total softie really,' Serena replied. 'But of course, you know that.'

The man's footsteps were now the only thing the viewer could see or hear. Then a woman appeared centre-screen, dressed in a flimsy white strappy dress. She was wearing no shoes.

'I've failed her, Serena.'

The woman in the white dress had broken into a run.

'She needed me here, and what did I do? I left the country to make money. Talk about having the wrong priorities.'

Unable to watch her step in the dark, the woman tumbled over a log, and fell hard.

'Yes, but you're here now. And it's not too late. I'm sure of it.'

Suddenly, the man was looming over her. He had something heavy in his right hand, raised his arm to strike...

'I hope so,' Pete replied, before aiming the remote control at the TV, and switching it off. That young woman would live to die another day.

'I'm so sorry,' Serena said, turning her attention to Pete. 'I should have been more on the ball, too. But honestly, since Patrick's death...'

'Don't be,' Pete replied, taking a sip of lemonade. 'You've been through hell.'

'Lou is so lucky to have you,' she said.

Pete looked across at Serena, to check that she was sincere.

'She isn't though, is she? I've let her down everywhere you look.' Pete stood up abruptly and made to leave.

'How's Patience?' Serena asked, before he reached the door.

'A bit better, they reckon. I think she might be pulling through.'

'That's wonderful.'

'Yes. Although this might be just the beginning. Who knows what damage this gene therapy might have done.' Serena nodded her understanding. 'I'll be gone by the time you're up in the morning, by the way. I want to get to the hospital before Lou wakes,' he said, looking back at her as he turned the door handle.

'She needs you,' he added, as an afterthought. 'She needs you more than anyone.'

'No, Pete. That's where you're wrong,' Serena replied. 'It's *you* she needs.'

28

Eliza and Patience

April

Eliza rang the doorbell of Morton Lodge and examined her reflection in the glass door. She'd just had her brown hair cut into a bob and it was so much easier to manage than before; she just washed it, brushed it and it fell into place. She'd had long hair for what felt like forever, but since deciding to keep the baby, she'd felt a surge of confidence in other areas of her life, a desire to ring the changes.

She had used the past few weeks to spring clean her flat and she'd also splashed out on new bedding from John Lewis. Ed had insisted that their bedding had to be white, with a high thread count. This new set was yellow, and she had deliberately ignored its labelling. Polyester-schmester – she had liked it and that was enough; this was a new Eliza and she didn't give a damn what people thought.

Shit, though. Was that Jimmy coming to the door? The last time she'd seen him was in that church when she'd yelled at him and run off. Far from her finest hour. He must think she was an idiot. An absolute fruit loop, frankly.

'Hi! Nice hair,' he said, as he opened the door.

Eliza took him in. He was wearing a pinny. It had a picture of a smiling Santa on the front and 'Christmas Cracker' emblazoned in huge red print over his chest.

'Thanks,' she said, smoothing her hair back from her face, colour rising to her cheeks. 'Felt like time for a change.'

'Well, it suits you. Unlike my pinny. I am no Paul Hollywood, so you must excuse me, we're making cookies.'

'No problem,' she said. 'I don't like him anyway.' They smiled at each other, and she felt like dancing. 'I've just come to check up on Patience. I hear she came out of hospital yesterday?'

'Yep, she's here with us for a bit, to give your mum a break. She's spent most of the day sleeping in her chair, actually, so we put her to bed after lunch. That lumbar puncture and all of the breathing shenanigans afterwards seem to have knocked the stuffing out of her.'

Eliza followed Jimmy down the hallway, trying her best to ignore the peaks his shoulder blades made in his crisp white shirt as he walked. Seriously, having a crush on her sister's carer was ridiculous. Primarily because he must think she was mad. He'd seen her in all states of disarray – in Patience's bed on Christmas morning, half-dead in her childhood pyjamas, in tears in a church. She was surprised he didn't want to give her as wide a berth as possible, like everyone else. When they reached Patience's room, Jimmy stood aside so that she could enter first. She smiled her thanks and walked in, taking a breath as she squeezed past him.

Patience's room was dark; the blackout blinds had been pulled down and Eliza could only just make out her sister's blonde hair on her pillow.

'I'll just pop this light on above her sink,' Jimmy said. 'That shouldn't wake her.'

When he'd done so, Eliza looked over at her sister – and gasped. Patience appeared to be panting and her face was incredibly pale. She walked over to her and grasped her hand.

It was freezing.

Where's Gary? He said he'd meet me by the park gate, and he's not here. Instead, he's sent Jason. We've been making small talk, mostly about unicorns, and that's nice and stuff, but Jason is not my favourite at all. And also, didn't he leave? Doesn't he live in anonymity in Manchester now? Oh, no, actually, that's not Jason. This guy has short brown hair, sort of floppy, and it's not Robbie. Hang on... Is it Jimmy? Has Jimmy joined Take That?

'Patience. Patience. Can you hear me, Patience?'

Everything changes but you, doo bee doo, doo bee doo. Where's my wheelchair? I thought I'd left it around here somewhere. Am I walking? How odd. I haven't done that since I was a toddler.

'Patience, it's Jimmy. Can you see me?'

If I reach out, can I touch him, this Jimmy-Robbie? My arms feel like lead, but I reckon I could try.

'Did you see her arm move just then? Shit, I only checked on her an hour ago.'

That's a shame, I've always wanted to feel Robbie's hair. And Jimmy's, come to think of it. These days, Jimmy has the edge. Oh no! Don't walk away. I'll try calling him back.

'Is she in pain?' Eliza asked. 'Is this related to the lumbar puncture?'

I don't think he can hear me. Bollocks. I learned that word from Eliza, by the way. It has a nice ring to it. I've learned lots from her, over the years. Like I know what an abortion is and that she's had one. It's the sort of thing I wish I didn't know.

'Why isn't she responding?'

Eliza's here too, right up against my nose, making me go cross-eyed. And it's just as well it's not Robbie here with me, you know, because I'm feeling a bit tired now, too tired to meet my childhood crush. I think I need a lie down, actually. Luckily this gigantic pillow is right here for me to fall back on.

'Can you check her pulse?' Jimmy asked.

Oh, Jimmy's not looking so good now. His face seems to be melting.

'It's racing. How long has she been like this?'

'Shit. How can she have deteriorated so fast? She was fine earlier. Totally fine. The hospital doctors said she was fine.'

'Fuck! Fuck!'

How funny, he's so hot when I feel so cold. I'm just going to walk over there, where... warm... sun... out...

'Eliza, go and get help, now!'

29

Louise

April

Louise was staring at the empty bottle of whisky which she'd just pulled out from behind the wrapping-paper box, which lived in the downstairs cupboard. When she last saw this bottle, it had been half-full. Now there wasn't even a dreg left. She had just fancied a snifter, a tiny amount, to celebrate Patience being discharged from hospital after the gene therapy, back into the respite care home. Eliza was there visiting her right now; she'd call her later to get an update. Moving one step away from hospital deserved just a little celebration, didn't it? But no, Serena had got to this, too. Were there no limits to her capabilities? Did she have X-ray vision?

Admitting defeat, Louise switched on the kettle and hunted for teabags in the cupboard. She had to remove several boxes of camomile, green and Red Bush before she located the English Breakfast – her friend had very hipster tastes.

Serena had now been in residence for three weeks. Louise hated to admit it, but she had transformed the place with her keen eye for detail, her obsession with cleanliness and her love of order. She had also set to work making Louise behave well, which included cracking down on her little booze habit. The latter had made her feel very indignant, but she saw that it was coming from a place of love, so she let it go. Serena was about to leave, anyhow, and it wouldn't be long before Patience would be able to come home and then life could resume as before.

Like before – and yet nothing like before. There would be no Pete. Not that he'd been around full-time since the children were teenagers, of course, but this was different. She was beginning to accept that this particular separation might be permanent. And although she missed him – she had allowed herself to acknowledge that at least – it was a relief not to have to consult with anyone any more, about anything.

She had been with Pete for nearly forty years. Wasn't it time for her to discover who she really was? More than just a mother; more than just a wife. She was finally getting the respect she deserved now. She had her own income. Life was back on track after years of derailment. And Pete's financial insecurities and infidelities were no longer her concern, thank God. And things were calmer this way. No one bothered her.

Pete had been trying to worm his way back in, though. While she had been staying in hospital with Patience during the gene therapy trial, he'd apparently come to the house with his tool kit and set about rectifying every outstanding piece of work, fixing down carpets, nailing down floorboards, plugging leaks. He had even painted the shed. He had said nothing about it and she'd only discovered it when she'd returned, exhausted and dishevelled, a few days ago. It had been a huge relief, admittedly, to find everything working and presentable and she was enjoying it.

She wasn't sure what he hoped to gain from it, though. He wasn't coming back, was he? He must be in clover at his brother's house, anyway; Steve had a huge six-bedroom house in Selly Oak, with a hot tub and a bar.

'Good morning,' chirped Serena as she walked past her, fresh from the shower, her red hair wet and freshly brushed, her body encased in a green towelling robe. 'How did you sleep?'

'Better.'

'Good. That will be the detox talking.'

'If you say so.'

Serena fetched herself a mug from the cupboard and lifted down a cafetière. 'Coffee?' she asked.

'Yes, why not? More caffeine is probably what I need,' replied Louise, stifling a yawn. 'I still feel like crap, though.'

'How's the appetite?'

'A bit better, now I've stopped feeling sick,' Louise slumped into a chair next to the kitchen table and put her head in her hands.

'Shall I get you some toast?'

'Sure,' Louise answered, rubbing her eyes.

'As you know, I need to go back today,' Serena said while filling up the kettle and putting sliced bread into the toaster. 'Mum can cope on her own for a bit, but I think she's lonely without me. I've probably been here long enough. And I hope you're now on a better path.'

'I'm fine, Serena. Really. It's all good.'

'Mm-hmm. Hang on, I have something for you.'

She abandoned her coffee-making and went into the living room. Louise could hear her open her handbag, followed by rustling as she searched through its contents. She returned within a couple of minutes, bearing a piece of paper. 'I picked this up from the library yesterday, when I was in town,' she said. 'I want you to go.' It was a leaflet advertising the services of a local branch of Alcoholics Anonymous.

'For God's sake, Serena!'

'Lou. I love you. You're my best friend. We have supported each other through everything. And I know you. And I know what you need. Please do this – for me. Go to these people. Just once, if you want to. But please go.'

Tess had now wandered in, in search of a snack in the form of crumbs on the floor. Finding none – Serena kept a tight ship – she rested her head on Louise's lap, begging for a stroke. Louise was happy to oblige.

'I am not an alcoholic,' she said, showering attention on the dog and avoiding Serena's gaze.

'So you say. And that's fine. Just please, *go*.'

'If it will stop you going on about it at every opportunity and destroying my booze supplies, I will. OK?'

Serena raised an eyebrow. 'Great.'

Louise leaned in and hugged her friend, realising as she did so how much she had missed human affection in the past few months.

'Will you be OK? On your own?' Serena asked as she plunged the filter in the cafetière.

'Oh, yes,' replied Louise. 'I'm used to it, as you know.'

'But there won't be Patience here, for a while anyway,' Serena said as she poured the coffee into two mugs. 'And so there won't be any carers visiting either.'

'Blessed silence,' Louise replied, smiling. 'I can hardly wait.'

'Be careful what you wish for,' Serena replied with a ghost of a smile which disappeared almost as soon as it had appeared. She put both coffees on the kitchen table, pulled out a chair and sat down opposite Louise.

'Is it really that quiet at home?' Louise asked.

'Put it this way – the bin collection every Wednesday is a thrilling event,' Serena replied, blowing on her coffee.

'You don't talk about it much, what it's been like, since Patrick... And I haven't been there for you, have I? Jesus, I am such a shit friend.' Louise reached out to hold Serena's hand.

'You had Patience to worry about,' Serena replied, batting her hand away. 'And it's my fault, isn't it, for always appearing together? Just because I painted my face on every morning and continued to wash, people thought I was fine. Some even said that it must be a relief. A relief!'

Louise looked closely at her friend, realising for the first time since her arrival how tired she looked. Her face was, as she'd said, usually a perfectly set mask of make-up; very few people ever saw what went on beneath the surface.

'Anyway, I know that talking about him makes people uncomfortable. No one knows what to say and nothing makes it better, anyway. Nothing is ever going to bring him back.' Serena ushered her hair back over her shoulders.

'You can talk about anything with me, you know that. I'm sorry, I should ask you more about you. I realise now that I've been utterly selfish for ages.'

'You bloody haven't,' said Serena, standing up and walking over to retrieve the toast. 'You devote yourself entirely to Patience. And that's how it should be.'

Louise knew that she had avoided talking to Serena about Patrick. That was partly because she felt guilty that she was the lucky one – her disabled child was still alive. And it was also because it made her even more anxious about Patience's fate. She had survived for all these years, but they all knew that just one major illness could kill her. It was like seeing your child play on a cliff edge every day, while you were forced to watch, impotent, hundreds of metres away. There was nothing she could do to protect Patience, apart from monitor her like a hawk and dive in with medical treatment at the very first sign of trouble.

'It's pain beyond anything I ever imagined, to be honest,' Serena said, filling the silence while reaching for plates, knives and jam. 'It's like someone's taken a sword to my soul.'

'Oh, Serena!'

'You know, I had all those years to get myself ready for it, I knew it was coming, but when he died, there was just… darkness. Nothing helped.'

Serena walked back to the table, placed her load on it, and sat down once more.

'Alec tried to help, but he couldn't fix me, and he wanted me to be "fixed",' she added. 'He was locked in his own personal grief, of course. We were both in our own personal hell, lashing out, angry.'

'I didn't know it was that bad,' replied Louise. 'I'm so sorry. I should have been there more…' She took a large gulp of coffee. 'Is it any easier now? Less raw?'

'Honestly?' Serena began to apply jam to her toast with vigour. 'When the fog began to clear – and my God that took a while – I decided that I hated everything. The empty house. My empty life. Alec. I know now of course that that was more about my anger at our situation rather than real, actual hatred. But of course, Alec has a new partner now. What's done is done.'

'I thought the fact that you were so quiet meant that you were doing well, enjoying your freedom.'

'Mum moving in means the house isn't empty, thank goodness,' Serena continued. 'But why do you think I'm able to stay here for weeks on end? I don't have to be *anywhere*. I'm a non-person. Women of a certain age without kids? We don't exist. No one needs me, Lou.'

'Oh, Serena, that's not true. *I* need you.'

'Only temporarily.'

'Well, Pete has gone, hasn't he? We're in the same boat in that respect.'

'Do you *really* believe that, Lou? Really? This is a man who slaved away fixing things in this house for days while you were in hospital.' Serena pointed out the remedial work Pete had carried out in the kitchen. 'I know. I was here. And he's living in some fleapit in Birmingham so that you have enough money, now he's jacked the Qatar gig in. It seems to me that he hasn't "gone" at all.'

'But I thought he was staying with Steve?'

'No. He's in a bedsit in Aston.'

Louise paused while she digested this new information. 'Well, you may be feeling sympathetic towards him, Serena, but what about the fact that he cheated? No amount of self-flagellation will ever make that OK, will it?'

'You have zero proof for that, sweetheart. You only have a feeling. He hasn't confessed to it, has he?'

'No. But the way he acted at the counselling session? I just *know*, Serena.' Louise looked down at her toast, which was now cold, and found, to her surprise, that she felt hungry. She hadn't felt truly hungry for months. She reached for the jam jar and spoon.

'OK, be that as it may,' Serena replied, taking a mouthful of her own toast. 'We'll park that. But do you think it's possible that you may be deliberately trying to shut the people who love you out of your life? This all feels like a mental health crisis to me.'

'Honestly! *Everyone* is bloody depressed these days. It's so fashionable. No. I'm just tired, busy, with a shit marriage and a disabled daughter. I have no friends, apart from you, and my healthy daughter is completely absorbed with her own life. But I'm not depressed, I'm just unhappy.'

'It takes one to know one, love,' replied Serena, getting up to retrieve a pack of pistachio nuts from one of the cupboards. 'I've been there. And I see the signs in you too. You've always been a doer, an achiever – but even superwomen need help sometimes. You need to fix your oxygen mask before helping others, as they say.'

'Have you got a leaflet for counselling in your bag, too?'

Serena snorted. 'I couldn't find one! But I'll email you some links to sites where you can find a local counsellor. You need one, for yourself, not just for your marriage.' Serena offered Louise a nut, but she declined.

'Yeah, well, whatever.' Louise had almost finished her toast and was considering putting on another slice.

'I'm a wise woman, Lou. Ignore me at your peril.'

Louise smiled, despite herself.

'Right, OK. How about you? Are you having counselling? Do you take your own medicine?'

'Yes, I am. And it's helping, you old cynic. I've been trying to work out what my future should look like. I may be in my sixties, but I'm not done yet. I need to take charge of my life, before society overlooks me completely.'

'Blimey, you do sound depressed,' said Louise, with a smirk.

'Ha, you joke – but life without hope is deadly. I know. I'm working on it. I'm thinking about dating again. About getting a job.'

'Yes to the job. I love mine. But blimey, dating? No thanks.'

'What I'm saying is that you should think about *yourself*, Lou, for a change. Ask yourself – how long will you be able to continue looking after Patience at home, with just these occasional respite visits? And how will you ever do anything for yourself ever again, if she never leaves?'

Louise's expression reflected her shock that this topic, of all topics, had been raised. There had always been an unspoken agreement between them that they should never, ever question each other's caring decisions. She was preparing to launch into her defence when she was interrupted by a hammering at the door.

30

Eliza

April

'Mum! Get your stuff, quickly, we've got to go. Now.'

Eliza was standing on the front door mat, tensing her fists, looking like she might sprint off at any moment.

'Where are we going in such a hurry?'

'Hospital. Patience.' There was a jagged edge to her words.

'But she's at Morton Lodge – she left hospital yesterday.'

'Not any more. She's heading back there in an ambulance right now. I've come to get you. I thought it was probably best if *I* drove.' As soon as it had come out of her mouth, Eliza realised she shouldn't have said it. But it was too late now.

'I am not permanently drunk, Elizabeth, whatever your father has told you,' said Louise, hastily putting on shoes and grabbing a coat to cover up her pyjamas.

'I didn't mean that, Mum. I just thought you'd be too panicked. Oh, Mum!'

'OK. Tell me in the car,' she said, searching for her handbag in circles, barely even looking in her panic. 'Serena! We have to go to hospital!' she shouted into the house. 'Can you find me a few things to wear and bring them to me in a bit?'

She found her bag and didn't wait for an answer from her friend, instead running straight out of the house and into the car. Seconds later, Serena appeared at the door.

'Of course!' she shouted at Louise's back, her concern registering in her voice. Eliza was still standing by the car, about to open the driver's door. '*Is it bad?*' Serena mouthed, both of them knowing what that meant.

Eliza grimaced. 'I'm not a doctor,' she said quietly, 'but Auntie Serena – I'm frightened.'

'Hello? Is that A & E? It's Mrs Willow. My daughter Patience has just been brought in... Yes, in an ambulance... Can you tell me how she is? ... Why not? I'm not asking for a full medical analysis, I just want to know if... Yes, I'm on my way in now... OK, OK, we'll be there as soon as we can.'

Eliza listened with increasing dread. The reception team obviously wouldn't part with any information on the phone, never a good sign. When the call had finished, Louise sat silently on the passenger seat with her head in her hands.

'We'll be there soon, Mum. Really soon. Have you called Dad?'

Her mum turned to look at her then. Her eyes were filling with tears.

'This is my fault, Eliza. It's my fault she did that trial. I can't call him.'

'Mum, you *have* to! He's her *dad*.'

'Can't you? You've both been talking about me behind my back lately, so you're clearly communicating.'

'We are worried about you, Mum! It's not a conspiracy. We care.'

'If you say so.' Louise reached down and retrieved a tissue from her handbag and began to dab her eyes. 'Why are you here, anyway? Why were you visiting Patience so early in the morning? What on earth is going on?'

Eliza took a deep breath. 'I've taken a week off work and I came down to have a chat with you. About something. But it can wait. This is much more important.'

Eliza hit the brakes as the car approached a notorious bottleneck on the ring road.

'I *knew* there was something up with you and I've been so worried. You are so distracted and so *thin*. Eliza, please tell me what it is.'

Eliza looked over at her mother in surprise.

'I didn't think you'd noticed.'

'I always notice.'

'But you've been so busy with Patience and all this stuff with Dad…'

'You're still my daughter, Eliza.'

Now it was Eliza's turn to cry. Not singular tears, but a whole river, interspersed with hungry gulps of air.

'Jesus, Eliza, what is it? *Pull over.*'

'We can't, Mum, we've got to get there.'

'A few minutes won't make much difference. And you can't drive in that state. Pull over here – there's a lay-by.'

Eliza brought the car to a stop where her mother had suggested. She unbuckled her seatbelt swiftly and descended into her mother's arms, sobbing. 'Oh, Mum,' she said, her whole body shaking as the tears fell. 'Oh, Mum. I am so *lonely*.'

'Shhhh, shhhh,' said Louise, rubbing her daughter's back, as she had done hundreds of times in Eliza's childhood. 'For heaven's sake, tell me what this is all about.'

'I can't. We need to get there! Look, I'm OK now, I can drive, let's go.'

'No. Tell me. Now.'

'You don't need to hear this at the moment. Honestly. It can wait.'

Louise raised an eyebrow. 'Eliza, the wedding is off, isn't it? You've broken up with him. Ed.'

Eliza pulled herself up off her mother's chest. 'How did you know?'

'You haven't mentioned it, or him, for months. I put two and two together.'

'Why didn't you say anything?' Eliza asked.

'I didn't want to add to your troubles.'

'I'm so sorry, Mum.'

'What for?'

'For letting you down.'

'Don't be ridiculous! Now, let's switch seats. I'm on the insurance so I'll drive and you can tell me what on earth has been going on before we get there.'

Eliza obeyed, her tears slowing. She could hardly believe that she had finally told her mum about the wedding and that the world was still turning. In fact, Louise appeared much calmer now, more focussed; not angry, or disappointed. Eliza was dumbfounded.

'Why didn't you want to tell me?' Louise asked.

'Because I knew you'd be disappointed. And then all of the stuff with the trial happened and Dad left and I just wanted to shield you from it all. I was hoping we'd get back together…' Eliza looked down and squeezed her hands together, rotating her thumbs first forwards, then back.

'But you didn't. And I'm glad,' said Louise after a pause, staring straight ahead.

'You're glad?'

'I was happy that *you* were happy, of course, but I never warmed to him. He seemed cold. And not very kind. Kindness is the most important thing in a relationship, you know.' Eliza was gaping at her mother. It had never occurred to her that her parents had their doubts about Ed. 'Your dad is very kind. It's one of the things I…' she swallowed '… really like about him.'

Eliza sighted the hospital sign straight ahead. 'Turn in here, Mum,' she said, pointing.

'I know, Eliza,' Lou replied wryly. 'I've been here many more times than you!'

'Oh, fuck.'

Patience was lying in a hospital bed flanked by medical equipment. She was wearing an oxygen mask, numerous lines criss-crossed her body, and monitors were issuing constant readouts on the activity of her heart, her oxygen levels and her blood pressure. Two nurses were working on her as they watched, noting down her readings and adjusting her machines.

Eliza and Louise stood at the foot of the bed, taking in the full horror of the scene. There was no room for them to sit by her.

'I know this looks really awful.' They both looked at the doctor who had shown them in, a tidy, efficient-looking young woman who had identified herself as Dr Fanning, in a sort of trance. This simply could not be happening. 'Patience was in a bad way when she came in,' she continued. 'She had a severe fever, her breathing was very shallow, and she seemed confused. She was making all kinds of noises which her carer – Jimmy? – said were unusual. She also vomited in the ambulance.'

'Jesus,' said Eliza.

'We're carrying out some tests, but at the moment we're working on the basis that Patience has an infection somewhere. A severe infection. We are concerned that it might be—'

'An infection? So it's not to do with the gene therapy?' said Louise, interrupting.

'I'm sorry?' replied Dr Fanning, her eyes flaring, displaying her shock. 'I didn't know that she'd had such a procedure.'

'A week ago,' Louise replied quickly, as if by doing so she could somehow speed up her daughter's recovery. 'She's one of the participants in the first human trial for Rett syndrome. She only left hospital a couple of days ago. She had problems with her breathing, but it had improved enough for her to be able to go back to her care home.'

'Then I must look into that. But at the moment, more than anything else there are very clear clinical signs of an infection, so we've started her on antibiotics. And we are concerned that this is sepsis. Do you know what that is?'

Louise swallowed hard. 'I do, yes. It's blood poisoning, isn't it?'

'Yes. It's what happens sometimes when an infection runs riot inside someone's body. It's a very serious condition.'

'It's what killed Patrick,' Louise said to Eliza. 'I'll call your dad.'

31

Pete

April

Patience was so pale, it appeared as if she was actually part of the white sheet which the nurses had draped over her and tucked in neatly at the corners. And if it hadn't been for the reassuring beeping of the heart monitor and the gentle sigh of the ventilator, he'd have believed she was already dead.

Pete knew all about sepsis. He and Lou had witnessed Serena go through that particular hell with Patrick a few years previously, so he knew what was coming. He drew closer to the bed, leaned over and kissed her cheek, feeling its warmth on his lips. Then he stroked her face with his right hand, tracing its contours: her mother's nose, her father's eyes, a mouth of her very own. Pete looked down and saw that her hands, usually clenched together in an irresistible embrace, were now lying singly either side of her torso. He held the hand nearest to him, noting how cold it was, how limp. She was not awake, and she was not aware. They had sedated her, and it was clear she was not feeling any pain. He was grateful for that.

'Mr Willow?' Pete turned round to see a female doctor in her forties, hair in a tight brown bun, standing next to him.

'Yes.'

'We have some test results. Would you like me to wait for your wife to come back?'

'Yes, definitely. Let me go out and call her; she just went for a walk.'

Pete strode out into the corridor, took his phone out from his pocket and dialled Louise's number.

'Lou. It's me. They've got results.'

'See you in a minute.'

He had arrived about forty-five minutes ago, having exceeded every speed limit on the roads between Birmingham and Oxford. He readily anticipated the speeding fines he'd be getting, and he absolutely did not care. Louise had met him in the corridor outside, her face puffy and red, her hair unbrushed and greasy, her pyjamas – a pair he'd bought her for Christmas about five years ago – askew. He had taken one look at her and swept her up into his arms and she had cried then, long and hard, against his chest. They had stood there like that for several minutes, neither of them in the least bit awkward. The bonds of a lifetime were, it seemed, automatic, and hard to break.

While she was there, right there in his arms, she'd told him, in rushed, hushed tones, that Eliza had split up from Ed. That made two life-changing pieces of news in one morning and Pete could barely take even one of them in.

His poor, lovely Eliza. When this was over, he decided he was going to try to talk to her about it. He knew he had often avoided talking about feelings, but now was perhaps the time to try, he thought. The poor thing must be heartbroken.

They had gone in to see Patience then. Eliza had been there, talking to her, holding her hand. They had all made ridiculous small talk and pretended, within her earshot, that the sky was not about to fall in. And then he'd looked over at his wife and seen how utterly exhausted she was, how broken, and he'd suggested that she should go for a walk and leave them there, on duty.

And now she was walking up the corridor carrying a white paper bag. When she reached him, she opened up the bag and revealed a giant bar of chocolate and a large bottle of mineral water. 'For us,' she said. 'I think we need it. Serena has told me that I'm not allowed gin, so…'

Pete appreciated her attempt at humour, and her choice of chocolate, which was his favourite. 'Thank you,' he said, 'for thinking of me.'

Louise put her hand on his arm, and squeezed it gently. 'And I wanted to ask you. Would you mind if we called the hospital chaplain? I know how you feel about church – but I – I would definitely feel happier if we had them here. For me, I suppose. Call it familiarity.'

'Of course. It makes no difference to me,' he had replied. His mum had not brought him up with any faith, and he had found Louise's father's vocation baffling, but if anything, he had missed the ritual of church after the big family falling out. It was at least a decade since he'd last said a prayer. He didn't know whether his thoughts went to a higher being or whether they went no further than his own brain, but in any case, he had discovered praying had helped him arrange his myriad fears and hopes in some order. Lou had often looked across at him during services and assumed that his uncomfortable expression related to his feelings about her father and his faith, but they had more often related to his own dissatisfaction with himself. He was a shit provider, a shit father, a shit husband. If she was still alive, his mother, who had single-handedly raised two kids by herself in post-war slum housing in Birmingham, would think he had failed, he was convinced of that.

'Let's go in,' he said, brushing his thoughts aside. Nothing ever came of self-pity. That had done him enough harm already.

The doctor was waiting by Patience's bed. Eliza was sitting nearby and stood up as she saw her parents approach. 'There you are,' she said. 'Mrs Willow, I thought you'd all like to hear the results of some of the early tests. We think at this point that Patience's infection may have started in her bladder. Her urine tests certainly show that there's a very bad infection there now. And there's scarring, so she may have had several of these before. Has she ever had one diagnosed?'

'No,' Louise answered. 'No one has ever suggested it.'

'Well, it can be very difficult to diagnose in people who are not able to articulate their own pain,' replied the doctor.

'So you think all of this started as a bladder infection? Cystitis?' Louise said, unable to take on board that something so apparently minor could bring about something so catastrophic. 'Nothing to do with the gene therapy trial?'

'We can't be absolutely certain, of course,' the doctor replied, 'but we think it unlikely. I've just spoken to Professor Larssen and he is devastated to hear about Patience's condition. But he reaffirmed that this is not a likely side effect of the treatment she's had. It might be just a very unfortunate coincidence, or it could be related to the catheter they inserted in the hospital during treatment.'

'Right,' said Pete. 'How long would she have had to have it, to make it get so bad? Have the carers been missing signs?'

'It might have started very recently, Mr Willow. It's impossible to say. These things can take hold very quickly, particularly if someone's had them before. And as for the sepsis – maybe the bacteria is particularly virulent, causing her immune system to go into overdrive? We're not sure.'

All four of them looked at Patience then, her mask-like face belying the epic battle going on inside her body. It didn't matter how she'd got it, Pete realised now. All the blame in the world couldn't make her better.

'Is she going to die?' Pete asked, suddenly remembering with crystal clarity the moment when Louise had put the same question to the consultant neurologist, all those years ago. He had been wrong, hadn't he? So, doctors *could* be wrong.

'It's impossible to say, Mr Willow. We have only just started the antibiotics. The next twenty-four hours will be crucial. We will simply have to wait and see.' She had moved on then, to see other critically ill patients, and left the three of them standing around the bed, like pallbearers.

It was Serena, coming through the door, who had broken the unbearable silence they were all sharing. 'I've brought you some things, Lou,' she'd said in the instant before she had fully taken in the tableau that lay on the other side of the room. When she had seen it, she put down the bag she'd packed and walked swiftly over to Patience's bedside, collapsing into the chair next to it. Louise had followed her, knowing that she would sink further when she heard which particular foe Patience was having to fight.

*

Pete and Eliza decided to leave them for a while. Serena had always been so private about her grief, so outwardly strong, that it was a shock to see her dissolve so quickly. Louise had whispered her thanks to them when they announced that they were going to go in search of a hospital chaplain.

'I think I saw a sign to the chapel this way,' said Eliza, her voice lightening and her face brightening the further away they walked from ICU. Pete knew exactly how she felt. It was like being on an alien spaceship in there, entirely separate from the rest of the world, surrounded by technology you didn't understand, people saying things you didn't understand. Seeing ordinary people walking around the hospital, visiting relatives, buying newspapers, delivering flowers, gave him comfort.

They found the chapel on the ground floor, tucked away behind the mortuary. Which was logical enough, he supposed. The relatives of those needing the latter would probably seek help from the former, if they had any faith at all. The chapel turned out to be a small room, no bigger than a living room, simply decorated with free-standing cushioned upright chairs and a small altar adorned with a simple wooden cross. There were windows along one side of the room looking out onto a well-tended garden full of wildflowers. There was no sign of the chaplain, but there was a contact number on a poster on the wall, so Pete texted it, asking them to come to visit Patience in ICU. Then he turned around, and saw his daughter kneeling in front of the altar, deep in thought. Or prayer. He hadn't raised her to pray, but these were certainly desperate times. He'd take anything that worked, frankly. He sat down on the front row of seats while he waited for her to finish.

'Sorry, Dad. I just thought... this might be a good time to ask for help.'

She had turned around and walked over to where he was sitting, and pulled out a chair. 'That's fine, love. Pray away. If it helps.'

'Grandpa taught me how to do it. You know, when we used to visit him.'

'Yes, I suppose he did.'

'You didn't like Grandpa, did you?'

'No, not very much. He never thought I was good enough for your mum. And... well, he wasn't a nice man, really.'

'Why?'

'Well, he said something horrible once. Something your mum and I have never forgiven him for.'

'Was it something about Patience?'

'Oh no. He was very nice about her. Although neither he nor your gran were very helpful, in practical ways. But they said nice things, at least.'

'Then who was it about?'

'It doesn't matter.' He swung his head around to look directly at her. 'Love, your mum told me about your news.'

Pete registered a look of panic in her eyes.

'About Ed leaving,' he carried on. 'Well, as your mum said, we had our doubts about him. As did you, I think? And you definitely don't want to marry someone if you have doubts.'

'But what about the money you've lost?'

'We'll get some of it back. And of course Great-Auntie Maud will be grumpy that she won't be able to debut her peach fascinator, but she'll just have to cope, won't she?'

Eliza laughed, and then looked at her dad in wonder.

'Don't look at me like that,' he said. 'You're human. Humans make mistakes. Why did you expect us to be so disappointed in you?' For heaven's sake, he thought, I've made enough mistakes for all of us.

'I just thought that you wanted me to do things properly,' she said. 'You've *always* wanted me to do things properly. Uni, proper career, good salary, pick a man with prospects, get married, have babies…'

'When did I ever say those things?'

He could see her thinking about it.

'Well, not exactly those words. But you did push me into going to uni. And wanted me to get a good job.'

'That wasn't for me, sweetheart, it was for *you*. I wanted you to be happy. And not make the mistakes that I did.' Pete looked down at his shoes, which were splattered with paint and dust.

'But you're a globetrotter, Dad. You work all over the world, see all sorts of stuff, meet all sorts of people. You have an exciting job.'

'Do you really think that? Love, I hate it.'

Eliza looked at her father in silence. Pete realised that he'd never really spoken to her about his own feelings, about anything. Their conversations had always been loving and caring, but practical, never emotional. He could tell that this shift had been noted.

'If you hate it, you should stop doing it.'

'I can't.'

'Why not?'

'Because we need the money.'

'But Mum's working now.'

Pete visibly sank, his shoulders and chin dropping. Then he gripped the bridge of his nose with his finger and thumb, cast his eyes down, and sighed. 'Oh, it doesn't matter now, does it,' he mumbled.

'Sorry, Dad? What doesn't matter? I don't understand.'

Pete looked around and made for a row of chairs to their right.

'Sit down, pet. Sit down and listen.'

Eliza did as he asked.

'So. Money,' he said, facing the altar, looking away from her. 'You'll be wondering why we're still hard up, given the work I've been doing abroad. The thing is, we did have a nice nest egg saved up. I'd worked hard on lots of foreign contracts and I had it squirrelled away. We were all set up for a nice retirement. And then, I met Chris.'

'Chris?' Eliza turned towards her father and he shifted slightly, meeting her gaze.

'She was another expat in Doha, a Brit.'

'Chris was a woman?'

'Yes, short for Christina, I think. I met her at the rugby club one night. She was friendly. Very friendly.' He remembered, with shame, that he'd allowed her to flirt with him. He'd even enjoyed the attention. 'We got on, you know? And she got me and my mates tickets for the golf via her firm. And we'd always wanted to go.'

'Oh?' Eliza's eyes had widened.

'It's not what you're thinking, pet, I promise. I'd never do that to your mum.'

Pete was worried enough about how this revelation

would affect his daughter's view of him; good heavens, he didn't want her thinking he would cheat on Louise, too. He'd had offers over the years – it happened, when you were away from home – but he'd never acted on it.

'Anyway. When we were there, she told me about this amazing investment opportunity she was working on, a new hotel they were building out there. Luxury development, beach-side property, all the bells and whistles. She said that if I invested in it, I could double my money. So I did, didn't I? I invested all of our life savings, all fifty thousand bloody pounds of them, in a hotel which never got built. Chris disappeared a few months later and I haven't been able to track her down. I have no idea if I even know her real name.'

Pete's eyes were brimming with tears. He had worked so hard over the years, not just to provide for his family, but also to present a strong, confident figure for them all. He had tried never to show any weakness, never to reveal how he was feeling inside. But now they knew the truth, he thought.

'Oh, Dad!'

'You know that saying? A fool is easily parted from his money? *I am that fool.*'

'Don't be ridiculous, Dad. You thought you were investing. You were trying to do your best for Mum.'

'That's all I've ever wanted to do,' he said. 'And just look at the mess I've made of that.'

They sat in silence for a few more seconds, before Pete sprang up and began to walk towards the door. The less said about all of this, the better.

'We'd better get back, don't you think?' he said, beckoning

for her to follow, and she was about to do so when a woman walked in.

'Can I help you?' she asked, with a gentle smile.

'We're looking for the priest, love,' he answered. 'My daughter is in ICU.'

'That's me,' said the woman, who Pete assessed to be in her early forties. She was wearing low heels, a knee-length patterned skirt, a white shirt – which he now noticed had a white clerical collar – and dangly silver earrings. Her highlighted hair was sleek and well-brushed. She did not look like any priest Pete had ever met before. 'I'm one of the hospital chaplaincy team,' she said. 'I'm a Church of England priest. What flavour of priest were you looking for?'

Pete's mouth twitched. 'We aren't regular churchgoers, I'm afraid,' he said. 'But my wife – her father was a vicar. He was C of E too.'

'OK, great. It doesn't much matter, to be honest, as long as you are comfortable,' the woman replied, her voice warm. 'I'm Theresa, by the way.'

'Nice to meet you, Theresa,' said Eliza, who had now joined them by the door. She held out her hand. 'I'm Eliza. Patience, my sister, is in ICU. She's really poorly. Could we go there now, do you think? Right now?'

32

Eliza and Patience

April

The priest had followed them immediately, her heels tapping on the stairs behind them as they'd climbed up the two storeys to the wards. Eliza took a deep breath before pushing open the door into ICU, genuinely frightened about what she might find when she entered.

She was relieved to find her mum and Screna sitting side by side, talking, a clear sign that Patience hadn't taken a turn for the worse. Louise looked up as they entered, and then stood up when she spotted Theresa coming in their wake.

'Thank you so much for coming,' she said, walking towards her, holding out a hand.

'Not at all,' Theresa replied, slowly and quietly, shaking Louise's hand as she did so. 'Now – can you tell me all about Patience?' she said.

The family made room for her beside the bed, and Theresa sat down so that she could look directly at Patience.

'Patience,' she called out, softly, carefully. 'Patience, my name is Theresa. I'm a priest here and your mum and dad asked me to come to see you. You're very poorly, but I wanted you to know that we are all rooting for you. That you are loved and watched over.'

Golly, the sun is warm here. It feels like it's closer to me than usual. It's HUGE. The grass I'm lying on is lush and not at all scratchy, and I'm watching wind-whipped clouds scudding over my head.

Eliza watched as the priest carried out her duty, offering comfort in the face of extreme fear. Her voice was incredibly soothing, and Eliza found that her own breathing – which she now realised had been rapid all morning – was easing.

I raise my hands in front of my face and wiggle my fingers, marvelling at the invisible patterns I can make in the sky, like I'm conducting an orchestra of the elements.

Eliza looked over at Patience's face. She appeared serene, as if she was having a lovely sleep. She thought that her breathing might have got a little easier in the past hour, but it was quite possible that she was imagining that. She wondered what Patience would say about her predicament, if she could speak. Probably a whole list of expletives – and fair enough.

'And what I'd like to do now is to say a prayer for Patience. If that's OK?' Theresa was now looking at Louise and Pete, seeking their approval. Louise nodded readily and a few seconds later so did Pete. Eliza looked at him closely and could not see any signs of discomfort in his face or body language. Theresa seemed to have had a calming influence on them all.

'Dear Lord, please watch over Patience,' she began, 'and give her the strength to fight. But please also look over her family.'

Eliza closed her eyes and, for the second time that day, pleaded with someone, anyone, to help her sister to continue to live.

That sun is growing larger by the minute. Is it... Is it... coming to get me? To take me home?

Eliza retreated from ICU after that and left her parents talking to Theresa. They hadn't asked her to leave, but there was something about their hushed tones and intense conversation that told her they would rather she didn't hear what they had to say. She also realised that it was the first time in months that she had seen them talking calmly to each other and she had no desire to disrupt such a rare event.

Hours spent in a hospital ward were definitely longer than ordinary hours, Eliza thought, as she walked out of the ward and into the corridor. At least twice as long. She had been taking turns with both her parents to sit beside Patience and talk to her, while they went to sit in the spring sunshine, or ate a meal in the on-site cafeteria. This time alone had given her plenty of time to think, not about Patience – she didn't even want to go there, it was too painful to contemplate – but about the peripheral stuff in her life that needed sorting. She had to make some decisions, some plans.

'Eliza?'

Jimmy was walking towards her down the corridor. She smiled at him instinctively, despite her worries about Patience.

'Oh, hi,' she said. They hadn't spoken since that morning,

when they had found Patience delirious in bed at the respite care home.

'I've just come off shift; I came straight here.'

Eliza was puzzling over whether it would be acceptable to embrace him, and couldn't think of anything remotely sensible to ask.

'Look, I'm sorry. Do you blame me? I wouldn't be surprised. We should have spotted it sooner. But we're short-staffed and we really did think she was just tired...' Evidently, Jimmy had misread her facial expression.

'Shall we take a seat?' she said, pointing to a bench further along the corridor. When they sat down, Jimmy's knee brushed hers, and she took an involuntary sharp intake of breath. Her knee felt like it was on fire. She sprang away from him.

'Actually, shall we get coffee? I'm gasping,' she said, walking away briskly, hoping to regain her composure before he caught up with her. Despite her turn of speed, however, Jimmy joined her in seconds, and kept pace with ease, like a marine on a route march. Just a minute later, Eliza was beginning to sweat. They were almost jogging now, she thought, smiling to herself.

'What's so funny?' Jimmy said, pursing his lips.

'Do you run regularly?' she replied. 'Because I'm knackered and you seem to have just warmed up.'

'It was your pace!'

'I know, I know. My fault. I am obviously very thirsty. Ah, here we are,' she said, grateful for a distraction. They had arrived at the café, a characterless white box furnished with uncomfortable metal chairs and white melamine tables, and decorated with posters advising visitors to wash their hands, get a flu jab, or check their cholesterol levels.

'I'll buy them,' said Jimmy. 'What do you want?'

'I'll have a decaf cappuccino, if they've got some.'

He turned around to look at her and made a face. 'Decaf? Are you sure?'

'Quite sure,' she replied.

'I'd have thought, given the day you've had, you'd be after all the caffeine you can get,' he said as he placed her cardboard takeaway cup on the table.

'Ah, well, *there's* a tale,' she replied, taking the lid off her coffee to see if the barista had sprinkled chocolate on top.

'Do you want to tell it?'

She considered this.

'Shit, you know, I might as well. Today is utterly surreal. It can't get any worse.'

Jimmy removed his jacket. He was wearing a short-sleeved shirt and the muscles in his arms danced as he lifted his coffee up to his mouth for each sip. Eliza was momentarily mesmerised.

'Eliza?'

'Sorry!' She tried to focus on her coffee instead. 'So, firstly, I told Mum about the wedding being off, and apparently it's no big deal. Can you imagine? I suppose that she's so consumed by Patience at the moment, she can't really get upset about anything else, can she? It looks like I picked a good day to bury bad news.'

'Or it could just be that she's really not that bothered.'

'Surely you know my mother well enough by now to know that she's never not bothered?'

Jimmy shrugged his shoulders.

'And then there's the other thing. The big thing, really...'
In for a penny, in for a pound, she thought. '... I'm having a
baby. In the autumn.' She looked at him carefully as she said
it, interested to see how he'd react.

Jimmy put down his cup and a broad smile spread across
his face.

'You are? That's amazing. Congratulations.'

She realised she'd been holding her breath waiting for his
response and let out a huge sigh.

'Thank you. I'm excited. Petrified, and excited. It's Ed's.
But he won't be around, so it's just... mine.'

'I'm sure you'll be a brilliant mother.'

Eliza raised one eyebrow.

'That just goes to show how little you know me,
Jimmy.'

'Oh, come off it. You'll be great. Are your parents made
up?'

Eliza bit her lip.

'You haven't broken that bit to them yet, then?' he said.

'Nope. Not quite yet.' Eliza stared down at her drink,
which the barista had decorated with a heart.

'About earlier,' she said, looking up at him. 'Of course
I don't blame you. There's little point blaming anyone.
Dad is blaming Mum for the trial, I blame myself for
the trial, and Mum is blaming herself, of course, and the
doctors are just blaming bacteria. It seems to me that we
are where we are and there's nothing that any of us can do,
except wait.'

'But if we'd spotted it earlier...'

'The medics said it must have come on really quickly.
Look, please, please don't beat yourself up about it. To be

honest, we've always known that this day would come. Patience has been on borrowed time for decades.'

'You're talking like she's going to die.'

'Don't you think she is?'

Jimmy looked at Eliza, his eyes wide.

'No. I've got to know P and she's got a fighting spirit.'

'No amount of fighting is going to make any difference to this, Jimmy. This is just about biology.'

'I know that. But I refuse to give up. I've watched someone die and I have no desire to see that again any time soon.'

'Fair enough.' Eliza put the lid back on her coffee and pushed her chair back.

'Hey, have you told P?' Jimmy's eyes were bright.

'About what?'

'The baby.'

'She knows I'm pregnant.'

'But does she know that you're keeping it?'

Eliza tapped her fingers against her cup. 'No. I suppose not.'

'Then you should tell her.'

'Do you think? But she won't understand it, will she?'

'How can you be sure? I know you share all sorts with her. And she loves it, I can tell. Go and tell her.'

Eliza didn't need to think twice. 'You know what? I will. Thanks. Thank you, Jimmy.' She pushed her chair back and stood up. 'OK, then. I'll see you back there in a bit, shall I?' she said, her head tipping in the direction of ICU.

'Sure. I'll hang out here, and come up in half an hour or so.'

Eliza pulled on her coat and strode off down the corridor.

*

Louise was sitting with Patience and she looked pleased to see that Eliza had returned.

'Your dad's taken Serena back to the house,' Louise said, sighing, patting the empty chair next to her, inviting Eliza to sit down. 'It's been difficult for her, seeing Patience like this. I think she needs to sleep.'

Eliza nodded. Sleep would also have been her preference, too.

'When did the priest go?' she asked.

'Oh, about half an hour ago. She was wonderful. So caring, so interested in Patience – and in us. Your dad and I had a good chat with her.'

'That must be the first time Dad has enjoyed talking to a priest,' Eliza said.

'Desperate times and all that,' Louise replied, leaning over towards Patience and rubbing her arm. 'He owned up to something, too. He's lost our savings, would you believe. All of them. *That's* what he's been hiding.'

Eliza tried to look surprised. 'Oh crikey, Mum. That's awful.' She had never been a convincing actress, but it seemed that her mum was so distracted, she didn't even notice.

'I know. Or at least, I *think* I know. Given today and how Patience is, I'm not sure I care that much. After all of that angst about our finances, trying to get a job so that I could help, sleepless nights spent worrying – it's only money, isn't it?'

Mother and daughter looked at Patience, immobile and attached to myriad different machines.

'Lots of money, though,' said Eliza, quietly.

'Yes. But we'll manage. We have somewhere to live, and an income. I'm just relieved he's finally being honest with me, really. For a while there I thought he had another woman.'

Eliza wrinkled her nose. It wasn't comfortable, knowing so much detail about her parents' private lives. They had never discussed their feelings for each other with her before, but she recognised that her mum's admission marked a turning point; and, after all, she had been waiting for her parents to be honest with each other for decades.

'I'm glad for you, Mum.'

They joined hands and sat in silence for a while, listening to Patience's machine-assisted breaths. And then Eliza decided to just come out and say it, the proverbial elephant in the room.

'Do you think she's going to die?'

'I don't know, sweetheart,' Louise replied after a pause, her voice a perpetual sigh. 'I really don't know.'

Eliza looked down at the floor for a few seconds, before taking a deep breath, her decision made.

'Mum, can I have a minute? With Patience?'

Louise looked at her quizzically.

'Of course, darling. Without me here?'

'Yes, please,' Eliza replied. 'I'm sorry. I'll only be a minute. I'll come to get you if anything changes. But I just wanted to have a private chat with her, if that's OK.'

'Of course. I'll just be outside.'

She placed her hand on her mother's arm. 'Thank you.'

When Louise had gone, Eliza looked around her, taking in the nurses who were looking after other patients, and the gaggles of relatives framing nearby beds. Craving privacy, she stood up and pulled the flimsy curtain around them. She knew that it would block no noise, but she felt better knowing that no one would be looking at her if – when – she cried.

'Patience – P. It's me,' she said, drawing her chair as close to the bed as it would go. She rested her chin on the mattress just a few inches from her sister's face. She watched her in silence for a minute, trying to focus on her golden hair, her porcelain skin and her luscious eyelashes, and doing her best to ignore the tubes, the mask, the machines. She wanted to remember her as she was, not like this.

'Patience? Are you in there? Can you hear me?'

It's a beautiful day. Summer's early glory: the air smells sweet with honeysuckle and a host of butterflies are dancing in our garden. I'm sitting cross-legged on the floor, rocking. And she is jumping, jumping high in the air.

'I don't know if you can hear me, Patience, but I have some things I want to say.'

She lets out a shriek of glee, and cups her hands. Then she comes to sit down next to me.

'Firstly, I want to say – I'm sorry I haven't been that brilliant a sister. I've made a lot of mistakes, and I've been resentful and distant and I haven't been to see you nearly enough. But I wanted you to know, to really know, how much you mean to me.'

She leans towards me and holds her hands up so that they are level with my face. And then she opens them just a crack. A tiny crack, but it's enough.

'I don't know how you feel about me at all, but you have been my constant, Patience. You have always been there, and I have needed you more than you know.'

The tortoiseshell butterfly which she'd been cocooning gently between her palms takes its chance and becomes airborne.

'And the other thing, the major thing, is that I'm going to keep the baby, Patience. You're going to be an auntie. And you're going to be awesome at it. So keep fighting, my lovely sister. Keep fighting.'

As the butterfly makes its escape, it miscalculates its flight path and heads straight for my face.

'Please don't leave me. I need you. I can't do this on my own.'

When it bumps into my nose, its wings tickle, and I begin to laugh; partly due to the strange sensation, but largely because she is laughing too, real belly laughs, and her joy makes me so happy. Then she drapes her arms around me, and we just sit there like that, laughing together. And I am happier than I have ever been.

Just as she had predicted, tears were now rolling down Eliza's cheeks. Pregnancy had made her even more emotional than normal; her hormones were wreaking havoc. She reached into her pocket to retrieve a tissue, mopped them up, and then stood up to give Patience a kiss. It was difficult to find a piece of skin that wasn't covered in a mask, surgical tape or tubes, but she eventually settled on her forehead.

'You make sure you stay, now,' she said, before turning and walking out of the ward in search of Louise.

When she eventually releases me, and then stands up and walks away, I wish with all my heart that I could reach out to her and bring her back.

*

'Mum?' Eliza had found Louise sitting on one of the benches in the corridor.

'Yes?'

'Thank you.'

Eliza took a seat next to her mother.

'How did it go?' Louise asked.

'Oh, you know,' Eliza had to find her tissue once again, to wipe away some more tears. 'As you'd expect.'

'Yes.' Louise reached out for Eliza's hand.

'And Mum?'

'Yes?'

'I didn't tell you the whole truth earlier.'

'Ah.'

'Ed and I have broken up, that's true. But also – there's something else.'

She paused. Was she really going to say it this time? Yes. She was.

'I'm having a baby, Mum.'

Louise gasped. She whipped her hand away from Eliza and used it to cover her face.

'Mum, I'm so sorry. This isn't the time to tell you about this, is it?'

'No.' Louise had now started to cry.

'I'm so sorry. So sorry.'

Louise put her hands back in her lap and looked at her daughter, her eyes wide.

'What on earth are you sorry for?' she said, sounding like a schoolteacher chastising a naughty child.

'For being a total mess,' Eliza blurted out. 'For not being the daughter I should be. The daughter you need.'

'Don't be ridiculous!' Louise said, wiping her nose with

the back of her hand. 'You are my wonderful daughter, and you are *everything* I need.'

It was Eliza's turn to cry now.

'Oh, Mum,' she said. '*Oh, Mum.*'

33

Patience

April

It is pitch black outside; the clouds are obliterating the moon. But in here, it is always twilight. The nurse's station has a desk lamp which illuminates charts, notes, and the face of the ward sister. It's casting shadows on the 2 a.m. creases on her face, making them look like crevices. The lamps above each bed are dimmed for night-time, but their white LED bulbs remain unforgiving, sending rays of bleached light onto the souls beneath.

Here is the realm of the hard, cold and functional; here is the realm of science and medicine, of evidence and analysis. It is not a place for dreams.

In each booth, green and blue lines on suspended screens undulate like mountain ranges and the bleeps that accompany them sound at their peaks and troughs, the human body writing its own music.

No one notices me watching them from up here. For you see, I'm light as air, a brief passing shadow, a veritable figment.

Beside my bed, Dad is sitting on a chair and leaning

against the safety rails, his head in his hands, as if in prayer. He has not moved for some time now, but he occasionally lifts his head to check the screens overhead, which, like airport departure boards, rarely seem to change.

In a room just down the corridor, a woman lies sleeping on a sofa bed. It's made up with hospital-issue sheets and pillows, but it's not a hospital bed. It is hard, and the springs chime whenever the woman turns over. Eliza, her stomach now swelling daily, has wedged one of the pillows between her knees to help her sleep. There are threadbare curtains at the window which the streetlights are permeating easily, and a blue plastic chair sits next to it, clothes slung over its back. There's a hook on the back of the door, and here hangs one threadbare white towel, barely large enough to reach around a small body. It is damp after use in the adjoining shower room, where one tiny tablet of soap was provided.

In the corridor outside, a young man sits slumped on a bench. Jimmy did not go home earlier when he had said goodnight; he found that he simply couldn't. His guilt is overwhelming and he wants to be here until the bitter end. He owes her that, at least, he thinks. And he also needs – wants – to be there for Eliza. He has fallen asleep even in that uncomfortable position, and the zip of his leather jacket is now burning a brand onto his face.

Miles away, in a semi-detached house in Kidlington, Mum is also sitting slumped, but this time on a large, comfortable leather sofa. She has a pile of notes beside her, the spoils of a frenetic couple of hours spent searching the internet for answers. She has found none. She fell asleep only an hour ago, and Serena has draped a large, crocheted blanket over her and propped her head up with a pillow.

Let's go back now into the ward, into my booth, and Dad with his head in his hands. Surrounded on all sides by banks of pillows and almost obliterated by the machines which are keeping me alive, my body lies there, sleeping. I am dreaming. In that dream I'm dancing, dancing madly, throwing my arms into the air and spinning with wild abandon, faster, and then faster. Now let's go deeper inside; look, there's my heart. Its chambers have been frantic, desperate to keep up the blood supply my body needs. The blood it dispatches is coursing through my veins and arteries, some of it becoming a tide that's making its way inexorably to the surface, venting its heat into the air. And if we look even closer, we can make out my minuscule army of white blood cells which have been involved in a relentless battle for some days now. They are exhausted.

But they are not giving up. In my dream, I'm now dancing a waltz, its tempo a beating heart which gradually, almost imperceptibly, is starting to slow.

PART FOUR

34

Louise

June

The churchyard roses were in full bloom, spilling their scent on Louise as she walked up the path. Interspersed between the graves were lilac, hydrangeas, golden marigolds and blushing pink asters, all planted, no doubt, by green-fingered parishioners. Bees flew from one flower to the next, gorging on nectar and sharing the glory of a perfect English summer's day.

Louise paused in front of one gravestone, dedicated to the memory of a woman who had died over a century ago, aged thirty-two, presumably in childbirth, for her baby had died a week later. He was buried with her. She said a silent prayer for a family she did not know, but for whom she now had a far greater empathy.

'It's time to go in now...' Pete had placed his arm on the small of her back, guiding her in the direction of the church entrance. Louise walked through the porch of the stone-built Norman building, which still felt cool, despite the rising temperature outdoors. She took a seat near the front on the right-hand side and looked around her; the church was packed and there were even spare chairs lined up at the back for latecomers. All of a sudden, a hush descended.

'She's coming,' several people near her muttered to their partners, the crowd standing up then and craning their necks to see.

Louise stood up then too, and her position giving her a clear view of Katy walking down the aisle on the arm of her father, Len. She was wearing a stunning, figure-hugging lace gown, and her beaming smile was aimed squarely at her husband-to-be, Matt, who was standing in front of the altar, hopping from foot to foot.

Following just behind her was Eliza, resplendent in a dress which had been adjusted several times in the past few months as her girth had expanded beyond expectation. Katy had not been bothered at all about the cost of the redesign, apparently; she had been a good friend to her daughter throughout her life, and for that Louise was incredibly grateful.

She had asked herself many times over the past few months why it had taken Eliza so long to tell her the truth, about both the failure of her relationship and the baby. It had been painful to admit to herself that it was absolutely, unequivocally, her fault. That was something she had started to work through with both her counsellor and her AA group; she had to learn to take responsibility for her own actions.

She acknowledged, now, that while showering attention on both of her girls, she had unknowingly smothered them. Her counsellor – a friendly, motherly Irish woman called Rosalie – had told her that she had to accept the anger she felt about the way her own life had turned out. If she did this, she said, she wouldn't feel the need to impose her suppressed hopes and dreams on her children. She realised now that she'd invested far too much of herself in Eliza, had piled on far too many expectations, and, painful as it was, it was time to let them go. She'd surpassed them, anyway – she was a wonderful sister, a loving daughter, and she would be an excellent mother, she had no doubt.

Louise turned to her right and looked at Pete, who met her eye and reached for her hand. She took it gladly, sharing their mutual relief at being able to be here at all today, to actually have something positive to celebrate.

Patience's hospitalisation had opened up a dark abyss for them all; time had stood still and they had all, at different points, worried that they would never find their way out of it. But it was also true that, facing their fears head-on and coming out the other side, had given them all a huge dose of perspective, and for that she was incredibly grateful.

She had realised that she'd lived without perspective for decades. She had been so caught up in the challenges of her life as a carer, as a mother of a disabled child, that she had been unable to look outside and think about what else mattered. Or didn't matter, come to that.

The medication her GP had given her had been helping restore her mental health, too. It was anti-anxiety medication, designed to take the edge of her stress levels, which had been permanently raised for decades. She'd felt a bit groggy to start with, but the side effects had now subsided.

This medication and her tentative steps towards sobriety had forced her to face the reality of the situation she was in – and that wasn't pleasant. As Serena had predicted, Louise *had* found their house unbearably silent after her friend had left, and she'd also realised that it wasn't the physical emptiness that disturbed her most; it was the emotional emptiness.

She had thought that Pete had left her alone for all of that time, but in truth, he had been a constant friend, a constant reassurance, a constant sounding-board, even when he hadn't physically been at home. And now that she was no longer self-medicating with alcohol, she had realised that she was left with a huge emotional void; trying to mend her relationship with Pete was something she hoped might fill it.

There was a long way to go. She was still processing the loss of their nest egg, for a start. But with the new perspective she now had, she could see Pete as a whole, as a good man who'd stood by them all. Her parents had been entirely wrong about him, she now realised. He was the kindest man she knew, far kinder than her own father. And she knew that Pete's own guilt about the loss of their savings was punishment enough. Adding her voice to that chorus would achieve nothing, and she had her own guilt to deal with, anyway. The only way to go was forwards – and the only way to do that was together.

She watched as Katy and Matt chuckled nervously while exchanging vows and rings, remembering her own wedding, which her parents had refused to attend. In the end, they'd got married at an ugly little church in Birmingham, which had bars at the windows and graffiti on the doors, instead of her father's neat little Saxon parish church in Oxfordshire. She'd worn a hired wedding dress and carried a simple, hand-tied bouquet of lilies. She hadn't cared at all, because her only focus had been the man waiting at the end of the aisle. Pete was the right man for her, she knew. They'd get through this.

It had taken her two decades to realise that her attempts at pleasing her parents were pointless. They had disapproved of their daughter's relationship throughout, from the early days of the engagement onwards, on the basis that Pete was working class and, therefore, to quote her mother, 'would not amount to anything'. They'd remained tacitly in touch, however, despite their refusal to attend their wedding, until things finally came to a head one appalling night in the late 1990s.

It was burned on Louise's memory.

Eliza had come to her in great distress after finding out she had become pregnant following a brief liaison with a feckless boy from her school. She had told Louise that she wanted an abortion. Louise had not argued with her – she was fifteen and had clearly been taken advantage of. She had found a private clinic near Serena's house, but she needed the money to pay for it. Louise wanted to pay, but she had a problem; if she took the money out of their joint account, Pete would ask what it was for. So, she decided to ask her mother for help instead.

Louise had approached her because she believed – hoped – that, as a fellow woman, she would see her granddaughter's need and do the right thing, quietly. But she had been wrong. Instead, she had referred the matter to Louise's father, who had refused any financial help whatsoever, before expounding on his moral views on the subject. He had shouted, as Louise was heading out of the door, that Eliza *must have become pregnant because she was clearly oversexed*.

Louise's outrage at that comment had been the final nail in the coffin of her relationship with her parents. Once their ample, antique front door had closed behind her, she had never been back, not even when they had become infirm and had moved into a care home. Some bridges could not be rebuilt. Some bridges were simply not worth rebuilding.

She had told Pete about the abortion after her own father's refusal, against Eliza's wishes. She'd had no choice. He had been horrified, utterly horrified. But he had understood. He had agreed that they should pay for the abortion, while also agreeing that he would never tell Eliza that he knew anything about it. She suspected that he would have found the subject hard to broach with her, at any rate, but his unwavering support had meant a great deal to her.

They had both been incredibly worried about Eliza after that, but she had appeared on the surface at least, to have made an admirable recovery. She had always been such an independent unit, so strident, so purposeful, and she had seemed to sail through her life – her exams, her degree, her friendships – with ease. It was only now that Louise was beginning to understand the truth…

The bride and groom were coming back down the aisle now, exuding pure joy. Eliza followed them once more, on the arm of one of the groomsmen, a rotund young man with a florid expression. Louise analysed her daughter's face for signs of melancholy, but saw none. Either she was unaffected by the moment, or she was hiding it well.

The congregation was beginning to file out, thoughts of a welcome drink and a large lunch beckoning them to the reception. Louise reached down to pick up her handbag, put her other arm through Pete's, and together they made their way out of the church.

Everyone around her was so happy, it was possible for her to ignore, briefly, the worries that haunted her.

Patience had recovered from sepsis, but what she was dealing with now was arguably worse. Her guilt weighed on her with every step.

Because, as it turned out, Pete had been right all along.

35

Eliza and Patience

July

Eliza unloaded the last bag of her belongings from her car. It had taken her two journeys to empty the flat, but it was all done now, with her father's help.

'Well done, love. That was hard, with all those stairs. Do you want a sit down?'

Pete had been asking her if she wanted to sit down all day. She knew he meant well, but she was not disabled, just pregnant, and the adrenaline boost she'd got after deciding to terminate the contract on the flat had given her enough energy to last for days.

'If you don't fancy a sit down, do you want a cup of tea instead?'

'Oh, go on then.'

They squeezed past the pile of bags in the hall and made their way into the kitchen. It was far tidier now that Pete had returned home, and Eliza knew her mum was grateful for that. She was back working full-time on the trial now, collating evidence and dealing with families. It was Dad, in fact, who had encouraged her to go back to work. It was clear that employment had given her new confidence.

'So, are you ready, then?' Her father was reaching into one of the bottom cupboards for the biscuit tin. Eliza took a seat by the kitchen table.

'For maternity leave? Yes. But not for motherhood. I feel like that may take some getting used to.'

Walking out of her office on her final day had felt like being released from prison; she had whistled the *Great Escape* theme tune under her breath. She wasn't sure whether she could bear the idea of going back to her job in twelve months, but she would worry about that when the time came.

For now, she had enough money to keep her ticking over, thanks to twin miracles. Her parents had given her the refunded money for the wedding booking, and Ed had – purely out of guilt, she suspected – given her not only her share of their honeymoon fund, but also the entirety of the deposit on the Battersea flat, to help her get back on her feet closer to home. Housing was cheaper around Kidlington, and she had found what she hoped was a perfect flat for her forthcoming family of two. It had one large bedroom, a small kitchen, a living room which looked out onto a park, and, crucially, a garden. She hadn't realised until recently how much she had longed to look out at green every day.

What she'd do for money after the birth was as yet unknown, but she had discovered significant inner strength in the past few months, and she knew now to trust her instincts. Ed had said he would help with childcare costs and she thought maybe she'd find a job closer to home, or try freelancing. Who knew, she might actually be good at PR if she wasn't trying so hard to be someone she wasn't?

'I'm not a mother, obviously, but fatherhood is hard enough,' said her dad, putting some biscuits on a plate and plopping teabags in two mugs. 'I'm not sure I've been very good at it.'

'Oh, Dad,' she said, getting up and enveloping him in a hug. Her father squeezed her tightly. 'You've been *amazing*. You've always been there for me and Patience.'

'I wasn't though, was I? I went off abroad, trying and failing to make money, thinking that was all you lot needed. But I'm home now, anyway. A bit late.'

'Yes, you *are* home, and exactly when it matters,' Eliza said, looking down at her bump, which was now so large she could no longer see her toes. 'I'll be needing you a lot, soon.'

'I know. And your mum and I will be very happy to help,' he said, pouring hot water from the kettle. 'It will be a nice change, caring for something so tiny. I've got so used to caring for an adult. I hear the nappies are smaller.'

Eliza rolled her eyes. She found the milk from the fridge and poured it into the mugs. 'So are you going back to work then, Dad, or is this it for you?'

'Well, your mum is bringing in money now, so that helps. But I think I might take Uncle Steve up on his offer of a job in the firm. Just part-time, consultancy stuff. Not really getting my hands dirty. It'll help us save a bit.'

Eliza took the mugs over towards the bin and removed the teabags. 'Sounds like a definite plan. I'm glad. For both of you.'

'I know, sweetheart. And thank you. We're getting there.'

Eliza smiled at her father, two adults acknowledging an elephant in the room. She took a sip from her tea and quickly changed the subject.

'So, do you know when Patience is coming home again?' she said, sitting back down, opposite her father.

'No,' he replied, avoiding her gaze. 'But Eliza, there's something else I wanted to raise with you, before we talk about her.'

'What, Dad?'

Pete shifted in his seat.

'How would you feel, love, if we sold the house?'

Eliza thought for a few seconds, holding her mug steady on top of her stomach.

'Seriously, Dad? I'd be relieved.'

'Really? You wouldn't mind us selling the house you grew up in?'

'You're not talking about moving miles away, are you? Like Spain, or somewhere?'

Pete snorted.

'No. Your mum would never move far away from Patience. We've just seen somewhere, a little bungalow out Woodstock way. It's got nice views of fields and it's cheaper than this. So we can have a bit of money back in our pockets. A new start. And there are no stairs, so Patience...'

'Honestly, Dad, you don't need to convince me. I'm all for it. This is *your* house. You do what you want with it. I'm getting my own place here now soon, anyway, aren't I?'

'You are, my girl. You are. Now, the other thing. Patience...'

'Yes?'

'How long is it since you last saw her?'

'A few weeks ago. Why?'

Pete put his mug down on the table and sank back in his seat.

'This past month has been bad. Very bad. For Patience.'

'But you told me she was fine when we spoke on the phone? That she was all recovered from the sepsis?'

'I didn't want to worry you, pet. And anyway, it's not that.'

'Then what?'

Pete looked up at the ceiling, and took a deep breath.

'She's shouting. Yelling. Crying. There's something up. Something really bad.'

'Have the doctors taken a look at her?'

'Yes, and they say she seems OK. Health-wise. But she's just... different, love. Really different. It's like she's not the same person. I just wanted to warn you before you see it for yourself. Your mum and I...'

'I can guess. *Shit*. What's going on?'

'I wish I knew, love. I really do wish I knew.'

Eliza was shocked to see that there was a tear brimming in her father's left eye.

'Do you think it's something to do with the gene therapy stuff?'

'Maybe, maybe... That's what your mum reckons.' The tear ambled down his cheek. 'What have we done?'

'You've done nothing wrong, Dad. Nothing. You stuck up for her. It was me, I allowed them to do it. *Me*.'

Eliza took a large breath, but it was not enough to stop the tears from falling down her cheeks.

'You mustn't blame yourself, pet,' Pete said, urgently, standing up and going over to Eliza, putting his arms around her. 'You mustn't. You did what you thought was best.'

'Did I?'

'Stop it, love. That's what I keep telling your mum, too. There's no use dwelling. Anyway, there's a meeting tomorrow, to talk about it. At the care home. Would you come with us? Safety in numbers and all that.'

'Yes, of course,' she said, as he patted her back. 'Of course I'll be there. It's the least I can do.'

Being pregnant in a heatwave was the worst kind of torture, she thought. Eliza had dressed in the lightest cotton sundress she could find, but the material was sticking to her sweaty body and the high temperature was making her feet swell. The pavement beneath her feet was radiating the heat it had been absorbing for over a week, and it felt to Eliza as if she was being grilled on both sides.

She had tried to park in the care-home car park, but it had been full, so she had been forced to leave her car further down the road. At the speed she was currently walking – make that waddling – several hundred metres felt like at least a mile.

'Hi, Eliza, come in.'

Beth had answered the door, her face sombre. Eliza wasn't used to that; Beth reminded her of Tigger, bouncing wherever she went, resolutely joyful. However, she was firmly grounded today. This did not augur well.

'She's in her room. I'll take you there.'

The inside of the bungalow seemed to be even hotter than outside; insulation had clearly not been the builder's top priority. Every window was open and industrial fans hummed from every corner, but they were only succeeding in generating even more warm, moist air. Eliza walked past at least four before she arrived at Patience's bedroom.

'Just you on shift today?' Eliza asked.

'Oh no, Magda's here with me. She's making lunch.'

'Ah.' Eliza tried her best to hide her disappointment that Jimmy wasn't there. She was now prepared to acknowledge that she had a crush on him; damn it, she thought, it was actually more of an obsession. She thought about him first thing in the morning, last thing at night and in her dreams, which were now becoming rather X-rated. She couldn't get him out of her head, because he was so kind, and funny and he cared for Patience, genuinely cared. And those broad shoulders, and strong arms…

Stop it, Eliza, she thought. None of this will come to any good. You have a terrible track record when it comes to choosing men.

'Here you go.'

Eliza walked into the room. Patience was sitting in her wheelchair, watching Take That's *Odyssey* tour DVD.

Or at least, that's what Eliza had assumed. But when she walked around to face her sister, she could see that Patience's head was lowered, her eyes resolutely not looking at the screen. And she looked – angry. She had never seen her sister look like that before. Eliza moved her face to try to catch her eye, but each time she moved, Patience moved her gaze. Oh my God, she thought, Patience is avoiding me.

Piss off, Eliza. Piss off. I want to be alone.

'Patience, it's me. Come on, darling girl. What's up?'

Haven't you noticed? I'm a cripple stuck in an

*uncomfortable chair, watching something I have no choice
over. It'll probably repeat when it finishes and the lazy
bastards here won't even bother to change it. So I'll have to
watch it twice.*

'Are you in pain? Does it hurt somewhere?'

*No, Sherlock, it doesn't. Not right now, anyway. It did
down below, for months, but none of you noticed. And then
I got sick and almost died, so…*

'Is it your bladder again?'

No. Bugger off.

'Have they sent off a sample again?' Eliza asked Beth,
who was still in the room, just behind Patience. 'She might
have another infection.'

'Yes, just a few days ago,' she replied. 'It came back clean.'

'Hmmm,' Eliza said. 'What else can it be, I wonder?'

*How about, you're going to have a baby, and you're
pretty, and you're clever, and you're healthy, and I'm none
of those things? Shall we start with that?*

'Beth – could you turn the DVD off for a minute? I want
to have a chat with her.' Beth nodded, switched it off, and
left the room.

Ah, thank fuck for that.

'Patience… Mum and Dad are worried about you,' she
began.

*I wish I could tell you that my internal world of green
fields and sunshine has become a rutted, muddy no-man's
land under dark skies. It's no longer a refuge.*

'They say you've been making funny noises…'

*I can only see shadows. Dark thoughts. I've never felt
frustrated about my life before, but now I go through
stretches of raging against my weak, bent body, and of*

screaming at anyone within range, disgusted that they can't understand me.

'… like you're almost shouting?'

You see, my previous dreamlike state was the reason why I was able to remain patient for more than thirty years, patient about the body I'd been given, patient about the entertainment I'd been offered, patient about the pain I frequently experienced, patient about being misunderstood and manipulated, over and over again.

'What is it, my lovely girl? What is it that you want to say?'

But now my dreams are nightmares. I have lost my small joys. And I want them back, Eliza. I want to have a reason to laugh, a reason to smile. I want my dreams back.

'They're all gathered in the office. Shall I bring them in now?' Beth said, putting her head around the door.

'Sure,' Eliza replied, too disturbed by what she had seen to even consider another option. Minutes later, her mum, dad, Patience's GP Dr Aitken, the care home manager, Maggie, and Professor Larssen filed into the room. The professor immediately sat down next to Patience.

'I'm just going to have a little listen, Patience,' he said. 'It might feel a bit cold.'

Bugger off. No amount of listening is going to make any difference.

He lifted up her T-shirt and began listening to her sister's breathing with a stethoscope. Everyone was standing in silence, watching him work. Her mum gesticulated to another chair in the corner. 'For you,' she whispered. 'You must be knackered.' Eliza smiled her thanks and took a seat. She needed it, after that encounter.

After a minute or so, Professor Larssen ceased his investigations and turned to them all. 'I think,' he said, looking once more at Patience, and then in the direction of her parents, 'that we are seeing some significant changes now. I know you have noticed some, and so have the nurses and carers, and I wanted to see it for myself.' He looked back at Patience, who was now staring blankly at the ceiling. Eliza was shocked to see that her sister appeared to be scowling. 'Shall we perhaps go outside? It might be easier to talk out there.'

Yes, you all bugger off. You don't care what I think, anyway. You never have.

The five able-bodied participants of the meeting did not disagree. There was a collective sigh when they emerged into the small garden behind the house. They sat down on two picnic benches. These were in the shade and there was a small breeze here too, which cooled the beads of sweat which were dripping down the back of Eliza's lower legs.

'So, as I was saying,' the professor continued, 'there have been changes. Some worrying. You say that Patience has been making a lot more noise than usual. There has been some yelling, I believe, and she has never done that before. You say she seems a lot less content. This is very concerning. But our monitoring, on the other hand, shows no obvious reasons for this; there is no raised intra-cranial pressure, no obvious source of pain. And conversely, her breathing now seems to have regulated – she is no longer breath-holding, as far as we can tell – and her legs seem more supple, perhaps stronger. Her heart has fully recovered from the infection and is beating normally and she has had no further seizures. So, I conclude – and you may all disagree with me – that Patience is depressed. Perhaps severely so. We have seen a mixture of reactions in the patients in the trial, but this is one of the outcomes we are seeing.'

'Depressed? Patience? But she has always been so happy,' replied Louise, her voice strangulated.

'Yes,' replied the doctor. 'We anticipated that it might be a side effect of the therapy. A symptom of an increased awareness of her plight, as well as changes in her brain.'

'Oh my God. What have we done?' Louise began to cry and Eliza moved over to sit next to her and hold her hand.

'It's OK, Mum. It's not your fault.'

'It is! She was always the one member of our family who could be guaranteed to smile, to laugh at life, even when she was uncomfortable. And now she's depressed? All the gene therapy has done is leave her pretty much the same as before, hasn't it? Except worse, because she now seems to know she's disabled. And I didn't think it could get any worse. I am such a fool!'

'Please don't upset yourself, Louise,' said Professor Larssen, his voice soft.

'It was on your bloody side-effect list! You knew it could happen,' Pete said, his voice raised.

'You're quite right,' the professor said. 'It was on our list, and we shared this with the trial participants. But we thought it unlikely.'

'Yes, well, whatever. It's too late now anyway. She's like this. We can't take it back. So, what are we going to do?' asked Pete, staring the professor down. 'More to the point, what are you going to do about it?'

'We have considered antidepressants' – the professor

looked across at the GP, who nodded her agreement – 'and we think that might be a good start. But one of my team has also suggested that we try a new communication therapy to see if Patience has things she wants to say. We know that communication problems greatly contribute to depression.'

'Oh, this is ridiculous! Patience is a child,' said Pete, his voice loud and determined. 'I know she's in an adult's body, but she's my baby. She has always been my baby. She laughs at things that toddlers laugh at, she thinks rattles are great fun to shake, and she thinks *The Muppets* is the best thing on TV. She's not going to be able to tell us anything.'

'But she doesn't laugh at those things any more,' said Maggie, speaking up for the first time. 'We have tried all of her DVDs and even Take That isn't making her smile any more. It's like she's switched off from life.'

'What do you mean by communication therapy?' asked Louise, who was still gripping Eliza's hand.

'It's a computer screen that's controlled by eye movements,' he replied. 'It starts off with simple choices, like different kinds of drinks or food, or asking to go to the toilet and so on, and then it gets more advanced as they learn. I understand that researchers are seeing great results, particularly with newly-diagnosed Rett patients. We are happy to pay for the equipment for her, to see if it helps.'

'But she's not a child, is she? Her brain is going to be hard-wired. So it's not going to work, surely, is it?' Pete was insistent.

'I think it's worth a try,' replied the professor.

'I think *anything's* worth a try,' said Eliza, taking in the absolute despair on both of her parents' faces. She thought of her sister, lying inside the superheated bungalow, occupying her own personal version of hell. 'When can you get it to us?'

36

Patience

July

This corridor is pockmarked by spots of absolute darkness. It's lit by far-flung gas lamps and these flicker as I pass by, heading deeper under the surface. It's no different from the many different routes I've taken this morning; each one is just as dingy, just as repetitive, just as obscure. The floor is damp and my feet are caked in mud, and each step sends dirt flying up in a cloud around my ankles.

'P? P? It's Jimmy.'

Now I need the loo. I hate it when I need it down here, because there are no toilets. I have to wet myself, and the urine is only warm at first. Then it chills quickly, sending sharp stalactites down to my ankles.

'P. I've got something for you.'

There are no beds down here either, but I find I can manage to doze off standing up, resting against the curved walls.

'P. Please open your eyes. I know you're not asleep. I have something I hope you'll like.'

I will do it for him. Only him. Even though I am disgusting

and deformed, the opposite of all beauty. He's only nice to me out of pity.

I open my eyes slowly, not wanting to let the world back in too quickly, because this world is not what I thought it was. It's far crueller than that.

'Ah, there you are. Hello P. Look at this. This is for you.'

He's holding what looks like an iPad in front of my face. It's got several pictures on it; there is a cake, a chocolate bar and an ice cream.

'This is an eye-gaze screen, P. If you look at something, it should light up. Come on, have a go.'

Jimmy is looking at me through his beautiful eyelashes and he seems so keen. Who am I to say no to him? And things can't get any worse, anyway, can they? I open my eyes a little wider and decide to look at the ice cream. After all, there's been a bloody heatwave for most of this summer. I am sweating like a pig.

There's a loud ping, like one of those sounds you get when someone receives a text message.

'That was the ice cream. Did you choose the ice cream, P?'

A strange sound escapes from my mouth. I swear I didn't make it, but it sounds like 'Arrrrrrr.'

'OK, OK. Right. Let's try this one.'

There are now three pictures. One is a glass of what looks like milk, the other is a bed, and the final one is a toilet. And that is just what I need, as I realise that I'm about to wet myself. I stare fixedly at the toilet.

'Do you need the loo, P?'

'Arrrrrrr.'

'Just a minute, P. Magda!' he shouts. *'I need you to take Patience to the bathroom.'*

★

I don't know what I've done to deserve it, but Mum, Dad and Eliza have all decided to pay me a visit this evening and they've brought ice cream with them. It's chocolate flavour, and there are chocolate flakes, too, but they don't give me one. In case I choke, of course.

I suppose it's time I owned up to a couple of things.

Firstly, I think I can bend my fingers. Wilfully, I mean. I've been practising at night when no one's looking (I don't want to freak them out – they've hospitalised me for less), and I've managed to get my hands to do my bidding a few times now. I thought it was a fluke the first time, but as I say, I've replicated it, so it must be real, right? I can scratch myself. I can even draw blood with my nails if I want.

The other thing is my tongue. For years, it's sat in my mouth like a slab of spam, unable to manipulate food properly, causing me to nearly choke to death several times. Now, though, it seems to be more mobile and it's responding when I try to move it to one side, or up and down. This is easier to do with no one watching – I don't want them panicking, see above – and I'm getting good at it. I've noticed, too, that if I exhale, I can make all sorts of different noises with it, which is fun to do. It's not quite working as well as it used to do in my internal world, but perhaps that was unrealistic?

I haven't shown them my new tongue control yet; it's sort of like having a hidden superpower. But I think perhaps seeing me eat ice cream has given me away; they watch me silently as I roll it around in my mouth, savouring its taste and texture, before swallowing it on my first attempt.

Jimmy has been showing Mum how to use the machine with the pictures on it. She's choosing some stuff to try now. When she's satisfied, she turns it round towards me and presents with me two pictures. One is Take That, and one is Kylie. This is an easy choice.

'Ha, Take That, I should have known,' replies Mum, wittering away delightedly, her mind already on the next choice she wants to put to me.

'Why don't we try words?' suggests Jimmy. 'We could read them out to her maybe?'

Dad raises his eyebrows, but Jimmy is undeterred. He takes the machine from Mum and selects a few options.

On the screen, there are the words, 'I feel'.

'Those words are "I feel",' says Jimmy.

Yes, I know that, you div.

'And then these words beneath are: tired, hungry, thirsty, sad, happy. Can you see those?'

I can. I have learned to read a bit over the years. I've had a lot of time to piece things together.

'OK, so take a look at them all and then stop at the one you feel like,' he tells me. Behind him, I can see Mum, Dad and Eliza leaning over in my direction, all of them apparently holding their breath.

I think for a moment. I am a bit tired, but I don't want to go to bed. I'm not thirsty, and for the first time in weeks I don't feel really sad. That might be the medicine they're giving me in the mornings now, but it might also be this little machine and the incredible gateway it has just opened. It makes me feel a bit... free.

I choose hungry.

'Hungry? OK. Take a look at these options.'

I now see a selection of foods. I choose the one that appears to be chocolate.

'Chocolate? OK. Right. And these?'

There is chocolate milk, chocolate cake, and a chocolate bar. Obviously, I choose the latter.

'You want a flake, darling?' says Mum, suddenly getting it. 'Pete, quick, for heaven's sake, get her out a flake.'

And I laugh.

And then the whole room laughs with me.

37

Eliza

July

'Holyfuckingfuckfuckingcrapfuckinghell...'

'I am getting there as quickly as I can, madam.'

Eliza raised her head slowly from its position between her knees and saw in the reflection in the rear-view mirror that Saleem – the unflappable, smiling, hardworking owner of Kidlington Kabs – was genuinely alarmed. And now that the wave of pain had subsided, she felt an inkling of embarrassment about screaming swear words in front of the man who usually drove her parents home from the pub. So she tried breathing deeply instead; or rather, as deeply as she could manage, given that most of her trunk was currently occupied by another human.

'That's good, madam, my wife was telling me that breathing helped,' said Saleem, beaming toothy encouragement into the mirror. 'And have you tried panting? She did a great deal of panting.'

Well, bully for her, Eliza thought. She was exhausted already and not in the least interested in trying to sound like the family Labrador. This was awkward enough.

Eliza scanned the back seat of Saleem's black Mercedes estate for her phone, which she had flung aside just as the last contraction had begun. She eventually found it in the pocket in the right passenger door, sitting pretty alongside a pack of complimentary tissues. She might be needing those, she thought. She speed-typed a text message.

Mum I'm in labour and you need to come back right now.

Hmm, on second thought, a text like that might cause her mother to have a coronary. Mum was not the type to respond calmly in a crisis. And it was hardly practical, anyway – she and Dad were currently about 33,000 feet up in the sky, en route to Dublin. The captain could hardly turn the plane around, even for the arrival of a grandchild. No, they'd have to get off and then immediately buy a ticket back and her SOS would ruin a long-awaited weekend away together, which they definitely deserved. She'd better not send it. Yes, she'd let them have at least twenty-four hours of peace before she told them the news. They'd be back soon enough. Refraining, coping on her own, was the grown-up thing to do, after all. She needed to grow up; she was going to be a mother.

But why, why did this baby have to arrive three weeks early? Everybody had told her that first babies took ages to come out, that she'd finish up the third trimester rolling around like a walrus, chugging raspberry leaf tea and chicken vindaloo by the gallon, desperate for anyone, anything, to get the sodding thing out. It was this certainty that had led her to assure her parents that it would be perfectly fine for them to squeeze in a mini break away together this weekend.

Yes, of course, she'd said: I'll look after the dog. Yes, no problem, I'll water the garden. You go and enjoy yourselves! I'm just going to sleep most of the time, anyway.

Sleep? Feck. Not much chance of that now.

Arrrgggggggggghhhhh, another one. *Fuccccckkkkk.* She needed someone to hold her hand.

Serena. She'd text Serena.

Help. The baby's coming and I need you to come! Mum and Dad are away.

Eliza concentrated on breathing in and out as she felt the pressure building in her abdomen and making its way inexorably upwards. That bloody witch at her NCT class had told her that this would feel wonderful and empowering, the pinnacle of her womanhood. But she had lied, damn her. This was excruciating and she was clearly powerless to stop it. This baby was forcing its way out into the world and she was merely its conduit.

Her phone beeped.

Oh crap – am visiting York with Mum but I'll set off now. With you asap. Hang on in there.

York to Oxford – what was that? Three and three-quarter hours, best case? More like four hours plus, if Serena was going to take her mother home first. Bugger. She was going to be on her own for a while. But that was OK, wasn't it? She had managed on her own for a long time. She was a strong, independent woman. Definitely. She had got this.

Oh, but should she call Ed? He was the father, after all. He could hold her hand and help her breathe…

Fuccccckkkkkkkkkk. Buuugggggeeeeeerrrrrrrrrr. Arrrrsssssssse.

Second thoughts, there was no way in hell that man was going to see her like this. Why should she let him see her at her most vulnerable? He'd hurt her deeply and she didn't need any more damage in that department. And it wasn't as if he'd been an enthusiastic expectant father; he had failed to attend every single ante-natal check, sometimes cancelling at the last moment. 'Work,' he'd said, every time. No, she'd tell him in a bit. He was only a few miles away and could get there quickly, anyway. It would be better if he came towards the end. Or even afterwards. That, actually, is what he deserved, she decided.

'We are almost there, madam. Just one more roundabout.'

Eliza was now staring fixedly at a speck of dust on the mat beneath her feet, but the way her body was slipping back and forth on the black leather seat told her that Saleem was now throwing the car around the bypass with wild abandon. He was probably worried that her waters would burst and damage his upholstery and, to be fair, she didn't blame him. It *was* quite likely. She was surprised they hadn't gone already; what had begun as period pains a few hours ago had developed quickly into an agony so severe that she barely had time to breathe between contractions. This baby clearly didn't want to wait.

Eliza raised her head and saw that they were approaching the hospital building. She decided to send one more text. Because when she needed comfort, she knew where to get it.

Hello. It's Patience's sister. I'm in labour. Please bring her to the hospital asap, please.

★

'Well, won't you look at that,' Natalie the midwife said, her hand and wrist currently exploring the dark recesses of Eliza's cervix. 'You're eight centimetres. Baby will make their entrance soon.'

Through the swirling mist of Entonox, Eliza pondered the midwife's use of pronoun. Eliza's grammar pedantry became worse when she was anxious or in pain.

The pain did, however, have one benefit. It was a distraction from her high levels of anxiety about this pregnancy. Having decided that she definitely wanted to keep her baby – how she could ever have thought differently baffled her now – her focus had shifted to an obsession about its health. She had feared that every twinge meant a miscarriage, and that every check-up would bring bad news. She had held her breath throughout her first scan at the hospital, examining the technician's face for any sign that she might be withholding information. She had drunk alcohol during the early days of pregnancy, had eaten goodness knows how much shellfish and unpasteurised cheese; there were so many ways in which she could have done this child harm. And in the back of her mind – no, who was she kidding, in the front of her mind, too – she thought of her mother's innocent joy at birthing two healthy children.

What if her baby was disabled and she just didn't know it yet? Even though all of the tests so far had come out negative, she knew she was far from out of the woods. There was still no in-utero test for Rett syndrome, and who knew how many other rare genetic faults.

'All done,' Natalie said, snapping off her latex gloves and walking over to the sink to wash her hands. 'After this, I'm just going to pop a monitor onto your tummy for a bit, to check how baby's doing.'

'Is that normal?' Eliza asked, her eyes wide. 'Is there something wrong?'

Natalie smiled and approached the bed. 'It's totally normal, sweetheart,' she replied, fixing the strap around Eliza's bump. 'Try not to worry. You're doing great. Have you got someone coming to be with you?'

'Yes,' Eliza said. 'My sister. She should be here soon.'

'Lovely,' Natalie replied, adjusting the monitor to locate the baby's heartbeat. 'That'll help. And I'll get someone to bring you a cup of tea. That'll calm you. And do you feel peckish? It might be good to keep your strength up. We could bring you toast?'

Eliza felt another contraction building, and with it a nausea which was now undeniable. She had never felt less like eating in her life.

'Just tea, please,' she replied, attempting a smile through gritted teeth. Natalie nodded and headed to the door as Eliza rolled onto her side, groaning.

Five minutes later, when she was in the only position she found even remotely comfortable – on all fours, hospital gown gaping wide, her naked bottom saluting the sun, or rather, the strip light above her bed – someone knocked on the door. Natalie again, she thought; what medical horror had she planned for her this time?

But it wasn't Natalie.

'Tea? And I've brought some toast in case you... Oh!'

It was a man's voice.

Shit.

And then it all happened at once. As Eliza yelled 'Jimmy!'

she rolled onto her side at speed in an effort to hide her elephantine nakedness. But she was too big, her body too unstable, and the bed too narrow. She screamed as she lost her balance and fell, as if in slow motion, off the side of the bed and onto the floor.

'*Shit, shit, shit, sorry. Shit. Hang on, I'll hit the button.*'

Suddenly, Jimmy was standing beside her. She felt a searing pain in her abdomen and howled. He crouched down and put his arms around her.

'Stay down here, just in case,' he said, as she tried to pull herself up. 'Wait until the doctors and nurses come to check you over.'

'OK,' Eliza replied, writhing in agony.

'What... the... hell... are... you... doing... here... anyway?' she panted. Oh God, she had finally started panting.

'I'm working as a healthcare assistant. I pick up the occasional shift here. I'm considering applying to study midwifery.'

'I... didn't... know,' she said, before trying to take in a long, slow breath as she'd been taught.

'No. I haven't told the care home yet. They don't know I have another job. I don't want them to get wind that I might leave.'

'Oh... I... see.'

Then suddenly there was a crowd.

'*Stand back,*' a voice said, and Jimmy complied. He was replaced with a smiling woman with a stethoscope around her neck.

'What hurts?' she asked. 'Or is that a silly question.'

Eliza would have laughed if she wasn't in such agony.

'Just... down... there,' she replied.

'Is it worse than before?'

Eliza thought for a moment. 'Maybe.'

The woman nodded to her colleagues and three of them stepped forward, took hold of Eliza under her arms, and hoisted her back onto the bed.

Eliza's head swam and stars appeared in front of her eyes. But even through the swirling patterns, she could see that the room had turned into a circus. There were at least six people staring at her. She could no longer see Jimmy.

'Just lie back on the bed for us, Elizabeth,' the woman said. 'We just need to check how your baby is doing.'

As two nurses helped Eliza into a reclining position, she realised that the monitor she'd been wearing had been ripped off.

'We're just going to attach a monitor to your baby's head,' the doctor said after she'd finished checking Eliza over. 'It's more reliable than the tummy monitor. It won't hurt the baby.'

'Is there something wrong?' Eliza asked once more, her anxiety levels now sky-high.

The doctor didn't answer her.

'That's it, Elizabeth,' she said in her best bedside manner, gesturing for Eliza to lie back on the bed. Then she put yet another latex-gloved hand where the sun didn't shine. 'That's it. I'm just going to... pop... this... in... there... Good!'

The woman removed her hand from between Eliza's legs and looked up at the screen beside the bed. Eliza was no longer able to turn around, but she could hear that the machine had begun to beep once more. All of the medical staff stood silently, their eyes glued to the monitor and the language it was speaking, a foreign language Eliza did not understand.

Eliza felt her face drain of colour and vomit rise up into her throat.

'I think I'm going to be sick,' she said.

One of the nurses swiftly placed a cardboard bowl beside her head. Eliza leaned over and retched into it. She brought up some liquid, but not much else; she hadn't eaten since breakfast.

'It's all right, love. You're fine. Lots of women are sick during labour. It's all totally normal,' the nurse said, putting her hand on Eliza's shoulder in an attempt to reassure her.

But Eliza felt as far from normal as it was possible to feel. She was also fixated on the faces at the foot of her bed, who were interpreting the squiggly lines behind her head. They were giving nothing away.

Finally, the female doctor spoke.

'Baby looks OK, Elizabeth, despite your tumble. We'll leave you to labour for a bit and come back to check in half an hour. You seem to be progressing well. OK?'

Eliza managed to find the energy to nod, just as another wave of pain and pressure began to sweep over her. She closed her eyes to block out the crowd. It didn't seem right that they were there. This was just about the two of them. The baby and her.

When she opened her eyes, the room had cleared. The only people who remained were Natalie and Jimmy, who had reappeared by her bedside.

'OK, love,' Natalie said, 'you're on the monitor and you're labouring well so I'll just pop out to check on one of my other ladies and come back in about ten minutes to see how you're getting on.'

Then the door shut behind her and Eliza and Jimmy were alone.

And then she started to cry; huge, shuddery tears.

Seconds later, Jimmy was sitting on the bed and putting his arms around her.

'Eliza, Lize, it's going to be OK. It will be, I promise. I'm here. You're not on your own. I'm here.'

Eliza collapsed into him, not caring that she was half-naked, or that she smelled of sick, or that her hair looked like an octopus catching a wave. And through the pain and the tears, she acknowledged that being held by him felt nice. Very nice. But she was still crying.

'Lize, please stop crying. It'll be OK. Just breathe.'

'Everyone... keeps... telling... me... to... breathe,' Eliza replied, 'but... I'm... so... frightened.'

'Why? You heard the doctors. Everything seems fine.'

'I... don't... deserve... fine.'

Jimmy withdrew from their embrace and sat down on the bed, lowering his head so that he was face to face with Eliza.

'What do you mean? Of course you do.'

'I... don't... I... got... rid... of... it.'

'Don't be silly. You're having it. We're both here, aren't we? You'll be holding your baby soon.'

'You don't understand,' she said, speaking quickly between pants, reckoning that if she said it as quickly as she could, she wouldn't feel the impact of what she was about to say. 'I got rid of a baby. Years ago. When I was a teenager. A perfectly healthy baby.'

'Oh, Lize.' There was a pause, during which Jimmy passed Eliza a tissue. 'Don't be silly. What's in the past is in the past. You are not some evil person. You're human. This is a new start.'

'The last time I was in pain like this was then. When I had the – the abortion. What if this baby dies, too?'

'It won't. It just won't. You heard them – the baby is fine.'

'But what if it's like – like Patience?'

'Then it will be awesome, like her,' he replied, not missing a beat.

There was a knock at the door. A woman Eliza didn't recognise peered around it.

'Are you Eliza?' she said. 'I'm Catherine and I have Patience with me. I'm sorry we took so long. Staffing problems. Can we come in?'

And so it was that Eliza went from no birth partners to three. She now had Jimmy, Patience and Catherine, a woman she had only known for a matter of minutes but who had now taken up a position at the foot of the bed next to Natalie, issuing regular updates from 'the business end', as she so delightfully put it. Catherine had, it transpired, birthed four children, one in the hallway of her block of flats, with only a postman for company. She was no-nonsense and Eliza warmed to her immediately.

Patience was parked to Eliza's right, as close to the bed as was practicable; close enough for Eliza to reach out her hand, which Patience was grasping. She had not brought her eye-gaze computer – Catherine was apparently a new member of staff and hadn't been told to bring it – but it didn't matter. Eliza knew her sister so well that her presence was enough. And having Patience actually hold her hand, instead of just resting it in hers, had an extraordinary power. The warmth of her hand felt like a transfer of energy. With Patience there, she felt as if she might actually be able to do this.

Jimmy was on Eliza's left and he was holding her other hand firmly. He had sprung away from her when Catherine and Patience had entered, like a little boy caught breaking the rules, but Eliza had decided that enough was enough. She had reached for his hand then and not let go, and Jimmy had not flinched. She hoped he didn't mind, because she had no plans to let go of it, ever.

'Just keep pushing, like you're doing a poo,' Natalie said. 'There's a good girl. That's it. Baby's coming.'

'Is it?' Eliza asked, breathless and exhausted.

'Yes, I can just make out the top of its head. When you feel the next contraction, push with all of your might.'

Eliza didn't feel like she had any might left. Her face was bright red, her eyes were bloodshot and she was exhausted. She had been pushing for at least an hour now. Never mind doing a poo; it felt like she was pushing all of her innards out onto the bed. She'd be entirely inside out so on, surely, and all that would be left of her would be a steaming pile of red, purple and brown organs, slithering onto the floor.

'Come on, lovey. That's it. Biiiiigggg push,' said Catherine.

'You can do it, my girl, you can do it,' said Jimmy.

My girl, Eliza thought. He said *my girl*.

And then Patience squeezed her right hand, an unmistakable message from sister to sister.

You can do this, Lize. You can do this.

Yes! I can do this, Patience. I will do this for you.

Eliza put her chin down onto her chest and pushed with every sinew in her body.

'That's it!' shouted Natalie. 'Now pant for me. Pant. Don't push.'

And so Eliza channelled the family Labrador once more.

'That's it. The head's out. You'll see baby with the next push.'

Eliza felt the now familiar tightening of her muscles and roared.

There was a feeling of release, of an emptying.

Then there was a cry.

She wasn't sure if it was hers, but it was a joyous cry, a cry which said fuck you to fear, and fuck you to failure.

'You have a perfect little girl!' announced Natalie.

Jimmy kissed her on her cheek and told her he was proud; Catherine cried happy tears and searched her handbag for her hankie; Patience squeezed Eliza's hand even tighter.

And then a red-faced, puffy and angry-looking infant was placed on her chest. Eliza looked down at her daughter's face, at her swollen eyes opening just a crack to take in her new world, and she vowed there and then that she would never look back.

38

Pete

September

The volume in the stadium was overwhelming and indescribable. If this was a work site, Pete would be mandating protective ear defenders for everyone, but looking around him, he could see that this was not a concern for the twenty thousand people who were currently singing Take That's 'Could It Be Magic' at the top of their voices.

He had agreed to come reluctantly, but even despite the inevitable hearing loss that he anticipated tomorrow, he was glad that he had conceded. He knew all of the songs, at any rate; more than thirty years of life with Patience had seen to that, and the sheer joy on the faces of those around him was infectious. And while he wasn't exactly dancing, his feet were tapping, unseen by anyone except Louise to his left, who leaned in just then and planted a kiss on his cheek.

They were here to celebrate the end of a landmark year. It was one he wouldn't like to live through again, that was certain, but it had brought unexpected blessings, too. One of those, little Orla, now two months, was at home in

Kidlington with a trusted babysitter. She was tiny, blonde and fierce, a whirlwind of mess and laughter.

Eliza seemed to have taken to motherhood with ease, and he hoped that from now on she would signal to them if she was unhappy. But he instinctively felt that things were different now. She seemed more honest; there was less front – and her confidence, which had been at an all-time low several months ago, seemed to be building. She had been talking about setting herself up as a freelance PR consultant, and his brother Steve was keen to get her to work her magic on his business. He hoped she would be OK.

And there was another reason for her improved state of mind, of course. Pete could see that Eliza's hand was currently resting in Jimmy's back pocket. That partnership had been a surprise for all of them – Eliza included, he thought – but it was having an extraordinary effect on her. His eldest daughter, previously so reserved, so independent, so closed-off, was now an emotional open house, loving wildly, fiercely and without fear. The relief he felt about this was palpable.

Sitting on the other side of Jimmy, was Patience. She had asked for a good seat this year (apparently the disabled ones she'd been allocated for the previous show had not been up to her expected standards) and he was gratified to see that she had a broad smile on her face. The counselling she was now having, combined with antidepressants, was bringing her out of the darkness. These seats were close to the front and they had a price tag to match, but Pete simply didn't care. She had been so recently plagued by nightmares he was only just beginning to understand, and he was so grateful to be able to give her something that brought her this much joy.

It had been an incredible shock to discover that she had been so aware for all of those years. He had experienced a cocktail of emotions when they'd discovered the truth. Mostly, he had felt ashamed. How could he call himself her father and not really know his daughter, at all? He struggled to even imagine what she had gone through in three decades of silence and the things she had witnessed, had heard. He thought of the many occasions when he and Louise had argued in front of her, about her. He was astonished that she still wanted anything to do with any of them.

And yet she did. In fact, she insisted that she had been quite content for all of those years. 'I really was happy, Daddy,' she had said to him recently, via the machine she now used. 'And now – this is a new beginning. For all of us.' She had smiled at him then. It had been a knowing smile.

He could see that Patience was experiencing this concert on a different level to the rest of them, soaring high above the crowds on a high-octane thrill ride, ducking and diving with the rhythm, revelling with the angels. And he suspected she'd be even more joyous when she discovered the surprise Eliza had managed to arrange for afterwards – a long-awaited, much-postponed meet-and-greet between three of the most famous pop stars in the world and their most fabulous fan. He couldn't wait to tell her. It would make her year. Or her life, perhaps.

The band were now playing their reunion single, 'Patience'. How kind of them to name one of their songs after his youngest, he thought. But it was fitting. The crowd at the O2 was now on its feet, swaying gently, mobile-phone torches raised up high. Patience's face was shining. Music had always transformed her absolutely. And despite all of the changes in her this year, it had continued to do so. And thank goodness for that, for she was the music in all of their lives.

She was now revealing herself to have a wicked sense of humour, and a mind thoroughly her own. She had issued them a wish list recently. She had told them that she wanted, in no particular order: a new haircut; Netflix; laser treatment on her facial hair; perfume; nicer drinks (including the occasional gin and tonic); prettier pants; a back catalogue of Robbie Williams' albums; and a ban on daytime TV programmes in the bungalow. He suspected the carers might fight her over that last one.

She had also told them that she wanted to leave home, permanently. 'I want my own life,' she had said, her eyes mirroring the defiance of the words she had chosen. 'And I want you to have yours.'

Louise had shed tears afterwards, but of course, they had complied. They could never refuse her wishes now. Patience had been offered a permanent place at the care home where she had always had respite, and they had taken it immediately, knowing that she felt safe and happy there.

He had been astonished by the effect the move had had on Louise. Instead of feeling bereft, as he had anticipated, she had become energised, seeking out new challenges. And, slowly, they were learning to live together again, beginning to put the house into order at last – not to live in, but to sell. With Louise's job and his consulting work for Steve, they had enough to get by, with a little to put away for a rainy day.

Patience was still very much a part of their lives, despite her move. They visited her several times a week and she often came home for weekends, although she now engaged with them in banter at the dinner table, and commented all-too-honestly on their apparently poor choices of TV shows, music and decor. There was a lot of laughter.

A speech therapist was now starting to work with Patience on what he suspected would be a very long project – teaching her to form her noises into words. Whether she would ever actually speak using her own voice was still an unknown, but what was certain was that she had regained at least some control of her muscles, and with it, some independence. She could now use her hands to steer an electric wheelchair, making her the menace of shoppers, walkers and joggers across Oxfordshire. She was also able to hold little Orla on her lap – with a little help – and watching the pair of them eyeing each other like this was a joy. She could also chew and swallow normally, and had recently begun to be able to pick up large food items by herself. Meals with her would never again involve a liquidiser, and he was glad of that.

The gene therapy trial she'd taken part in had been judged to have been a success. All of the trial participants had gained something from it, although none had so far experienced the Lazarus-style resurrection that some of the families had hoped for. Phase two of the trial was being rolled out across the world, and experts reckoned that eventually, even more targeted therapies could be introduced, with the potential of even more incredible results.

But for now, this was enough for her, he thought. Patience was content. She had found her startling, sparkling voice.

And William. She had found William.

39

Patience

September

'I think it should be green.'

There is a pause while I assemble my response on the machine.

'I love you,' the computerised version of me says, 'but your taste is appalling.'

William laughs raucously and trundles over in his electric wheelchair, parking himself alongside mine and taking my left hand, which nowadays is more of an independent agent than a Siamese twin.

'Seriously, you should have whatever colour you want,' he says, squeezing it. 'This is your home now, after all.'

Yes, it is my home. This room is mine.'

Yesterday, when William was out having physio, I sat in here and took myself onto a glorious, sun-drenched hillside. I inhaled the scent of baked fern and grasses and made a necklace from the wildflowers beneath my feet. I felt extraordinary afterwards; rested, revitalised, free. My counsellor – who's luckily very patient with my still very inept usage of the eye-gaze tech – says that what I'm doing is meditating. I suppose she's right, although I never knew that was what it was called. I have always just done it instinctively, but I know now that I was self-medicating with it, maintaining my mental health. Clever me.

I've only been able to get back to it recently, however. It took me a long time to find my way out of that dark tunnel. Antidepressants and counselling are an amazing combo, though, it turns out. With their help I've gone from feeling like the walls were closing in, to rejoicing in the four walls I now call home. And now that I'm emerging from that dark tunnel I found myself in, I feel like marking that transition.

Decades of decor not of my choosing has left me craving something different, something... *out there*.

I know! What I need is wallpaper. And on it I want big, bright, colourful butterflies. Hundreds of them, a whole kaleidoscope. I will tell Maggie later. I know she hates my to-do lists; I enjoy hearing her sigh when I read them out to her. She may perhaps be regretting her enthusiasm for the gene therapy now. It's made so much extra work for her.

'I'm going to watch *Coronation Street*. Want to come?'

I nod. William and I love to watch the soaps together; we chuckle over the outrageous storylines, the dreadful clothing choices, the unlikely affairs.

It was TV that first brought us together, actually. A few months back, I watched as a minibus drew up outside our bungalow and a young man in a wheelchair was lowered down slowly on its rear-lift, alongside a modest collection of boxes and suitcases. He was particularly notable because he was holding a TV screen on his lap. It was a large one, at least thirty inches across, and I couldn't even see his face.

As he steered his way to the front door, effectively blind,

I was worried that he'd drop it. He wobbles, you see. I've learned since that William has cerebral palsy, a physical disability, coupled with completely normal brain function, just like me. But unlike me, he can talk; his speech is slurred but audible. And that's fine. Compared to the groans I'm currently managing to produce, he's got the diction of Benedict Cumberbatch. Actually, I reckon he looks a bit like him, too.

He tells me that he had insisted on carrying that TV himself. He doesn't trust anyone with his beloved Sonia, a Sony smart television. He's spent most of his life living in care homes and he tells me that he's discovered that the secret to his sanity is having his own set. Sonia was bought for him by his foster parents who love him with an intensity I admire deeply. They've looked after him on and off since he was a toddler. They visit him several times a week, and they always bring us treats.

It was a Saturday when he moved in, and as I steered myself to dinner that night, I heard the opening chords of the *Strictly Come Dancing* theme tune emanating from his room. I love *Strictly*, so it was a moth-to-a-flame situation. I simply couldn't stop myself, and when I looked through the door in search of the screen, the man I'd seen arrive that morning suddenly had a face. And it was lovely.

William has short brown hair, a sexy smile and sparkling hazel eyes. He's twenty-seven, so he's technically a toy boy: result! And he loves music. When he spotted me gawping at the opening number of *Strictly* that night, he beckoned for me to join him. Before I knew it, we were attempting a wheelchair version of the first dance that night, which was a samba. Wheels clashed, brakes screamed, and laughter echoed off the walls and down the corridor. When the carers came to check up on us, I had hiccups from laughing so hard.

I don't think of Jimmy much these days. It helps that I don't see him often. He's left the care home to do a foundation course, to help him get into university. I won't pretend that watching him fall in love with Eliza was easy – it smarted, God, it smarted – but I'm glad for them both. She deserves to be happy. And I now realise that what I felt for him was simply a harmless fantasy, the equivalent of a teenage crush. I was exercising my emotional muscle, on a dummy run. And frankly, when I discovered that he didn't like Take That, I knew it would never work. Eliza is welcome to him, and his strange, unpleasant obsession with R & B.

No, William is the real deal. He doesn't mind my stubble or my wonky back; I don't care a jot that he's clumsy and prone to dribbling. We have accepted each other, warts and all.

Like my parents, I suppose. They are now making a decent go of it and I'm glad. I think their caring responsibilities meant that they focussed almost entirely on me, rather than each other, and I hope that me leaving home has changed that.

'Chocolate?'

William has a box of Quality Street in his room this week, a gift from his foster parents, and we're working our way through it. I nod and he gives me the strawberry cream, because he knows they're my favourite. I tell you, the man is a keeper.

As the familiar *Coronation Street* theme tune floats

around the room and I roll the chocolate around in my mouth, its rosy sweetness romancing my taste buds, I realise, with a start, that I am extraordinarily happy right now, in this moment.

I am happy, you know, and yet still not 'normal', not by any means. The gene therapy didn't 'cure' me. I still look about as disabled as you could imagine. But William says that this is my superpower; I keep my abilities under wraps, putting them to use only rarely, shocking people around me. Take, for example, the self-important man who parked illegally in the only available disabled space at the supermarket last week. My computerised voice shouted 'Wanker!' at him repeatedly as he scurried back into his Range Rover and drove off at speed. Who knew you could teach an eye-gaze computer to swear? Me, of course.

It turns out, you see, that I'm funny and clever. *I* knew this (I'm also not very modest) but the rest of the world thought I was an empty shell, didn't they? And that, for me, is the true benefit of the gene therapy and the hideous side effects I endured. I'm now able to ask for a back scratch, or to go to the toilet, or for some paracetamol if I have a headache – by mouth! Oh, I know, the luxury of it! And, crucially, I can also tell the carers if something hurts, as soon as it begins to hurt. So no more untreated bladder infections for me, I hope.

And do you know what? People laugh *with* me, and not *at* me, these days. I'm thinking of asking to go to college. Oh, and I quite fancy writing a book. It would be nice to put my overactive imagination to good use – and, let's face it, my internal monologue, honed over the decades, gives me plenty of rich material to choose from.

Hang on a sec – what's that? Oh my *God*, they're playing 'Pray' on the juke box in the Rovers Return! I hear the familiar chords and, just like that, my heart swells, my pulse quickens and I'm cloaked in the warmth of my memories.

But then William wraps his hand around mine and I am certain, absolutely certain, absolutely determined, that my future will be even better.

Author's Note

In June 1980, my parents celebrated the birth of their second child, Clare. A young professional couple with their lives and careers ahead of them, they were both relieved and delighted that she was, according to the hospital, 'normal' and healthy. Our mother Yvonne wrote almost exactly this in a memory book she'd begun just after Clare's arrival. I discovered that book years later, locked up in a cupboard gathering dust, because it was an unwanted reminder of a period of innocence that was desperately short lived.

Clare was one of the first children in the UK to be diagnosed with Rett syndrome. It's an incredibly cruel disorder. Although she gained some skills as a toddler, she eventually lost them all, and her profound disability has shaped and buffeted all of our lives ever since. Bringing up – and living alongside – a disabled child is a unique mixture of joy, frustration, exhaustion and fear, and I hope that *Patience* helps shine a light on that experience. Growing up, I always felt that none of my friends really understood what my family and I were going through. I really wish a novel like *Patience* had existed then for us all to read.

For all of Clare's childhood, our parents were entirely in the dark as to the cause of her disability. Doctors assumed it had a genetic basis, but had no proof. At the turn of the millennium, however, a scientist called Dr Huda Zoghbi in the USA published a paper pin-pointing the exact gene that was at fault – MECP2. This was followed in 2007 by groundbreaking research by a team at Edinburgh University led by Professor Adrian Bird, which showed that it was apparently possible to 'reverse' Rett syndrome in mice.

This development sent shockwaves through the global Rett community, giving families hope for the first time that their relatives' condition might be treatable. It was also the spark that ignited my desire to write this book.

The gene therapy experiment threw up all sorts of questions for me. Would it be painful? Would Clare be frightened? And would she welcome it, or refuse it, given the choice?

Writing *Patience* allowed me to explore these questions, as well as to examine the potential of another recent breakthrough in the Rett world – eye-gaze technology. Many Rett families are now finding that its use, particularly when started young, is transforming their relationships. Unfortunately, Clare started to use it only recently and is still getting to grips with it. So for now at least, her inner-world remains a mystery, and that's frustrating (for both of us, I suspect.) The unspoken communication we've developed over the years can only go so far. I realise now that one of my main motivations for writing this book was to try to inhabit her wonderful brain, and learn to see the world from her perspective. I yearn to know her every thought, and there's so much I don't know. But what I am certain of, however, is that she has a wicked sense of humour. Her eyes convey that perfectly.

At the time of writing, gene therapy for Rett syndrome is still at the research stage, but I have no doubt that it will eventually become a reality. I know that hundreds of thousands of Rett families around the world are waiting patiently for that day to come.

Victoria's website: www.toryscott.com

You can follow Victoria on Twitter @toryscott and on Instagram @victoriascottauthor.

Book Club Questions

1. Louise reflects that many medics and carers involved in her daughter's life think she's 'nuts' and Eliza acknowledges that people often refer to her mother as 'superwoman'. How do Louise's drive and determination make you feel about her?

2. Patience's chapters are written in the first person, while Eliza, Louise and Pete's perspectives are written in the third person. How did the use of the first person perspective affect how you felt about her character?

3. Eliza feels like she has to try to be the perfect daughter. To what extent do you think this view reflects reality? Could this ambition actually be entirely of her own making?

4. Pete believes he has been a terrible father to both of his girls. Is this true?

5. Patience's Best Interests panel decides to give the go-ahead for the gene therapy trial, despite their concerns. Would you have made the same decision?

6. Now that you've spent some time in Patience's head, how do you think society can better support and integrate people with disabilities into communities?

7. Despite being unable to talk to each other, Patience and Eliza still have a very strong bond. How do you think Patience's disability affects their relationship?

Acknowledgements

I started writing *Patience* more than a decade ago, and a great many people have helped me with it along the way.

Firstly, a huge thanks to my amazing family. It was my husband Teil who encouraged me to take the Faber Academy Writing A Novel course, led by tutor Lee Weatherly, in 2019. It was the push I needed to finally get on and finish the first draft of *Patience*, which had been sitting for years unfinished on my hard drive, simply entitled "Rett novel". Thank you, Teil, for believing in me, and for making me so many excellent cappuccinos while I write.

Thank you also to my parents Yvonne and Chris Milne, for their support, love and supply of thick socks and a heated blanket to keep me warm in my author's shed. Mum was one of my earliest interviewees for this book, and her real-life experiences have undoubtedly added to its power. Also, a big thank you for gifting me the money to do the writing course (alongside Auntie Juliet and David Artal) – definitely my most useful birthday present ever.

Secondly, I'd like to thank Louise Walters, whose excellent editorial advice set me on the path to finding my agent, the brilliant Hannah Weatherill at Northbank Talent Management. Hannah's passion for Patience's story won me over immediately, and her support, editorial assistance and friendship have been absolutely invaluable.

Thirdly, I'd like to thank Hannah Smith, my editor, and all at Head of Zeus. Their decision to publish *Patience* has genuinely changed my life.

I'd also like to thank the many author friends who gave me advice and support as I was writing, including the wonderful Clare Mackintosh, whose early encouragement meant a huge deal to me. Thanks also to the #Debut20 and #Debut21 crews – every novelist trying to write, edit and publish a novel in the time of Covid-19 deserves to be a bestseller.

I also want to thank the many people who read early versions of this book and offered great feedback – Vicki, Catherine, Theresa – as well as those I interviewed as part of my research, including the fabulous Dr Hilary Cass OBE. Her advice helped me to make this book medically accurate. Any errors that remain are all mine, I promise. Thank you also to those I interviewed who wanted to remain anonymous – your honesty and knowledge were much appreciated.

Finally, a huge thank you to my sister Clare, for inspiring me, putting up with me trying out make-up on her, and keeping my secrets.

To find out more about Rett syndrome, or to support research into therapies and work supporting Rett syndrome families, go to:

Rett UK www.rettuk.org

Reverse Rett UK www.reverserett.org.uk

About the Author

VICTORIA SCOTT has been a journalist for two decades, working for outlets including the BBC, Al Jazeera, *Time Out* and the *Telegraph*. She lives on a Thames island with her husband, two children and a cat called Alice, and when she's not writing she works as a university lecturer and copywriter. She has a degree in English from King's College London and a Postgraduate Diploma in Broadcast Journalism from City University, London. Victoria's debut novel, *Patience*, was a Booksellers' Association Book of the Month.